Disney

AS OLD AS TIME

A TWISTED TALE NOVEL

LIZ BRASWELL

AUTUMN
PUBLISHING

Published in 2022
Published in the UK by Autumn Publishing
An imprint of Igloo Books Ltd
Cottage Farm, NN6 0BJ, UK
Owned by Bonnier Books
Sveavägen 56, Stockholm, Sweden
www.igloobooks.com

0822 001
2 4 6 8 10 9 7 5 3 1
ISBN 978-1-80368-472-7

Printed and manufactured in the UK

Disney

AS OLD AS TIME

A TWISTED TALE NOVEL

For my husband, Scott. Without your support,
love and presence these books – and certain days
ending in y – would be a whole lot harder.

And a gigantic, fluffy THANK YOU to my editor,
Brittany, whose sense of fun and brilliant ideas
made over a thousand pages seem to just fly by.
– L.B.

PART I

ONCE UPON A TIME

Once upon a time in a faraway land, a young prince lived in a shining castle. Although he had everything his heart desired, the Prince was spoiled, selfish and unkind.

But then, one winter's night, an old beggar woman came to the castle and offered him a single blood-red rose in return for shelter from the bitter cold. Repulsed by her haggard appearance, the Prince sneered at the gift and turned the old woman away, although she warned him not to be deceived by appearances, for true beauty is found within. And when he dismissed her again, the old woman's ugliness melted away to reveal a beautiful enchantress.

The Prince tried to apologise but it was too late, for she had seen that there was no love in his heart. As punishment she transformed him into a hideous beast and placed a powerful spell on the castle and all who lived there.

"You have until the eve of your 21st birthday to become as beautiful on the *inside* as you were on the outside. If you do not learn to love another – and be loved in return – by the time the last petal of this rose falls, you, your castle and all within, will be cursed and forgotten *forever.*"

Ashamed of his monstrous form, the Beast concealed himself inside his castle, with a magic mirror as his only window to the outside world.

As the years passed, he fell into despair and lost all hope, for who could ever learn to love a beast?

It was a very good story.

It often entertained the woman who lay in her black hole of a room, manacled to a hard, cold bed.

She had enjoyed its repetition in her mind for years. Sometimes she remembered bits differently: sometimes the rose was as pink as a sunrise by the sea. But that never resonated as well as *red as blood.*

And the part at the *very* end, where the Enchantress is waylaid upon exiting the castle, thrown into a black carriage and spirited into the night – well, it didn't sound as epic and grand. She never included it.

Almost anyone else would have run out of thoughts by this point. Almost anyone else would have given in to the finality of the dungeon until she forgot herself entirely.

A few of her thoughts *were* crazy, spinning round and round the dried kettle that was now the inside of her head. If she wasn't careful, they would become too speedy, break free and seek escape through the cracks of her mind. But that way lay madness, and she wasn't quite there yet.

Ten years and she had *almost* forgotten herself. But not quite.

Footsteps down the hall.

She shut her eyes as tight as possible against the madness that tried to intrude upon her black personal madness.

Chattering voices. Another set of footsteps. The *swish swish* of a rank mop against the endlessly slimy floors. The clink of keys.

"No need to do that one. It's empty."

"But it's locked. Why would it be locked if it's empty?"

She had to scream, she had to shake, she had to explode – *anything* rather than let the dialogue repeat itself yet again as it had for the last 4,000 days, in only slightly different iterations:

"This one's locked. But do you hear something inside?"

"This door's closed. You think it's locked?"

"The one down here is locked – but I don't remember anyone being put down here."

It was as if God were trying out all the different possible lines in the farcical play that was her life and still hadn't got it quite right.

The next two minutes were as predictable as the words from a parent to a child who knows she has misbehaved and chafes under the inevitability of the sentences hurled at her.

Turn of the key in the lock.

Door creaking open.

A hideous face, hideous only in its familiarity, the same look of surprise as always and every day since forever began. The face's owner carried a tray with her in the hand that didn't have the keys. Behind her, in the hall, stood the woman with the mop. And behind *her* stood a large and silent man who was ready to subdue any of the prisoners not tied down.

The prisoner found herself opening her eyes, curiosity getting the better of her survival instinct. Today's tray had *four* bowls of broth. Sometimes it was five, sometimes it was three. Sometimes there was only one.

"Lucky for you I got an extra," the one with the tray said, settling herself down in a filthy tuffet of skirts and aprons.

This line never changed. Ever.

The prisoner screamed, unable to contain herself, unable to keep herself from looking forward to that one thing each day – the thin gruel that passed for nourishment.

The woman with the mop muttered indignantly.

"I didn't hear nuffink about a new one, I can tell you that. Thought they done a right good job clearing these sorts out of the world."

"Well, there's one now. There you go, finish up now."

The woman said it with the same false tenderness she expressed every time. The bowl tipped faster, broth trickled down the sides of the prisoner's neck and, despite herself, she got desperate, straining against the chains and sticking her tongue out to get every last drop before the bowl was removed.

"This one is old enough to be a mother," the gruel woman said without a trace of emotion or sentiment. "Think of that, them having children and raising them."

"Like animals, all of them. Animals raise their children, too. I don't know why they keep them around. Kill 'em and be done with it."

"Oh, soon enough, soon enough, no doubt," the broth hag said philosophically, getting up. "They don't last long around here."

Except, of course, it had been ten years now.

This time the hag didn't bother to toss some platitude over her shoulder as she left; the prisoner's existence was forgotten the moment she touched the door and was on her way out.

It would be all new again for her and her horrible companion tomorrow... and the next day... and the day after that...

The prisoner screamed one last time, finally and uncontrollably, as the darkness closed in.

She had to start the story again. If she just started the story and played it through, everything would be all right. *Once upon a time in a faraway land, a young prince lived in a shining castle...*

BEFORE THE BEGINNING

Once upon a time, slightly longer ago than before, there was a kingdom whose name and very existence have long since been forgotten. While the rest of the world was fighting for control of new lands across the seas, inventing ever more deadly weapons and generously gifting their own religion to foreign people who didn't want it, this kingdom just splendidly *was*.

It had fertile croplands, dense hunting forests, a neat little hamlet and the prettiest picture-postcard castle anyone had ever seen.

In happier years, because of its removed location in an out-of-the-way valley, it was a lodestone for the artistic, the different, the clever: *les charmantes*. They fled there as the modern world closed in on the rest of Europe. The little kingdom passed the Dark Ages and the

Renaissance peacefully and uneventfully. Only now were the diseases of civilised man finally catching up.

Even so, here there were still fortune-tellers who could actually tell your fortune, farmers who could pull water from stone during a dry season and performers who could really turn boys into doves. And sometimes back.

The kingdom also drew those who didn't have *powers*, precisely, but their own unusual natural talents and quirks – those who felt comfortable among the other folk. Misfits and dreamers. Poets and musicians. Nice oddballs, finding refuge there in a world that didn't want them.

One was a young man named Maurice. The son of a tinker, he had both the will to wander and the skill to fix and invent. Unlike his father, however, he felt a change in the ancient air of Europe. Wonderful, mechanical change: a future filled with weaving mills powered by steam, balloons that could carry people to far-off lands and stoves that could cook meals all by themselves.

Determined to be part of all this, Maurice looked to both the past – the steam engines of Hero – and the present, desperately chatting up anyone who had a first-hand account of the marvels he had read about. His longing took him all over, chasing down gears and pistons and demonstrations of science.

But he realised that a life of wandering would get him

nowhere; he needed a place where he could sit and think for a while and tinker with really big things – machines that required huge fires and mighty smelters. Somewhere he could store all his junk. In short, he needed a *home.*

Following his heart, and rumours, he found his way to a corner of Europe that was just a bit out of sync with the rest of the world.

First he stopped at a tiny village on a river that was perfect for powering waterwheels. But after observing the provincial little lives of the people there and enduring their horrified looks at his handcart filled with goggles and equipment and books, he realised that it was not the right place for him.

He crossed the river and went on through the woods, ending up in the strange kingdom where it wasn't unusual for someone to be seen whispering to a black cat – and the cat whispering back – or having a drink at the local pub, still covered in silver soot from the day's work and wearing dark mica goggles. Where he would fit in.

Maurice immediately struck up a friendship with some local lads and ended up renting a place with one of them. Alaric, more into animals than machines, managed to get them a cheap room at the back of one of the stables where he hired himself out as a groom.

While the lodging itself was tiny and reeked of horses,

it did include access to a large common yard. Maurice immediately set about constructing a forge, kiln and tinkering table.

He happily betook any hard labour that would bring him closer to getting the right bits for his latest project. While he picked rocks out of fields or hauled sheaves of grain on his shoulders, his mind was far away, thinking about the tensile strength of different metals, the possibilities of alloys and how to achieve the perfectly cylindrical, smooth shape he needed for the next step.

"Old Maurice Head-in-the-Clouds", his fellow strong lads would say, clapping him on the shoulders. But it was always said with a smile and respect, the same way they called Josepha the tavern maid "the Black Witch". Her punch was strong and the shocks she could deliver with a snap of her fingers to irksome customers even stronger.

At the end of summer, all of the able-bodied young men were working in the fields – even Alaric, who preferred horses to the oats they ate. Sunburned and with aching backs, they staggered into town every evening, throats parched but still singing. And, of course, they made their way directly to Josepha's.

One night, while his friends piled into the tavern, Maurice hung back to dust himself off as best he could – and to get a better look at a bit of a commotion occurring just outside.

A giant and solid-looking man stood with his legs spread aggressively and a dangerous look in his eye. This was interesting, but not as intriguing as what *else* was going on.

Sticking her face into the man's was one of the most beautiful women Maurice had ever seen. She had the poise of a dancer and the body of a goddess. Her hair glowed golden in the sunset. But bright spots of rage flushed her beautiful cheeks, and her eyes flashed green with indignation.

She waved a slim alder wand in the air for emphasis:

"*Nothing is unnatural about us!*" Her words were perfectly formed and accented; it was emotion that caused her to nearly spit. "Anything God makes is natural – by definition. And we, all of us, are the children of God!"

"You are the children of the devil," the man said calmly, lazily. Like someone who knew he was going to win. "Put here as a test. You shall be wiped from the earth like the unnatural dragons of old, you mouthy hag. Unless you purify yourself."

"*Purify?*" The girl *actually* spat this time. "I was baptised by the *monsignor* himself – so that is at least one more bath than *you've* ever had, you son of a pig!"

The man made a movement, a very slight one, reaching to his waist. As good-natured as Maurice was, he had travelled enough to know what that signalled: a knife, a pistol, a backhand across the face. *Something* violent.

He acted immediately, moving to run over and help her.

But it was all over before he took a single step: there was a flash brighter than lightning, completely silent. Everything went stark white.

After a few moments, Maurice could see again. The girl was storming off angrily but the man still stood there. There was indeed a pistol in his hand that he had meant to use. It fell to his side, now forgotten. More pressing business occupied the man's attention. Where his nose had been, there was now a bright-pink snout.

"*Son of a pig...*" Maurice repeated slowly, beginning to smile. "*Pig!*"

He chuckled to himself and finally went into the tavern.

He found Alaric with the usual gang, along with someone new: a thin, drawn-looking young man who folded his body over and brought his shoulders together like an insect, a very unhappy one. His clothes were dark and the expression on his face nervous and dour – in every way the exact opposite of the fair-haired and sunny groomsman.

Maurice moved towards them slowly, still thinking about the incident outside. Not the flash or the fight or the pig's nose, but the way the setting sun had gleamed on the girl's tresses.

Alaric impatiently pulled him down into a seat between himself and the brooding fellow.

"Here, sit down! Have you met the doc yet? I don't think

you have. Frédéric, Maurice. Maurice, Frédéric."

Maurice nodded absently. He hoped he wasn't being rude. Without being asked, Josepha placed a tankard of *cidre* down in front of him.

"Pleased to meet you," Frédéric said crisply, if gloomily. "But I am not a doctor, I keep telling you that. I was *meant* to be one, once..."

"What happened?" Maurice asked, trying to remember his manners. Frédéric, he noted, had a tiny glass of something expensive. He must have come from some learned, professional background.

"My parents sent me away before I could complete my studies. They sent me to this... *lovely* little place. They paid me off to come here."

"Frédéric here has a talent," Alaric said meaningfully, tugging on the end of his cap. "He can see the future."

"Oh, aye?" Maurice asked, impressed.

"Not really, not always, only a little," Frédéric protested, shaking his head. "Just enough for my family to exile me here... with 'people like myself' who would 'understand it'. Or, possibly, remove it with more magic. I was at university. I was going to be an apprentice to a great surgeon. I was *going* to be a doctor."

Alaric caught Maurice's eye and made a face.

"I've been trying to get him to move in with us," the

groomsman declared, taking a swig of beer and then wiping the foam off in one easy, well-practised motion.

"I don't need to," Frédéric said, but not meanly. "I have money and I don't wish to live with animals, thank you very much. Also, I already have a bit of an additional income. The king and queen summoned me to attend to their royal infant. A *cold*," he added quickly. "Nothing else wrong with him, and nothing I – or a real doctor – could fix. *Ignoramuses!* Anyway, they have hired me as their occasional consulting physician, and I do not require your charity, thank you."

"C'mon, don't you want to bunk with a couple of lads your age who can show you round? Rather than rent a room by yourself at the top of some widow's draughty attic?"

"Thank you for your concern," Frédéric said, again, not unkindly. It was more like he didn't know any way to be other than perfectly polite. But it left a strange hole in the conversation.

"Alaric, that girl..." Maurice began. "Outside the tavern before... there was a beautiful girl with golden hair... she turned a man's nose into a pig's snout..."

"Oh, you must mean Rosalind! That one's a card!" Alaric said, laughing.

"It's a bit excessive," Frédéric said, making a sour face. "That's the problem with witches."

"He was being very insulting," Maurice said, finding himself rising to the defence of a girl whose name he hadn't known a moment before. "He was accusing her of being unnatural and saying that magic was impure."

Alaric clicked his tongue. "Ah, there's a lot of that these days, I'm afraid. Before you came, there was a terrible row. Two boys, a *charmante* and a normal one – like us – fought over a girl. It came to blows and the *charmante* won and the other boy died. By magic. The palace guards were sent to break up everything and there was a bit of a riot, accusations being flung back and forth. Some of the guards got caught in the crossfire… and ended up with rather more permanent afflictions than pigs' snouts… which, knowing Rosalind, she will remove the next time she sees him."

"You can hardly blame the *normal* ones, 'like you'," Frédéric said with bitterness. "Here these people are who have powers and can do things that you can't. There's no control over their behaviour and nothing anyone – palace guards or people with muskets – can do about them. They… *we,* I suppose… need to be controlled. Or made less dangerous."

"It was two boys fighting over a girl," Alaric pointed out patiently. "It happens all the time. Boys die over that sort of thing in normal duels. This one just happened to involve magic. You can't get all worked up about it."

"At the very least, if there must be… unnatural things… people should hide it rather than flaunt it. Besides, magic always comes back on itself. Everyone knows that. *She* should know that. Rosalind, I mean."

"*Rosalind*," Maurice said, trying the name out on his tongue.

"Oh, no," Alaric said with wide eyes. "Maurice! Say it isn't so! Not so soon in our relationship!"

"Her hair," Maurice said thoughtfully, "is the exact colour of the inside of my kiln, when it is hot enough to melt iron."

"Oh, good, we're all safe then," Alaric said with a sigh, shouldering Frédéric companionably. "With lines like that, we don't need to worry about coming home and being forced to find another place to stay the night."

"I have said I am not sharing a room with you," Frédéric repeated patiently.

But Maurice was no longer listening.

THE GIRL IS STRANGE – NO QUESTION

Belle always forgot to take the hidden path to reach Lévi's bookshop. Either she was reading or dreaming or singing to herself, or just genuinely interested in what the world was like outside her house and the quiet life she and her father led. So she always ended up on the route directly through the village, and therefore talking *to*, and being talked *about* by, the villagers.

And if she was honest, she might have done it a little on purpose. It was pleasant but lonely on their tiny farm. Belle was always eager to start conversations and always disappointed by how they ended the same way, every time.

"That's nice, Belle."

"Buy a roll, Belle?"

"Think it's going to rain, Belle?"

"Why don't you stop reading and… do something with your hair?"

"Isn't my baby beautiful, Belle? She's just like the other six."

"Have you said yes to Gaston yet?"

She wished, just once, someone would show an interest in the same things she did. But that just wasn't possible in the tiny village with the same hundred or so people who had always lived there and always would.

Today at least everyone was a bit more subdued, and there seemed to be fewer villagers milling about, gossiping. Maybe someone's batch of *cidre* was finally ready, or some cow had given birth to a calf with two tails.

No, even that *would be too exciting to happen in this place.*

She sighed and stepped into the bookshop, pushing a stray strand of hair behind her ear.

"Good morning, Monsieur Lévi."

"Good morning, Belle!" the old man said brightly. He always had a kind smile for her, and was always glad to see her, no matter how many times she visited. "How is your father doing?"

"Oh, he's putting the last touches on a steam-powered log chopper for the fair," she said, spinning daintily on her toes to look round the shelves. Her brown ponytail lifted behind her and, for a moment, she almost felt like a child.

"Wonderful!" Lévi said, his mouth breaking into a big toothy grin. "He's a man who deserves a prize. Or some recognition of his genius!"

"You're the only person here who thinks so," Belle said with a sad smile. "Everyone else thinks he's crazy, or wasting his time."

"Everyone thought I was crazy for opening a bookshop here, of all places," Lévi said with a smile, pushing his spectacles up his nose and looking at her over them. "But it's certainly quiet without so many customers. I can get quite a lot of reading done."

Belle gave him a smile back, the half-sarcastic one that she was famous – or infamous – for.

"Speaking of reading –"

"Nothing new this week, I'm afraid," he said with a sigh. "Unless you'd like to read one of these religious pamphlets that Madame de Fanatique ordered."

"Are they philosophical?" she asked, desperate for anything. "Like, responses to Voltaire? Or Diderot? I wouldn't mind reading opposing views."

"Ah, no. They're the usual sort. Not even any songs or hymns. Really fairly boring. I also have some… rather morbid… treatises for Monsieur D'Arque to pick up and take back to the, ah, asylum," he said, mouth pinched in extreme distaste. "But I'm afraid I can't let you even touch those. He's very particular."

Belle sighed. "All right. I guess I'll just borrow one of the old ones, maybe?"

"Feel free," Lévi said with a smile, indicating his whole shop. "Any book."

She would have to make it a good one. Life would be even sleepier and quieter with her father gone. She saw nothing between now and his return other than bright, cold autumn days, feeding the livestock, and the occasional disappointing long walk to the village.

Belle needed something fantastic, something exciting to last her until her papa got back, or until life finally began to happen.

HAPPILY EVER AFTER

Whether by chance or not, Maurice began to see the pretty girl with the blonde hair everywhere: attending to magical fixes of ordinary things for farmers and shopkeepers, distributing bespelled roses to cure this and that ailment, laughing with friends, spending time at the tavern chatting with Josepha or, more likely, reading a book by herself.

He always managed to pick her out of the crowd, though she didn't always have blonde hair.

Or green eyes.

Or that height.

Or that colour skin.

It was bewitching.

But even *more* marvellous than that was the way she would chat with other boys – then turn away. Maurice was stunned that they didn't run after her.

His friends began to call him "moon-eyed". Frédéric pestered him to find a nice normal girl instead. One without powers. Alaric, on the other hand, encouraged him to actually go up and talk to her. To introduce himself. To let her know that he existed.

But as it turned out, Maurice didn't have to.

One day he went to the tavern early, by himself, bringing in little pieces of metal he had been working on to fiddle with as he sat there. At first glance they looked like a bar-puzzle of forged nails, of the type a country gentleman might play with while having a drink, but the pieces were much stranger-looking: a tiny bit of tarnished copper pipe and a dull-grey metal blob he was trying to fit into it.

He was still staring owlishly at the smallest end of the blob when he was suddenly aware of someone sitting down in the chair next to him, adjusting her voluminous skirts to fit the space.

"You know, you need to *speak* to the metal."

He looked up at the vision next to him and blinked.

The girl with green eyes and blonde hair regarded him calmly, a little smile on her face and a book half-closed in her hand.

The normal thing to do at this point would have been to offer to buy her a drink, to tell her how he had seen her around town, or even to gibber nervously about how pretty she was and question why she was sitting next to him.

But she was talking about the metal.

"*Speak* to it?" he asked. "What do you mean?"

"Ask it what it *needs*, to do what you want it to do. At least, that's what a friend of mine who knows about such things says."

"Well, I've tried everything else," he said with a sigh. He held up the ugly little bits of metal and cleared his throat. "*HELLO, METAL. WHAT DO I NEED TO DO TO GET YOU TO WORK?*"

The woman laughed, a throaty, honey sound that wasn't mean in the slightest. Maurice found himself chuckling as well, and even the grumpy bartender managed a smile.

The girl pushed a stray golden lock of hair out of her face and closed her book all the way, setting it beside her.

"Not like that, I don't think. At least not in *our* language. You need to know the language of metal. I'm Rosalind, by the way." She held out her hand.

"*Enchanté*," Maurice said frankly, not bothering to pretend he didn't know it already or that he whispered it at night sometimes, just to see how it felt. He took her hand and kissed it. "Not my name, of course. *Maurice* is my name."

"I've seen you around," she said, indicating the

world outside the tavern with the tip of her alder wand. "No matter what you're doing – pulling turnips, laying stones, digging – you're always thinking about something else: your metal. You're always carrying bits of it – and you're always covered in the soot of a blacksmith. Whatever are you doing?"

"I am trying to develop a *use–ful steam en–gine*," Maurice said, clapping the metal bits down on the bar on each syllable for emphasis. "The problem is that thus far it's all about someone opening valves and closing valves and drawing up water… They're trying to use them to drain mines over in England and Scotland – a lot of water problems they have over there – but it could do so much more. Instead of pushing and pulling water, you could push and pull a piston, and then, of course, there you are."

"Of course," the woman said with another smile. "There we are."

Maurice stared at her for a moment, trying to figure out if she was making fun of him. Then he laughed self-deprecatingly. "I don't speak as well as the pictures in my head do. I can't… fully… the possibilities… It's too much to explain all at once. It would be world-changing."

"Ah," the woman said. "Like gunpowder."

"No, *not* like gunpowder. This would be for building

and making, not killing and conquering."

"Not all gunpowder is for killing. I have a friend who makes the most amazing fireworks. And who, a little like you, spends all her spare time trying to launch things higher and higher into the air, using gunpowder and a thing like a cannon aimed at the sky."

"You have a lot of interesting friends, it seems," Maurice said, sighing. "I wish I could meet them."

"I'm not sure I would like that," the girl said thoughtfully. "If I introduced you to my friends, you would spend all your time talking to them and not to *me*."

Maurice stared at her for a long moment, trying to decide if what he thought she meant by that was what she actually meant by that.

And, with a smile, it became apparent that it was.

With a feeling of unreality approaching straight-up wonder, Maurice began to court Rosalind. Or perhaps it was the other way around. It didn't matter and he certainly didn't care.

He took her to a festival dance and offered her a rose he had painstakingly hammered out of metal. She graciously pinned it to the bodice of her dress – which, honestly, was pulled down almost indecently by its weight.

Then Rosalind took him to see *her* roses, a delightful garden hidden by magic inside a little park, filled with perfectly healthy, perfectly formed roses in every shade of pink and red and a few colours Maurice wasn't sure he had seen before on *any* flower.

She often grew bored with her own appearance, he discovered, which was why her looks and outfits seemed to change of their own accord so frequently. So if she was helping Maurice with something dangerous, hot and sticky in his kiln yard, when they emerged to take a stroll round town her apron and old skirts would disappear and she would appear attired in the robes of a fashionable lady wearing the latest style from Paris – but one with purple skin.

Maurice never caught the transformation as it happened; it was always done by the time he noticed.

Her powers weren't limited to roses and fashion and pigs' snouts, however. When the freshwater spring on the western side of town went sour in late summer, a delegation from the town came to *her* for a solution.

Just like Maurice spent weeks on end with his kiln and metals and tools, she pored over ancient texts day and night, mumbling to herself and waving her wand in what looked like the same pattern again and again. And in the same way Maurice wrote to great scientists and inventors around the world, she spoke with timid creatures who looked like water themselves, and sought out ancient, powerful crones for advice.

It all culminated with what *looked* like a simple, quick enchantment that made the water sweet once again. Everyone cheered, but few understood the amount of time and effort that had gone into those few minutes of chanting.

But it wasn't all work and inventing. Some nights Maurice spent carousing with Alaric and Frédéric, and Rosalind with Adelise and Bernard, when science and magic were forgotten and drinking and laughing were the subjects of the night.

So the two lovers spent long afternoons in each other's company or tending to their own pursuits and long evenings in each other's arms, surrounded by the heady perfume of roses.

And then came the day that Maurice witnessed two young men dragging a teenage boy into an alley. It was in a quiet part of town and they were trying to do it furtively, but not having much success as he kicked and screamed.

"*Stop!* Right where you are! Put him down!" the inventor shouted. "What is all this now?"

"None of your business," one of the men snapped. "Do yourself a favour and pretend you never saw this."

"He's one of those *charmantes*," the other one said heavily, as if everyone would understand what was going on just by hearing the word.

"So? Since when is that a crime?" Maurice asked, both angry and mystified.

"It has *always* been a crime against nature, as you should

know already if you're... *naturel*... uncorrupted by evil."

Maurice put down the shaft of the cart he was pulling, making it clear he was ready to fight. His clothes, though dirty, did a nice job of highlighting his thick upper arms and solid legs.

Plus there was the long knife he kept on his belt, as all labourers did. He twitched his thumb at it.

The thugs tried to look defiant. It didn't really work.

"I suggest you run along," Maurice growled. "*NOW!* Before I call the guards or teach you a lesson myself."

"Friends of those who consort with the devil are as cursed as the devil himself!" one spat. "You will get yours too!"

They stalked off and Maurice sighed deeply. He turned to the now-freed prisoner. "You all right, boy?"

"I am for now." He didn't say it with ingratitude; it was more like wry irony. Maurice could see, as the teen stretched and shook out his bruised body, the high cheekbones, pearly skin and delicate jaw that made him look *different*. "They will come after me again, when no one is around to save me. I suppose I will have to... run away... for good."

The inventor ground his teeth, frustrated. "And the palace guards are just letting this sort of thing happen? To citizens?"

In answer, the boy tossed his chin, pointing across the way. There, lolling in the shadows like they were unemployed, stood a pair of castle guards who had been watching the whole thing. They gave Maurice twin looks of distrust and disgust.

"Something must be done about this," the inventor began to say, turning back to the boy.

He had disappeared.

But Rosalind was there, suddenly, running forward and throwing her arms round him.

"I saw the whole thing. Marry me," she said.

"What? Yes. What?" Maurice said.

"You are the best, kindest, bravest, nicest man I have ever met. I want to make sure you can't ever leave me – by oath."

"Well, of course. I mean, I was planning to ask you mys..."

But his words were cut off by a passionate kiss.

He only pulled back once, to ask the one thing that bothered him.

"You weren't the boy there, being beaten up, were you? You weren't testing me, were you?"

"Don't be absurd! I came looking for you, using a 'find friend' spell. I need you and the cart to haul back some rather big packages for me."

"Oh."

"Besides, those two hooligans would have been blind, finless fish if they had tried to attack me. Now shut up and kiss me!" she added, planting her lips firmly on his again.

And so they were married. The wedding might have been hidden, both by its secret location and protective spells. The attendees might have been a trifle strange: tiny men who had advice for Maurice on the workings of metal; long-eared girls with hooves for feet who stamped impatiently for the priest to finish; bespectacled librarians and students; and the heavy-drinking young men Maurice still hung out with. But the party afterwards was as enthusiastic as any the kingdom had ever seen.

Except, perhaps, for Frédéric, who was not enthusiastic and spent the whole night looking uncomfortable and sour about the presence of so many *charmantes.*

But besides his general grumpiness, there was only one real mishap the whole night: a wild boar, enticed by the smell of the food, managed to work its way in from the woods and root through quite a bit of the magical rose garden before the drunken guests could contain it.

"That's an odd thing to happen," Maurice commented.

"Magic," a tipsy faun said, pushing her finger up on her nose to make a snout, "always comes back on itself."

Maurice then remembered the man whose nose Rosalind had changed. His new wife was swearing roundly at the pig in her garden now – but not using any magic to shoo it away, he noticed.

"Wait – that's not *him*, is it?" Maurice asked, alarmed.

"No!" the girl giggled. "Issa *pig*! But's all the same. Everything comes back on itself again. Love, hate, magic, pig noses. S'how it works."

"That seems reasonable," said Maurice thoughtfully, who might have also been a little more in his cups than he appeared at first.

What a wonderful place this is, and what an amazing woman I've married, he thought. *And what a magnificent wedding. Pigs and all.*

ALWAYS THE BRIDESMAID

Belle stomped off over the hill, wanting to run, wanting to maintain her dignity, not managing either. She kept up a strange fast-march in too precise a straight line that neither got her away from everything fast enough nor let her appear to be unaffected by it.

Behind her, on the lawn by the side of the house, was a wedding party.

Her wedding party.

It was beautiful; she had to admit that.

There was a very tasteful canopy woven with sweet-smelling flowers. Paper bells and pink ribbons festooned a high arch. Tables were draped with shining white cloths and pink bunting, and spread with an array of savoury delicacies. Silver buckets held bottles of chilled champagne; perfect little beads of moisture covered their gleaming sides like pearls. Like a painting.

There was a band, which was actually kind of terrible but enthusiastic.

There was an absolutely amazing-looking cake, the only thing Belle was really sad to leave behind. It had three tiers and its white-and-pink fondant perfectly matched everything else. Crowning the top was a tiny wedding couple, which she would have tossed aside, unexamined, in her haste to get to the cake underneath. Monsieur Boulanger might have been irksome in person but his skills as a baker were definitely on top form that day.

There was also a disappointed would-be groom sitting splay-legged in the pig wallow.

She hadn't meant to push him that hard. But having done so, she wasn't precisely displeased with the results.

The noise behind her was terrific: the squeaking of the blonde triplets; the squonkings of the tuba and accordion, which now had no purpose; the not-quite *sotto voce* assurances of LeFou to Gaston; the apologetic titterings of the priest.

The priest.

For some reason *his* presence upset Belle the most.

She could almost dismiss the ridiculous band, the cake, the table and everything else as all the accoutrements of a love-smitten madman but a priest meant Gaston was deadly serious. He had every intention of "till-death-do-they-part" marrying her.

"*Amor* does not *vincit omnia,* you ignorant man," Belle muttered, "…when the woman doesn't *amat* you back!"

She took a quick, undignified step aside to hide behind a scrub oak, then peeped out from behind it. Her heart sank. Besides the main characters in the wedding party, it looked like all the rest of the town had shown up to bear witness to Gaston's triumphant day. There was the silversmith, Monsieur LeClerc; Monsieur Hebert, the wigmaker and haberdasher; Madame Baudette, the couturier… the butcher, the baker, the candlestick-maker – *everyone* was there.

Everyone except for Monsieur Lévi.

His absence was extremely notable. He knew the kind of boy she would eventually marry, if she married.

And it certainly wasn't Gaston.

Absent, also, was her father, of course, who was on his way to the fair. And her mother, but Belle hadn't seen her since she was a baby, so that part wasn't really so surprising.

Drifts of conversation came to her as the breeze shifted.

"Terrible, but is it really surprising? That girl isn't right in the head…"

"Turning down Gaston? The most handsome, eligible bachelor in town?"

"Stupid hussy. I'd give my right pinky to wear his ring."

"Who does she think she is?"

"Does she think she can do better?"

"Maybe she'll try Dupuis's son instead, you know, the simple one who counts pebbles all day. More to her taste."

Belle balled up her fists and threw herself against the tree trunk in rage. *None* of them thought she was good enough for Gaston, the town's favourite son… the most handsome boy, with the bluest eyes and best physique, the best shot with a gun…

No one ever asked if he was good enough for *her.*

That was just the way the townspeople were.

On the one hand, they did nothing, had done nothing, but gossip endlessly about Belle and her father. How odd they were. How odd *she* was. Always reading. No friends. No suitors.

How Maurice rarely came to the pub for a drink. How he didn't have a respectable trade. How his wife had disappeared.

How, some whispered, he consorted with the devil down in his basement.

Her father had finally put an end to *that* rumour by inviting a select few to come by and inspect his house for evidence of demonic shenanigans. They had been carefully chosen: Monsieur LeClerc, who knew a bit about technology and metal, and Madame Bussard, the town gossip, sure to spread the news of what she had seen. What they saw were the half-built contraptions and engines of someone they immediately assumed was a madman. Later, Belle wasn't sure if she preferred the fear the villagers exhibited before this experiment, or the pity and ridicule after.

But on the other hand, there was Gaston, who, despite Belle's strangeness, came after her with the relentlessness of a crazed hunting dog after a boar. It wasn't that he overlooked the oddity of the father and daughter; it was more like it was irrelevant compared to Belle's status as prettiest girl in town.

Plus he felt he could fix her. Make her *normal.* His overwhelming masculinity and presence would exorcise her desire to read and think and be alone.

Was there a tiny part of Belle just a little bit tickled to be the centre of attention of such a handsome boy, the town favourite?

Of course. Yes.

Boulanger had clearly spent a lot of time on that cake.

But she would trade it all in immediately for being left alone… for being treated by Gaston the same way the rest of the town treated her.

The crowd looked so tiny from up where she was.

Belle backed away from the tree, watching the wedding party grow even smaller. In the strange, honey-like softening of the afternoon sunlight, the scene looked both more brilliant and less real, like a miniature painting. She held up her thumb and managed to block out everything with its tip, erasing everyone from the landscape.

It was like what she did when she read.

As soon as she opened a book, this little town disappeared into a vast map of countries both real and imagined.

The people down below, cleaning up from the non-wedding and erased by her thumb tip, didn't think anything interesting or important lay beyond the next bend in the river. They had no curiosity about the new lands beyond the sea or the ancient lands to the east. They had no regard for the recent discovery that other planets had moons just like the one that smiled down at them.

Belle wanted more. She wanted to *see* more. She wanted to travel to the lands she had read about, where people ate with delicate sticks, not forks.

At the very least, she wanted to be carried there in her imagination.

Belle lowered her thumb, and the townspeople reappeared.

She plopped herself down on the grass, defeated.

The truth was… reading wasn't enough any more.

It wasn't enough to catch a glimpse of these lands and ideas through the small window of the pages she turned. She wanted to step through and feel the yellow waters of the Yangtze *herself*, to hear the celestial music of foreign pipes, to taste the foods described by adventurers who travelled purposefully into the areas on maps labelled *Here there be tygres.*

Looking to the west, where the late afternoon was drawing to a dark close, she didn't see the endless landscape that often set her dreaming.

Instead she saw thick black clouds that stretched to the heights of the sky, roiling and boiling with wind and winking with lightning. *Fine.* It suited her mood. She clenched her fists unconsciously, wishing she could bring the storm faster, like a wizard or enchantress in one of her books. She wished she could stand on top of the hill in the midst of the winds and the thunder, untouched, alone, as all the would-be wedding guests fled for the safety of their homes.

And then she remembered her father, who was somewhere out on the road, heading to the fair.

Guiltily, she unclenched her fists and forced her shoulders to relax as if she really did have some control over the weather.

She rolled over on to her stomach and scanned the road as best she could, but either he was already too far into the forest or the dust in the air had obscured him and Phillipe and the cart.

She sighed and desultorily picked a dandelion. Under a protective tarp on that cart was her father's masterpiece, his finest invention. When fuelled up and working properly, it could split a pile of logs in half the time it took two men. An amazing achievement, sure to win a prize.

Belle puckered her lips and blew on the dandelion.

Either you could see how many feathery seedpods were left stuck to the head and pretend it was that o'clock, or you could make a wish.

She chose the latter.

If Maurice won the prize, and *if* it were a big one, then maybe she could convince him to move to a bigger city. Maybe even the one that he sometimes talked about, where they had lived when she was a baby. There her father could spend all his time inventing, not trying to eke out a living for himself and his daughter among countryfolk who thought he was mad.

And then Belle could have all the books she wanted. And no one would look at her as being odd; not in a city full of odd people.

Or maybe some rich member of the nobility would see his invention for the genius it truly was and sponsor him… take him and Belle away like a fairy godmother and whisk them into a world of academics, science and people just like them. They would be part of all the exciting things this century promised, far away from this provincial town and its stupid ambush weddings.

(She was glad her papa wasn't around to see *that.* He wouldn't have been angry, the way she had been; he would have been merely very, very confused. It wouldn't have helped things.)

She rested her head on her hands, watching the wedding party quickly disperse as the winds picked up. LeFou tried to grab some bunting as it whipped round branches and chairs like an eel. The villagers would all be gone in a few minutes, but she wished she could head down sooner, somehow sneak around them, to be inside when the storm finally hit. Maybe she could try going down to the east side of the house, through the rose garden…

She sighed, turning to look at the pretty pink-and-white dots that mottled the scenery just out of view of the wedding party. *They* were the main reason her father was reluctant to leave their little house in the country. Part of him still believed there was a chance that one day his wife would come back, to her roses and her husband and her daughter. If only he just kept tending the bushes and keeping the flowers pretty and healthy, maybe she would be tempted to return.

If they left, how would she find them?

But despite the automatic watering contraption Maurice had built for the garden, the roses that were usually so healthy, blooming even in deepest winter, were beginning to look a little brown and peaked.

Belle grumpily got up. She barely remembered her mother. She had the best father in the world. That was all she needed.

She took one last look at the horizon, bidding the storm and the lands beyond farewell – when she saw a strange commotion on the road.

It was Phillipe, galloping out of control towards the house, still attached to the cart.

And her father wasn't on it.

A KINGDOM SOURS

Maurice and Rosalind immediately began their happily-ever-afters. They moved to a snug little third-floor flat in the castle district, right in the middle of the most fashionable and bustling neighbourhood. A tiny garden at the back sufficed for most of Rosalind's immediate magical needs, and Maurice worked out a deal with Alaric to continue using the kiln yard despite his no longer living there.

For the first year the flat was crammed with work and parties, late-night academic discussions with friends and loud drinking songs, days and nights of research, roses and metal. Then, when the newlyweds' lives calmed down a little, their place became a serene and peaceful retreat from the world.

It was just high and removed enough to be unnoticeable from the street, and surprisingly quiet for the part of town it was in. Rarely did a random person follow the narrow, shaded alley to the back of the building and clamber up the old wooden steps to the third floor, friends knew how to step around or otherwise disengage Maurice's clever, and loud, alarm system.

Which was why he was surprised and unprepared the day the alarms went off.

Pots clashed, broken bits of ceramic broke further, and a horn, powered by an old accordion-like bellow, blasted away the sleepy late afternoon hush in the garden and sent creatures and moths flying.

"See? Told you it would come in handy," Maurice called over his shoulder to Rosalind as he went to see who it was. He had ideas about the door, too – installing a sort of periscope or monocular that would allow the inhabitant to see who was outside without, say, letting the cold winter air in.

Yes… something with a reflector inside a tube, maybe…

He opened the door and was surprised to see a young boy standing there, shocked and startled, his hand hovering in the air.

"Hello," Maurice said amiably. "Did my alarm system frighten you?"

The boy said nothing.

"Because I am trying to decide whether it should be

silent to those who approach, so I may better surprise them, or if it should be loud to frighten them off before any mischief can be achieved. What do *you* think? Can you – oh!"

Maurice suddenly noticed what was in the boy's hand. It was a piece of charcoal. He followed the direction of the hand to the lintel and saw the beginnings of a poorly written, rather rude word scratched out there.

"What," the inventor asked, at first more confused than angry, "is the meaning of this?"

"It's said that a great and terrible witch lives here!" the boy shouted, scared and defiant. There was a nasty look in his little piggy eyes.

"Oh." Maurice was by nature a generous and charitable person, travellers and dreamers and tinkerers by needs must be. But he remembered the man who had tried to threaten Rosalind the day he first saw her. And the bruised, beaten-up boy the day she had asked him to marry her. "Ah… so… so what?"

"*SHE TURNED A MAN INTO A PIG!*" the boy cried.

"No, she just turned his nose into a pig's nose. And he was very rude. *And* she turned it back, by the way. He's just fine."

"*DEVIL WORSHIPPER!*" the boy spat, and turned and ran away.

With a sigh Maurice went back inside and closed the door, locking it, something he rarely did.

His lovely wife was reclined in a rocking chair, glowing but tired, using the end of her pinky to make a stirring motion and thereby encourage the spoon across the room to put honey in her tea and mix it in.

"Darling," he said, sitting down on the stool next to her, "I think we're in for some trouble… Some strange young lad was making a mess above our door… swearing all up and down about magic, it seems."

"Oh, those ignorant peasants," Rosalind growled tiredly, putting a hand to her head. "I grow so tired of them. They're everywhere now. Some are vicious brutes, too. I thought it would just simmer down after that whole incident with the girl…"

"That happened long before I came here and it still doesn't seem like it's simmering down. I don't think that boy knew how to write. I think someone made him learn that one rather nasty phrase."

"Is he still here? Where is he?" Rosalind demanded, colour beginning to flush her cheeks as she forced herself to sit up.

Maurice made shushing noises and took her hand. "Don't grow excited. It's not good for you *or* the baby. It's over now."

Rosalind took his hand and squeezed it and kissed it, then put it on her belly.

"You're *sure* it's a girl?" he whispered.

"As sure as anything," Rosalind said with a wan smile.

"An enchantress knows these sorts of things. Don't forget, when you go out this afternoon, stop by Vashti's. I want her for my midwife. She was my aunt's, and my aunt just loved her."

"Absolutely, dear. *Anything* for you and my baby daughter."

But the midwife wasn't to be found.

When Maurice called at her house the door was open, hanging there like an ill omen.

"Hello?" Maurice called out tentatively.

After a few moments and no answer, he let himself in, keeping one hand casually on his knife.

"Vashti? Hello? It's Maurice, Rosalind's husband…"

The midwife was old but in good health. In the back of his mind Maurice feared finding her on the floor with a broken hip or worse, but he suspected that was not the case. Here and there things looked out of order in the tiny house: one chair of three was pushed far aside, a single crock lay broken on the floor. And on the table lay half a baguette, a nice piece of cheese and some grapes. Dinner, untouched.

"Hello?"

The inventor fretted. It didn't look like a robbery, nothing was stolen, not even her fine woollen blankets. It was like she had just… vanished.

After a few more minutes of looking round, he left and asked her neighbours about her whereabouts, but no one knew where she had gone. Or even that she *had* gone.

Or, he gathered as he watched some sets of shifting eyes, they didn't *want* to know.

He decided to see if any of Rosalind's other friends had heard from Vashti, perhaps there had been some sort of emergency, a birth gone wrong, that she had been summoned away to.

But as he walked through the town Maurice noticed other doors that had nasty graffiti smeared on them, sometimes in charcoal and occasionally in something that looked very much like blood.

If the friends he sought were home, they ushered Maurice in off the streets quickly, or made a big deal of talking to him loudly where others could hear, about nothing in particular, emphasising again and again how nice it was to have such a normal friend who wasn't one of *les charmantes.*

None of them knew where Vashti was. No one even knew she was missing.

With a confused and heavy heart, Maurice decided before he went home empty-handed that he would at least fortify himself at the tavern with a drink and a chat with his friends.

There was a sign on the door.

"*Under new management. No dogs, Italians or charmantes*"

Maurice hesitated, unsure what to do. But habit took over his feet, and he found himself continuing in.

The place seemed darker. Small groups spoke in loud, lively tones, but it sounded forced. A new and sour-looking young woman made a big pretence of wiping down the bar with an already filthy rag.

Frédéric and Alaric were in their usual seats. The doctor had never moved in with the groomsman, even after Maurice had moved out; there were some differences of station that were insurmountable beyond drinking at a bar together. Yet they had still managed to stay friends. Both brightened upon seeing Maurice.

"Where is Josepha?" he asked in a low voice, indicating the barmaid with a tilt of his head.

"She was… bought out," Alaric said distastefully. "Not of her own free will. Told to move to a more… accepting part of town."

"She was paid," Frédéric noted. But he regarded his cordial glass with a sceptical eye, obviously unconvinced of its cleanliness.

"Where did she go? Has she set up elsewhere yet? We should go and see her…"

"No one has seen her since… this happened," Alaric said. "Some suspect foul play."

"Or she has merely seen which way the wind is blowing, taken her fee and left town," Frédéric suggested.

Alaric rolled his eyes.

"This is getting out of hand," Maurice said. "All of it! This… *boy*… wrote some very nasty things on our door. Lots of doors, it looks like. And my wife is dead set upon this Vashti woman for her midwife, and she's nowhere to be found. And no one will talk about her. I have a terrible feeling about it. What is going on around here?"

Alaric sighed and played with his cup. "Things are growing worse between… *regular* people."

"*Les naturels*," Frédéric interrupted primly, "and *les charmantes*."

Alaric gave him a black look, then continued. "I've never seen it this bad. It's out of control. Idiots are hassling anyone even the slightest bit unusual – from a self-declared goodwife peddling love potions, to Babbo, who sings to himself and makes those little toys out of twigs and moss. They are badgering them, pestering them – and, occasionally, beating the tar out of them."

"Things are *not* out of control," Frédéric said with the patience of someone who had been arguing the same thing with a friend for a long time. "*Any more.* That is precisely the point. Normal people are trying to keep control of things, to keep things safe. And they are not hassling anyone who is innocent."

"Innocent of what?" Maurice demanded. "Magic? Since when is that a crime?"

"It's a crime against nature."

"But you yourself are…"

"Tainted!" Frédéric hissed. "Yes, I know! *Keep your voice down!*"

Maurice slammed his fist on the bar, exasperated.

"But… but what about Vashti? Rosalind will be terribly upset if I don't procure her for the birth. Where did she go?"

"She probably left after finding pig's blood smeared all over her door," the groomsman said moodily. "*Les charmantes* are leaving… disappearing out of the last safe haven for the fey and magical left in this world."

"I would suggest that your wife choose another for her imminent birth, and seek her no more," Frédéric suggested crisply. "Find a good *doctor*, perhaps."

Maurice ignored him. "But surely the king and queen… I mean… well, the whole *point* of this place is that it's safe, and different, and…"

"The king and queen are doing nothing about it," Alaric said with a sigh. "Just like they are doing nothing about the salt scarcity and the trade embargo with Guerende. Perhaps they feel threatened, ever since they lost a couple of guards to errant spells. Or maybe they're lazy and just don't care. I'm not really sure *what* they do up in their towers all day. Guess I'll find out. They certainly don't give their precious stallions enough exercise." He brightened suddenly. "Which reminds me! I have great news! Drinks are on me tonight, old friend!"

"What's the occasion?" Maurice asked, cautiously hopeful for something to offset the gloom of the day.

Frédéric gave a thin smile. "You are looking at the new Master of the Royal Stables. Bow, as is only appropriate – but do not breathe in, for the aura of horse is hard to avoid."

"And it's all thanks to this chap here," Alaric said, toasting his drink rather sloshily at the doctor. "He put in a good word for me to the king himself!"

Maurice smiled and shook Alaric's hand formally but heartily.

"Marvellous news, Alaric! You're moving up in the world!"

"Oh, in more ways than one," the groomsman said with a suggestive waggle of his eyebrows. "There's a head maid there in the castle, soon to be the housekeeper…"

Frédéric rolled his eyes. "No good deed goes unpunished."

"And you? Any good news in your life?" Maurice pressed.

Frédéric's dour face looked strangely, timidly pleased.

"As a matter of fact, yes. The king and queen, still impressed with my ability to cure their son – utter hogwash, by the way – have given me my own facility for research. It's all hush-hush, but trust me when I say the freedom I have is more than I ever thought possible going to a traditional college… Let us leave it with the fact that I am able to practise my skills in surgery at leisure, in cutting out that which is too infected to save. I may even be able to cure… *myself,* someday."

Alaric and Maurice exchanged a look and a shudder.

"The downside is that it's all the way out near that boring little village on the other side of the river," the groomsman said quickly, trying to change the subject.

"We will never see you any more," the inventor protested.

"I am not disappearing off the planet," Frédéric said primly, though obviously pleased that someone cared enough to miss him. "I came today specifically to see you and congratulate you on your wife's pregnancy."

"Thank you kindly, Monsieur Doctor!" Maurice said with a little bow. "Have you had any visions about my baby girl? Can you tell me her future?"

Frédéric looked away. "It does not work like that, and I do not encourage their… coming to me. Frankly, the very fact that you know your baby's sex is disturbing."

Alaric flushed at the word *sex*. Maurice just sighed and

shook his head at his friends. It was strange to think of them as possible uncles to his little daughter. Well, maybe she could learn something from them at least the – skills of a physician, perhaps some basic horsemanship…

AN ENCHANTED CASTLE

Belle ran to Phillipe, carefully staying out of the way of his hooves. She tried to keep from panicking but the big horse's fear was infectious. Usually nothing could spook the staid, untroubled beast. He was from an ancient line of war mounts who were bred for size, stamina and most of all *calm* in the midst of battle.

Phillipe had also spent most of his life around Maurice's often exploding inventions. Almost nothing could distract him from a nice patch of clover or a nap.

But now he bucked and snorted and rolled his eyes like a pack of wolves was after him.

"Where is Papa, Phillipe? Did you make it to the fair? What happened?"

The log-splitting device seemed to be more or less in one

piece on the cart, though some of the more delicate pieces were missing. Had it been a robbery, the thieves would have likely taken whatever seemed precious, including the thing's grill, which gleamed gold. Belle carefully disengaged the cart and pushed it aside, still holding the reins.

"You've got to take me to him, Phillipe," she said, throwing herself up on the big horse's back. She pulled his bit firmly, forcing his enormous head back round towards the forest.

Phillipe resisted at first, trying to yank his neck out of the old rope. When he finally gave in, it was with a weary chuff, as if even *he* knew they needed to go back for Maurice.

Belle had only been on the road through the forest once or twice, and never alone and never that far. Although instinctively she started to direct Phillipe to the left, where the path divided and eventually led to the next town, the horse snorted and pulled to the right, down an ancient, overgrown road that obviously led to places less visited.

The storm had already lent an eerie darkness to the end of the day. That, coupled with the thick, almost monstrously exuberant foliage around them, left the path unnaturally shadowed. Little white moths that should have waited until much later to emerge from their daytime sleeping spots flapped round Belle's face like it was a lantern they were drawn to. Strange, nearly invisible insects made very different noises from their cousins in the fields or carefully cultivated orchards of the village. Dry leaves crackled in the underbrush, disturbed by things Belle couldn't see.

She found herself, very much against her will, thinking about how useful it would be to have someone like Gaston along with her on this quest.

Or, actually, someone else *with a gun.* Anyone *else, really.*

Minutes played out into what seemed like hours on the lonely black path. Belle's initial excitement and adrenalin rush were worn down by time and the lack of anything imminently dangerous. The forest was sinister, nothing more.

Her fear for her father grew, however; there was no sign of him at all aside from the occasional cart track that revealed itself in a sandy bank or thick wedge of mud.

Slowly the land began to change around them: the ground rose up steeply on either side of the path, making a ravine that widened out into a small valley. Whatever was left of the sky was obscured by high, sharp hills and black pines. Thick and thorny plants clustered unnaturally at the squat, square roots of trees.

Wait. Square?

Belle gasped as she realised that what she had mistaken for particularly unnatural growth were the ruins of old buildings. She stopped paying attention to where

Phillipe was heading and tried to distinguish outlines and patterns in the stones and bricks. The vines that covered them weren't thick; certainly not more than 50 or 100 years old. But Belle had never heard of a village this far into the forest and no one in town had ever mentioned it.

"What *is* this place?" she murmured.

Phillipe stopped, huffing nervously. They were in front of a massive rusted iron gate that hung a little open – but it was not so far decayed that it fell off its hinges. The gap was just wide enough to fit through.

Phillipe pawed the ground with his hoof and snorted.

He would not be going in.

Belle took a deep breath and dismounted. She gave his warm, comforting flank a pat and regretfully left him behind. Then she slipped through the crack in the gate, unwilling to make it squeal by trying to open it farther.

Beyond was a twilit courtyard, wide and grey with a dry and dusty three-tiered fountain in the middle. The whole scene possessed but one splat of colour: a dirty mustard-yellow sun hat that lay discarded on the ground.

"Papa!" Belle cried, rushing over and picking it up. There was no other sign of her father – of anyone, really – and no footprints on the cobblestones. She looked round, up at the main building, and started at what she saw.

No inn or hunting retreat this; what she had thought

was the entrance to a mews was the base of what appeared to be a small but perfectly preserved castle.

In the gloom it was hard to see the whole thing, but there were shadows of turrets, towers, parapets and delicate roofs with merlons and crenels too slim and decorative to be of any real use.

Belle frowned. While she hadn't travelled the world or gone on "The Grand Tour", she had read enough to know that this wasn't an ancient castle. It was too tiny, too perfect and too battlement-free to be from the dark times of yore when neighbouring kingdoms often battled each other.

It wasn't unreasonable to imagine her father, having noticed the mysterious ruins, deciding on a whim to investigate them. *Like Don Quixote and his golden helmet of Mambrino*, she thought, looking at his yellow hat. *Off on a silly quest.*

That idea and the notion that he was somewhere in the grounds gave her courage.

"Papa?" she called, slipping through the giant iron-banded, and strangely unlocked, front door.

The abandoned building was almost pitch-dark, of course.

"Papa?"

Her voice quickly echoed back at her off tapestry-covered walls, and furniture and statues that she could barely see…

statues with seemingly dead eyes, claws and *fangs*.

Did she hear footsteps up ahead, pattering and quick?

Was that the golden glint of a lantern, shining briefly off a slick, cold mirror?

"Hello? Papa?"

Unsure it was the right thing to do, she hurried after it.

The carpet under her feet was cold but soft and mostly unworn. The columned loggias beyond the foyer were unlike anything Belle had ever seen in person; she had only sighed over pictures of them in books about warm foreign countries. Suits of armour, alabaster urns and enormous ancient paintings decorated every possible inch.

Not paying attention at all to her feet or where she was going, Belle almost tripped over the giant formal staircase that led up to the mezzanine.

There it was again, the slightest tap against the floor. Normally she wouldn't have said her father was delicate or light-footed, but noises echoed strangely in the castle…

And there was no one else there… *right*?

Thieves, she told herself quite reasonably, *and highwaymen – they would have accosted me already.*

Right?

They would have already grabbed her and divested her of… whatever it was they wanted from her. She had been yelling; they would know where she was.

She climbed up through the castle, heading towards where she thought the sounds were coming from. The walls grew closer and the stairways became narrower until finally the steps began to spiral steeply and she had to stoop. *I'm probably in one of the towers*, she thought. The air was colder and damper here, and the cobwebs thicker.

She unconsciously put her hand to her neck, forgetting for a moment that she hadn't brought her cloak and therefore couldn't clasp it any closer.

"*Papa?*"

A niche in the wall was lit by the happy glow of a little candelabrum, which should have cheered Belle. Instead it only made her shiver. W*ho lit it?* And left it there? Wouldn't her father have taken it with him?

More pitter-patter. The slide of something wooden against an uncarpeted floor.

"Hello?" she called out, trying to make *her voice*, at least, seem brave. "Is anyone there? I'm looking for my father! Please…?"

"…*Belle?*"

Her heart leapt as her father's voice echoed weakly through the stone halls.

"*PAPA!*"

She ran down a bleak corridor whose dire accoutrements hinted at the cruel purpose of this place: iron manacles and rotting, long-unused stocks. Ringing the room were a number of identical doors that were heavily banded and locked.

A single torch flickered in a sconce next to the first one and Belle hurried towards it.

"Papa!" she cried.

"Belle!"

He stuck as much of his face as he could fit through the narrow bars in the door. Then he pulled away as a paroxysm of coughing overcame him.

"Oh, Papa..."

Belle reached through the bars and he clasped her hands eagerly. She gasped in shock.

"Papa! Your hands are so cold, we have to get you out of here!"

Maurice, despite his pallor, gave her an ironic look. "Belle, my dear, I think my health is the least of our issues right now. Listen, please: go and get help."

"Absolutely not! I won't leave you!"

"Belle, you *have* to get out of here! I mean it! *Run!*"

And then it was as if the shadows themselves suddenly congealed and took form beside her.

Something black and clawed grabbed Belle's shoulder and spun her round.

"*WHAT ARE YOU DOING HERE?*" the shadow roared.

But, a part of her noticed, it didn't threaten her. Not outright, anyway.

"Who's there?" she demanded, squinting into the gloom. "Who are you?"

"*I am the master of this castle. And once again, I demand to know what you are doing here!*"

"I've come for my father," Belle said, a little spark of anger igniting within her. "Let him out. He's sick and he's done nothing wrong."

"*He shouldn't have trespassed!*"

The voice sounded petulant. Not diabolical.

It gave Belle hope, how human it seemed. In all of her fairy tales and adventure books – the ones with the heroes who were clever rather than strong – *this* was how you outwitted an opponent. By finding a chink in his armour, a personality flaw to exploit. Then you got him to show off his power by turning into a tiny (and easily stompable) mouse, or slitting open his own stomach.

All she needed was a flaw, and time.

"Is there *nothing* we can do? I can pay you..." She thought back to their house, full of bits of metal, books, dust and occasionally food. "Something," she finished, a little lamely.

The voice roared with laughter. "*I am the master of all that you see. What could you give me that I don't already own?*"

Belle looked round desperately.

"Me," she said without thinking.

"Belle, no!" Maurice shouted.

"Me. Take me," she repeated, with a deep breath. "I'll be your prisoner. Just let my father go."

She would think of something eventually. All the heroes did.

"Belle, no! I forbid it!"

"*I agree to this*," the voice finally said. "*But you must promise to stay here forever.*"

Wind roared in Belle's ears as this strange tipping point in her life suddenly rose before her, consumed her and passed by. Just a few hours before she had avoided an ambush wedding and dreamed about what life would be like far from the village when her father won money at the fair.

And now she was trading all those possible futures for a life behind bars in a haunted castle.

She needed to see what she was up against. All the heroes in her stories were granted *that*, at least – a last request.

"Come into the light," she ordered.

The voice chuckled nastily.

With the complete silence of a terrible predator, *something* dragged itself into the orange glow of the little candelabrum.

Belle caught her breath in shock.

Disparate parts of creatures that didn't belong together

were combined in one horrible body: a monstrous clawed foot, bigger than that of a bear's or a lion's; a narrow waist; a massive chest. An even more massive neck. Thick, matted brown hair… *a cloak.*

It wore a ragged purple cloak with a gold pin clasped at its neck. Torn blue trousers hung in tatters down legs like a giant dog's.

It had a face the size of an oven. A shiny black nose, flaring and wet. Tusks that protruded out of its skull like a mistake. Startlingly blue eyes… with intelligence behind them…

Wet, hot breath and slavering tongue.

Belle fell back despite herself. If it was entirely an animal, she might have been able to deal with it. Like a dog. If it was a demon or ghost, she would have at least known where she stood with her opponent. She had read many, many stories about those sorts of things.

But *this*…

Some sort of monstrous, sick, half-human, half beast…

Belle forced her head up, though she could not look the thing in the eye.

"I give you my word."

She said it slowly… doling out each syllable with weight.

"No, Belle!" her father cried. "I won't let you do this!"

"*DONE!*" the Beast roared.

Moving faster than something of that size should have been able to, and in utter silence, the Beast flowed forward and opened the cell door with a single swipe of his massive paw.

Maurice ran to his daughter.

"No, Belle, listen to me, I'm *old,* I've lived my life!"

But the Beast grabbed him and began to bound down the stairs, pulling the old man with him.

And Belle sank to the floor and began to weep.

THE END OF FAIRY TALES

Maurice dutifully told Rosalind everything about the growing violence towards *les charmantes* and how he couldn't find the midwife – despite knowing what would come of it. From the widening of her eyes upon hearing about Vashti's disappearance to a cool narrowing of their mossy green pupils at the news of Josepha and her tavern, Maurice could have easily predicted each facial tic and where it would all lead.

"I must find her," Rosalind announced, standing up with the awkward slowness her rounding belly and strange joint pains gave her. Her eyes darted seriously round the room, searching for things: a cloak, a walking stick, maybe… "There are too many of these 'disappearances' lately. I will get to the bottom of this *now*…"

"Rosalind," her husband said firmly.

"You cannot stop me!" she cried, eyes flaring and cheeks flushing pink. Some women grew calm and peaceful during pregnancy; Rosalind seemed to become more of what she already was: fiercely happy, fiercely angry, fiercely productive. "Vashti was godmother to my cousin! She is like family!"

"I'm not going to try and stop you," Maurice said. "I am merely urging caution. You are… well known… for what you do. This doesn't seem like the safest place for people who wield magic any more. Going round knocking on doors and demanding information out of people might not be a good idea. It would draw too much attention to yourself."

"I was not going to knock on doors and demand information," Rosalind said, with such hauteur it was obvious that had been precisely her plan. "We… who do what *we* do have more subtle means of procuring information."

Maurice waited patiently.

"I… shall go to Monsieur Lévi," she said after a moment of quick thinking. "With his books and scrying glasses, he should make short work of this."

"That is an excellent plan. Just be… discreet."

"*Of course* it's an excellent plan. And *yes*, I shall be discreet!" she snapped, magicking a cloak round her shoulders in exasperation.

Slapping her swollen feet on the uneven, hard cobbles of the kingdom's best-kept roads was more tiring and strenuous than she had imagined. Still, thousands upon thousands of mothers and grandmothers before her had laboured in the fields and gardens and hunted in the woods and still had perfectly healthy children. She would not complain.

Monsieur Lévi's shop did not need to be in the centre of town. Those who wanted to visit him managed to find him. Even if his shop was never in the same location twice.

"I don't have time for this," Rosalind said, blowing quickly through her puckered lips, trying to calm her heart. She closed her eyes, shook her head to clear the universe of silliness, then strode forward to the closest shop door.

Whatever the sign had advertised outside, the interior was filled with paper and glass. Piles of books and clusters of scrolls competed for space with polished silver hand mirrors, tiny square windows sized for a doll's house, and bowls like small stone ponds with perfectly still water – water that *stayed* still, despite the door-slamming and bell-jingling at Rosalind's dramatic entrance.

None of it was ordered; all of it looked like it had been pulled from the empty shelves round the room quite recently.

"Rosalind!" the shopkeeper said with a twinkle in his eye as he turned to greet her. He had been polishing a lens and continued to do so, breathing on it to fog the surface.

The man was thin, and probably ancient, but didn't look a day over 70. Scruffy hair grew round his pate and from the end of his pointy chin. "How are things?"

Despite the urgency of her quest, Rosalind was distracted by the state of the place.

"Monsieur Lévi, what is going on here? Are you *closing*?"

"Well, the way things are heading… I'd rather disappear myself before someone *else* disappears me. It's time for me and the old girl" – he looked round the shop lovingly – "to pick up and move on."

"No, no," Rosalind said. "Things aren't so bad…! Are they?" she added, less sure.

"Bad enough," Lévi said bleakly. "They just shut down the Midnight Market… everyone is worried about safety and pogroms. Florent was found on a doorstep, black and blue and beaten to within an inch of his life. And I believe the only reason my shop has escaped the rocks and arson other places have endured is because of our tendency… to move…"

Rosalind let this news sink in and churn through her recently sluggish mind. "Stay and fight, then. We can change it before it gets worse."

Lévi gave a chuckle. "Spoken like a spirited young lady who will change the world one way or another. My dear, I am *old*." He leaned forward on his counter for emphasis.

"And… I have seen this sort of thing before. And I have seen it happen again. I do not know if I shall survive the times after next. But while there is life, there is hope. And with life, and hope, go I… and the books they will no doubt be trying to burn soon. Hopefully we'll find a place where that nasty fever everyone is talking about hasn't reached yet. I don't know if I could survive an illness like that at this age."

"Oh, you'll live forever," Rosalind said with a dismissive wave and a smile. "But where else in Europe have you experienced this sort of thing before? Are there other places where magic is still strong?"

"You don't need to be a witch to have them hate you," he said lightly. "Now, how may I help you? I just got in an absolutely delicious stack of not-strictly-accurate historical fictions about the late Republic. Er, Roman, that is… far from serious, but good for a cosy evening in front of the fire. What do you say?"

"I'm afraid I'm not here for books this time," Rosalind said sadly, looking round at the luscious stacks. "I'm here for a reading. I mean, the *other* kind of reading."

Lévi's face seemed to tighten away from her, towards the back of his head, as if all his features were trying to escape. He turned pale.

"Things must be dire indeed, if the great Rosalind comes to *me* for such a thing."

"Vashti is missing," Rosalind said, unconsciously putting a hand on her belly. "I wanted her for a midwife. Maurice found her flat empty, her dinner still on the table. I suspect the worst."

"Very well," Lévi said with a sigh. He carefully put down the moon-shaped lens he was working on.

"What is that?" she asked, curious.

"Oh, just a little idea I have," he said as he rummaged through a recently packed box. "Something to let me do my thing while blending in with the natives. Ah, this one will do."

He pulled out a silver hand mirror, the sort a gentleman might own, with a not-very-ornate handle and simple, bold lines around the reflecting surface. "Here, *you* hold it and ask. You knew her better. She was… not much of a reader. The *usual* kind of reader."

Rosalind took the mirror. It was heavier than it looked, or she was weaker than she expected; it caused her hand to dip.

"Show me Vashti," she ordered.

Lévi peered over her shoulder, curious.

Nothing happened.

The mirror remained a mirror, reflecting her face with just a hint of fog. Her nose, Rosalind noticed distractedly, was red and unattractive in its current state.

"Mirror," she said, more loudly this time. "*Show me Vashti.* Where is she?"

The gleaming surface *did* fog this time. But it revealed nothing beyond a matt, stark black. Eventually this, too, dissipated and it went back to being a mirror.

"It's not working," Rosalind said stubbornly, holding the mirror out to its maker.

"Rosalind," Lévi said softly. "She is gone. You know that."

Rosalind bit her lip, determined not to cry. Her face felt huge, as if all the tears she was keeping back were filling up her skull and her eyes and forehead. If Vashti was dead, there was nothing she could do now.

The Enchantress thrust the mirror into Lévi's hands and turned away, sobbing and retching. Her morning sickness, magically gone on the first day of her second trimester, suddenly came back with a vengeance.

"Oh, Rose," Lévi said sadly without looking at the mirror. He put an arm round her.

"She would… she would *never* have just left her home that way," Rosalind sobbed. "She would put her things in order. Her family has been here for centuries as healers… she would have known she was going to die… of something *natural.* Something has happened to her, Lévi. Someone has *done* something to her."

The bookseller didn't say anything but watched her

quietly, seeing the change on her face that reflected the emotions roiling within her.

"She will be avenged. I will have justice," Rosalind growled, torn between throwing up, being comforted and destroying everything in a great inferno. "*This isn't the dark ages!*"

"Every age has its darkness," Lévi said quietly. "Rosalind. Take your family and move far away from here. I mean it. You're not safe. None of us are. I myself am going to the New World. I think they're mostly done with their witch trials there. And Providence is supposed to be a city of great religious freedom."

Rosalind's mind spun. She was the greatest enchantress in these magic-poor times, but she didn't have the power or ability to defeat the anonymous, loosely connected bands of ruffians and hatemongers who seemed to be taking over the kingdom. Once she found them, she could turn them all into pigs or stones or insects, of course.

Rosalind thought. "I shall go to the king and queen. They are the only ones who can stop this. They *must*. Surely unrest and crime have to be a threat to the kingdom. Even… even despite what happened to their guards. They have to see this can't go on."

"And how will you get in to see them?" Lévi said curiously.

"Their… son. The little prince. I did not attend the christening," she said, warming to the plan even as she thought of it. It felt right. Ancient. Grand. "I will come bearing some sort of charm or blessing to bestow. Just like we used to, in the old days, when there was newborn royalty."

Lévi sighed. "It's not a bad idea. Just don't expect too much. And maybe have an escape plan ready."

He looked round at his half-packed boxes and then at Rosalind's belly, which she was holding with both hands.

Outfitted in the most impressive, angelic and magicked outfit she could manage, Rosalind walked into the castle with head held high, alder wand gripped firmly in her right hand. The guards stepped aside as she approached; she ignored the distrustful look in their eyes.

In the throne room the young king and queen sat with their princeling – well, the toddler was held by his wet nurse – all three in deep shades of matching velvet.

"Your Highnesses," Rosalind said with a mild head nod – generally unacceptable as a way of greeting royalty, but, after all, *she* was an enchantress.

"Enchantress," the queen said in an equally neutral tone. Her features were beautiful, if harsh: white-blond hair and razor-sharp cheekbones, ice-blue eyes. Motherhood had softened her looks not at all.

"This is an unusual visit," the king said with a smile

that did not reach his eyes. He had long, dark-brown hair drawn back into a ponytail, with the front part curled over his forehead in a way that was currently very fashionable. Neither one wore a crown, for it was not considered modern. But they were each covered in sparkling pins and jewelled brooches, golden buckles and rich, rich cloth.

"I have come to offer a blessing on your child, the royal prince," Rosalind began, turning to him.

"That will not be necessary," the king said languidly. "These are modern times. We appreciate your sentiment and allow your presence out of respect for ancient traditions, but your blessing is no more than words, your charm no more than meaningless well-wishing."

Rosalind stared hard at the king, trying not to show how taken aback she was. In *this* kingdom! The last refuge of ancient traditions and *les charmantes.*

Magic was being forced out of the world entirely. She shivered, was this really the end?

"In that case, let me attend to the other issue I came here for," she said, spreading her hands and now lowering her eyes. "I beg your intercession on behalf of my people. They are being harassed, beaten, sometimes murdered. Let their persecution come to an end and defend your innocent citizens."

"And which citizens would that be, Enchantress?" the king asked mockingly. "The good and natural citizens of this kingdom? Or are you allying yourself with some of the more unpatriotic and unnatural creatures who dwell in our fair land, threatening our citizens and disrupting our peaceful life?"

Rosalind ground her teeth, trying to keep the look of a mild petitioner. Trying to control the anger Maurice always warned her about. She looked round the room but the servants and royal entourage all seemed to be doing a very good job of not paying attention to what was going on. The Prince was playing with a ball that looked like it was made out of real gold.

She took a deep breath. "If I may be so bold, what *unpatriotic* creatures? Who has been threatening *you*?"

"Their *existence* is threat enough," the queen said. "They – you – all have abilities which make our muskets and swords seem like toys. And they show no hesitation in using these powers at the slightest provocation... as if this is some medieval fairy tale and not the age of laws and reason!"

"A boy is dead because of his interest in a *charmante* girl and the anger of her warlock boyfriend," the king pointed out. "And the unrest that followed, the attacks on our own soldiers, destroyed even more lives."

"You're allowing the complete subjugation of a people because two boys fought over a *girl*?" Rosalind demanded. "A woman is dead because of this insanity, this... prejudice!

An innocent woman who never hurt *anyone*… who wasn't even there when the fights broke out. What has a midwife ever done besides keep young mothers healthy and deliver babies into the world? Her death is on your hands!"

The king shrugged.

"I have no idea what you're talking about. Such things do not concern us. We have other, more important affairs to attend to. The business of running a kingdom. Business of the state. The re-emergence of what looks very much like the plague in countries far too close to us. We need to consider shutting down our borders."

"So if one or two… of the more… odd… residents of the land disappear, and thus keep the others in line in this time of trouble and possible quarantine, *c'est bon, n'est-ce pas*?"

The queen made a little kissy noise at her son.

The princeling babbled incoherently back.

Rosalind regarded the scene with disgust, hate and rage. She wanted to turn away, leaving with some juicy retort, like *you will regret this*, and become a golden ball of light and explode out of there.

But the way things appeared to be going, maybe it wouldn't have been a good idea to make such a display.

So she turned and stalked out like a…

…like a *human*.

Like a failure.

THE ENCHANTED CASTLE

Belle wept on the floor of the cell.

A surprisingly large part of her thought that maybe if she just closed her eyes and cried hard enough, it would all disappear. Everything was so unlikely anyway – the castle, the monster, her imprisonment… It could easily be a nightmare she was having after falling asleep reading one of those horror stories her father warned her about.

But the floor was ice-cold under her knees and wet from her tears.

There was no denying reality.

Any dream she had of escaping the boring little village she grew up in to go on adventures was gone forever; she would spend the rest of her days chained in a dark room, lost and forgotten. She wondered, briefly, if Gaston would look for her… if he would mount a search party even after the whole wedding business.

I'll never see Papa again.

Belle leapt up and dashed to the one tiny window, pressing her face against the cold stone frame. In the courtyard below, what looked very much like a dusty, wheel-less old carriage crept along on its axles like a giant bug. Belle gasped at the strange thing. Her father was inside, desperately trying to open the door; she could just see his anxious face. Then the gates swung open of their own accord and the carriage scuttled away, carrying its passenger into the woods.

Belle could *feel* rather than see the silent presence of the Beast. He was terrifying, to be sure, but far less immediate than the waves of despair engulfing her.

"You didn't even let me say goodbye," she sobbed, not looking away from the window. "I'll never see him again."

There was a strange whispering noise, as if the Beast was shuffling his feet.

"I'll," he paused, coughing. "I'll show you to your room."

Belle swallowed her tears in surprise. Did she hear him right?

"My *room*?" she asked, looking up. She glanced round the cell. "But I thought…"

"You *want* to stay in the tower?" the Beast growled

at her impatiently.

"No, of course not, but—"

"*Then follow me!*"

With a movement that was graceful and powerful the Beast spun to leave, the candelabrum in one hand. Seamlessly he switched from two legs to four, then to two again, depending on what the terrain required: fitting through the door, gambolling down the stairs, holding the candles high to light the way. His movements were unnatural and strange, like a poodle walking on its hind legs.

Seeing no other choice and utterly exhausted, Belle followed. They walked in silence for a few moments, the only noise her own feet on the floor.

"I..." The Beast coughed again. "I hope you like it here."

What?

He hoped she *liked* it here? Like a guest? What an odd thing to say to a prisoner. This monster was conversing with her almost like a human. A human that could be reasoned with. Hope began to rear its shining head.

"Excuse me?" she asked politely.

"The castle is your home now, so you can go anywhere. Except the West Wing."

"What's in the West Wing?"

But apparently she had grown too hopeful, too expectant, too quickly.

The Beast turned on her and bared his fangs in her face.

"*IT IS FORBIDDEN!*"

Belle shrank back against the wall. His hot breath engulfed her the way she imagined a lion's would have, right before it ate a Christian in ancient Rome. With a final, barely audible growl in the back of his throat, the Beast withdrew from her and continued down the stairs.

Belle reluctantly followed him. What choice did she have?

Mention of the West Wing ended all conversation on the long walk through the dark castle. She tried to look around, get her bearings and pretend she wasn't being led to what was essentially just a nicer prison cell by a creature that could devour her in two gulps.

Eventually the Beast stopped in a long hall of apartments and opened a door, beckoning her to step in.

Belle was surprised at the grandeur of the room. In the centre was a beautiful canopied bed that looked like it had just been made up that morning, not abandoned years ago. Thick velvet curtains hung in front of delicate oriel windows and enclosed a comfortable-looking tuffet for watching the world outside. A gilt wardrobe the size of her pantry back home stood to attention next to the bed. Fancy paint and plaster medallions graced the walls. The room was ringed by golden-mirrored sconces, which the Beast lit from his own candelabrum. Soon it was a merry and cosy place indeed.

The Beast swept out into the hall again silently and stood for a moment in the doorway as if unsure what to say.

Belle was unsure too. *Thank you* didn't seem appropriate. Not to her jailer.

"If, um, there's anything you need…" the Beast growled uncomfortably, "my servants will attend you."

Servants? What servants? Except for the Beast and Belle and her father, there was no sign of any other life in the castle. What if, on top of being monstrous, her captor was insane as well?

"*YOU WILL JOIN ME FOR DINNER!*" he suddenly roared. "This is not a request."

And with that, he swooped out of the room and disappeared into the shadows, slamming the door behind him.

As much as she tried to resist, this sent Belle into another fit of weeping. Her confused, exhausted brain laboured under the painfully strange duality of "little girl being punished in her room" and "terrified prisoner of a beast".

In between her sobs she heard the faintest tap at the door.

It didn't sound right. Too bony to be a normal human

knuckle. Too small to be even the eldest, weakest hand. Almost fragile-sounding. Delicate. A claw maybe?

What other horrors and mysteries did this night hold?

Belle took a deep breath and forced herself to rise.

"Who is it?"

"It's Mrs Potts, dear. The housekeeper."

Ah, so there are *other people here.* Feeling another surge of hope, Belle patted down her hair and tried to make herself look presentable. She opened the door. Maybe she would find some solace in...

"I thought you might like a nice cup of tea."

Belle's heart nearly stopped.

The voice came from below, close to the floor.

A ceramic teapot, sugar bowl, milk jug and cup came hopping into the room like a tiny porcelain army, chiming *tink tink tink*. The teapot kept its spout – *nose?* – pointed towards Belle as it – *she?* – spoke.

Belle backed away, into the wardrobe.

"You, but, you..." she stammered.

"Hey, be careful," the wardrobe said, in a feminine voice that boomed.

Belle sprang away from the thing and landed on the bed.

She immediately leapt off the bed, terrified that it would begin to speak too.

"This is all... impossible," Belle whispered. She wondered

if recent events were making her delusional. Somehow the Beast was easier to believe than talking furniture.

The teapot was very calmly pouring her insides into the cup. She spoke as she did so, sounding a little gurgly.

"Slowly now, don't spill…"

The little teacup had a chip in it, Belle noted absently, as it hopped over to where she sat on the floor. It waited patiently, its – *head?* – tilted up towards her.

Dazed, Belle put out her hand and carefully lifted the teacup, one pinky extended like she had always practised after reading a book on fancy etiquette. Where she touched the cup it was hard, smooth, warm from the tea, and utterly immobile. Solid porcelain. How did it move?

"Wanna see me do a trick?" the cup asked, shifting in her grasp.

Belle almost dropped it. The thing had no face at all but the voice sounded so real, so full of life. Like a little boy or girl. And the pottery still felt hard under her fingers; it wasn't pliable at all.

The cup shivered. Bubbles began to come up through the tea. They nearly overran the rim.

"*Chip!*" the teapot chastised.

The teacup shivered again and Belle could have sworn she heard it giggle.

Feeling strange about it but not seeing that she had

much of a choice, Belle took a little sip. It was excellent tea, black and fresh and strong, with just enough sugar. Very restorative.

"That was a very brave thing you did back there," the teapot said confidentially. "Trading yourself for your father. We all think so."

Belle blinked, trying to focus on *what* the teapot was saying rather than the fact that it spoke at all. The cup felt strange in her hand and hung there, still mostly full.

"Not that this isn't amazing," Belle said, holding it up and looking at it closely. Chip flinched and giggled again, making it hard to keep a grip. "This is like… I don't know *what* this is like. The most incredible fairy tale I've ever read. Papa will be so…" She stopped, remembering that she wouldn't be seeing him again. "But I'm stuck here forever."

"Cheer up, child. It will all turn out all right in the end. You'll see," the teapot said sympathetically. Then she jumped, steam coming out of her spout. "Look at me jabbering on, when there's supper to get on the table for the first time in I don't know how long!"

Belle tried to process the teapot's cheery, if bland, words of comfort. They seemed completely out of place in a dark castle ruled by a beast.

Mrs Potts hopped clumsily out of the door and her little

retinue followed. Belle sucked down the rest of her tea and set the cup at the end of the line. He hopped quickly to catch up with the others.

She felt strangely let down after the door closed behind them. Belle wished the teapot could have stayed a little longer and told the story of the castle, of whatever wizard had breathed life into their inanimate forms, of whatever the Beast had to do with any of this.

Because except for ordering the others around, Belle had seen no indication he could perform any magic himself. Definitely not a Prospero managing his little islands of conjured sprites. No, the Beast was more like a princely squatter, haunting the ruined and bespelled castle as it slowly wore itself down over the centuries.

Magic, Belle suddenly realised, *must have a lot to do with why I've never heard of this place.*

Magic.

Magic was *real.*

It was a thing not confined to German fantasies about the Black Forest or ancient stories involving giants and golems.

She was in a castle *full* of magic, completely hidden from the outside world.

And so close to the normal, boring little place where she had grown up!

If it were a "haunted" castle of the more prosaic, actually

*un*haunted type usually found in the woods, no one in the village would have been able to *stop* talking about it. Teenagers would have dared each other to spend the night within its walls; people like Gaston would have marched in and shot everything that looked even remotely interesting. The place would have been looted of all its mirrors, sconces and statues years ago. And no doubt British tourists would be thronging through on a weekly basis, begging to be taken to the romantic abandoned castle to paint pictures, smoke opium and write terrible poetry about their experience.

No, this castle had camouflaged itself well. She wondered how her father and Phillipe had managed to find it the first time. Clever old Phillipe…

Belle bit her lip, feeling another surge of loneliness. What was so important that the teapot couldn't have stayed another moment to talk to her? And just how *did* a teapot cook dinner? She had introduced herself as the housekeeper, so maybe she merely ordered other servants around. Were *they* real? Or other *living* objects? Or beasts? Or…

The wardrobe cleared her throat.

"Well, now, what shall we dress you in for dinner?"

I'm dreaming, Belle told herself again, a little hopefully.

The wardrobe threw open her doors. Inside were a few interesting things, one of the largest, clearest mirrors Belle had ever seen, some moths and an extremely pretty collection of gowns that would have made the blonde triplets, Paulette, Claudette and Laurette, swoon.

Belle examined the dresses sceptically. Of course, if things went the way they did in fairy tales, they would all fit her perfectly. The question was, was this a "Bluebeard's Wives" situation? Or something else?

The tired girl turned and walked over to the bed. So far *it*, at least, seemed to be inanimate.

"I'm not going to dinner."

"Oh!" the wardrobe said, shocked. "But you must!"

"No. I'm a prisoner, that's fine. But he can't make me do something I don't want to."

Well, maybe he could. Belle really had no idea. She would find out just what the limits of his powers – and anger – were. More clues to help her escape.

"But… you can't decline a royal invitation!" the wardrobe sputtered.

"*Royal?*" Belle asked quickly, sitting up. "That… *beast*… is a member of *royalty*?"

The wardrobe somehow managed to look guilty.

"I… I mean…" she stuttered. "We can't really talk about these things."

"Is it forbidden? Like, by a curse or a spell?" Belle pressed, eager for any information.

"No, it's… *déclassé*."

Belle raised an eyebrow.

The wardrobe shrugged.

"Help is supposed to be seen, not heard," she said apologetically. "Anything the master wants you to know, he will tell you himself."

"Who *is* he? Really?"

"Anything," the wardrobe repeated patiently, "the master wants you to know, he will tell you himself."

"Well, what *can* you talk about? *Yourself,* maybe? What kind of wood are you made from?"

"Honey, if I knew about wood, I'd be an enchanted axe," the wardrobe said with a sigh. "I know corsets and ribbons and hand-spandable waists and what shoes to wear to what sort of occasion and how to tie a thousand different girdle knots and which hat to wear to what sort of outdoor entertainment."

Belle's quick mind reviewed what she had just heard.

"You know, I've never known much about fashion, living in the country and all," she said innocently. "What sort of hat would a lady like myself wear to an afternoon tea outside, in the garden, with other ladies? Assuming I'm ever invited, of course."

"Oh, that's easy… a lovely straw number, with a wide brim, *en grecque* curls if you're dining among the ruins, or piles of flowers and feathers, and tipped, just so…"

Belle allowed herself a little smile.

"No one has worn hats like that, even in this remote part of the world, for at least ten years. Not even Madame Bussard has pulled one out of her own wardrobe recently. And she is very thrifty with her accessories. So *whatever* happened here must have happened at least a decade ago."

The wardrobe shifted nervously.

"You're a clever girl," she said with some grudging admiration. "I like that. But I think… maybe… I'd better hold my drawers with you for a while. Unless, of course, you'd actually like to get ready for dinner?" she added hopefully.

"Nope," Belle said with a firm shake of her head. "My father and I both wound up here by accident and it is incredibly uncivilised, even *evil*, to hold us accountable for such a simple mistake. I gave my word about not leaving, but that is all. I will starve to death before I consent to having dinner with such a monster."

And with that she lay back down on the bed, head turned away from the wardrobe, lest she see the traitorous tear leaking down Belle's otherwise brave face.

The wardrobe didn't say anything. In fact, when she was quiet there was no way to tell she *wasn't* just a piece of furniture and Belle wasn't just making up conversations in her head like a madwoman.

Her eyes shot open.

Just because the bed didn't talk didn't mean it couldn't. And what about the windows, the rugs, the very stones in the walls? *Anything* could come alive in this strange place and address her. Or just watch her…

She closed her eyes tightly shut again and clutched the pillow. *I just won't look, then.*

Beyond that, Belle was out of ideas. She didn't have any real plans aside from a hunger strike.

Eventually the door creaked open. A new voice, high and nasal, announced officiously: "Dinner is served."

Another servant. Possibly a butler. She was curious what he would turn out to be – a brush, a hanger, a serving plate maybe? – but decided to stay firm in her resolve to sulk and ignore any communication from the master of the castle who kept her prisoner.

She remained lying down but opened her eyes a crack. Fortunately, nothing moved on the wall, not even a spider.

"Miss?" the voice persisted.

"Young lady?

"Dinner…?"

Eventually he went away.

Castles, even more modern ones, didn't creak like houses. Or at least this one didn't. Wind picked up for a moment outside; she could hear it past the very expensive glazing in the windows. But nothing squeaked or rocked or shifted. Solid.

The silence was absolute.

Belle might have drifted off to sleep; it was hard to keep track between the hush of the shadows, her tears, her hunger and, if she fully admitted it, fear. She lay on her side like a lumpy, sick child. Just like the time Maurice tried to get her to go out and play with the three little girls he had rounded up as companions for her. She hadn't *needed* companions. She had *him*. And her books. That was all she ever needed.

"They're meanies," she had insisted with a pout. She could hear her father making stuttering, muffled apologies in the kitchen, either to the girls or to their mother.

"You just need to get to know them," Maurice had said brightly, coming into her room to get her. "It's human nature to avoid what's new... Maybe they just need to get to know *you*... to see that you're no meanie... yourself."

"*You* don't have friends," Belle pointed out.

"Well, I'm too busy now. But I had some... rather odd friends once," Maurice said. "Can't for the life of me remember their names... or what they looked like... Ah, well. A lifetime ago. But the point is we got to know each other and became thick as thieves. The scariest, most frightening person can turn out to be quite a lovely character... if you give him time."

Young Belle sat up, considering this. There was that

one time Gaston had bumped her into the puddle… and Paulette had let her borrow her hankie to get the worst mud spots off. Maybe there had even been a flicker of sympathy in the girl's eyes.

She took a deep breath and wiped her face. She opened her mouth to call out to the other little girls.

"We don't want to be friends with her anyway," came the unexpected chirp of a voice. Probably Laurette's. "We're here because Mama and *le prêtre* said to. *For charity.*"

Belle threw herself back down on to her bed with a solid finality.

"*I DON'T WANT FRIENDS.*"

Trying not to weep at the other girl's callous statement, she pulled out her latest book and deliberately and firmly turned to the last page she had read, the one right before the picture of the galleon being tossed about in the waves.

A quick pitter-patter of six feet sounded in the next room, away into the outside world. The girls were gone, free to enjoy the day as they chose, which probably meant avoiding the sunshine so they wouldn't ruin their creamy complexions.

Belle's father sighed and sat down heavily at the edge of her bed. He smiled when he saw what book she was reading and shook his head.

"Belle, you can't find real adventures that way. You have to go out into the world… you have to *meet* people…"

"*You* don't," she protested.

"I did when I was younger," he said gently. "That's how I met your mother. True love doesn't just fall into your lap. You have to go out and find your other half."

"But your… my… she fell *out* of your lap. She just kept going."

Maurice blinked, obviously surprised by this pithy, intelligent observation from his daughter. Then he put his arms round her and pulled her until she was sitting in his lap like a much younger girl. She didn't resist, snuggling into him.

"You can't have adventures without risk. You can't have great things if you constantly fear loss. And I am a much, much better person because of your mother. If nothing else, she gave me you."

He kissed her on the forehead and hugged her tight.

"Oh, Belle, what are we going to do with you, my little dreamer?"

Adult Belle shifted uncomfortably on the bed and shed a few more tears at this memory. She was finally having her adventure and it had cost her *everything*: her father, her home, her books, her life. It was too much.

She was shaken out of her reveries by a loud banging on the door. Thundering, really; the whole thing shook. A lesser door would have been torn off its hinges.

Of course it was the Beast this time.

"*I THOUGHT I TOLD YOU TO COME DOWN TO DINNER!*"

"*I'M NOT HUNGRY!*" she screamed back, rage billowing out of her more forcefully than she had imagined possible. Thinking of the triplets and their behaviour hadn't improved her mood.

"*YOU'LL COME OUT OR... I'LL BREAK DOWN THE DOOR!*"

"*HUFF AND PUFF ALL YOU LIKE, YOU MONSTROUS WOLF!*" she spat. "*GO RIGHT AHEAD! IT'S* YOUR *CASTLE, AFTER ALL. DO WHATEVER YOU WANT WITH IT. I'M JUST YOUR* PRISONER*!*"

There was a pause. She thought she heard voices in the corridor besides the Beast's own, entreating him.

"Willyoucomedowntodinner?" the Beast finally muttered, rapidly.

"NO!"

"It would... give me... great pleasure... if you... would... join me... for dinner. *Please.*"

"No. Thank you," Belle replied just as formally and twice as icily.

"*YOU CAN'T STAY IN THERE FOREVER!*" the Beast roared.

"JUST WATCH ME!" Belle spat back.

"FINE! THEN GO AHEAD AND *STARVE*!"

"I ALREADY *PLANNED* TO!"

The Beast let out a wordless snarl. He made no noise leaving, no stomping off. Much like the now-still wardrobe, there was just the utter silence of an absence of presence.

THE CHRISTENING

Maurice hadn't thought it possible to fall in love with another human even more than he had with his dear wife… and yet he had to be forcefully persuaded to give up tiny infant Belle when it was time to feed her. He handed her over reluctantly, utterly taken by twinkling topaz eyes and chubby pink cheeks.

Her mother loved her differently: with a fierceness that grew warier as the days drew on.

Smoke from arson fire was a more than occasional sight first thing in the morning, and always of a *charmante* business or house. It was not safe for *charmantes* to walk the streets alone at night now; disappearances were becoming more common and their bodies rarely showed up.

It was hard to say which was more frightening, the

growing list of the missing – or the utter mystery of how it was done.

The fever that had taken out several towns to the north had finally reached the little kingdom; the king and queen did close the borders, but perhaps too late. And so the place seemed more claustrophobic and inescapable – and at the same time frailer, like it was slowly diminishing from the inside out. Vanishing, along with *les charmantes*.

Far fewer friends than Rosalind would have liked came by for Belle's christening, not even any of her old nemeses who might have jokingly cursed the baby with a penchant for hating carrots or a tendency to sneeze when suddenly exposed to sunlight.

"There were supposed to be seven of us here," Rosalind fretted, rocking little Belle protectively in her arms. "Seven to weave the charms to keep the baby safe. It has always been thus."

"I am only still here because of you, and the baby and the celebration today," Adelise the faun said. She crossed and uncrossed her goat's legs, stretching them out after taking off the giant boots she now felt inclined to wear around town. "When we say farewell tonight, I shall depart for islands south of here, to join my cousins in the Summer Lands, if they still even live. Rosalind, you are not being kind. Your friends would come if they could.

Some cannot because they *cannot.*"

Her gift was an acorn, blessed to grow quickly into a tree that would protect the new family. Rosalind had it in her fingers and was rolling it anxiously.

"I'm going to stay," Bernard said. There was nothing outwardly *charming* about him – at least literally. He had to hunch over to fit in the house, and squeeze his arms round his knees to fit in the circle of friends. "My family has been here for centuries. We have always been peaceful. Surely people will remember that. It will all pass. It always does… this sort of foolishness."

His gift was a plain-looking stone that would guarantee the help of the earth for whatever the family endeavoured, wherever they buried it.

"Yes? And what about the fever everyone is coming down with in the eastern quarter?" Adelise demanded. "How soon is it going to be before someone blames a witch for cursing the kingdom, or a goodwife for cooking it up in her cauldron, or a dryad in return for something a wood-cutter's done? Leave now, I say, before the quarantine is fully in place and you cannot."

"If we turn the cheek, as it were, and cooperate… and show we are as good and loyal citizens as everyone else, we'll be fine."

"*Cooperate?*" Monsieur Lévi laughed. "Perhaps if by

'cooperate' you mean 'politely stick our heads out for the peasants to bludgeon…' No, my dears. This is why I moved my own bookshop to the village beyond the woods, near the river."

His gift was a pretty picture book whose brightly painted images seemed to move whenever you weren't looking straight at them. And perhaps its stories didn't always end the same way.

Rosalind spun to look at him. "I thought you were going to the New World."

"Well." He took off the little moon-shaped spectacles he now always wore and polished the lenses carefully on his shirt. When he put them back on, he looked meaningfully at the baby. "Since you named me godfather, I thought it would be best if I stuck around long enough to see her grow up… in the neighbourhood, at least."

Rosalind sat down but continued to move nervously, dandling Belle on her lap. The baby clapped her hands as a large pink butterfly appeared, its languorous and unlikely wings propelling it in slow circles round her head.

Maurice was refilling everyone's teacups and cordial glasses in the kitchen and listened carefully to everything.

"I don't want to leave," his wife said. "I love it here. I love the people, I love…"

"The people you love are gone," Lévi said bluntly.

"Everyone else is either looking the other way or helping to harass the remaining *charmantes*. The countrymen out where I have moved may be uneducated farmers who have their own prejudices, but they certainly haven't locked anyone up over it yet. They're sane, if boring, *naturels*. No disrespect, Alaric."

The groomsman shrugged. "There is no such thing as different kinds of people, except for the good ones and the bad ones. And the bad ones do seem to have the upper hand these days."

His gift was a perfectly forged horseshoe, to hang above the door to Belle's room for luck.

The door jangled open; a twitchy and nervous Frédéric fell rather than walked in, like a scarecrow looking for shelter.

"Sorry I'm late," he mumbled. His attire was, as always, perfect; his hair back in a neat, unshowy ponytail tied with a sober black ribbon.

"Frédéric!" Maurice cried delightedly, coming in and clapping his friend on the shoulders. "I thought you weren't going to make it!"

Frédéric gave a thin smile at his reception, both embarrassed and pleased by it. Then he looked round at the room and his face went pale.

"You were going to weave a charm with *this* as one of the seven?" Adelise whispered dramatically to Rosalind.

"*Weave* a *charm?*" Frédéric demanded, horrified. "What is this? What are you doing? I never agreed to be part of any… *magic…*"

"And what do *you* have against magic?" Adelise said, standing up and putting her hands on her hips. "I thought , besides actually being a *charmante* yourself, you were educated, unlike the ignorant pig-people who are running round like thugs, murdering everyone!"

"Now, now, settle down, everyone," Maurice interrupted, standing between them. "This is a christening celebration. That is all, as far as you are concerned, Frédéric. Can we please just drop it, for a few moments? For *Belle*?"

Guiltily all the grown-ups turned their regard to the baby. She had passed out despite all the noise and slept with a perfectly peaceful face against her mother's breast.

"I have a gift," Frédéric said awkwardly in the silence that followed. He held out his hand. It clutched an expensive, delicate-looking little toy carriage.

Even Bernard the ogre looked sceptical.

"She's a *baby*," he said in his deep, rumbly voice. "She could eat that."

"We'll keep it for when she's older, really, a lovely gift," Maurice said quickly, taking it and obviously admiring the workmanship.

"I, uh, also used my own accursed… 'gift'," Frédéric

admitted. "For the last time… before I remove it. I have discovered a cure! But more on that later. I called forth a vision… for you."

Everyone in the room looked at him in surprise.

"Thank you…" Maurice said in wonder. "But… why?"

"Because you're a friend. And because she is innocent." He pointed at the sleeping baby with one long, skinny finger.

"And what do you mean by *innocent*, Monsieur?" Adelise demanded with thinly veiled disgust.

"You know precisely what I mean," Frédéric said. "The child has no powers whatsoever. She is pure."

"*Pure?* You…"

But as Adelise started forwards, Bernard put a gentle, giant hand on her foot.

"Please listen. I saw her future – you have to go, Rosalind," Frédéric said bluntly. "Listen to your friends. Get out. The fever will spread. No one will be able to leave because of the quarantine. Things will… get out of control. They will look for someone to blame. They will come here. You should never have revealed yourself to the king and queen. That was a foolish move."

"I had to stand up for my people!"

"*YOUR PEOPLE*," Frédéric said sarcastically. "Your sick, diseased versions of true humanity? Your community of supernatural lepers?"

"That's enough, Frédéric!" Alaric swore, standing up. "I am 'pure' and have never felt threatened by *les charmantes.* And they are your people too, do not forget. They will come after you just like everyone else, no matter how much you wheedle and whine to join their ranks – or try to treat yourself with sulphurs and bloodletting."

"You have seen this?" Rosalind demanded of the doctor, ignoring everything else.

"Yes," he said without taking his eyes off Alaric, whose hand had started to go to his belt. "You and the baby will be trampled escaping a riot. Maurice will be beaten nearly to death and lose his sight."

He tried to speak as coldly as he always did, but there was a catch in his throat.

"Even if you left now, there is no guarantee of *your* safety, Rosalind," he added quietly. "Only Maurice and the baby. Things get… hazy as the future opens up and paths multiply, but you cannot entirely escape your fate."

Everyone in the room was silent for a moment.

"You did your best, Enchantress," Adelise said gently, putting a hand on her arm. "You always have. But the war, I think, is over, and our time in this place is done. Your priority now is raising that child, safe and free and made to understand that things like we seem to be enduring are not right and shouldn't be. And should never happen again."

"We *should* stay. And fight..." Rosalind half-asked, half-said to Maurice.

"Then you will lose," Frédéric said simply. "*Everything.*"

BE OUR... OH, YOU KNOW THE REST!

Belle refused to give in to hunger.

But when she had slept and cried as much as her body could stand, her *mind* grew hungry.

All your life you have been waiting for adventure, it said. *And now that adventures have found you, you're just* lying around*?*

If Belle closed her eyes and curled into a fetal position, she could pretend she was in her own bed, back home.

This is dumb, her inner voice persisted. *Lying in this – albeit ridiculously comfy and beautiful – bed when you're in a castle with talking teapots and wardrobes who gossip. Did Gulliver do this when a prisoner at the Brobdingnagian court? Just sulk and lie around? No, he enjoyed the adventure while doing whatever he could to get home!*

Belle sniffed one last time and realised her mind was right. She was acting like a baby.

She had given her word she would stay here forever.

But what, precisely, was 'here'?

Certainly not the cell – he had led her out of it.

Certainly not this room; he expected her to go to dinner.

So…

She took a deep breath and rose from the bed as quietly as she could. The wardrobe did nothing; it didn't speak, it didn't bend its wood in strange and elastic ways imitating human movement, it didn't so much as creak. Perhaps it was asleep or hibernating or doing whatever talking furniture did when it wasn't talking.

Belle quickly smoothed out her dress and pushed her hair out of her face, tucking it behind her ear. Then, with gentle, stealthy moves, she tiptoed over to the door and let herself out.

Where to go first?

The teapot. Find her and see if she will talk to me.

Belle frowned thoughtfully. In smaller homes the kitchens were often at the back of the main building so the heat wouldn't suffocate everyone in the summer. She decided to just head that way and descend any staircases she found.

The rich carpets on the floor seemed mostly clean but

still puffed up little clouds of dust every ninth or tenth tiptoe. She put her finger out on the handrail as she went down the smooth, potentially deadly stone steps and her fingertip came back a little grey. What a beautiful place this could have been, cleaned and polished, the sconces filled with beeswax candles.

Belle's mind populated the castle with royalty from all the eras she could imagine:

Recent ones with great powdered wigs and hats in the shapes of fanciful things like ships, great skirts that billowed out, ugly garish make-up on the faces of those who gossiped behind embroidered silk fans.

Renaissance rulers with thick curled collars and poison rings, intellect and conspiracy at every dinner.

Ancient kings and queens in long, heavy dresses and cloaks, wise looks on their faces and solid gold crowns on their heads, innocents in a world they believed to possess unicorns and dragons, and maps whose seas ran off at the edges, beyond where the *tygres* were.

Of course, maybe around here there *were* dragons and unicorns. Who knew? They had talking teacups.

Belle froze at that thought.

The wardrobe looked like just a wardrobe when she was still. How many of these other things were just biding their time, silently watching her, until they were called to awaken?

She waited a long moment… the same amount of time a child stalls in the half-light of a spooky hiding place, or a bed, or an empty road, to see if the shadows are indeed a monster coming to get her, or just her father.

Wait. What was that?

She put a hand to her mouth to stifle a scream. Her heart pounded in her chest as though trying to break free.

"Nothing has tried to harm me yet," Belle whispered aloud to give herself courage.

She tried to be calm and just listen to the darkness.

Nothing.

But then she turned her head a fraction of an inch, willing her ears to pick up the sound again. Gaston, a superb hunter if nothing else, would probably have had no trouble at all stalking this prey.

There.

It wasn't anything in the room with her; it was somewhere beyond. In the direction she was heading, the faint jabber of voices and clinks of pottery being put away. Belle shuddered in relief. Nothing deadly.

She started moving again, still tiptoeing awkwardly.

The noises grew louder as she drew closer. Several voices were arguing. None, thankfully, were the Beast's. She recognised Mrs Potts and the high one she had heard before, the butler or whatever…

A set of stone stairs led half a floor down. Wonderful smells and heat drifted from a large open doorway at the end. Belle descended cautiously and peeped round the frame.

Just a metre or so away, on the servants' dining table, was one of the most wonderful and unsettling things she had ever seen.

The teapot, a mantel clock and a small candelabrum were arguing with one another, bowing and gesticulating and emoting as charmingly as a trio of children who didn't know they were being watched.

Belle bit her lip. This really *was* the adventure she had always been looking for. If she wasn't just going mad.

"But if the master doesn't learn to control his temper, he'll never break the…"

Belle coughed politely.

Suddenly all three dropped into a hushed silence and spun round to stare at her, just like servants caught in the act of doing something clever but illicit in a Molière play.

"Splendid to see you out and about, Mademoiselle," the little clock said and it was indeed the voice from outside her door earlier. He waddled forwards on his strange, rubbery wooden feet, gilded flourishes below his dial unfurling to become arms as he dipped into a small but graceful bow.

That's odd, Belle thought. *Wouldn't the hands on his face make better* hands? *At least philosophically?*

"I am Cogsworth, head of the household."

He put his little golden hand out to hers, drawing it up for a polite kiss.

The candelabrum was suddenly between them. He had three arms; apparently the middle one was both his head and his body. The other two were, well, arms. And the flames, hands.

"This is Lumière," the clock said with a disgruntled sniff.

"*Enchanté, ma chérie,*" Lumière said, kissing the back of her wrist. Her skin felt hot for a moment, like an ember from the fire had popped and landed on her. But it wasn't unpleasant.

The candelabrum turned as if to throw a look of triumph back at the clock. But Cogsworth obviously thought it was too much and tried to shove Lumière out of the way.

The candelabrum responded by just touching the clock's wood edging with one flame hand.

"*YOWCH!*" Cogsworth shrieked against his will.

Belle wasn't sure whether to laugh or pity them. Were they grown-ups? Were they children? Were they something else entirely?

The little clock recovered himself and, with slightly bruised dignity, swished his minute and hour hands like they were a moustache he was resettling. "If there's anything we can do to make your stay more comfortable… extra pillows, maybe a pair of slippers…"

"Well," Belle said, "I *am* a little hungry, actually…"

"Do you hear that, dears?" the teapot said excitedly to the rest of the room. "*She's hungry.* Stoke the fire, break out the silver, wake the china!"

Belle looked up at the sudden noises in the rest of the room, a little alarmed.

Almost everything was fluttering and shuffling: the china was indeed waking from whatever slumber it enjoyed; dishes were very carefully shuddering themselves to life; teacups were bouncing and trying to get out of their glass cabinet prison. The stove, which seemed so cheerful and warm and fiery at the end of the room, now began to yawn and stretch its great black iron arms and exhaust pipe. Belle drew into herself a little, alarmed. Stories of witches with their fires and stoves and terrible, terrible endings played through her head. Baba Yaga, Hansel and Gretel…

"Remember what the master said," Cogsworth reminded them sternly.

"Oh pish tosh," Mrs Potts said back. "I'm not going to let the poor child go hungry."

"If you absolutely must, then. Glass of water, crust of bread, and then…"

"Cogsworth, I am surprised at you," Lumière said,

chastising. "She's not our prisoner. She's our guest. We must make her feel welcome here."

"Actually, I'm pretty sure that's exactly what I am. A *prisoner*," Belle said wryly. But she was distracted by the commotion around her. Pots were shifting themselves on the hob, cracking their lids to let steam out. The whole stove seemed to be holding its breath – or forcing it back down into its oven; suddenly, the fire expanded and grew more orange. The stove began muttering disgustedly to itself, something about preparing a feast and then being forced to abandon it and having everything cool off.

Silverware was marching like little soldiers down the long length of the table towards Belle. Pieces of china were shoving each other precariously out of the way, vying to be in the single place setting in front of her. Little pots of mustard and chutney and other condiments hopped one after another off the shelves lining the room, landing surprisingly intact on silver trays.

Too many things were moving round the room, things that shouldn't have been moving at all. It was dizzying, and more than a little ominous.

"Really, this isn't necessary..." Belle said, getting ready to bolt. A fresh *boule,* the cracks in its crust emitting amazing-smelling steam, was carried to her by a spidery basket with alarming silver legs.

"No, no, no, *ma chérie*," Lumière said, gesturing for her

to sit. The back of her own legs were whumped out from under her and she fell into a not-uncomfortable chair. It was still spooky and unnerving. The scents from all the different dishes were making her head spin. In fairy worlds you weren't supposed to eat the food or you would be trapped there forever…

But then again, what fairies offered you *pâté*?

"Our master, he is a little… *ungentile*," the little candelabrum said tactfully. "And he has been alone for so long… his manners may have grown a little rusty. He truly wished you could share this feast with him."

"He threw my father – *my harmless old father* – into a prison cell and then exchanged me for him. That's not bad manners – that's behaving like a pirate," Belle pointed out. "Also? The claws… and fangs…"

"Try the *gougères*," Lumière interrupted, popping a pastry into her mouth before she could continue. It was warmed by his flame and melted on her tongue, nothing at all like the perfectly good but usually rock-hard ones she and her father baked.

"Ohhh…" she couldn't help saying.

"It's been *so long* since we had a guest!" Mrs Potts danced around on the table happily, somehow managing to fold a napkin with her spout-nose. She tossed it into Belle's lap: a swan shape that gracefully unfolded as it fell, almost like it was flying. Belle shrank back, worried it was actually going to fly.

"I can't imagine why," she muttered.

And then she was distracted by the food.

Piles of it. More than a feast – a banquet.

There was a whole leg of lamb, multiple terrines and soufflés, three soup courses, a delicate fish in white wine broth, an orange ice in between to clear the palate...

There was a water glass, a golden glass for red wine, a crystal one for white, and a saucer for consommé. There were seven forks of descending size and different numbers of tines, the last three whose use she couldn't even begin to work out.

This was what the Beast was planning to have for dinner with her? As what, an apology for keeping her prisoner? For the way he had treated her father?

Maybe... maybe the little accessories *were* right. Maybe he just didn't know how to ask nicely.

No.

Belle shook her head. She had read about this. The victims of kidnapping often ended up sympathising with the perpetrator. It was a sickness, a very scientifically predictable one.

This was the 18th century. The age of reason. And a man-beast had thrown her father into prison for simply trespassing. This wasn't just about a failure to be polite. This was about breaking the laws of France.

Even if the little magical castle was hidden far from the worlds of Paris and Versailles.

But…

The broth was nearly clear and colourless, singing with notes of the sea – and Belle had never actually been to the sea. When she broke her bread to dip, the crust shattered, the crumb inside moist to the point of almost being a custard.

The terrine was so rich she managed only one tiny teaspoonful.

She and her father didn't eat fancily but they ate well enough and even had meat once or twice a week. The herbs that still flourished in her mother's garden spiced up dishes more than it seemed like they should have. They supped well, like all Frenchmen and women.

But even Christmas was nothing compared to this.

Belle suddenly realised she was shovelling it all in like a character from one of those stories who was tricked into eating magic food until he exploded or grew too large to escape.

And a slightly more down-to-earth part of her spoke up warningly, in what she liked to pretend was her mother's voice: *You are, at the very least, going to have an* extremely *upset stomach from this rich new food.*

"You really made this all for me?" she said, pausing to wipe her mouth.

"Of course, dear," the teapot said glowingly.

"You're our first guest in ages. Years of bouncing round this dusty castle with nothing to do and no one to serve."

"No one? But your master… "

"He, ah, doesn't have very refined tastes or desires," the candelabrum said tactfully, admiring the flame on one of his hands. "He didn't really put us to work, as it were."

"He doesn't even sleep in a proper bed," Mrs Potts said severely. "Just curls up like a kitten wherever it's soft or warm."

Cogsworth shot her a look, even with numbers instead of eyes, it was easy to tell he didn't approve of this sort of gossip about their employer.

But he didn't disagree, either.

"Are there no human servants here at all?"

"Why?" Cogsworth asked, a little offended. "Do you require one?"

"We do everything ourselves," Mrs Potts explained gently. "The dusters take a bit of prompting, and getting the mops to do the job properly requires some direct supervision on my part, but on the whole, yes, we take care of the castle ourselves. Not that there's been much to take care of for the last…"

"Ten years?" Belle suggested innocently.

"Yes, ten years," the teapot continued, lost in her memories, unaware of the desperate headshakes and looks the other two were giving her.

"Why ten years?" Belle asked. "What happened ten years ago?"

The three little creatures looked at each other warily.

"Well, let's just say that's how long it's been since we've been graced with a visitor," Cogsworth said.

"You're not going to tell me," she said with a sigh.

Lumière seemed to be on the brink of saying something.

"It's quite late," Cogsworth interrupted, stretching strangely as if to look at his own face. "Time enough for stories another night. Off to bed now, eh?"

"Oh, I couldn't possibly go to bed now," Belle drawled teasingly. The food had settled in her stomach – and the rich wine, too. It was hard to be afraid of anything with a full tummy and adequate rest. And how much of a threat could these three adorable talking objects be? "This was delicious, thank you. I think I'd like to take a look round the castle where I will be imprisoned for the rest of my life."

"Oh, forever is just a word," Lumière said philosophically, whirling one of his hand-flames around. "To a candle burning at both ends, forever is an hour. But if you want a tour, *ma chérie*, we would be glad to assist."

"I don't know if that's such a good idea," Cogsworth said quickly. "We wouldn't want her… poking round… *certain places…*"

"Oh, but couldn't you take me?" Belle asked, tickling

Cogsworth under his dial. He giggled like a pleased toddler. "I'll bet you know *everything* about the castle."

"Well, I do, of course, I do, yes, of course," he spluttered. "I'd be delighted to impart some of my knowledge. No harm in that. Right this way."

The little clock hopped off the table and began to waddle out of the room and down the hall.

"The kitchen," he began, "is, of course, like most castles, the oldest part of the main building still remaining. We have found markings on the walls near the back indicating that it might even date back to Roman days..."

Lumière cocked his middle candle, his head, at Belle.

"Well, you certainly turned him upside down in a moment, *ma chérie*," he said with appreciation. "There is a lot more to you than it would appear."

"Don't judge a book by its cover," she retorted, following the clock out.

Lumière barked out laughter, and sparks sprayed harmlessly to the stone floor.

FLIGHT

Maurice packed up the cart with all of their worldly belongings and harnessed their newly acquired foal to pull it. With a final tearful goodbye to the little apartment on its bustling street, he and his wife and their baby began the journey to their new home.

They had taken Lévi's advice and decided to move to the pleasant, if dull, little village where the bookseller himself now lived, trading friends and excitement for a safe country life of chickens and weather and farmers as neighbours. And very little magic. Belle would grow up in a place without witches and enchanted crystals, but also without the violence and dangers of the tumultuous kingdom.

It was tricky driving their fully loaded cart through the

busy streets at first. Besides the usual traffic, people often just stopped and stared: Rosalind had a kind of fame. Seeing her leave gave some people pause, and others a triumphant grin.

Approaching the border, where the road began to rise out of the forest, things grew quiet. But at the border, guards blocked their way.

"What is this?" Maurice demanded, pretending ignorance.

"Quarantine. No one is to leave or enter the kingdom without royal permission until the fever has passed," one answered, not a hint of kindness in his voice. His black eyes flicked over Maurice and Rosalind and the baby – and even the horse.

Rosalind ground her teeth. She clutched her alder wand under her cloak, but there were at least ten soldiers.

"We bought a nice little farmhouse on the other side of the river," Maurice said amiably. "For our growing family. Our plan was to escape from the plague. All of us are well, you can see that."

"Escape from the plague," the guard said nastily, putting a finger to his chin as if in thought. "How convenient. The sickness that rose up just as we began getting a handle on the situation of *les charmantes.* And now you flee."

"We have a baby," Maurice said, indicating Belle. "Of course we're fleeing. It's not safe."

"Are you sure it's the plague you're fleeing, precisely? How many *naturels* did your wife kill or ensorcell the night of the riots?"

"I did no such thing!" Rosalind said, trying to keep her voice down. "I wasn't even in town when the fight over the girl happened, I was deep in the woods, picking mushrooms."

Two other guards closed in behind the cart. Maurice began to reach inside his belt for his knife; Rosalind, her wand.

A fourth guard spoke up, almost impatiently. "Are you not Rosalind, the one who keeps the garden of magic roses in the park?"

Rosalind looked at her husband. Was this it? Was this where they took her but let her husband and baby go free? Was this the end?

There was no point in lying, either way.

"I am," she said.

The young man regarded her for a moment. His eyes were unreadable, but unlike his partner's, they were thoughtful.

"My mother had a cough. It wasn't consumption but she couldn't breathe properly, and sometimes blood came out. You gave her roses. Each fortnight, for two months. She put them in a vase and breathed in their perfume. It cured her completely."

"Madame Guernbeck," Rosalind said, remembering.

"Her lungs were ailing. She loved my simple pink beach roses best, because she had never been to the sea. But the ones that cured her were yellow. I brought her both."

"*Alan*," the first guard hissed, seeing where this was going. "Who cares? We have our orders. No one in or out. *And* she is a *charmante*, she just admitted it!"

Alan waved his hand without looking at his partner, as if he were no more than a fly. "Move along," he told the family. "Leave and if you take my advice, never come back."

Maurice let out a breath he didn't even realise he was holding, the buzzing in his ears so loud he forgot his manners and didn't wish them a good day. Rosalind squeezed her baby tightly.

"Magic always comes back on itself," Rosalind whispered.

"And also kindness," Maurice pointed out.

So the little family rolled quietly out of the forest and into their new life. Belle sat on her mother's lap, reaching for the tiny white moths that fluttered at the periphery of light and dark where the sun just began to meet the forest floor. Hours passed in contemplative silence for all three of them.

Maurice felt some of the weight he had been bearing lift away as they crossed the bridge over the river and into the little village. They were running away, yes, but it was to a new beginning. Their house was a nice, sunny little place on the outskirts of town where the fumes and noises from his inventions wouldn't bother anyone and the occasional showy spell wouldn't be seen. Rosalind would, for now at least, cast off the role of *enchantress* and confine most of her magic to plants and research. Until the world was safe again.

The first moonless night they spent there she paced out a new garden and circled it three times widdershins, chanting. She also planted the magic acorn and ancient pebble, singing to them as she did. Maurice held the baby in his lap so she could watch, wondering if his daughter would pick up some of the magic, despite the fact that, as Frédéric had accurately deduced, she was not a *charmante*.

The next day, under the full sun where everyone could see, Rosalind began planting normal things. Roses, herbs and even more roses.

Maurice rigged up a wheel in the nearby stream to pump water into the house and the new garden. He mounted a small windmill to the top of the roof and ran belts to various things in the kitchen: the roasting spit and a mechanical spoon over the stove, for instance, to ease their household tasks now that magic had to be hidden.

The little family went into the village proper as often as they could to visit their old friend Monsieur Lévi. He loved his little god-daughter Belle, and played with her and made her laugh and gave her all sorts of treats: books and pretty mirrors and tiny kaleidoscopes. But Maurice and Rosalind tended to restrict their visits to market days when there was so much else going on they wouldn't attract much notice, when gossip about *everyone* flowed as freely as the *cidre.*

Alaric was one of the few friends from their old life who ever visited, using 'trying one of the horses out' as an excuse to make the half-day journey to the village over the river, breaking the quarantine with the king's permission.

Whenever he came it was a happy time for all. Maurice and Rosalind stuffed him with wine and cheese and pulled their chairs close to hear news about the kingdom they had exiled themselves from. It was mostly bleak tidings, however; fever had established a firm grip in the poorer sections of town, and those few who could have done something about it – *les charmantes*, witches and the like – were missing.

But the stablemaster had also wed his merry housekeeper, and that was cause for some joy. He showed the little family a miniature of her that he kept in his pocket, next to his journal, and swore they would all celebrate together properly one day.

And then one day Alaric showed up at *night*, long after Belle had been put to bed.

There was a rider behind him on the horse, a small,

terrified-looking woman-thing with eyes that were all black, even the whites, and long, folded-over green ears that spoke of goblin lineage.

"Ah," Alaric said uneasily to Maurice and Rosalind, who came to the door in their dressing gowns, "a thousand pardons for the interruption of your evening... I was wondering... maybe you could give my friend here a night's stay... and maybe a loaf of bread to start her on her way in the morning?"

"Of course," Rosalind said, glancing uneasily over to her daughter's room to make sure she was asleep. "Any friend of yours is a friend of ours."

"But why?" Maurice asked, oblivious as always to the finer nuances of emotion in the air: his old friend's barely concealed nervousness, the *obviousness* of deep night outside, the hastily thrown-on aspect of the woman's clothes: it looked like she wore everything she owned, all at once. "What's wrong?"

"*They come for me,*" the woman rasped in the hissing, guttural tone of a goblin. "*Thona saw them. A pair of men, all in black, with masks and whatnot. Coming for me in silence like the dead.*"

Alaric nodded grimly. "I found her hiding with a rat – uh, *Thona* – in my stables. It seems as if whoever is targeting *les charmantes* is getting sneakier. Just clubbing them over the heads or whatever and dragging them off in the middle of the night. And no one's finding the bodies."

"*Like ghosts, they are and God knows what happens to them that gets taken*," the woman said, shivering.

Alaric gave her a pitying look. "She had to get out, it wasn't safe for her to stay. And with the quarantine, no one can leave now. Legally. So..."

"Oh my goodness, you poor thing," Rosalind said with a sad shake of her head. "Why don't you go on inside, wash your hands and face. We'll get you a blanket and some hot tea in a moment."

The woman pushed past them into the warmth without a thank you – that was not the goblin way – but then turned and looked back for one piteous moment, her black eyes wide and begging as if her hosts could do something.

"*I lived there all my life. I sold swamp herbs. Good, honest swamp herbs. Wild begonia for colds and moss for packing into wounds. I never did black magic or poison arts. Everyone knows that. Everyone knows old Jenny!*"

Then she hobbled in through the door, coughing back tears, crying, which was the human way.

THE EXTREMELY FASCINATING TOUR OF A HISTORICALLY AND ARCHITECTURALLY IMPORTANT LANDMARK CASTLE

"... And then the problem was obviously that the main keep had grown too organically from its medieval origins, and so the symmetry needed for a true baroque makeover was impossible. I speak, of course, of the high-middle-gate and flanking annexes you see elsewhere, as in Mansart's *Chateau de Maisons...*"

Lumière was hopping ahead to light the way, obviously bored by the direction the tour was taking. Belle *was* interested; she had read all about Mansart and dreamed of seeing his palaces in Versailles. But Cogsworth's stories were also strangely banal. Here was a talking clock, for heaven's sake. And everything he was telling her seemed straight out of a normal history book. There was nothing about evil wizards, angry gods, or why the castle was the way it was: enchanted and forgotten.

"All of these weapons and armour don't *seem* to be very baroque," she interrupted gently, waving her hand at a pair of crossed battle-axes on the wall. The hall they were in definitely had a medieval slant; tarnished suits of armour lined each side and she was pretty sure she heard them squeaking despite their apparent stillness.

"Ah, yes, well, you can never entirely strip the gothic influence from the French," Cogsworth said proudly. "We're not ashamed of our heritage."

Belle pretended to ignore the suits of armour as she passed, which were now quite obviously turning to watch her. She felt less threatened by their martial stance than unnerved by their attention. It was like the first market day after she had developed a figure. That was the moment the tone of the villagers' gossip about her had changed: from *look at that strange little child* to *what a waste looks like that are on one like her.*

"*AS YOU WERE!*" Cogsworth snapped at the armour, seeing her distress.

Immediately, with dozens of identical clacks, the suits resumed their original watchful positions.

They entered a wide foyer but walked right by a grand marble staircase that was an exact duplicate of the one that led to the wing where Belle's room was.

"What's up there?" she asked.

"Oh, uh, nothing important," Lumière said quickly. "Nothing to interest *Mademoiselle*… and all the… uh… stairs…"

Aha.

"Ohhhh. *Stairs.* My goodness. So tiring for a delicate girl like me. So… if there's nothing there, then it doesn't matter if we go and see or not," she said, turning to go up.

"*NO!*" Cogsworth stuttered, running forwards. "The West Wing is utterly boring. Nothing up there to interest you!"

Lumière whacked his friend with the brass end of one of his hands.

"So," Belle said, hesitating a moment with relish. "This is the *forbidden* West Wing."

"What he meant was… we have so many other places to go first," Lumière amended quickly. "The gardens, for instance."

"Too cold," Belle said, continuing to move forwards.

"What about the armoury?" Cogsworth said hopefully. "Or the orangerie?"

"Too spooky. Too late," Belle said, not turning back.

"What about… the *library*?"

Belle whirled round. Somehow Lumière managed a look of pleased satisfaction in his flames.

"Library…?" she asked slowly.

"Oh yes, the master has *so many* books," the little candelabrum drawled.

"Yes, yes!" Cogsworth said, leaping forwards to stand next to his friend. So close, Belle saw distractedly, she was surprised he didn't catch fire. "Rooms and rooms of them!"

"Really?" she asked despite herself.

Rooms of books.

When other children dreamed of mansions with fountains and big silky beds and servants to do their bidding, *this* was what Belle dreamed about. The money to buy all the books she ever wanted from all over the world and a place to keep them.

"Yes, yes, yes, come," Cogsworth said. "You can spend the whole night there if you want. Biographies, histories, twelve different translations of the Bible, romantic adventures…"

It was tempting.

But the library would be there tomorrow. She had *forever*, right?

These little guys were trying to hide something. Just like they tried to hide whatever had happened ten years before… She just *knew* all of the answers she sought would be revealed upstairs.

Including why I have never heard of this castle and kingdom… And who is the Beast? How did he come to rule all of these inanimate objects? Where are all the actual people who should be living here? On what grounds is it considered acceptable to throw a harmless old man and his daughter into prison…?

…And why did no one want her going into the West Wing?

She started climbing the stairs again.

Lumière looked stricken. "*Please*, don't go… the master asked…"

"I only gave my word to *stay*. Nothing else," Belle repeated firmly.

Nothing would stop her from satisfying her curiosity about the most interesting thing that had ever happened to her.

DEATH AND A CURSE

In the sleepy little village, Maurice kept improving his inventions and Rosalind refined her bespelled roses, all the while both were learning how to properly feed (and butcher) their chickens, milk the goats, tend the bees and other new and unfamiliar chores of country life.

Belle grew, reading voraciously, running round barefoot, watching the clouds and dreaming of a life beyond the fields and the plants; the days so similar they all seemed rolled into one.

Meanwhile, in their old kingdom, the fever redoubled its strength and began to spread faster, just like the plague had in horrible days long before. It utterly destroyed the population; young or old, rich or poor, man or woman, it didn't matter. People were dying like rats in the town below while the king and queen hid themselves in their high castle and barricaded their doors against potential contagion. No one was allowed in or out, including the servants… and therefore Alaric.

But the village where Rosalind and Maurice and Belle lived seemed strangely unaffected by the disease rampaging around them. Perhaps it was because of the other town's closed borders and quarantine.

Or perhaps it was because of Rosalind's wards. Or a certain quick-growing oak tree. Or the special broth made by another relocated goodwitch.

Whatever the reason, not a single person west of the river was affected. Nor were the other villages that received the fleeing *charmantes*.

And then, late one dire, rainy night, long after Belle was put to bed a *third* time after trying to read under her covers with a jar of fireflies, there was a knock on the door.

Rosalind and Maurice looked at each other at once and leapt up, expecting to see their dear old friend again.

Instead, an unknown person stood hunched over in the cold, a pale and milky moon making his tired eyes seem even more sunken.

"You are to come to the castle. At once. The king and queen would see you."

"We are no longer citizens of that fair kingdom,"

Rosalind said with a barely contained snarl. "We do not need to obey any demands or requests of the rulers there. They hold my allegiance no longer."

Maurice put his hands lightly on her shoulders, curiosity always stronger in him than outrage. "What do they want?"

The man sighed. "The disease which ravages the countryside is now inside the castle walls, killing royalty and servants alike."

"I don't..." But Rosalind trailed off whatever she was going to say. Her anger deflated in the face of needless death, and the worry in the messenger's eyes. Perhaps he too had a loved one who was sick.

Rosalind looked back at Maurice.

"You should go," he urged. "People are in trouble. And you can see Alaric once you're inside the castle! That would be good..."

"All right. My husband is a kinder man than I." Rosalind was suddenly swirling a warm grey cloak round her neck. "But I shall make my own way there. Just as you must make yours wherever you would go now."

After she disappeared into the dark night, Maurice was left alone, somewhat awkwardly, with the exhausted messenger.

"Can't have you in," he said apologetically.

"Plague. And all. I could... get you a cup of tea? Which you could take. With you. As a... souvenir?"

The castle was very different from the last time Rosalind had been there. Lights were dim and servants kept to the shadows; the deep chanting of priests echoed in the corridors. There was so much incense clouding the air she almost couldn't breathe.

The king and queen were on their thrones, looking tired. The boy prince was nowhere to be seen.

"Enchantress," the queen said, her voice a little scratchy but otherwise as firm as ever. "You are forgiven for the high crime of breaking quarantine. In return, we would ask you use what powers you possess to secure the safety and health of our royal selves and the castle."

Rosalind blinked.

"*What?*" she asked, for once in her life at a loss for words.

"The queen stated it quite clearly," the king snapped. "We have, out of the graciousness of our hearts, cleared you of illegally crossing the border to fly like a coward from our kingdom in distress. In gratitude, *perhaps*, you will... fix... this..." He waved a hand vaguely round the room, trailing a handkerchief that no longer smelled of perfume and flowers but of salts and bitter medicines in hopes of warding off the plague.

"I am not a criminal," Rosalind stated as calmly as she could. "I fled this… *nightmare* of a place and live in a new one now, where no one smears insults on my door and my neighbours don't just disappear without investigation because of their background. You can forgive me of imaginary crimes or not as you like. I have no desire to come back here ever again, and your words are meaningless. Go fetch yourself a doctor and be done with it."

"The… doctors… who remain… have been unable to affect any cure or treatment," the king added, choosing his words carefully. "Frédéric is apparently a gifted surgeon but a terrible healer."

"All who *could* have helped you have disappeared or been forced into exile," Rosalind hissed. "If one were more religious-minded, one would think God had brought this down on you to punish you for your sins."

"I am a king," the king said, his arrogance returning. "God alone may judge me."

The queen waved her hand at him. "If you *must* blame us, do so. But *help* us. We beg you to save what is left of us… what is left of the castle."

"Never," Rosalind spat. "The last free country of *les charmantes* is gone because of the atrocities perpetrated while you looked on without so much as lifting a finger…

I will never help you."

The room was silent, though because all within it were stunned or just weary, it was hard to tell.

"We ordered you here for a spell, not a lecture," the king finally said with a sniff. "Do not try to debate morality with *us*, you base creature."

Rosalind spun round and began to walk out.

"Wait!" the queen leapt up. "My son. I have a… son. You have a daughter. I don't care what happens to the rest of the kingdom. I don't care what happens to us. But please… he is truly innocent of anything we've ever done…"

Rosalind spun back. "Innocent? *MY DAUGHTER* was at risk in your kingdom because her *mother* is one of *les charmantes*… And you think your *son* should be safe because you are a *queen*?"

"Please," was all the queen said, her eyes lowered.

The king looked away and said nothing.

"I shall consider it," Rosalind said coldly. "While I am here, considering it, I wish to see your stablemaster. He is an old friend of my husband's."

"Who?" the king asked, sounding utterly uninterested.

"Your stablemaster. Alaric Potts. We haven't seen him since you barricaded your gates and hid yourself in the castle with your trusted servants, forbidding them to leave."

"Oh. The horse fellow. He's gone," the king said,

rolling his eyes. "Disappeared. Just upped and left when things grew tough, I assume. Ran away from his family and the quarantine."

"If he's dead, it isn't of the plague; they haven't found his body," the queen added. "I almost hope he *is* dead. The Prince has been inconsolable without his daily ride. All he does is cry about his horse. Servants never consider the consequences of their actions, how it affects others."

"Alaric. Potts. Would never. Just. Run. Away."

A wind of rage and agony built inside Rosalind, threatening to tear her and everything in the room apart.

Instead, the Enchantress let it take her and carry her home.

Weeping and exhausted, she related all that had happened to Maurice while he held her. When she had no more to say, Rosalind straightened up and jerkily made the motions that cleared the house of pestilence. Then she went over to Belle's doorway and made additional signs that hung green a moment in the air before trailing to the floor like vines. *Safe.*

Maurice clapped her sadly on the shoulder.

"I understand your decision not to help them, especially after hearing about Alaric," he said quietly. "But overall I'm not sure that was the kindest thing to do."

"They didn't protect my people, *their* people.

Their subjects. There are repercussions for actions. Magic comes back to you, just as the actions of people do. The bigger the person, the more their actions affect the world. If they live, perhaps they will learn that."

"And if everyone dies, no one learns anything," he pointed out gently.

Rosalind remained silent, but her fingers started twitching, working.

Deep in the castle in the woods, silver sparkles fell over those ignorant of the doings of enchantresses and inventors.

"The Prince is... safe?" her husband asked.

Rosalind nodded. "As are the servants and their children."

The couple was silent for a moment.

"If something were to happen to me..." Rosalind began slowly.

"Nothing's going to happen to you, my dear!" Maurice said, giving her a kiss. "You can't get the fever."

"But... if it were... something *else*. Anything else," she said, thinking. "I would want... Belle to be safe. I would want my people... to be safe."

"I don't know how you could do that," Maurice said with a sigh. "You're the most powerful sorceress left in the world... but even *you* can't protect everyone."

"I would make everyone... else... *forget*," she said slowly, thinking. "Forget about me and *les charmantes.* We would become nothing but fairy tales, and hide forever from the eyes of men."

"That seems sad, but pragmatic," Maurice said, putting his arms round her waist. "Just don't include me in the spell. I don't care *what* happens to me, I never want to forget you."

Rosalind smiled and kissed him…

… but didn't answer.

THE ROSE

Cogsworth and Lumière frittered at the edge of the stairs, debating nervously about going up after her.

Belle left them behind.

This part of the castle was… different. If every other room seemed a little musty, cool, dark and abandoned, the West Wing felt like a cave. Also moist, as if a window had been left open despite the early winter weather. Strange, if not strictly unpleasant, barn-like smells assaulted her nose. Vaguely reminiscent of animals.

Belle realised she was holding her breath.

What must have once been a truly spectacular mirror, framed in gold, took up the entire wall at the top of the stairs. Its silvered perfection had been destroyed long ago; shards of deadly glass stuck out like teeth in the otherwise empty frame and littered the floor. There wasn't a single piece remaining that was as large as Belle's hand. But all of them, every single one, from the finger-sized remainders to the tiniest gem-like droplet, reflected her face and the pale, worried look she hadn't even known she wore.

Something was building in the back of her head, thrumming and pulsing. Fear or panic or excitement that she was about to learn something important. It was obvious she was on the right track.

Next to the mirror was a pair of monstrous wooden doors. Their bronze handles were in the form of strangely familiar demons. Belle was reluctant to place her hands over their uncomfortable and jagged forms. But she did.

A sudden gust of wind caught the doors and slammed them all the way open. Belle fell through, tumbling helplessly into the room.

At first she thought she had found a bizarrely cluttered attic: furniture was scattered round like a drunken giant had come through, smashing his way to the window. Hard chairs were knocked down and broken, soft ones were strangely unharmed but pushed together in unusual clusters. Rugs were bunched back up over themselves like something had tried to burrow beneath them. The floors beneath were scored with silver scratch marks, four in a line, like a giant claw. Streaks of dust striped tapestries that hung torn and off-kilter from splintered rods. Scattered here and there were eerily white objects: bones, picked clean.

This, Belle knew without even thinking, was the lair of the Beast.

A handsome four-poster bed was the only thing in the room that seemed untouched, unused. It was sized for a young child, the rosewood poles would have been like a cage for someone like the Beast. A ten-year-old, maybe.

Ten years.

Everything had begun to happen *ten years* ago.

Belle's heart started to race.

Had the Beast invaded this castle, consumed everyone alive in it, and taken this prince's room for his own?

She jumped when another gust of wind caused the shredded curtains to suddenly whip out like angry ghosts. As clouds scuttled away from the moon outside, everything was illuminated in pale white light: besides the general disarray, there were more *violent* signs of destruction now made obvious. Some of the chairs were deliberately smashed. A desk lay in pieces in a corner. Side tables were torn apart, their marble tops cracked like ice.

Belle swallowed.

Were all of these things once animated, like the teapot and clock?

Had they been lively and talkative, moving and

adorable – but were now stilled in a strange death?

How had it happened?

Was there some sort of war to protect the castle?

Were these soldiers, somehow killed in the battle?

Or were they just victims of the Beast's rage?

Belle bit her lip and pushed farther into the room despite every instinct telling her to *run away*. But she would get no answers by remaining at the edges. And there was something comforting about the moonlight streaming in from the window. Belle made her way to the far wall, hoping for a gulp of fresh air.

She tiptoed around mouldering piles of clothes that lay undisturbed by mice. She tried not to shudder at a broken-down wardrobe, a smaller version of the one who had spoken to her: this one lay silent and covered in cobwebs, its doors pulled off its hinges and drawers askew.

Past that was a portrait almost as large as the mirror in the hallway, and almost as destroyed. Great shreds of canvas and peeling oil paint hung from its elaborate frame. Four very deliberate claws had done this. Belle reached forward without thinking and tried to reposition the two largest remaining pieces, like a puzzle, to see who the subject was. It seemed to be a young man with piercing blue eyes in what looked like royal clothes…

Belle frowned. He was too old to be the last occupant

of the child-sized bed in the room, but also too young to be the boy's father. Who was it? Mystery upon mystery…

Something sparkled at the corner of her eye.

There, farther into the room, in front of the windows she was trying to reach, was a little white stone-topped table completely free from the destruction that had torn apart everything else. On it sat two things glittering in the moonlight. One was a pretty silver hand mirror.

The other was a red rose under a bell jar.

ENDGAME

Despite their walls and doctors and priests and incense and wealth, the king and queen took ill and died.

Their son, by some twist of fate, was spared. As were all of the children in the castle. Some called it a miracle.

A year passed. The fever ran itself out, though not before taking a staggering percentage of the townspeople with it.

The time of mourning finally ended and a coronation date was set. There would be a new king and, hopefully, a new beginning for the beleaguered little kingdom.

Meanwhile, in the village, Rosalind was trying to make a dress for Belle. Sewing was not one of her talents; her fingers were covered with little ruby-red pricks of blood and she said many un-enchantress-like things as she went. But Belle's birthday was coming up and, as happened occasionally, Rosalind felt a need to do some sort of 'normal' motherly thing for it.

Maurice had suggested several times they have a dress tailored for their daughter instead. His automated thresher had won some money at a fair and for once they had coin to spare for little luxuries but Rosalind stubbornly refused.

And so she cursed and sewed in the lantern light, cleverly magnified by a system of mirrors and lenses, as a storm blew outside and she wrestled with something that was plaguing her subconscious.

Maurice caught her eyes flickering to the window. Not to the storm he knew, but to what lay east of them.

"Why do you care about the coronation?" he finally asked with a sigh. "Our life there is over, you told them you were never coming back."

"It's just… I just…" Rosalind bit her lip. "If there's any chance at all of saving the kingdom, of making it the way it used to be, it all rests with the Prince."

"He has a hard road ahead of him," Maurice said sympathetically. "And few people left to help. Honestly, it wouldn't surprise me a bit if he just gave it all up and went to university instead. German princes do that all the time."

Rosalind threw down what she was working on.

"I need to go and see him. Now. Before he is made king."

"Dear…" Maurice began.

"I need to make sure he's not like his parents," she said firmly. "If that land is to have any future, it needs a ruler who is kind and generous and forward-thinking and energetic and kind."

"You said *kind* already."

"I have to go," she said, grabbing her green cloak.

Maurice didn't even protest about the weather. Enchantresses had a way of dealing with those sorts of things.

"You've managed to go and escape twice already," he said. "Remember what Frédéric said."

"I'll go in disguise," she promised, giving him a quick kiss.

Maurice grabbed her hands and pressed them to his heart.

"Darling," she said with a patient smile. "I'll go and come back before Belle wakes up. She won't even know I was gone. And we'll all celebrate her birthday together."

Then she hesitated over a pitcher of roses on the table, debating silently. Finally, she selected a glorious red blossom that surpassed perfection but was merely average for *that* household.

Her husband gave her a knowing look. "Magic… always comes back on itself," he reminded her.

"What? I know that. Who said anything about magic?" she demanded.

And then she disappeared.

Because she didn't take the normal road, she never saw the black carriage with the thick windows that was also making its way to the castle.

CURIOSITY KILLED THE BEAST

The rose under the bell jar wasn't in water, nor was it dried; it seemed to be just floating there under the glass, glistening a little in the moonlight.

Entranced, Belle drew closer. She had never seen anything like it before, were there magnets? Lodestones? How was the trick accomplished?

And even stranger, there was something familiar about the rose. Something about the colour of its petals. Like she had seen it somewhere before.

The mirror lay ignored on the table; she reached out her hand and carefully lifted the glass cloche up by its top.

The rose did not fall, as she expected, nor were there invisible strings or wires connecting it to the glass. Still it floated, glittering and twirling slowly above a small pile of petals that had already fallen.

Belle reached out a finger to touch it.

"*NO!*"

Where there had been silence a moment earlier now it was all rumble and roar, sudden and terrifying. The Beast rushed at her upon all fours.

But Belle couldn't quite focus on him; she *had* to know how the trick worked.

She grabbed the rose.

WHAT BELLE SAW

Once upon a time there was a dying magical kingdom hidden deep in the forest. Inside its once-shining castle lived a young prince who had everything anyone in the world could want but despite this, he was selfish, spoiled and unkind. Then, on the night before he was to be made king, an old beggar woman came to the castle and offered him a single blood-red rose in return for shelter from the bitter cold. Repulsed by her haggard appearance, the Prince sneered at the gift and turned the old woman away, although she warned him not to be deceived by appearances, for true beauty is found within.

When the Prince again dismissed her, there was a loud clap of thunder and the old crone disappeared.

Standing in her place was a beautiful woman with

hair as gold as the Prince's mother's necklace, wearing a beautiful dress all shades of the sea. She still held the rose in one hand. In the other, where she had clutched her cane, was a wand of white alder wood.

She was brilliant as the sun, terrible as an avenging angel.

"My – my lady," the Prince stammered, falling to one knee. "Forgive me..."

But it was too late, for she had seen into his soul and knew what sort of person he truly was. As punishment she transformed him into a hideous beast and placed a powerful spell on the castle and those who lived there.

"There is no love in your heart at all, Prince, just like your parents, who utterly destroyed this kingdom with their selfishness and cruelty.

"You have until the eve of your 21st birthday to become as beautiful on the *inside* as you were on the outside. If you do not learn to love another, and be loved in return, by the time the last petal of this rose falls, you, your castle, and all within, will be cursed and forgotten *forever*."

Ashamed of his monstrous form, the Beast concealed himself inside his castle, with a magic mirror as his only window to the outside world.

As the years passed he fell into despair and lost all hope, for who could ever learn to love a beast?

A CURSE DESCENDS

Belle stumbled in confusion. As clear as if it were occurring right there behind her eyes, she saw the truth: the Prince who was the Beast, the spell, the rose, *the Enchantress.*

Her mother.

The rose was from *her* garden. That was why it had looked familiar.

Belle held the blossom before her face in wonder. Her mother had held it exactly ten years before, the same way.

But under her look and the light of the moon, the rose began to fall apart. The petals fell and shifted into glittering red sand that disappeared before it hit the ground. The stem dissolved inch by inch until there was nothing left.

And the Beast howled in despair.

PART II

ESCAPE

The castle shook. There was a mighty clap, like the largest crack of lightning in the history of the world struck the tower. Strange loud noises erupted from everywhere at once; somehow familiar, they touched the very core of Belle's soul. Something between a cracking and a crack*ling*, but much, much bigger.

Ice.

It sounded like ice breaking across a pond, and brought with it the accompanying dread: as when a foot steps down and lines shoot out from under it into the white distance and death is in the frigid air.

Somehow, Belle wouldn't have been surprised if the whole palace began crumbling around her but that wasn't what was happening.

"*MY ONE CHANCE!*" the Beast cried. "*MY ONE CHANCE TO END THE CURSE. IT'S* GONE. *YOU'VE RUINED IT!*"

She was only half paying attention to him; he was standing still and screaming and not accosting her. More immediate things were happening outside. She ran to the window.

Strange bone-white *things* were coming out of the ground just beyond the perimeter of the castle walls. Too angular and thick to be vines, too solid to be ice. At first Belle thought they were something like antlers or bones being forced out of the dirt by whatever forces were now at work. But they *kept* coming up, unending and sickly. They twisted and turned as they shot forth, whipping around and sticking to whatever solid object they touched. Once they came in contact with the wall, they slowed. But then they grew like frost on a window, criss-crossing each other and spreading unnaturally.

Spiderwebs.

Somehow Belle knew without even wondering.

Not the ones that hung in neat circles and octagons and whatever-other-gons in bushes and on flowers with a pretty little spider sitting in the middle. The *other* ones – the messy ones that covered the ground and grass like snow on dewy mornings, all random peaks and valleys and impossible to see where the spider hid. Three-dimensional. Complicated.

Her mother... had liked... roses... and natural things... Belle remembered this vaguely. Her mother the *Enchantress.*

It made sense that she had cursed the castle with webs.

Belle turned to look at the Beast.

His eyes were empty of everything except for animal-like anger. There was no spark of intelligence or humanity left in them. He stood on all fours and bellowed madly.

Belle was paralysed for a moment. Then instinct kicked in and she ran, pushing past him and out through the door.

Without wasting a moment to look behind her, she dashed down the steps, two and three at a time and raced through the great halls.

She had to get out of there.

"*Ma chérie!* Where do you go? What is happening?" Lumière plonked awkwardly out of the shadows after her.

"*What have you done?*" shrieked Cogsworth.

"I'm sorry," Belle sobbed. "I'm..."

She didn't know why she was sorry. Maybe it was because she was leaving the cute little things back with that monster, to be sealed up with him, to face his wrath once she was gone. Here she was, on her first and only adventure, and somehow she had ruined everything immediately.

She flung open the front door and ran through the courtyard, past the fountain, to the gates. A single strand of webbing as thick as her wrist had grown over them, holding them mostly closed. She reluctantly reached out to touch it.

Sticky.

Just a little.

And cold.

Belle swallowed her revulsion and tried to pull it aside, but it didn't give at all in the way she imagined a giant piece of spider silk should have. It was hard and unyielding. She pulled her hands away and scrambled underneath it instead, forcing her body through the small crack, pushing the metal bars apart with her legs. Her clothes brushed against the gluey surface of the webbing and it grabbed her like it was alive.

Belle kicked and screamed and forced herself out, entirely giving in to panic. Her dress tore with a sound that seemed to rip the world. By the time she got up and brushed herself off, the webs were already re-covering the gap, thicker, behind her. Almost as if they sensed the breach and strove to fix it.

Belle shuddered.

Phillipe, bless his horse heart, was still there. And more than ready to run himself, ears cocked and eyes rolling, at the strangeness of what was happening.

Belle grabbed his reins and leapt on his back. He didn't need to be told twice.

In a turn and gallop that would have made his warhorse

ancestors proud, Phillipe dashed into the woods. His long legs pushed hard against the ground, hooves smashing into dust everything that lay beneath them. They were going to make it and she was going to ride triumphantly through the snow back home.

Then he stopped, rearing up. Belle was almost flung from his back and that's when she saw them.

Wolves.

There were, of course, still wolves left around the village where she lived. Once in a very great while, driven by hunger, they would come down out of the hills and mountains and forests to grab a sheep if a shepherd wasn't watching properly. But unless it was sick or desperate, none would appear in broad daylight to a human on a horse, a human whom it knew probably carried a gun. Wolves were bad guys only in fairy tales and legends to scare young children at night.

These, however, didn't look like the grey wolves she and her father had once seen trotting in the distance.

They were *huge.* And white. With red eyes that seemed to glow.

Seemed?

She had just fled an enchanted castle with talking furniture and a beast prince ruling them all… *whom her mother had cursed.*

These were *not* normal wolves. They were magic, too. They were trying to stop her from leaving the castle.

Belle grabbed the reins and pulled hard, spinning Phillipe the other way.

The wolves howled and bayed like nightmare creatures as they took off in pursuit.

Belle could barely hold on, much less direct Phillipe. She let him go wherever he needed to for escape and didn't try to stop him from running over a snowy pond like it was nothing more than a field. The ice broke beneath them, with thundering waves of noise that rippled out to the banks on the far side, echoing what was occurring back at the castle.

Unheeding of the danger, the wolves followed.

One of Phillipe's hooves struck a weak spot. A moment later the horse was floundering in the freezing water, churning his front legs desperately and trying to get back up.

But several of the wolves were also caught in the shifting sheets of ice; they had lost at least two of their followers to the blackness below.

Phillipe managed to clamber to the edge of the pond and pull himself out on to solid ground. Belle gritted her teeth as the icy water sloshed in her shoes. She couldn't feel her lower legs.

The horse threw himself forwards, galloping into the forest again. Belle hunkered down, trying to avoid being knocked off by low branches or taken out by vines.

They burst into a clearing and saw three more wolves already waiting for them there.

Surrounded on all sides, Phillipe began to panic in earnest, making terrible shrieking noises, his eyes rolling. He bucked wildly, slashing his hooves at the enemy. Forgetting about his rider.

Belle flew off his back.

The wolves came closer and closer and snapped at his feet and legs.

Belle shook her head, which was ringing from her hard landing. Otherwise nothing seemed to be too badly damaged. She dragged herself to her wobbly feet and looked round for anything that could be used as a weapon. A large forked branch lay on the ground nearby. She grabbed it and stood with her back to the panicking horse, trying to fight off the wolves that were closing in.

"*Stay back!*" she ordered. "I am the daughter of an enchantress!"

The wolves didn't think much of her declaration.

One wolf leapt at her and grabbed the branch in its teeth, pulling it out of her grip. At the same time, another hurled itself into her chest, knocking her down.

Belle rolled away, trying to make sure she didn't end up under Phillipe's deadly hooves.

Another wolf stood over her, its slavering mouth inches from her face, its yellow teeth glinting like poison in the moonlight. It snarled and opened wide, ready to tear her to pieces.

Belle turned her face aside and covered her head with her hands, waiting for the finishing bite.

And suddenly the weight was off her.

She peeped through her fingers to look.

The Beast was there, throwing the wolf he had picked off her to one side. He roared and howled, louder than the pack. The rest of the wolves leapt to attack him. One lunged at his leg, another at his shoulder.

In movements that were too quick to follow, the Beast shifted from two feet to four, shaking the wolves off him like water.

But he bled from ugly wounds where they fell away.

Belle crawled to the safety of a large tree and hid behind its enormous roots.

The Beast was *saving* her?

He stood for a moment, silhouetted against the moonlight, claws out. They were longer than a bear's and glittered ivory and ruby from raking through the belly of a wolf.

Then he was all shadows and blurry movement again, throwing himself among the remaining wolves like a reaver.

With yelps that didn't sound properly dog-like at all, the wolves began to sense the battle had turned. The Beast grabbed one of the last and flung it against a tree like a sack of apples. There was an ugly wet-sounding *crack* as it crumpled to a heap right in front of Belle. She flinched at its closeness.

Without a signal or a noise, the wolves admitted defeat and loped into the shadows, disappearing back to wherever they had come from.

Belle looked up at the Beast, who was on two legs now, growling a final warning. His fur was torn and one ear didn't look quite right. His stance, never normal to begin with, looked more misshapen and awkward than before. There was a small pool of blood forming in the dirt below his right forepaw.

He opened his mouth to say something to her…

… and then, slowly, like a falling tree, collapsed at her feet.

A DECISION AND ITS CONSEQUENCES

Belle stayed as still as a rabbit, looking with wide eyes upon the scene before her, replaying in her mind what had just happened.

The Beast, the big, malformed and grotesque thing that lay unconscious in a patch of its own blood before her, had imprisoned her father just for trespassing and then traded Maurice's life for hers like some sort of medieval despot. He was not, by any stretch of the imagination, a *good* creature.

And yet… he had saved her from the wolves.

Snow began to fall.

Belle suddenly had no idea how long she had been sitting there, frozen.

Phillipe's reins were caught up in strangler vines across the clearing. He chuffed unhappily, pacing back and forth. The lingering scent of wolves and death were making him fractious.

Belle blinked the snowflakes out of her eyes. Now that the shock of the battle was wearing off, she was beginning to feel things again, including how numb and aching her wet feet were. If she stayed out much longer, she wouldn't be able to walk. She would freeze.

Slowly she rose, stomping her feet, trying to work feeling back into them. Then she stumbled across the clearing to Phillipe and worked the ropes out of their snarl with stiff, unhelpful fingers. Murmuring calming words, she managed to get the giant horse to back up and slowly turn around.

The bodies of the wolves, and the Beast, were lifeless mounds gradually whitening in the rapidly increasing snow. She turned to go.

The Beast would freeze if she left him there.

He had saved her life.

Cursing, she led the nervous Phillipe over the carcasses and piles of bloody innards. He did not shy away from the Beast as she was afraid he might; something about his body was less terrifying than those of the wolves.

With a lot of difficulty, Phillipe had no desire to kneel in the snowy, bloody muck, and a strained back, Belle managed to shove the Beast on to the horse so his head and hind limbs dangled off opposite sides. As loathe as she was to touch him, his fur didn't smell as bad or as animal-like as she expected. It had a faintly wild, barn-like whiff to it but was neither greasy nor dirty. She idly wondered if he licked himself clean like a cat or dived into ponds like a dog.

But now, where to?

As she looked round the woods through whirling drifts of snow, she realised she had no idea where she was. She had just made Phillipe run through woods, willy-nilly. Belle frowned and stared at the sky but, of course, there were no stars. Between the gloom and the snow there was no way to find any familiar landmarks.

She couldn't stop shivering.

The toes of her shoes, she saw, had hardened with ice and were dusted with hoarfrost – echoing the webs that had crawled up outside the castle. She felt like one of the luckless peasant girls in some Russian hagiography, left to fend for her family in deep Siberian snows.

Ever a logical girl, she didn't like where the hints all around were leading her.

Apparently, I'm the daughter of an enchantress, she thought. *So… maybe I can enchant?*

She closed her eyes and imagined *warm*. Sunny skies, still clouds and snow swept away.

Nothing.

She clenched her fists hard and imagined *fire*, even at the risk of it consuming the tree in front of her. *MAKE IT BURN!*

She opened her eyes.

Nothing.

"I command you, winds!" she shouted imperiously. "Take me home…"

"… please?" she added after a moment.

Nothing.

With aching slowness she turned Phillipe and his burden round and followed their tracks back to the castle.

It was very hard going. Belle tried not to panic about not being able to feel her feet any more, tried to put away little fairy tale horror stories she had read about girls freezing in the wilderness.

I'm the daughter of an enchantress, she told herself to bolster her courage. Also just to taste the feeling of it. That had been *her mother* in the visions, whose role in Belle's broken memories was merely that of a pretty face and loving smile and soft lap. There was nothing magical about her, beyond the extra layers of warmth that nostalgia and loss applied to fond remembrances.

When they finally made it back to the castle, she saw with a shock that all the perimeter walls were now shrouded in white, thick ribby drifts. Strands were still growing up out of the ground, much more slowly now, but with a frightening relentlessness.

Where she had squeezed out through the gates there were now many more ropes of webbing. But when she reached out to try to push them, they broke off in her hand, shattering. Belle was shocked, before she realised the truth of it: they were there to keep the Beast *in*, not out.

A few deft swipes and they were gone. She threw the gates open and led Phillipe in. When the gates clanged shut behind her, the webbing had already begun to grow back.

A funny, sad little scene greeted her at the door to the castle: Cogsworth, Lumière and – was that a *dust* mop? – drooped in despair, looking out into the night. Lumière had a carefully placed candle-hand on Cogsworth's back in sympathy.

They all gawped and jumped as soon as they saw her.

"Get him inside. He needs a fire and bandages," Belle ordered. "Right away."

"*Certainement*," Lumière said briskly, marching off.

"First aid immediately, of course!" Cogsworth added, looking grim.

All sorts of little creatures and animated bric-a-brac that Belle hadn't seen earlier came to life, whisking and scampering this way and that to help out. She caught sight of Mrs Potts, steaming with purpose, ordering the lesser kitchenware to help out with boiling water and hot towels.

Once the Beast was inside and being tended to, Belle reluctantly returned to the courtyard.

"Thank you, old friend," she said to Phillipe, patting his soft nose. "Now go home. Go to Papa."

She led him to the gates, shuddering at the sight of the icy webbing that was slowly continuing to spread. After both of them carefully stepped through she gave his flanks a firm but friendly slap.

The horse neighed, then trotted off into the woods, towards home.

Belle felt a pang. But she had made her decision.

"I need some rope," she said to Cogsworth as she entered the study, shaking herself into action.

"Yes, of course, right away," the little clock said. "Wait, what?"

"I'm not letting him free until I get some answers," Belle said, gritting her teeth. "Help me tie him up."

"Tie up? The *master*?" Cogsworth stuttered.

"He threw my *father* into a cold prison cell, then took me in his place! I think tying him up in front of a warm roaring fire is plenty generous, considering!" she snapped.

The little clock started to protest, but Belle simply glared at him.

"Yes… I can see your point…" Cogsworth boggled.

"All right… *PANTRY? Storage?* You're needed…"

He waddled off, still mumbling about the inappropriateness of the whole thing.

Belle watched the castle busy itself, a little surprised at her quick acceptance of the whole thing. From discovering the existence of an enchanted castle to ordering its occupants around like she had been doing it her entire life, had all taken less than the span of a day. She wondered for a moment what would have happened if she had never gone up the stairs to the forbidden West Wing. Would she have remained a prisoner of the Beast? Or would she have become the queen of this place?

She never did see the library…

Belle didn't trust the silverware and oversaw each of the knots as it was being tied and pulled. Sometimes when they ran out of money for metal, her father had to cobble his inventions together with leather thongs and rope. She was good at lacing things tightly.

Mrs Potts had a cart of hot tea and brandy wheeled in, along with a dish of broth and a covered tureen of what, from the smell, Belle was pretty sure the Beast ate on a regular basis. Meat. Not cooked much.

Belle took it upon herself to help wash his wounds; except for an animated mop and broom, there wasn't really anyone large enough or with strong prehensile digits to gently dab a wound and then wring out the cloth in boiling hot water.

Could my mother have just healed him, with a snap of her fingers?

Belle tried to remember some incident from her childhood where she was hurt, but it was always just Maurice bandaging her wounds or putting salves on them or giving her a kiss to make it feel better. She couldn't remember her mother doing *anything*. Or being there at all, really.

Belle helped herself to some tea in between, putting in plenty of sugar. They never had enough of it at home; here there was a whole pyramid of shining brown lumps.

Do enchantresses drink tea? Or did my mother only have tisanes and wild concoctions made from forest things? She hadn't seemed like a woodsy sort in the vision. The dress she wore when she turned back into herself was a little showy but otherwise quite fashionable. As if a modern, well-to-do lady wanted to impress a snobby prince with her enchantress-ness.

Sorceresses with bustles, witches with frothy white wigs... Belle drowsily tried to figure out what a modern wizard would look like.

Eventually, she must have dozed off, kneeling on the floor with her body resting against the giant chair the Beast was lying in and tied to. When she woke, the Beast's eyelids were fluttering open.

Funny, Belle thought. *He has eyelashes.*

The moment of drowsy calm didn't last.

As soon as he was fully awake, the Beast roared and strained to get up and then roared again when he realised he couldn't.

"Hush!" Belle chastised. "The entire castle can hear you."

"*WHY AM I RESTRAINED? WHAT DO* – arrrgh!" He fell back into the chair, one of his wounds having pressed against the rope when he strained. He bit his lip and whimpered like a dog.

"Thank you for saving me from the wolves," Belle said mildly. But she was a little cautious; it wouldn't take many more attempts like that for the Beast to break free. One of the ropes grew taut and frayed as he struggled.

"If you're thanking me, why have you tied me up?" he grumbled.

This was the Beast she could reason with; it was a tone of voice she recognised from before. Human but grumpy.

"Let's see." She ticked off reasons on her fingers. "Because you made my father your prisoner. Because you then made *me* your personal prisoner. Because you are cursed, and I feel like maybe with reason. And also I have questions."

"Doesn't matter. Tie me up or not. I'm trapped here forever, in this," the Beast mumbled.

He began to lick one of his wounds moodily.

"Stop that," Belle said, lightly slapping his arm.

The Beast jumped. "Ow!"

"Please." Belle rolled her eyes. "I saw what the wolves did to you. *That* hurt?"

He remained grouchily quiet. In the flickering light of the fire the Beast looked both more monstrous and more human. His head was massive – *massive* – and not, on second look, canine or wolfish as one would expect of a werewolf. It was more like a bull with longer fur; his horns went a long way towards completing that image. But his eyebrows were large and expressive, and if one didn't look *too* closely one could mistake the lower part of his mane for a beard. His eyes remained intelligent and unreadable in the orange light.

"Wait," he suddenly said. "How did you know I was cursed?"

"When I touched the rose… sorry!"

The Beast had immediately wilted, somehow becoming small in the giant chair. His brow furrowed in pain and something like a whimper might have escaped around his mighty tusks.

Now she understood his rage.

Not all the details, of course. But she had accidentally destroyed the only way he had of freeing himself from the monstrous form he was in.

"When I touched the rose I saw what happened. I saw you, as a boy, in the castle being cursed by an enchantress. I'm… very sorry for what I did," Belle said, much more gently. "But… it didn't look like you were ever going to break the curse on your own. Most of the petals had already fallen, isn't that right? We must be very close to your 21st birthday. So unless you were going to somehow make me fall in love with you in… I don't know… a month or less, it was all over already."

The Beast looked away. Possibly in embarrassment.

"And," Belle added wryly, "I have already almost been the victim of *one* involuntary wedding today. So. I can tell you. I'm not that easy a catch."

The Beast looked at her, surprised and interested for a moment – before grinding his teeth and looking down at the floor again.

"Why did she curse you?" Belle pressed.

The Beast didn't answer.

"Come on… why?"

"Crazy enchantress, I don't know." The Beast shrugged angrily.

"*Please*," Belle said.

"I was eleven years old!" he roared. "What *could* I have done?"

Belle was silent for a moment. He had a point. The boy in the vision seemed, in truth, a terrible little human being. But he was still a boy.

And also a prince, apparently.

And what was it the Enchantress – her *mother* – had said?

There is no love in your heart at all, Prince, just like your parents…

"Did she… did the woman who cursed you know your parents?"

It looked like he was going to stay sulkily silent, but then he seemed to think about it, as if this were the first time he had considered the whole thing. "My parents ruled the kingdom. Of course she knew them."

Belle rubbed her temples in frustration. "Was the Enchantress famous? Did she bear some sort of grudge against your parents, or the kingdom, for some reason?" She didn't like to think the woman she had suddenly learned so much about was one of those irrational fairies or witches or sorceresses from legend who went around cursing people and their babies out of spite.

"What… does it matter now?" the Beast asked.

"It *matters* because I'm trapped here with you, because of whatever happened ten years ago, and, oh, yes, it turns out the Enchantress was my *mother*!"

The look of surprise on the Beast's face was almost comical.

No, *actually comical*, Belle decided.

"Wh-what?"

"The Enchantress was my mother," she repeated, a little more patiently.

It was strange to say it aloud.

She had these new images in her head of a woman maybe ten years older than Belle herself was now. She wondered at the cross of sublime, angelic determination and hair-trigger anger that had caused her to test and then curse a boy prince.

Rash. That was the word Belle would have chosen to use for a woman who did things like that.

Oh, a tiny voice in her mind said, *you mean things like marching into a haunted castle and trading your life for your father's. Acting without thinking about consequences.*

She waved her hand as if to physically brush the thought away.

"Your mother?" the Beast repeated, still dumbfounded. He scrabbled in his chair like a restless dog. "Are *you* an enchantress, too?" he asked eagerly. "Can you free me from this?"

"I'm *not* an enchantress," Belle said softly. She was surprised at how much it bothered her to see the Beast's look of disappointment. "And up until today I didn't believe such things as *enchantresses* existed. Or curses. Or enchanted castles."

As she said this a pair of silver teaspoons marched

out and, using a cloth napkin they held like a sheet to be folded, delicately wiped up some spilled tea before marching away again.

"Well, where is she? Is your mother at home? Can we go and see her?"

He was leaning forwards eagerly, hopefully.

"I… never knew my mother," she admitted. "I have no idea where she is. She left us years ago. I'd love to see her again. Especially now that it turns out she's an enchantress. I have a lot of questions I'd like answered."

"Why are you here then?" the Beast growled. "If your mother came and cursed me, isn't it unusual that *you also* show up at my castle's door ten years later?"

"Well, yes," Belle agreed. "But I'm here only because of my father. Phillipe – the horse – came back without him and I went out to search."

"You're lying. You could have come to make sure the curse would come true."

Belle raised an eyebrow at him. "I am *not* lying. I'm not sure what the point of me doing that would be. After, you know, bringing you back to the castle so you wouldn't freeze to death."

The Beast, chagrined, didn't say anything.

"What… what do we do now?" he finally asked in a small voice.

Belle looked at him in surprise.

He threw out his hands as best he could, indicating the room, or the castle, or the world.

"We're… stuck here. Forever. The… spiderwebs will cover the whole castle soon. Completing the curse."

Belle looked up at the ceiling, at the walls, hoping an answer or something would materialise. The corners of the room were shadowy and angles leapt back and forth as the fire danced and cast eerie lights. She realised, with a slow blink of her eyes, that her overwhelming feeling at that moment wasn't fear. It was exhaustion. It was being overwhelmed. It was her brain, the one that her father always praised her for, suddenly being overtaxed and overfull.

All she wanted to do was to sit quietly in a corner and *think*. Think about the wisps of ideas she had about her mother.

For instance, she had somehow always thought of her mother as having auburn hair.

Sort of like her own hair but redder. *Not* blonde. Why had she got it so wrong? Isn't the first thing a child describes about a parent the hair colour? She had no idea what it smelled like, either. She couldn't summon a single sensory image of her mother holding her; all her mind did was shortcut the memory by alluding to loving scenes in books she had read: everything from nursery rhymes to fairy tales to picaresques.

The picture she had in her head now, of angelic retribution, didn't exactly conform to what she thought her mother, *any* mother, would be like. She wasn't a mother at all in the scene; she was a woman, a person, doing things that had nothing to do with Belle.

Nothing to do with me. She never had anything to do with me.

She rubbed her temples and glanced over at the Beast.

She *should* have been afraid. He was a big, violent beast who could easily kill her in a dozen different ways. But he had saved her life from the wolves. Surely he didn't mean to hurt her? And he spoke like a mostly normal human. Something that could be reasoned with.

She thought about Gaston, the only other big beast-like thing she knew who spoke.

He would have been a lot slower on the uptake about everything. Their conversation would have been a *lot* longer and more frustrating. And he would have tried to marry her at some point. He was human and utterly impossible to communicate or negotiate with.

With a sigh Belle got up and began to untie the ropes.

The Beast stayed still until she was finished, being careful not to move at all while following her movements with his wide and suspicious eyes.

"What… why are you doing that?"

She shrugged. "As you say, nothing much matters any more. We're here for… a while, at least. May as well trust each other."

When she was finished, he flexed his claws experimentally. As he rose out of the chair, he winced, grinding his teeth at the pain from his wounds.

"If we *could* find my mother," Belle said slowly, thinking, "if she's not dead, or something. Maybe she could reverse the curse."

"How would we find her?" the Beast grumbled, massaging one paw with the other.

"Do you still have the mirror, the one she gave you?" Even as she asked, she remembered the other thing on the table with the rose. The ornate silver hand mirror, lying there so innocently. "That lets you see everywhere?"

"The magic mirror," the Beast said, eyebrows rising. "Yes! We could consult it!"

"Great, let's go and consult the *magic mirror*," she repeated, unable to believe she was saying those words aloud. "Why not. And maybe afterwards we can go and visit the witch in her woods and break off a bit of her gingerbread house for a snack."

The Beast looked at her, confused, his eyebrows rising even higher, like dark clouds above his blue eyes.

"Never mind," Belle said with a sigh. "It was a joke."

For the second time Belle found herself going up the stairs to the forbidden wing. Her feelings were entirely different now: she was exhausted and unafraid. The whisperings of shadows and creakings of animated suits of armour held no terror against the whirl of images and thoughts in her head: blonde and green and lightning-coloured thoughts with her mother's face, again and again, that look of disappointment and triumph that wasn't altogether pleasing.

The Beast hesitated a moment at the demon-handled doors of his room. It made Belle think of a scene from some book in which a boy, somewhat embarrassed, showed his family home or private room to a girl he liked. Fear of disappointing the guest, fear she would discover something uncouth about the host.

Like there could be anything worse than torn-up furniture 'nests' and bones everywhere, Belle thought wryly.

He let her go first, which was chivalrous although unwonted. The room was cold and the curtains still flapping. Not inviting in the slightest.

"What picture is this?" she asked, indicating the carefully mangled one, the portrait of the young man with blue eyes.

The Beast deflated, his giant shoulders hunching over his neck and head.

"It's me."

He reached out a delicate claw and pulled all the strips of canvas back into place. The Prince was revealed yet again: tall and handsome and arrogantly looking into the viewers' eyes, challenging them to keep looking.

"The Enchantress put a spell on it so it would age *with* me and show me how I would look if I was still human. If I hadn't failed her test. I'm… always reminded of who I *could* have been."

Belle cocked her head and really looked at the picture. It was painted by a consummate artist; the velvet on the Prince's jacket looked soft and furry enough to touch. *But those eyes…*

"I'm not so sure it should make you feel bad," she finally said. "The man in that picture looks contemptuous. Self-important."

The Beast looked at her, shocked.

"Well, he *does*," she said, waving a hand to indicate the Prince's face. "It's supposed to show what you would look like on the outside. But does it show how you really are *now*, on the inside?"

The Beast dropped the canvas strips in disgust and swung away, muttering something about "meaningless words". Belle almost smiled despite their circumstances. There were moments when she almost *enjoyed* talking with the Beast… poking at him gently…

She followed him over to the table. The wind had dropped and now everything was strangely still; there wasn't enough breeze to flutter a single rose petal. The Beast took one sharp breath upon seeing the destroyed flower, then made himself look away.

Belle felt her heart sink. It really *was* all her fault. Maybe he only had a few more weeks until the curse was complete anyway – but those would have been a few more weeks of hope. And who knows? Maybe the magic would have sent someone, some nice peasant girl, to lift the hex. Maybe her mother had a plan that wouldn't have kept this poor beast in his damned state for ever.

With far more gentleness than she would have guessed those massive paws were capable of, he picked up the mirror and cradled it lovingly. At first it seemed like no more than a fancy princess's vanity object, decorated with roses and what looked like abstract beastly faces on it.

"What can it do?" Belle asked politely.

"Oh, it can show me anything," the Beast said eagerly. "Anything real. I've seen mountains in the Far East that are always covered in snow and Paris at Christmas time with all of the lights and festivals and markets."

Belle pushed a stray bit of hair back behind her ear. "You can see the entire world in that?"

"Yes. Look!" He held it out for her.

At first, there was nothing but the silvery surface and her own sceptical face. Belle couldn't help stroking another stray lock of hair neatly behind her ear. She had rarely examined herself in such a fine glass and wasn't thrilled with how a few blocked pores looked in its illuminative depths. And was that a tiny scar next to her eye? She had never noticed it…

"Mirror, show me Paris," the Beast commanded.

Mists fogged the image like he had breathed on it. When they cleared, Belle was so surprised she was glad she wasn't the one holding the mirror or she might have dropped it.

As real as if it were happening right in front of her through a window, she could see shining carriages hurtling through cobbled streets, fancy ladies and gentlemen dressed in fashions she had only read about, buildings and shops and fountains and streets like the entire world was filled with them. *So many people!* From aristocratic doyennes attended by uniformed maids to merchants with smart but patched hats…

… to waifs, beggars, little hungry children with feral eyes, dodging among everyone, trying to earn a few pennies… or steal them…

Belle was speechless. If she had a mirror like this, she might not ever have bothered to read. She could see an entire world full of stories, right here.

Then she realised she was leaning in, trying to hear what people were saying, to smell their perfumes, to feel the city air on her face.

Nothing.

It was a strangely cold experience despite the beauty of the picture.

"This is my favourite thing," the Beast said sadly. "My only thing. I can see the world I am missing – the life I would have had."

Belle frowned as he took the mirror back to look in it himself.

"But… if you have this mirror, and you know what you need to break the spell, why didn't you use it to help you?" she asked. "You could have used it to find a girl, maybe… or…"

With a snarl the Beast shoved the mirror back in her face.

"Mirror, show me the red-headed boy!"

The image changed. Now it was of a child whose hands were grotesque: like a lobster, with only two large thick fingers on each hand and a thumb. He was behind bars that he gripped with his awkward digits, and stood in a tub of water. In front of him, people were laughing and jeering and, in the case of one 'gentleman', poking at his claws with a cane.

The saddest thing was not the restrained violence of the scene but how resigned the boy looked; how empty his eyes were, how he could see this was his lot in life for ever.

"If they do this to a child, what do you think they will do to a beast?"

Belle bit her lip. She had no answer. Besides the meanness and small-mindedness of the townspeople, she had never seen any real cruelty. At least not outside a book.

She wanted to touch the boy's cheek. She wanted to throw up. She wanted to…

The Beast took the mirror away.

"Just like that stupid hunter in that village over the river probably wants to put my pelt on his floor like a rug," he muttered.

"Gaston?" Belle asked, shocked. "You mean Gaston?"

"I don't know anyone's names. Can't hear anything," he said, shaking the mirror. "He always comes into the forest and shoots anything large, pretty, or different-looking. Or just *moving*. Other hunters come and go, getting deer or birds… for meat… I have no problem with that. But this man just wants to kill and stuff everything. He doesn't need the meat."

Belle decided to file away how the Beast said 'meat' to think about more fully later. He was a hundred-kilo-plus beast and obviously didn't eat toast to keep his weight up.

"If I tried to leave the castle, they'd do that. Tie me up and make me a display at a circus… *if I was lucky*," the Beast continued. "So I watch the world from here. It's safer."

"Safer, except that's no way to break the spell," Belle pointed out.

The Beast shrugged impatiently. "You want to find your mother?"

"Yes, yes," Belle said. "Let's see."

"Mirror, show me the Enchantress who put this curse upon me!"

The image faded and the mirror became foggy – a strange grey that didn't reflect, a silver that wasn't shiny.

"It's never done that before," the Beast said in wonder, shaking it again as if to fix it.

"Can I try? Mirror, show me my father," Belle commanded before the Beast could answer.

Maurice appeared, looking miserable, bouncing round the inside of the wheel-less carriage and trying to look through its windows back at the castle.

Belle felt her heart would burst.

"Papa!"

"Does *he* know where your mother is?" the Beast asked eagerly.

"What? No," Belle said, distracted. "He… never talked

about her, really. I thought it was because he was upset by whatever made her leave… but now I think maybe he just… somehow… doesn't *remember* her. The same way I don't."

"Hmph. *Show me the Enchantress*," the Beast said, pulling the mirror away from her.

But the image faded again to the same strange grey.

"But my father…" Belle began again.

"What about him?"

"He *needs* me…"

"He raised you by himself, didn't he? Seems like he's done a more than all right job. He'll be fine for a few days on his own," the Beast pointed out.

Belle glared at him.

Her father couldn't… he didn't…

… make their meals, tend their garden, earn coin for comestibles they couldn't grow or forage themselves, spend days inventing – all things he did before she was old enough to help him… when he was taking care of her…

Her lip quivered. Of course he was fine.

Wait…

"You think he did a *more than all right job*?" she couldn't help asking.

The Beast shrugged, suddenly embarrassed.

She found herself smiling.

Was he *almost* smiling back? In his eyes, at least?

But after a moment, grim reality set in again.

"Now what?" the Beast asked, indicating the failed mirror.

But Belle was exhausted and out of ideas. "I don't know. It's been a long day. I'm very tired."

He *did* give her a smile this time, albeit a wan one. "Me too. Might as well… go to bed…" he said, shrugging.

"I guess we have forever to figure this out," Belle said softly.

As they turned to go back through the door, they walked, side by side, in companionable, if wistful, silence.

They didn't speak until the Beast had walked her all the way back to her bedroom door.

Belle started to open the door, then stopped. She never found words hard; her whole life she had always had a pert answer or a gentle insult or a funny riposte to anything the villagers said to her. Now she found that pulling them from her heart and not her mind, felt like dragging something jagged and reluctant out of a well.

"I'm… sorry," she said quietly. "I really am. I shouldn't have touched the rose."

She made herself look straight into his eyes. His very *un*animal eyes.

The Beast gave her a sad smile. "You were my prisoner. Why *would* you listen to anything I said? And… it wouldn't have mattered… Anyway… you're right. I wouldn't have broken the curse on my own."

He looked down at his feet. Silence gathered over them like soft snow.

"Good night," Belle said finally, opening the door and stepping inside.

But the Beast, black as shadow and twice as silent, was already gone.

A CASTLE, HAUNTED

As soon as Belle closed the door behind her, a complete and heavy hush fell over everything. She leaned back against the firm wood and closed her eyes. Maybe she would push a chair up against the door, but somehow she didn't think the Beast would come back that night. It was unclear what she would be barricading against.

She rubbed the palms of her hands over her face. She felt dry and drained. Remembering the princess-pretty basin and pitcher on the bureau, Belle went over and poured some water into her cupped hand and smoothed it over her face.

"There's a towel, there, if you like," the wardrobe said helpfully from behind her.

Belle didn't so much jump as *shiver* at the sudden voice. Also, she felt a little foolish: hanging right there was a lovely, soft facecloth.

"Thank you."

"If you want some hot water, we can order it right up for you," the wardrobe added helpfully.

"No, I'm all right, really, thank you."

The idea of a *hot* bath was, in fact, incredibly appealing. To get one at home Belle usually had to time it just right with making dinner or breakfast; they only had two pots and one had the meal in it. Her father's automatic watering system made it easy to get cold, clear, pure well water any given moment of the day, heating it up was what took the effort. Sometimes she put a pot on top of his forge if it was going.

But she couldn't deal with any more odd little animated 'inanimate' objects right now. The wardrobe's… *presence*… was enough.

Before she could even finish that thought, however, there was a tap on the door.

"Come in," she found herself saying politely before she could stop herself.

"Sorry to bother you, miss." A funny leather-and-metal thing whose original use she couldn't even begin to guess at came waddling in with several stout logs balanced carefully on its… back. Lumière came hopping behind.

"I thought we would… top you off, so we wouldn't disturb you tonight," the little candelabrum said. His companion carefully stacked the logs on the hearth and then fiddled with some twigs and other kindling in the fireplace itself. Bowing gracefully and dramatically, Lumière managed to light it with a single flick of his flame-hand. In no time it was roaring, orange and friendly.

"Thank you, Lumière," Belle said warmly. She could have lit the fire herself, of course, and she could certainly tend it herself, unlike the sort of princesses who had probably stayed in this room long ago. It was the 'not disturbing her tonight' bit that made her grateful.

He gave her another bow, less inclined to chattiness than usual, and hopped out of the room. The other thing, perhaps once a footman, followed close behind.

The fire crackled happily now, more highlighting the quiet than breaking it. Belle stretched and yawned and began to unlace the back of her bodice.

"I have some lovely nightgowns, if you like," the wardrobe said eagerly.

"Ah… no… not tonight, thank you," Belle said. "No offence."

"No, of course not," the wardrobe said, a little too promptly.

"It's been a strange... very long... day," Belle said as patiently as she could. "I just want to... sleep. In my own clothes tonight."

The wardrobe moved in ways Belle couldn't have described: *softened* somehow, rubbery round the edges.

"I understand, honey," she said in a much more sympathetic tone. "You get some sleep. It *has* been a long day. Even for us."

"Thank you," Belle sighed. She carefully took off her apron and pinafore, then her shirt, and carefully folded them and put them on the chair. If the wardrobe thought they would be better kept inside her drawers, she wisely didn't say anything.

Clad in her slip and underthings, Belle pulled back the incredibly warm and soft coverlet and slipped underneath. The pocket her body made against the silken sheets was icy cold initially, but she knew that in a few short minutes it would be warm enough from her body that she could uncurl out of the fetal position she was currently in.

She thought about her mother.

Belle tried to dismiss the same quick, almost violent succession of images she had seen when touching the rose. She tried to concentrate on what she *did* remember. It was very, very little. She thought she recalled a smile, wide and warm, and far less toothy than that of the woman in the vision. She remembered the smell of roses and the feel of sunlight. The roses and sunlight and her mother were all mixed in together, like they were all part of the same thing, and one couldn't exist without the other two.

Which woman was real? The one she didn't really remember, or the one in the vision?

But before she could even begin to ponder the answer, another question asked itself immediately:

Of the two, who was more likely to leave her baby daughter and husband?

Belle couldn't pin down when exactly her mother had left. It was all a continuum, and at one point her mother was there and most of the time she wasn't, and Maurice was *always* there. And Phillipe. And the rose garden.

When the townspeople were feeling kind, they told Belle how sorry they were she didn't have a real mother to raise her. Some even offered to take her under their wing, to teach her how to be a 'proper' girl. Obviously she was a little bit… *off*… having been raised by her papa, like a boy. It wasn't really her fault.

Were they right? Even just a teeny bit?

If her mother had stayed, how would it all have been different?

Would she have brushed Belle's long hair at night while her daughter talked about her day and the mean girls in town? Would she have taught her how to bake pastries, take care of her nails, milk the goats more efficiently?

Or would she, Belle thought bitterly, *have taught me how to grow magic roses and curse people and summon lightning from my hands?*

That would have been something.

Despite the warming of the bed, Belle grew less comfortable, tossing and turning as these jagged thoughts tore at the inside of her mind, opening holes and letting in painful new ideas.

Eventually sleep found her anyway, inserting its curling tendrils into her eyes and nose and mouth and consuming her, even as she resisted.

Her eyes shot open in the middle of the night.

Belle had no idea what time it was. Maurice had clocks, several of them, and even without those she could tell by the movements and noises of the chickens and the animals and the *feel* of the house which hour of the watch it was.

Here it could have been five minutes after she fell asleep, or five hours.

The room was dark except for the orange bubble of space illuminated by the fire. Outside that she could feel it was also cold. All was as silent as when she went to sleep; there wasn't even the scurrying of a mouse or a rat to remind her of a normal night at home.

She couldn't remember ever waking up anywhere besides the little farmhouse she shared with her father or the woods on a warm summer night, if they stayed out while foraging. And there she would have been surrounded by the familiar songs of insects and night birds.

Belle…

It wasn't a sound, it wasn't a thought. It was like a wisp of a memory of an idea – *almost;* something you catch the faintest hint of that reminds you of something else. But when asked, you can't explain what it was.

Belle sat up.

The wardrobe stayed still. Asleep? Drowsing? Dreaming?

Hardly aware of what she was doing, Belle threw her legs over the side of the bed.

Shadows crackled along the ceiling – they were just the result of firelight playing over the objects in the room. Probably. She frowned, squinting at them. There was no way there were little… *things*… running back and forth between the other shadows, slim as smoke – right?

Slowly she rose out of bed. After debating a moment, she took a thick taper out of a sconce and lit it in the fireplace, cupping her hand round so the flame wouldn't go out when she pulled back.

Taking one last look round the room, she opened the door as silently as she could and let herself out.

Belle stood in the utter darkness of the hall, feeling foolish for a moment.

As her eyes adjusted she could just begin to make out the dim and hazy outlines of things. With no light except for her one tiny candle flame, it was surprising how those *things* shifted and moved so much out of the corner of her eye. She could have sworn strange, thin feelers of blackness had begun to web the corners of the walls and ceiling.

Belle…

She drifted into the great hall beyond, trying to follow or escape whatever it was calling her. Dark, rich carpet softened her footsteps and only added to the eerie feeling.

The statues that she had initially dismissed as Greco-Roman replicas did *not*, she suddenly realised, depict gods and heroes; they were actually of howling, toothy demons.

She stopped, blinking at them. Had they always been like that? Even when she first came inside the castle? And she just hadn't noticed?

Even the most normal, angelic-looking one had a mouth open in a vicious snarl, revealing sharp, inhuman teeth.

Above, what she thought were alabaster cherubim supporting vaulted arches now had hideous expressions on their faces and strange closed eyes. Their hands reached out as if to grab anyone who came too close. Candlelight flickered off their frightening details: eyes and fangs and claws.

She backed away, bumping into a table behind her. She felt a vase tip and spun round to catch it… and then caught her breath. The legs of the table it was on looked like slavering monsters, wretched and angry to be supporting such a weight.

Belle…

Something was in the once-forbidden West Wing. Something was left there, something they missed.

It wasn't forbidden now, but that did not mean she wanted to go up there alone, in the middle of the night. Even the Beast's presence would have been acceptable. Maybe he would even *be* there, asleep.

The thought gave her courage.

Trying to steel her nerves, she walked forwards more forcefully, as if this were *her* choice. As if she were just going to seek out a mystery she forgot. Not a scared, lonely girl with a candle, like some daft heroine from one of the lighter romance books she read. This thought, too, gave her courage; she was *Belle*, not an idiot.

She started to march up the stairs and then thought…

Wait, who else but an idiot would just be propelled forwards by her overactive imagination?

The castle was getting to her. Something about the shadows made it look like she was ascending into a gigantic cage, reminding her of the ivory webs on the outside walls. The stairs resembled nothing more than a ramp up into a trap like the one for rats her father designed.

Maybe she should just go back to bed, or see if one of the little serving creatures was up. She turned round.

There, in the middle of the steps, as if it had always been there, was a statue made entirely out of ivy.

Belle was too frightened to even scream. She put a hand over her mouth and bit her knuckles – a tiny, dim portion of her mind saying, *Aha, that's why people in stories do that. It's so they don't break down into useless, screaming piles of insanity.*

Little pools of water were forming from snowmelt. For some reason, watching the slow drips was the most frightening thing of all. *It must have come in from the garden*, Belle thought insanely. There didn't appear to be anything under the leaves and vines; they wove round themselves to make the vague semblance of a person. Perhaps a woman. Its green and amorphous arms were lifted up, entreating.

Belle stumbled up the stairs backwards, away from the thing, keeping her eye on it. It didn't move.

Shaking and making little whimpering noises in the back of her throat, Belle kept moving, backing all the way up to the top of the stairs, almost tripping as she reached for the next step that wasn't there. Her foot came down hard on the floor instead, sending a shivering jolt through her ankle and up her spine. She let out an involuntary cry and stumbled on to the landing, barely catching herself. But she managed to keep a firm grip on the candle, not daring to let it go.

Realising she had taken her eye off the statue, she stood up quickly and spun round.

It was now farther up the stairs, just metres behind her.

Belle sobbed.

Its arms were by its sides, like it knew Belle would just finish going where she was being herded, of her own free will. It was there only as a reminder.

Belle took a deep breath and then ran the last ten metres to the Beast's lair. She started to put her hands on the ugly, monstrous bronze handles that opened the door to his room… and then stopped, a different sharp pain suddenly in the sole of her foot.

She looked down: a giant shard of glass was stuck into her flesh. Blood slowly crept along its edge and dripped. With a wince, Belle reached down and pulled it out. The piece was from the giant mirror on the wall, the one that had been shattered by the Beast, no doubt after he caught his reflection in there.

Belle looked up at what was left of the mirror now, raising her candle and moving it round. It was hard to tell exactly with so little light and all of the shards pointing every which way, but even so Belle could see that they weren't reflecting her, or anything around her. She frowned and looked closer.

One piece of glass showed a blonde lady carefully guiding a little girl's fat hand over a hole in the ground, to drop seeds in…

… another had the woman throwing leaves on the girl like a snowfall…

… a third showed the woman and the girl in matching outfits, spinning and laughing…

Belle suddenly realised with a shock that these were all scenes of *her and her mother* doing things together: her mother squeezing her tight; her mother running after her with Belle running away, crying; her mother and Maurice both cuddling her together on their tiny bed…

Some showed Belle as a baby, the little family in a smaller apartment that she didn't recognise, with no rose garden at all and an eerily familiar castle in the background.

Belle gasped. She had lived *here*? In this *kingdom*? *This* was where she and her father had moved from when she was a baby?

She didn't remember any of it. It was like watching

something else, like seeing other people through the Beast's magic mirror. This was a different family, something that happened another time to someone else.

"No," Belle whispered. "Why can't I remember this? *Maman? What is all of this?*"

As if in answer, suddenly all the shards went dark.

A single face appeared in the blackness, scarred and shadowed and monstrous – even more monstrous than the Beast, for this was at least part human. Mangled, scarred, bloody and torn apart, whatever features remained were erased, deep in shadow.

Belle…

It croaked and then suddenly lunged towards her…

Betrayed was betrayed stay away stay safe away from dark…

Belle fell back, screaming.

She couldn't *stop* screaming. All of the terror and insanity of the night welled up and burst out of her. She felt like it would never end, the screams and terror and the blackness would just roll up out of her forever.

The large doors opened and suddenly the Beast was there. He gathered her up in his big, revoltingly furry arms and she began to kick and scream louder. He held her carefully at arm's length so she couldn't reach him and loped away, back to her own room.

"*NO!*" she shrieked. "*I'M NOT GOING BACK IN!*

The shadows! It's too dark!"

The thought of being shut up there with the blackness outside, the fire and the talking wardrobe and the shadows and no easy escape, was too much.

The Beast paused for a moment, then carried her into the study where she had tied him up earlier. Sleepy-looking objects peeked round corners, fluffed up the fire, and generally watched, curious, as the Beast set her down on a divan.

"Here, have a drink of this," Mrs Potts said. She wore, Belle noticed distractedly, a knitted tea cosy, the way one might wear a dressing gown. The cup she offered was not Chip, and the liquid in it was not tea.

"No," Belle protested.

"*Ma chérie*," Lumière said gently, "really? Don't you think if we wanted to poison you, we could have done it earlier?"

Through the thick muddle in her head, Belle could see the logic in this. She could also see how ridiculously she was behaving, a hysterical girl among the closest things she had to *friends* at the moment.

She took the cup and drained it in one draught.

"Easy, *mon petit chou*," the little candelabrum laughed.

She didn't even cough or choke. The fiery warmth hit her stomach in an explosion of comfort.

Calmness returned to her eventually. The tick-tock of Cogsworth's face helped slow her own heartbeats. Sleep came back, to claim what it had been denied.

"*Don't leave!*" she whispered before she finally succumbed, begging *someone.*

Maybe even the Beast.

THE LIBRARY

The study had no windows to let in morning light or to reveal the creepy, bony netting that was taking over the outer castle walls.

The fire was banked low, emitting a steady orange glow. All the shadows were calm.

Someone had thrown a – *silk?* – coverlet over Belle and carefully put a down pillow under her head. She was, despite everything that had happened, ridiculously comfy, warm and sleepy. Safe.

Somehow her soul knew that it was day and that all of the demons and nightmares had been banished back to where they came from for the next 12 hours and there was nothing to be afraid of.

She pulled her foot round to take a look at the injury.

It was still there.

Everything was real.

Belle sighed.

She had read too many romantic novels of a dark and dreary bent to really be surprised, *The Castle of Otranto* was one of her favourite English reads. For all intents and purposes, she was the overwrought, terrified heroine wandering round a cursed castle at night, seeing things in the shadows, jumping at noises. Plus she could not, even in her most imaginative moments, have come up with the idea of an ivy statue that sneakily followed her when she wasn't looking.

She rubbed her hands over her face. Was her mother dead? Was she haunting this castle? Was it somehow filled with her soul or her memories?

The scenes shown in the shards weren't just happy, archetypal mother-daughter moments she could draw from any well-written book; the two fought in some instances and they did *nothing* in others. Although details were hazy in the tiny visions, Belle could see her mother frowning and her hair was askew. Imperfect.

And what about that other home? The tiny flat, the one she didn't remember, somewhere in the town below? There was no doubt that these were fragments of real memories she no longer had.

So what had happened to them?

Belle rose and went over to the fire and took the poker. She knelt before it like a supplicant and began prodding the coals lightly, not out of any real need for more heat as much as for something to do.

Moodily, she felt little wisps of thought try to sneak into her consciousness. Irritating ones. Ones she had dismissed long ago.

Why *didn't* she have a mother, all those years? Where did she go?

And: maybe, just maybe, she would really have actually *liked* to have a mother. Just a little bit.

There should have been no perceived difference between a father brushing her hair and a mother.

And yet there was.

"Good morning, dearie." Mrs Potts came waltzing in, steamy and bubbly. Behind her Cogsworth himself was pushing a trolley of breakfast things: chocolate, pastries, the smell of rich, fatty bacon, a bowl of warm compote.

"What are you doing there, in the ashes?" she clucked. "That's James's job! Get up, you'll ruin your pretty slip!"

Belle wondered how they had known she was awake. Was something in the room secretly alive, transmitting the message through the house somehow, like telepathy? Or was it a purely natural instinct of good servants?

Either way, she would've liked a few more minutes

to herself.

Although the bacon *did* smell delicious.

"Here are your clothes," a dustmaid said, dancing in on her feathery skirts. She carried Belle's pinafore and apron, all cleaned and pressed. "The… wardrobe thought you would like them."

"Thank you," Belle said politely. "Sorry about last night…"

"Oh pish," Mrs Potts said, turning her head. "First night in an enchanted castle! Who could blame you?"

Belle regarded the three little objects looking expectantly up at her and realised she wasn't awake or chipper enough to deal with them.

"I think I'd like to get dressed now," she said delicately.

"Of course!" Cogsworth said, flustered. He practically tripped over himself bowing and leaving backwards.

"Let us know if you need anything, dearie." Mrs Potts used her spout to indicate to the maid that she should leave as well.

When the door closed behind them, Belle sighed. *An eternity of that? Is it worth bacon?* She had read about how servants and general entourage members fought among themselves for the privilege of handing the Queen of France her underwear in the morning while the queen herself remained shivering, waiting, in her bed.

Belle slipped the rest of her clothes on quickly, unsure

when the next interruption would be.

She had just poured her chocolate and begun to nibble a croissant when there was a faint but animal; *fleshy* knock at the door, and it opened a centimetre.

"Can I… come in?" the Beast asked softly.

"You may."

She was surprised by the relief she felt that it was *him*. There was nothing normal about him, or this situation, or particularly pleasing about being thrown in a room and told she was a prisoner but there was, ironically, something slightly more *human* about the Beast than his servants.

"You… all right?" he asked gruffly, looking round, as if asking the question embarrassed him.

"Yes. Thank you. I hope this doesn't happen every night of my eternal incarceration. Chocolate?" she offered primly.

"No."

The Beast didn't seem to be able to stay still for very long. He went over and sat in his chair, twisting this way and that in it, looking at the fire, and then got up again.

"I want to go out and hunt," he finally admitted. "I can't."

Belle felt her stomach rise. But whatever thoughts she had about the Beast's more beastly habits were swept aside by what he said next.

"All the gates are blocked. There's no way off the grounds."

Trapped!

Belle felt her heart begin to race in an ugly, stuttering tattoo. Her decision to bring the Beast back home had sealed her own fate as well. Forever.

Belle swallowed and tried to calm herself. Panicking wouldn't solve anything. She sat carefully back down on the divan, the coverlet neatly folded next to her. "I saw some strange things last night," she said.

The Beast didn't say anything; he just raised an eyebrow.

"I think… if I didn't know better, I would think that my mother is trying to reach me somehow. I don't know if she's dead or living but *something* from her is trying to contact me. Warn me. Through this curse, or through… something else. She said something about being *betrayed*. And that I should stay away from the dark."

The Beast visibly brightened despite the creepiness of her words. "You think she might still be alive?"

"Before last night, I never thought she was *dead*. I thought she just left us," Belle admitted, realising it was true as she said the words. How easy it would have been for everyone to simply have told her that her mother had died! Sad but simple and *done*. Poor little orphan girl with no mother. The townspeople would have pitied her and she never would have questioned it.

"I think we lived here," Belle said slowly. "In this

kingdom. When I was a baby. I saw it in the mirror upstairs, the broken one. And I know we moved to the village when I was young, so that… makes sense."

The Beast continued to look at her. "So?"

"So… I have to believe that a powerful enchantress who lays curses and deals with magic roses and mirrors was probably pretty well known in this… strange… kingdom, if she was from here. *Lived* here. If we could find out more about her, maybe it would help. Maybe she cursed you because she was betrayed by someone? Maybe if we figure it out, we can put her soul to rest, or something? If only there was someone else we could talk to, or maybe search my old house… Except that we're *trapped* in here…"

She slammed her hand down on the trolley in frustration, causing the things on it to rattle and clink. The Beast's eyes widened and he seemed to draw back a little.

"How can we figure out *anything* without any ability to… research anything?"

The Beast frowned: she could practically see the cogs turning in his gigantic furry head.

"A… book?" he finally said, hesitantly.

Belle blinked.

"A book about people in this kingdom. A *history*." The beast grew excited as he spoke. "Maybe stories? Maybe… records?"

"Sure. But where would we find these books?"

"In the library," he said with a shrug, pointing over his shoulder. It was such a casual, human gesture that it took Belle aback.

And then she registered his words.

"Library," she said slowly, remembering what Lumière and Cogsworth had said while trying to lure her away from the forbidden West Wing.

"*You have a library! Oh. Mon. Dieu.*"

Belle didn't make it past the library door.

At least not immediately.

The Beast stood to the side, having chivalrously pushed the doors open for her, holding Lumière above her head to light the way. They both looked perplexed as she just hung there, not going in.

The far end of the library looked like it was miles away. Furnishing it was a huge fireplace, overstuffed velvet reading chairs, colourful landscape paintings and squat little tables upon which to lay out the really big volumes.

And the distance between that and the door where Belle stood was… filled… with… books.

From floor to the incredibly high ceiling, books.

Three storeys of books.

Golden balconies and delicate stairways that allowed readers to climb to the higher levels of books. Belle stopped trying to count the number of shelves after 20.

Unlike the rest of the castle, which was dark and foreboding, this room was all bright: pearly inlaid stone on the floor, white and gold plaster on the walls, silvered ceilings that reflected the dim light let in by tall, narrow windows. Behind their heavy curtains were benches that allowed readers to hide away from the rest of the world with their finds.

"OH MY GOD!"

Belle finally fell into the room and began to spin dizzily, overwhelmed.

"This is like… this is like… I don't know *what* this is like! A university! A library in Paris! A…"

The Beast shuffled in on his inadequate legs, looking round the room as if for the first time.

"A library in a castle?" he offered.

Belle stared at him, trying to figure out if he was teasing her. His face was as beast-y and unreadable as ever, but were his eyes dancing, just a little?

"Forget your magic mirror," she decided to say. "If I lived here, I would spend my whole life in here, reading."

"They're just… books…"

He carefully lit the candelabra at the front and placed Lumière on the floor, dismissing him.

"*Just books?* That's like saying Alexandria is *just a library.*" She ran over to the closest shelf and tilted her head, reading titles. "You don't understand. I don't understand how you don't understand. Look, here's an ancient text in Greek about astronomy... and next to it is everything Galileo Galilei ever wrote! This whole section is about the stars and planets and the *entire universe*!"

The Beast stood, looking slightly embarrassed, scratching the back of his neck with his hand.

Belle grabbed a book and ran over to him, shoving it in his face. "Up until *this* man, Copernicus, everyone thought the entire universe rotated round the earth – that we were the centre of it all." She flipped open to a page that had an engraving of planets and their paths, little callouts to their names and the length of their orbits. "Thanks to men like him and Tycho Brahe and Kepler, we now know *nothing* revolves round the earth, except the moon."

"Books can tell you all that?" the Beast asked, taking the book from her and frowning at the words.

"Books can tell you almost everything that mankind knows. Or imagines," she added after a moment.

"I don't think I could have grown up in the small village I'm from without books. Life is... was... um... *small* there. Provincial. The same old people, the same old gossip, the same *food*... always the same... Reading books let me realise there was a world beyond the river, beyond the people who made fun of me and my father. There were scientists and writers and explorers, and all sorts of fascinating people out there… somewhere… leading interesting lives…

"*You* had a magic mirror that let you see life outside your tiny world. Your castle. *I* had books. Reading them is like travelling to other places. Being other people. Living other lives. It made life far less… sad and lonely for me."

The Beast flipped through the pages of his book and frowned suspiciously.

"My tutor read to me sometimes," he admitted, squinting at a sentence in his book. "Never liked reading. Rather go hunting or ride my horse. I didn't know… I didn't know they could do these other things."

Then he looked at her with a strange expression.

"*You* were sad and lonely?" he asked.

"Yes," Belle said, suddenly feeling shy as she put the book back on the shelf.

He was still looking at her, puzzled, as if trying to draw out of her body some secret of her existence.

"Are we here to find my mother and your enchantress or *what*?" She put on her most serious frowny face and ran a finger along the line of books. They were dusty, but not overwhelmingly so. The little animated creatures must have taken spins through there occasionally on their cleaning rounds, dreaming of a day when someone who actually cared about books came in…

She wondered if there were any enchanted *books*. Now that *would* be really exciting! And also useful, since she couldn't quite figure out how anything was organised. There weren't any headings over any of the shelves, and she didn't have Monsieur Lévi to guide her.

"I can't find *anything* here!" the Beast complained after only a minute or two, echoing her own thoughts. She couldn't see him but the sneeze he emitted caused all the shelves to shudder, as well as the ladder she was standing on.

"Well, let's see… Where would *history* be…" Belle said, thinking. "Like… ancient kings lists, or chronicles of battles, or a history of land division, or maybe something from the church? Sometimes they record things others don't."

"There's nothing like that. Just a whole section on '*po-pul-ation cen-si*'."

Belle waited.

The Beast was silent for a moment.

"Oh," he finally said. "Guess I found it."

AND HER NOSE STUCK IN A BOOK

Ten minutes later they were in front of the cosy library fire. Lumière had come in at the pull of a bell and, with the help of a crusty poker, lit and fanned it for them. Snacks were *not* allowed – that was a law older than the Beast's parents – but a kettle was wheeled in at Mrs Potts's insistence, and, at Lumière's, a flagon of spiced wine.

Piles of giant ancient books lay around them; the Beast might not have been a fast reader but he was certainly a strong one, carrying shifting stacks of records that spanned hundreds of pages in one trip.

They were quiet for a little while, companionably flipping through their finds. Belle looked up now and then, amazed at the sight of a monster so bizarre and huge and dangerous-looking bent over a book, running a claw along a sentence as he read it, mouthing the words. She tried not to giggle at the image of him wearing a pince-nez.

And the Beast really tried.

He *tried* every possible sitting position in his chair, including almost upside down, with his legs hanging off the headrest. He took many, many breaks for tea. And then he would yawn and declare it was time for a stretch, or some exercise, or that he smelled a rat and was going to chase it down.

Or his foot began to tap, and then his ear began to shake, and then he even began to hum an annoying little tune, looking round the room, anywhere except at the book in front of him.

"*Beast*," Belle finally said with a gentle admonishment.

"Sorry," he answered, chagrined.

Belle had to admit her own book was astonishingly boring: *Tracts of Farmable Land and Tithing to the Church from 1623 to Present.* But she chose the less interesting ones on purpose. She had given the Beast *Oral Traditions of the Principality as Recorded by an Interested Vicar.* Surely there was a story or folk tale in there that would help them and keep him interested.

Non.

"Why did you never look for your mother before?"

the Beast asked after less than a minute.

Belle blew the annoying strand of hair out of her face. "Didn't have a reason to. She left when I was a baby. Or very young. It's always just been Papa and me and that's been just fine."

But the words sounded rehearsed and tired, even to herself. The revelations of the night and the mirror put a very different spin on things and woke up questions she thought were long since buried and dead.

Like: didn't her mother love her?

Of *course* she did. In fact, from the visions it seemed as if Belle's was a *very* loving mother, if at times impatient.

So why did she leave? Was life in a tiny rural village too much for a great enchantress? Was she this big, glamorous, powerful woman who had other places to be, spells to cast, curses to distribute?

Did she long to go and find adventure elsewhere, the way Belle did?

The Beast was leaning forwards now like an attentive dog, eyes wide, watching the thoughts she was having drift to the surface of her face, waiting for her to say something.

"I think I was *made* to forget her," she said slowly. "Everything she touched seems utterly forgotten. I think there is magic involved in the same way no one knows about your kingdom, or you."

"That was… the end of the curse. She said '*If you do not learn to love another – and be loved in return – by the time the last petal of this rose falls, you, your castle, and all within, will remain cursed and forgotten – forever.*' "

It was the most the Beast had spoken yet. He recited it perfectly, closing his eyes in pain at the memory.

Belle felt her heart clench. True, he *had* thrown her father into a prison cell. But… since they had sort of… come to terms with their situation, he hadn't shown any signs of being the kind of monster that might cause an enchantress to curse a little boy.

Can an 11-year-old even truly understand the concept of that kind of love?

The silence dragged on. The Beast eventually opened his eyes and went back to looking at his book, and she to hers.

"Hey, hey, Belle, hey," he said after a moment, tapping her on the knee with one of his claws.

"*What?*" she demanded, surprised out of her concentration.

He gave her a grievous look. "I think I found something," he said piteously.

"I'm sorry. Please share it. That's great news."

The Beast cleared his throat and held up the book, delicately indicating his place with one claw while he read.

"*… And the long-failing spring on the western side of the town at Parson's Rock was restored to its original vitality by a local woman of sorcerous nature known to many. It was said she was the most powerful of all hereabouts and thus entreated to carry out the job. Whether or not all the stories concerning her are true, everyone agreed that her magical abilities were only exceeded by her beauty; her golden hair and green eyes that caused some to call her Angel…*"

"You see?" the Beast said excitedly. "Golden hair and green eyes. It has to be her!"

"Fantastic!" Belle said, grinning. "What else does it say about her?"

The Beast's face fell as he scanned the text. "Nothing. It's mostly stories about fairies and woods people, folk doctors who could heal better than city doctors. It's all sort of mixed up… someone was collecting interesting local legends and personages. But at least we know this was real. It happened around the time I was born."

"But… hang on… just…" Belle's mind spun dizzily. "Besides my *mother* the *Enchantress*, there were… ah… just, like, fairies and stuff? Around here?"

"Sure," the Beast said, shrugging. "Not a lot. And I guess they were dangerous. I remember my mother and father talking about how they just wished they would go away."

At first, that sounded utterly horrible and barbaric to Belle. Wishing for fairies to go away? Belle had spent most of her young life wishing to see one, and reading every book about them she could get her hands on. And they were *here* all along!

And yet…

If they were all like my mother, powerful and ready to dispense curses at the drop of a hat… Well, she could sort of see the king and queen's point. Was whatever her mother had been angry about *worth* what was essentially the destruction and erasure of the last magical kingdom in the world?

"Maybe we don't have to find my *mother*," Belle said slowly. "Maybe we just need to find *another* powerful enchanter."

The Beast shrugged. "There aren't any. Any more. I remember people saying she was the last."

"Of course. I should have guessed. All right, back to looking for Maman, then…"

"What was her name? Maybe we can find more about her in one of those books of tax records."

Belle put her book down and drew her legs up into her chest, wrapping her arms round them.

"I don't know," she admitted in a small voice.

"*WHAT?*" the Beast roared.

But it wasn't that which made Belle shudder. It was

her realisation. She felt cold and strangely terrified. Maman and Papa. Maurice and…?

How could she not know her own mother's name?

"I don't know her name… I don't know why, I just don't. Remember the whole 'magic' thing? I would bet it has something to do with that… and forgetting…"

The Beast stared at her for a long moment.

From frozen in shock to blurry motion, he let out a roar of rage. The books she had just been looking at were suddenly sliced into ribbons of paper and leather. She gasped and drew back her hands – but his claws had been nowhere near them.

"*That* wasn't very helpful," Belle said as soon as she got her voice back.

"*Neither is looking for a woman whose name we don't know!*" the Beast roared. "*THIS IS USELESS!*"

"*DO I LOOK HAPPY ABOUT THIS?*" Belle shot back. "I'm not! This is the first time I ever even *realised* I don't know her name! How strange and horrible is *that*?"

The Beast lowered his eyes, and his ears drooped.

"*You're right*," he mumbled.

Belle shook her head and rubbed her temples. "All right. We know she used to live here and was, obviously, well known. We know I was born here, from what I saw in the broken mirror. So if we search the census books we should be able to find some record of *my* birth or baptism, and my father's and my *mother's* names." She took a deep breath. "And possibly the record of her death and its cause. I don't know what knowing that will get us, but it's *something*."

"That… makes sense," the Beast said grudgingly.

"*You* can start with that one right there," Belle said primly, pointing at the ruined mess. "Try to figure out at least what years it was for."

Meekly, the Beast obeyed.

At first it all looked the same to Belle… rows and rows of taxpayer names, peasants who apparently didn't even merit being named at all, and an absolutely astonishing number of people named Jacques and François.

On top of that she realised that only very rarely were older *women* recorded at all, it was mostly only male heads-of-household.

The handwriting of the archivist was so tight and cramped and crowded that Belle often missed when a season turned, and it was from this that she had to figure out when the year changed.

But long before she got to her own birth, about 20 years before the curse, she noticed something that had nothing to do with what they were looking for. Some of the people listed started getting the addition of funny little symbols next to their names. Curious, Belle flipped back and forth between different seasons, trying to see if it meant an increase in tax, a change of life status, or some other thing that would have been important to the castle's treasurer. Nothing.

The only thing that linked them was that generally the people who received these symbols didn't show up anywhere later, either as a death or anything else.

They were all different ages, both sexes, and held different occupations. She couldn't see any connection between them.

"*Found it!*" she suddenly cried, forgetting the symbols for a moment. "I found me! My birth record!"

The Beast swooped over in his silent, unbelievably predatory way to stand behind her on the sofa and peer over her shoulder.

" '*Belle, female, born to...*' Oh." Her face fell. "*Maurice.* Nothing else."

The Beast started to let out a roar. Without looking, Belle put her hand up over his mouth to stop him.

"What *is* it about your mother?" he demanded around her fingers. "It's like she doesn't appear anywhere."

"She erased herself, somehow. For some reason." Belle sighed. "I guess this is what happens when you have an enchantress in the family. But look, here's something. This little symbol I've been seeing everywhere. It's in the place where my mother's name *would* be. Like it was supposed to be associated with her."

"So?" the Beast said.

"So does it mean anything to you? Do you recognise it?"

"No," he said, frowning.

"It must be something important. Everyone who has one by his or her name disappears from the records eventually. See?" She flipped back and forth to show him a few examples. "Where did they all go?"

"There was a plague," the Beast said bleakly. "When I was a child."

"No," Belle said, shaking her head, gazing back and forth between two books.

The Beast gave her an incredulous look.

She suddenly realised how awful that 'no' sounded.

"Sorry! I didn't mean... I didn't mean to seem so callous. I just meant that doesn't explain these people all disappearing from the town records. Look: here it clearly says the person died of *fever*. And here, and here. There are *hundreds* of entries that say that. The people with the symbol don't... *die* of anything. They just don't appear again."

"Maybe they moved, like you did."

"*All* of these people? I think, despite the world being made to forget about your kingdom, someone would have noticed a mass exodus around these parts. The peasants in the village where I grew up don't like *anything* new or strange. They would have at least complained about it."

The two lapsed into a depressed silence. Belle felt like there was no solidity anywhere, that even the chair she sat on was just going to tip her over and disappear. Nothing made sense; there were no facts to hold on to. Only a pile of ancient paper confetti on her lap, words and information now rendered useless.

"Alaric," the Beast suddenly said.

Belle looked up. He was staring into the space in front of his head.

"Alaric, the stablemaster. He disappeared, a few years before… before the curse. See if he has one of those little marks next to him."

"What exactly do you mean, disappeared? What do you remember?" Belle asked, pulling up one of the undamaged books.

"He just… didn't show up for work. And his family didn't know what happened to him, either. My parents said it was my fault. They said I was too nice to him and now he was leaving us and his family for a new life, the way 'his type' always did whenever they had a little gold."

"That is a *terrible* thing to say to a child," Belle said, aghast.

"I *did* sneak him coins," the Beast admitted. "And little treasures. Just like I sneaked carrots and sugar to the horses. I didn't think I was hurting anyone."

This was a child 'with no love in his heart'?

"You gave sugar to the castle horses on the sly?" she asked with a smile.

"I loved them. I always loved the horses," the Beast said sadly. "When… this happened… I let them all go free. They were terrified of me in this form."

That was a strange image: the big monster opening up a bunch of stalls so his childhood companions and pets would go away forever now that they couldn't stand him any more. Not a *beastly* thing to do at all.

"Well, let's see if Alaric is in here," she said, trying to sound businesslike again. He looked so sad… "What was his surname?"

"Potts."

Belle stopped, blinking.

"What?" she asked, unsure if she had heard correctly.

"Potts. Alaric Potts."

"Like… *Mrs* Potts?"

"Yes. That's his wife. Or… widow."

Belle dropped the book.

"*All of those creatures were real people?* Cogsworth? Lumière?"

The Beast looked at her as if she was an idiot. "Of course. They were all my servants. What did you think?"

"And all of these… *people*… were turned into what they are because of your curse?"

"Yes, the entire castle was enchanted," he said, still confused by her reaction.

"My *mother* turned an *entire castle* of *people* into *furniture* when she was punishing *you*?"

"Well…" The Beast thought about it. "I suppose the idea was to freeze them in time or something so they wouldn't age while the curse lasted. Maybe? Why are… why are you so upset?"

"Cursing a spoiled eleven-year-old prince is one thing!" Belle groaned. "I mean, it's terrible. But what did *these* people do to deserve their fate?"

"I never thought about it before," he mumbled. "They were just… servants."

"'Just servants'. Well, *thanks to me*, your 'just servants' will remain wardrobes and candles forever! God's *BLOOD*!"

She collapsed into the sofa, pulling a pillow over her face. Tears began to roll down her nose.

"It's not… " the Beast started.

"You didn't," he tried again.

Belle knew she was being self-indulgent. Feeling bad

wouldn't help the servants. Only somehow breaking the curse would help them now. She took a deep breath.

Then she forced herself to sit up, crushing her hands into her eyes, making the crying stop.

The Beast had his face shockingly close to hers, she noticed when she could see again. His jaw was working, still trying to find something to say.

A small voice below them cleared its throat.

They both looked down. Cogsworth was standing there, wringing what passed for his hands.

"Just thought I would ask if there were any preferences for the dinner menu tonight," he said with a meek cough.

"We were just about to see Mrs Potts ourselves. We will talk to her about it," Belle said with as much dignity as she could muster.

She quickly rose and walked out of the room, before looking at Cogsworth any longer caused her to break down again.

MRS POTTS LOSES HER TEA

Belle made her way back to the kitchen, the Beast silently keeping up with her. Cogsworth awkwardly waddled behind them, obviously unsure whether to address his master or leave well enough alone.

Lumière appeared from behind a curtain – Belle could have sworn she heard giggling – and cocked his middle candle inquisitively at the expressions the strange little party had on.

"Everything all right, *mon chéri*? Enjoying your stay?" he asked, making a magnificent little bow.

"As much as I can," Belle said politely, trying not to sniff. "You were right about the library, it *is* fantastic. I'm enjoying it immensely."

She tried to see the human in the little three-branched

candelabrum, but when he was still, he merely looked like a normal, if misplaced, taper holder, albeit with an arm twisted askew. There were no discernible eyes or features, not even in his flames. His name couldn't possibly have been *Lumière* before the change, could it have been? Belle had read in books by Defoe and others that in England, masters of great houses often renamed servants when they entered their hire. Manservants went by the names John and James far too commonly to have been just randomly called that by their mothers. Had the Beast taken away his name once the Enchantress had taken away his body?

"We're on our way to the kitchen," she said gently, kneeling down. "Would you like to come with us? I can carry you..."

"Oh, no, *Mademoiselle*," Lumière said with another little bow. "I am on my way... elsewhere... duties..."

Belle could actually hear the giggling behind the curtain this time. She tried not to smile nor imagine what furniture could do behind closed doors. She would never look at a writing desk the same way again.

Cogsworth was still, his face pointed at Lumière. Belle wondered if he was frowning sternly.

"I didn't realise you... We're trying to find a way to break the curse," Belle began awkwardly. Things had become so much more desperate and complicated now that *these* people's lives depended on her as well.

"Of course you are!" Lumière said gamely. Was it just projecting, or did she hear a little bit of strain in his voice? "Where there is life there is hope, no? Come along anyway, Cogsworth. Let's let these young people… *work*. And please, let us know if there is *anything* we can do, *mon chéri*."

"Of course," Belle said. It was all she could promise.

The two little creatures hopped off together, what passed for their heads pressed close, like two old soldiers hobbling off into the sunset. They whispered as they went, strange, high little sounds that both chilled and saddened Belle.

The Beast just waited expressionlessly for her to move again, and followed behind her.

The kitchen was cheery and warm, a welcome relief from the dark hall and the sad revelations in the library. The stove was murmuring to itself, stirring the pots on its hob and occasionally popping open its oven to adjust the temperature and check what was going on in there. Bright orange firelight sparkled against the spotless glass on the cabinets, and a bubbling tub full of soapy water had a brush that was vigorously scrubbing cups in it.

"Goodness," Mrs Potts said, spinning round from her perch on the prep table where she was addressing a cohort of silverware, surprised by her master's appearance. "I just sent Cogsworth after you to see if you had a hankering for anything in particular for dinner. It's so nice to have a real guest after all this time!"

She moved and bounced and burbled. Belle could have sworn there was a pink glow to her rounded cheeks.

"We saw Cogsworth," Belle said politely, "but we were coming down to talk to you anyway."

"Is everything all right?" Mrs Potts practically hopped up and down, coming perilously close to the edge of the table to get closer to Belle. "Was the tea cold? I know we're not supposed to serve biscuits in the library but if you had asked, maybe..."

"What really happened to Alaric?" the Beast interrupted a little impatiently.

Belle shot him a look. Could he really be *that* rude?

Mrs Potts *also* gave him a look. It was harder to read her because she had no eyes or mouth, but if Belle had to guess what expression it was, *slack-jawed stupefaction* seemed likely.

"My... Mr Potts?" the teapot stammered.

"Yes. Your husband. Alaric Potts. The stablemaster. What happened to him?" the Beast said.

"What I think he's *trying* to say," Belle broke in, "is that we're working on a... different angle to break the curse and could use whatever information you have about any disappearances that may have occurred some years ago."

"Alaric Potts. The stablemaster. Your *favourite* servant. Out of all of us," Mrs Potts said slowly and calmly.

"Yes. What happened to him? Why did he leave? My parents said he just abandoned you and his job. Possibly because of me."

"Because of you…? It's been over a decade since his disappearance and you're just asking that question *now*?"

Thus far, Belle's only view of the housekeeper was of a lovely, fat little animated teapot, sympathetic, motherly and kind.

The tone she used now was not that of a housekeeper or anyone sympathetic to anything. It was a dignified older lady filled with righteous affrontment.

"I was a child. A lot was going on," the Beast said defensively. "The plague, my parents…"

"I see. Yet… *now* is the first time it has occurred to you to inquire what happened to a wayward servant? A *favourite* wayward servant?" she persisted, trilling her consonants. "*LET ME TELL YOU* about Alaric Potts."

She hopped up to the Beast so violently that her lid clacked up and down. Belle was tempted to reach out and steady it so it didn't fly off and break. But she was paralysed by the woman's anger.

"Alaric Potts was the most kind, honourable, decent,

caring man I ever met," Mrs Potts declared. A little puff of steam came out of her spout after each adjective. "Sometimes *too* kind. He didn't believe in treating anyone differently, whether he was a prince or a gnome. He loved me and Chip and everyone in our family – everyone in the castle. He loved *you*, Master, almost as much as his real son. And he loved his job in the stables. He loved those horses.

"I don't know what happened the night he never came home. I never found out. No one did. He was just gone, into thin air like everyone else. But through the plague and this wretched curse for over *ten years*, I've put on a brave face for our son who lost his father. Surely you can sympathise with *that*, can't you?"

Belle risked a glance at the Beast. He looked shocked… and perhaps a little guilty.

"And then… *blurble*… to come… *blorb* ten years later… *glug*… and *ask* me…"

Mrs Potts was quite literally boiling over.

Belle was horrified and unsure what to do. Scalding hot tea began to bubble up through the teapot's spout and out of her top.

The Beast also looked taken aback and moved slightly away.

Eventually Mrs Potts grew silent, shuddering and bubbling until she seemed to calm down.

She stopped moving entirely, in fact. Completely frozen.

After a moment, Belle began to grow worried.

"Mrs Potts…?" she said tentatively.

Belle looked over at the Beast, he was also alarmed. The teapot looked like… just a teapot now. There was nothing at all animated about her.

And then she suddenly shook to life again, as if nothing at all had happened.

"I… I need to go and rest. This is just too much," she cried, spinning round and hopping off, spout in the air. Trying to retain her dignity. Belle and the Beast watched her hop down on to a chair and then to the floor and back to the pantry, her ringing clip-clop diminishing until they could hear her hopping up on to a shelf.

LA CUISINE DE LA MAISON

The stove busied itself, loudly stirring something it probably didn't need to, casting angry ember eyes at the couple.

Everything else was awkwardly silent.

"I just… I always thought it was my fault," the Beast finally said halfheartedly. He sank down into the closest chair. It staggered under his weight, readjusting itself on bent, fat little legs. "I was too ashamed to talk to anyone. I didn't even think to talk to her or Chip. I was afraid they would hate me. I didn't think about what *they* felt. Losing him."

He ran a large, ungainly paw through the fur on the top of his head. Belle thought about the portrait in the West Wing; his real hair would've been a dark blond now.

She put a hand on his shoulder.

"I think you can explain that to her later, when she's calmed down," she said soothingly.

"Maybe your mother was right," he whispered. "I never thought of most of the servants as anything other than… *things*. Things that made my life easier. That's why she did this to me."

"Perhaps." She still didn't like the use of real people for a morality lesson, however.

The Beast growled at her.

Then Belle saw the sheepish look on his face and realised that the sound had not come from his mouth. He put a defensive paw over his belly.

"Actually, I'm kind of hungry too," she realised. Her stomach felt emptier than usual and there was a slight dizziness in her head. She had successfully ignored it while working.

"We were supposed to come down here to talk about dinner," the Beast said plaintively.

"Well…" Belle looked over at the stove. "Maybe… *we* should make dinner. For ourselves."

He stared at her.

Belle put her hands on her hips. "You were just saying: these servants have been waiting on you hand and foot all their lives… And the last ten years they haven't even been human for it! They *still* serve you, make you dinner, clean the castle… all while they're spoons and mops and teacups and whatever. And they are only those things because of *your* curse. Maybe it's time you eased up on them a little, huh?"

The Beast opened and closed his mouth a few times, obviously stunned into speechlessness by the strangeness of the suggestion.

"I don't know how to make dinner," he finally admitted.

"I will *help* you. We'll do it together," Belle said, going over to the washbasin.

"Cooking. Reading. Is there anything you *can't* do?"

Belle grabbed his big paw and shoved it into the water as well. "Oh yes, I'm a veritable domestic demi-goddess," she said archly. "You should see me turn invisible and walk on water. Come on, let's get you an apron."

There probably wasn't any real point in making him wear something over his fur and ragged clothes. Still, she tied a tablecloth up and round his neck, trying not to make him look ridiculous.

Actually, if the thick white cloth had leather straps, he could easily be Hephaestus or one of his titan helpers working the forge on Olympus.

But they were going to make ratatouille, not swords for heroes.

"… And buckwheat crêpes, and an onion tart, and

coq au... um... Riesling, in a skillet," she added thoughtfully, looking at the time. The clock in the kitchen didn't talk, thankfully. "We don't have time for a true *coq au vin* or cassoulet. Oooh, and a *tarte tatin* for dessert!"

The Beast looked sceptical.

She turned, regretfully, to the stove. "I... guess we'll have to use your services," she said apologetically. "There's no other heating source in here."

"My skills are yours to command, Mademoiselle," the chef said with a lowering of his pipes. "But only once. Otherwise, *nobody touches my stuff in this kitchen*."

"*Unless you're too drunk to do it without hurting yourself*," something called from the back pantry.

"*MAYBE IT'S YOU WHO DRIVES ME TO DRINK!*" the stove shot back. "*YOU AND YOUR OVERUSE OF CUMIN!*"

"All right. Beast," Belle said quickly. "Let's get you peeling some apples."

She thought handling something dangerous and manly like a knife would be more interesting for him than trying to work with something fiddly like pastry dough. And at first he did seem excited. But he clutched the little paring blade awkwardly in his paw, which, despite its five 'fingers', was nowhere near as nimble as a human hand. He struck at the apples in little jabs, trying to put what passed for his thumb on the back of the handle. He obviously had skill in whittling at some point.

But after two and a half apples, and three cuts he tried to hide from her, the Beast gave up, throwing the knife on the table so hard that it stuck deep into the wood.

"This is *useless*!" he growled. "This knife is too small. These apples are too soft. I can't do this."

"All right..." Belle said, taking a deep breath. "Let's have you mix up some dough. That should be fun!"

She found the largest bowl she could and tried to measure out correct amounts of everything; it was hard to keep to scale. But the Beast was delighted by the process of rubbing the butter into the flour; he could use his big, ungainly paws to mash them together. And he only tried to lick the bits off his fingers when she wasn't looking.

They worked for a while in companionable silence. She wondered if this would have been what it was like if her mother had been around during her childhood. The two of them cooking side by side, Belle, a tinier version of her mother, maybe both of them with matching kerchiefs in their hair...

Of course she had cooked with her father. But would it have been different? Would it have been the same?

"So... everyone... who's... not a... prince... can do this?" the Beast asked, breaking the silence.

"More or less," Belle said with a shrug. "My father can.

I think generally girls are taught more than boys… but most people can fend for themselves."

"Because you get married and cook for your husbands," the Beast said, showing what he knew almost like he had read it in a book somewhere. *A Spoiled Prince's Guide to Life Among Peasants.*

"Sure. Yes. Cook for our *husbands.*" Belle slammed a cleaver down on a chicken leg, separating the drumstick from the thigh in one stroke. "Good little wives."

The Beast's eyes widened at her unexpected violence. "What did… what did I say?"

"Oh… nothing," Belle said with a sigh. "I don't want to be a *good little wife.* I want adventure. I want… to be the hero in the story. But everyone else just wants me to… *get married, obey my husband, have seven or eight kids, wash his socks… YOUR SOCKS ARE DISGUSTING, GASTON!*"

She whacked off another leg.

If her mother had been around, would she have been home for the would-be wedding? Would the Enchantress have turned them all into pigs for accosting and embarrassing her daughter?

"Gaston? The… hunter you mentioned before?" the Beast asked meekly.

"A wedding ambusher. A surprise groom. An utter clown." Saying this aloud made her stop. *Clown.* That was exactly correct – why hadn't she thought of that before? Hiring a band, getting a cake and throwing a surprise wedding wasn't normal or romantic. Especially since she didn't return any of Gaston's affection. He couldn't even seem to see that. The whole thing was creepy and bizarre. And, in some ways, not that far removed from throwing someone into your own private prison for trespassing on your property.

"He's the big man in town," she said more calmly, putting the cleaver down for a moment. "*Everyone* wants to marry him. He's tall, handsome, strong, deadly with a shot, has these absolutely *amazing* blue eyes, is always the life of parties…"

The Beast stopped mixing for a moment to regard her. She noticed that there was a telltale fluff of flour on his muzzle. He saw where her eyes went and discreetly flicked out his long pink tongue to take care of it.

Belle shook her head and rolled her eyes.

"But," he began, confused, "if he's so… handsome and perfect and everyone else wants to marry him, why doesn't he marry someone else? Someone who *wants* to marry him?"

She smiled, blushing, and turned back to the chicken. "This is going to sound positively vain, but he thinks I'm the prettiest girl in town. He doesn't want *me*… he wants, you know, *the prettiest girl in town.* He feels he deserves it, because he's the handsomest man in town."

The Beast looked down at his big ugly paws covered in dough and then up at her again.

"You are… pretty," he said gruffly. "So don't you want to marry the handsomest man? Don't *you* deserve it?"

"Haven't you been listening to a *word* I've been saying?" Belle asked, putting her hands on her hips – carefully, so the chicken juice wouldn't get all over her. "He's dumb, he's arrogant, he's self-centred, he kills a *lot* of things, he's loud, he doesn't read…"

"I don't read, either," the Beast mumbled, looking into the bowl.

Belle sighed.

"I'm also big," he continued, even more softly. "And loud."

"And apparently self-centred enough to make this all about yourself, instead of *me,* which is whom we were talking about," Belle said with a not-quite-serious glare.

The Beast immediately looked contrite.

"*Betyouwouldhavemadeaprettybride,*" he added under his breath, working at the dough, pretending to use all his concentration.

Belle laughed. "Thank you." She hadn't even really thought of that point. Had Gaston arranged some flowers or a veil for her as well? She couldn't imagine him not caring how the prettiest bride in town would look next to the most handsome groom. It was funny to imagine him speaking with the hatmaker, maybe figuring out what to order…

"*DAMMIT!*"

Her thoughts were cut off by an explosion from the Beast: he had grabbed the bowl of dough and now threw the whole thing to the ground, smashing it into a thousand tiny clay pieces. The *pâte brisée* stayed as one ugly lump on the floor – splatted so thin she could almost see the design of the stones below it.

The Beast was roiling, in full beast mode, on two legs but about to drop down to four, his face contorted in a snarl that almost made her afraid.

"What just happened?" she asked slowly.

"*I JUST TURNED TO GET SOME MORE BUTTER AND IT TIPPED!*" he howled. "It was my… *paw*! It got caught! *STUPID!* I shouldn't be doing this!"

"You're right. You *shouldn't* be doing this. You *shouldn't* be acting like a big spoiled child who throws a tantrum whenever things don't go his way. How old are you? Twenty? A twenty-year-old *prince* acting like this?"

"*I'M NOT A PRINCE. I'M A BEAST!*" he roared at her. His hot breath gusted over her like the fetid wind of a rotten summer – or one of her father's steam experiments gone horribly wrong and getting ready to blow up.

"Really? Then why do you bother trying at all?"

She reached up and tugged on his cloak's golden clasp. "Why do you bother wearing *any* clothes? Or living inside? Or fighting your curse? Why not just give up and become a real, total beast?"

His mouth moved silently, gaping like a fish – whether to keep from biting her or out of being unable to find the right words she wasn't sure.

"*IT'S HARD!*" he finally shouted.

"Of course it's hard. You've never cooked before," Belle said crisply. "I suppose being a prince also means you can do everything perfectly on the first try?"

She turned and walked back to the chicken and prepared to begin working on it again.

The Beast was silent.

He started to lean over and peel the dough up off the floor.

"Don't you *dare* put that back in another bowl," Belle said without looking at him.

"I wasn't!" the Beast said immediately. "I was just… going to go and get a new bowl," he added quickly.

Belle couldn't quite hide her grin as he shuffled awkwardly over to the dustbin.

DINNER IS SERVED

Two hours later the kitchen was full of complex, amazing smells. Belle felt slightly drunk from the warmth, the scents, the complete exhaustion. Making dinner with a beast was hard work. And then making him clean up even harder. He didn't protest, but handled an inanimate mop even more awkwardly than a beast with malformed hands should, having never touched anything like it before.

Belle wiped her brow. It was kind of amazing to cook in a kitchen like this. She never had any particular desire to pursue a more culinary life; food was fuel to be enjoyed in between books. *But if I had to cook, boy, a kitchen like this would be amazing. The space… the ingredients… the size of the stove…*

"Just what on earth is going on?" Cogsworth demanded,

stomping into the room as giantly as his little padded wooden feet would allow. He stopped as soon as he saw the Beast, who was ripping off his apron. "Oh, Master, I'm so sorry, I was just…"

Lumière was close behind.

"Well, well, what have we here?" The candelabrum made a noise like he was taking a great sniff. Belle wondered if he – if any of them – could smell. Or taste. They could obviously see, but how much of the rest of their lives were deadened by the curse? "Chicken? Mushrooms? *Love?*"

His flame flickered like he was waggling his eyebrows. Cogsworth hit him.

Belle smiled. "Your master and I made dinner for *ourselves* tonight."

Cogsworth spluttered. "That's highly…"

"… *enterprising* of you," Lumière said with a bow, cocking a questioning eye at the Beast.

"It wasn't *my* idea. But we did it," the Beast said proudly.

"Well, then, we shall leave you to it," Lumière said, ushering Cogsworth out with a wave of his flaming hand. "A night off! What shall we do?"

"…Cribbage, perhaps?"

Belle watched the two of them go almost fondly, then checked the dining room.

It was stark and formal-looking. Despite her insistence

they do it all themselves, someone had set either end of the very long table with a full dinner service. The Beast looked at Belle. She gave him a smile and shook her head, gathering up all the spoons and forks and plates in one gentle sweep to bring them next to each other.

When they went into the kitchen to fetch the food, they found Mrs Potts laying everything out on a tray to bring in. She spun round guiltily.

"Mrs Potts," Belle said, gently chastising. "We're serving ourselves tonight. You deserve a break."

"Oh, I was just, I felt bad about before, I just..." she sputtered. "You've got an excellent skill with cooking, my dear! This is all amazing!"

"If a bit *élémentaire*," the stove called out helpfully.

To the Beast's credit, when he lifted the lid of the *coq* and inhaled its glorious scent – and a fair bit of steam – into his wide, animal nostrils, he did not reach in his paw and scoop up a mouthful. It looked like he sorely wanted to. Instead he put the lid back down – maybe a trifle harder than was needed. Belle smiled her approval. She was busy gathering up all the other dishes, balancing the onion tart awkwardly on one arm.

Without straining, the Beast reached over with a casual paw and took the tart from her as if it were no larger or heavier than an egg. She laughed and he smiled, overcome by the little moment's absurdity.

"Dinner is served," Belle announced grandly, marching into the dining room.

The Beast watched her carefully as she put the food out on the table and then served herself, using all the proper implements, then sat there for a moment before realising she wasn't going to serve *him*.

He quickly grabbed a ladle and did the best he could, spilling only a little.

Belle took hearty sips, pleased with her cooking. She hadn't had to skimp or substitute ingredients like she often had to at home.

"It's very good," the Beast said. "*Élémentaire*," he added, quoting the stove. As if he thought it was a compliment.

Belle raised an eyebrow at him.

"I don't like fancy stuff," he went on quickly, suddenly realising how it sounded. "I like… meat."

Belle slumped a little. So much for her attempt at haute cuisine. *Well,* I'm *enjoying it*, she thought.

The Beast's eyes widened in horror.

At first she thought maybe he bit down on a peppercorn, wasn't there something about dogs hating pepper? Then she saw that he was staring at something in particular, *above* the table.

Rose petals.

Black rose petals were falling softly out of the air.

They made a little pile in the middle of the table. All in utter silence. Against the dark wood of the table and the shadows on the walls, it was like a Dutch still life made real, one of the sombre ones, with a skull or the like in the background.

"Not… very… romantic…" Belle tried to joke weakly.

But in the back of her head, she was counting.

Wild roses had five petals, generally; cabbage roses could have as many as one hundred. A normal 'fancy' rose had between 25 and 40. Ten had fallen already, and the look of alarm was growing on the Beast's face.

Nineteen… twenty…

Insomuch as the Beast could turn pale, he did; frozen with his mouth open in purely human apprehension.

Belle started to get up, to try and grab them…

Twenty-one.

The petals stopped.

Of course. Twenty-one, for his age when the curse is completed.

Where they landed on the table was now a sizable heap of velvety-black tatters.

"I'll just…" Belle said, rising to brush them off, away from him. The part of her that wasn't also transfixed by the terrible apparition was mildly stunned at her own reaction. While her first instinct was to be terrified, her second was to comfort the Beast and protect *him*…

But as she touched the petals, they glittered and vanished, just the way the original ones had.

The Beast sat perfectly still this whole time, but something about the way his claws gripped the table made Belle think he was about to bolt.

"Maybe it's my mother, trying to tell me something," she offered.

"Maybe it's just more effects of the curse," the Beast said darkly. "The castle grows more haunted, reminding me of my doom."

"All right," Belle said, taking a deep breath. She thought quickly, trying to come up with some topic to take their minds off the horrible apparition.

Or… not. They *had* to figure out how to break the curse. This was a not-so-subtle reminder of that. She might as well grab the elephant in the room by its tusks.

Or something.

"Let's review the facts. One, my mother cursed you ten years ago. We do not know if she is dead or alive. She's feeling a little… ghostly, though, I have to say. We *do* know that she had a symbol next to her name in the record book, and everyone else who did seems to have disappeared. We know Alaric Potts disappeared… damn. I forgot to check next to his name, to see if there was a symbol.

I was too upset. We should do that straight after dinner.

"How am I doing so far?"

The Beast shrugged. But he seemed to have relaxed a little. "Sounds right. Not sure how it helps."

"I don't know either, but there's a *ton* of mysteries here, like boxes inside boxes, which are just begging to be solved," Belle said, sighing. She scraped at the bottom of her bowl, playing with what remained of the gravy. "At least… now I know that all of your servants were… people. That means we can ask everyone here about what went on before the curse. Makes things a whole lot easier."

"It never even occurred to me to talk to them before," the Beast said thoughtfully. "Mother and father always told me… servants were tools… possessions, almost. To not get too attached to them because then they would use you… That's why they were so mad about me and Alaric…"

"Oh. Huh."

Belle put a bite of chicken in her mouth while she thought of something else to say. Could you blame someone for their views if that was the way they were raised… and then turned into a beast for ten years? Frozen in time, in some ways? Did her mother understand that was a possible result of her curse? That it wouldn't fix anything – and maybe make things worse?

The faults of all the parents involved…

"Your mother and father don't sound very… enlightened," she eventually observed. "Or modern."

The Beast twitched his shoulder uncomfortably.

The words from the vision came back to her: *There is no love in your heart at all, Prince – just like your parents.*

"What were… the king and queen… like?"

"They were my parents. They ruled the kingdom," he said with a shrug.

"But… like… *How* did they rule? What did they do during the fever? Can you remember?"

The Beast stopped eating and looked bleakly at his dish. "They locked up the castle and had everyone stay inside, safe. With priests and… no, there were no doctors. I don't remember why. I remember the incense and not being allowed to ride my horses."

"Did they do anything for the people? To help alleviate the suffering?"

The Beast gave her a blank look.

"They… closed the borders," he said slowly. "I was upset because I couldn't have the fresh berries from the north that I liked so much. No one in or out, for any reason. To try to contain the sickness. To keep it from spreading."

"Well, that was smart. But did they… build makeshift hospitals? Provide food for those too afflicted to leave their homes?"

The Beast shifted his feet under the table.

"Did your parents give *anything*, like…"

The Beast roared, suddenly standing up and throwing his chair backwards.

"They gave *everything*!" he snarled in her face. Belle turned away and put her hands up to protect herself, suddenly terrified of his yellow teeth and murderous look.

And then, without another word, he leapt away – silently, on all fours, tearing his way through the castle.

Belle looked at the ruined remains of dinner, sloshed all over the table.

A little stunned, she began to take a napkin and slowly wipe up the mess.

Never forget he's still a beast, she told herself sadly.

ASK THE DISHES

By the time she had finished cleaning, Belle was beyond exhausted and all alone in the silent kitchen. The stove seemed to be asleep, frozen in his unlit 'off' position. The furniture was also hushed or otherwise unmoving.

For the first time in the haunted castle, Belle began to feel lonely. Not scared or desperate for some other sign of life, but just lonely for companionship. Things had seemed to be going so well with the Beast… What had set him off so dramatically?

She peeked into the servants' dining hall. To her relief, most of the senior house staff and some of the more prominent junior staff were sitting around the table, enjoying the large banked fire at the end of the room. Mrs Potts, Lumière and

Cogsworth sat together at the head. The rake – presumably the former gardener – and the shaving strop were trying to play a game of cards. Dustmaids and a parasol gossiped.

"Hello?" Belle ventured.

They all immediately stopped what they were doing and looked over at her.

"Oh child, is your dinner over already?" Mrs Potts asked in concern.

"I think I… pushed him too far," Belle said wearily. She indicated an empty chair. "May I?"

"It's highly—" Cogsworth began.

"Yes, of course," Lumière interrupted, leaping down and pulling it out for her.

Belle sank into the chair gratefully. "Apparently, I just… rush into things…" *Totally not like my mother. Rushing to curse someone, rushing into a creepy castle… Totally not the same thing at all.* "I may as well apologise to all of you right now. If you haven't heard yet, it turns out *my mother* was the one who cursed your master and all of you. And, of course, it's me who brought the curse to fruition. I am so very, very sorry."

Those who knew at least some of it already, like Lumière and Cogsworth, studiously didn't react. The rest dropped everything in shock.

"I feel terrible. I can't even describe how sorry I am.

I didn't realise when I first came here… that you were all human once. I thought maybe you were just… things that were animated to life."

"I am a *Christian*," Cogsworth said indignantly. He pronounced it *Chris-tee-an*. "A man with a soul, trapped in this unforgivable clockwork prison."

"Oh, I'd say it's fairly forgiving of some of your less attractive features," Lumière said casually.

"We were all people once," Mrs Potts said sadly. "Even my boy, Chip. He was just a lad when it all happened. And he still is, after all these years. Maybe, in its own way, that's a blessing."

"So you are the great Enchantress's daughter," Cogsworth said thoughtfully. "I find it… very odd that *you* came back here…"

"Magic always comes back on itself," Mrs Potts clucked. There were general murmurs of agreement and nodding of head-like appendages around the table.

"What?" Belle asked.

"Oh, it's just something Mr Potts used to say," she said, shaking her spout. "Every curse, every charm, every little bit of kitchen magic, comes from somewhere and doesn't go… *away* when it's finished. There's always a price to pay – and it usually involves the one who cast the spell."

"Was he an enchanter?" Belle asked politely.

"Him? No," Mrs Potts chuckled. "He wasn't one of *les charmantes*. His only magic was with animals, and it wasn't *magic* magic, if you know what I mean."

"Wait – *les charmantes*?" Belle pressed, suddenly alert. "What are those?"

"It's just a general term," Lumière explained with a candle-like shrug. "It means anyone... just a little bit touched. By magic."

"Could be the ears and tail of a wolf," Mrs Potts said. "Could be a tendency to float rather than walk. Could be a great enchantress, a kitchen witch, or that strange little girl at the market who never aged and always had those lovely mushrooms in the autumn."

"*Fairies*," Belle said in wonder, remembering what the Beast had said. "*Les charmantes.* They lived here."

"We were famous for it," Cogsworth said with a sniff of pride. "At one time."

"So... my mother... was one of those *charmantes*," Belle said slowly. "That funny mark next to where my mother's name would have been in the record book... I wonder if that's what it meant. Did the kingdom keep track of *les charmantes*?"

Everyone looked a little uncomfortable.

"Not... officially," Cogsworth said delicately. "All, er, minority groups have had... good and bad relations with the crown… at different times in history. This particular reign was not… thrilled… with the idea of people with potentially greater strength and power than their own soldiers…"

Belle racked her brain for other names that had the symbol next to them.

"Have you heard of… Girard? François Girard?"

Everyone looked blank.

"Aimi Duprée?"

The little objects gave various versions of shrugs as their anatomy allowed.

"Christophe Lambert?"

"Werewolf," Lumière said immediately. Several other people around the table nodded. "And what a *drinker*! The whole family was a bit touched. With drinking, I mean. Mostly harmless, except for that time with the sheep. He tended to go on a spree before the full moon and then decamp to the hills. It was quite a sight, some nights."

"I wonder what happened to him," the old gardener said. "You used to hear his howls – some hated it, but I thought it was rather lovely. Forlorn and magical, like the old days."

"Oh, they were all mostly gone by the third year of the fever," the shaving strop added.

"That was a bad time," Mrs Potts said, shuddering.

"I was in bed for a month, do you remember? And I was one of the lucky ones! A fever so high you'd like as to burn your thumb feeling a patient's forehead. And just wasting away with terrible, shallow breathing."

"Less than half the kingdom was left when it was over," Cogsworth added bleakly. "It ran us through. Didn't matter if you were a peasant or a king or a queen."

Belle's throat went dry.

"King… or… queen?"

"Yes, it took both of them, poor things," Mrs Potts said, clucking. "Left the master an orphan at age ten."

"Oh, *oh my God…*" Belle rubbed her face with her hands, feeling panicky and nauseated. "The plague killed them. That's why he was so upset and rushed out. And there I was, just chattering along about what terrible people they were for not helping… *I am an idiot.* I am such. An. Idiot. I need to find him and apologise…" She started to get up.

"Don't bother," Lumière said gently, grasping at her sleeve. "If he is in one of his… fits… it would just be best to leave him alone until he calms down."

"Wait until tomorrow morning, dear," Mrs Potts said, nodding. "It's for the best."

Belle reluctantly sat back down. *Research, ask, investigate,* she told herself. *That's what you're here to do, so do it!*

"All right… But you said there were almost no

charmantes left by the end. The records tend to indicate that it wasn't the fever..."

"Ha! *Non*," a dustmaid spoke up. "It didn't touch them at all. Because it was *started* by them. It was started by a witch!"

"Pish and nonsense," Mrs Potts said. "You have no idea what you're talking about, child."

"It was a terrible, deadly disease, plain and simple," Cogsworth added firmly. "There was nothing magical about it. It didn't discriminate in its victims."

"So what happened to them?" Belle pressed.

Suddenly, the room grew very quiet. The objects became still, only Lumière's flames flickering and Cogsworth's dial ticking.

"Look, I think it might have something to do with breaking the curse," Belle said, pleading. "I think it might have to do with my mother's leaving us, or disappearing... I really think she's trying to tell me something. But if we're going to try at all, you need to tell me!"

"Besides... our king and queen... not everyone... liked *les charmantes*," Mrs Potts said slowly.

"For obvious reasons!" the dustmaid said with a snort, indicating everyone in the room.

"There's always been tension in the principality, as I said," Cogsworth put in primly. "Usually everyone got on all right. But… there have been periods… when people were on… worse behaviour than usual, let us say. Just before the curse was one of those periods. There was an incident involving the death of a normal boy at the hands of one of *les charmantes.* Violence ensued. Many people already believed *les charmantes* were the cause of all the trouble in the kingdom. Whenever there was a drought, or a crop failure, or livestock weren't breeding…"

"Or a plague," the dustmaid put in icily.

"Some said they were leaving, going back to the Fair Lands or wherever they came from," Mrs Potts said with a sigh. "But in reality, they were probably *being* disappeared. One week you'd hear of a goodwife being beaten half to death and the next week the nice man with the claws who sold the lovely China silk would be gone, just gone, nothing else missing. It doesn't take a lot of guessing to figure out what probably happened."

"If you weren't a *charmante*, there was nothing to fear," the dustmaid pointed out.

"That's foolishness," Mrs Potts said. "Think of Mr Potts. He went the way of the rest of them, and he wasn't magic."

"*Bah,*" the dustmaid said. "You prove my point. He was well known for his views. If he wasn't so friendly to those freaks of nature, maybe he would be fine. And do not forget that it was one of *les charmantes* who cursed you!

Who cursed all of us! You see how they are all insane and powerful! How can you forgive them?"

"It was one person," Cogsworth said patiently, "who had to watch as her people were… harassed and hunted down. In her own twisted way she was doing what she thought was right to protect them and save what was left of the rest of the kingdom. And you cannot blame an entire group for the actions of one."

"But…"

"*We are all 'charmantes' now!*" Lumière said, pounding a brass fist on the table. It was the first time Belle had seen serious, strong emotion in what seemed like an otherwise laid-back little guy. "It doesn't matter any more! It's just as well the rest of the world has forgotten about us, because if they hadn't people would swoop in and kill us for being tainted by the devil or lock us up in a circus!"

All of the creatures looked round at each other and then at the ground awkwardly after his outburst.

"I don't understand," Belle said, resting her weary head on her hands. "No one in the village where I grew up even believes in magic. The village right over there, across the river. From all of this. And my mother disappeared *after* we moved there. So it couldn't have been some… sort of… witch-hunt… right?"

"It's a lot to take in for one night," Mrs Potts said

kindly, waddling forwards. She seemed tired, like just moving took effort.

"I think, maybe, we should *all* retire," Lumière suggested, trying to sound like his old self again.

All the spoons, cups, mops, garden equipment and assorted animated household things clipped and clanked and clopped stiffly down from the table, on to the chairs and finally to the floor. Some of them weren't moving too well at all; one of the spoons seemed so sleepy and stiff that she had to be carried by her friends. Belle wondered about that – but then Cogsworth's face chimed. It was late. They were probably just tired, and didn't show it the way normal people did. Maybe, like Cinderella, the magic changed at midnight.

"I just have a few more dishes," Belle said, also getting up.

"Leave it, dear," Mrs Potts said. "We'll deal with it fresh and early in the morning."

"But the whole point was to give you all a night off!" Belle protested.

"You've done enough, I mean that sincerely," the teapot said, turning this way and that but keeping her spout directed at Belle. The gesture seemed to be the equivalent of a knowing smile. "You've done more to bring life and change into these walls than anything has in the past ten years."

Belle's look turned dark.

"I wonder if maybe your whole kingdom was cursed long before my mother showed up. Disease... ethnic cleansing... a king and queen who didn't care for their people..."

Mrs Potts sighed. "It wasn't always like that. It used to be quite a magical place, in all senses of the word. Ah, well."

She struggled to waddle her way to the edge of the table, the end of the parade of creatures retreating back to the kitchen. With some alarm Belle reacted before she thought, gently picking up Mrs Potts and setting her on the floor. She wasn't sure if it was breaking some sort of unspoken code among the cursed, but it just felt right.

Mrs Potts felt warm but unmoving in her hand – just like a real, normal teapot. If it weren't for the twitch of her spout, Belle never would have known she was anything but.

"Thank you, my dear," Mrs Potts said, shuffling off into the kitchen.

Belle wondered who babysat the baby cups during the dinner party. *A nursemaid pitcher?*

Sighing at how crazy her life had become in the last few days, Belle tiredly – and stiffly too, in her own way – headed up to her room.

She held the balustrades tightly as she ascended the stairs, pulling herself along, deep in thought.

In adventure books there weren't awkward pauses or

embarrassing social scenes. In morality plays and farces there were rarely serious discussions of racial tension, mob mentality, pogroms, or plague. In scientific books there were no dinnertime revelations of a terrible matter.

Life is a strange mixture of all of these genres, she mused, *and it doesn't have nearly as neat and happy an ending as you often get in books.*

When she got to her room, the wardrobe was asleep. Or very still.

Belle undressed slowly and climbed into bed, head spinning with all she had learned.

A kingdom at the end of its time, corrupt with evil and disease.

A king and queen so removed they were as bad as Nero, literally doing nothing while their kingdom burned.

A curse on an 11-year-old, delivered by an enchantress probably enraged by the treatment of her people and angry about the neglect of the kingdom as a whole.

But did the boy prince really deserve his fate?

And here was Belle, who had hurried that unhappily ever after along. Unless they found out what happened to her mother, or managed to find some equally powerful member of *les charmantes,* the Beast and his servants would be stuck that way forever, riding out the remainder of time in the forgotten castle in the middle of the woods.

Magic... always comes back on itself...

One last thought occurred to Belle before sleep finally claimed her:

What if, since her mother was the one who cast the spell, Belle was the only one who could *break* it?

MEANWHILE, NOT AT THE CASTLE...

Maurice looked out of the window of the automatic carriage with a strange mixture of desperation, revulsion and regret.

Regret because despite the dire circumstances, he was being carried home by a marvel – a magical thing that figured out the way without eyes or ears and trotted along without a horse. He wished he had more time and the ability to observe it properly, poke at it, tinker with it. See if it obeyed anyone other than the Beast.

Revulsion because when he dreamed of a world filled with carriages that could drive themselves and carts without horses, he never imagined such a sickly insectoid thing. The magical conveyance didn't roll, it didn't have wheels at all. Instead it crept along on its shafts and axles, making a terrible scurrying noise. Like a giant cockroach.

And *desperation* because he had to go and find someone to help him get Belle immediately!

But who?

He didn't really have any close friends, and he suspected that Monsieur Lévi probably wouldn't be up to a raid on a magical castle. The man was easily 20 years older than Maurice himself.

Who was young and strong enough to help? Who could round up a posse of helpers to go after the Beast?

And then it hit him. There was only one person, really, and it should have been obvious.

As the carriage turned on to the main square, Maurice began pulling at the door. He needn't have tried so hard; it was unlocked and swung open easily, and he tumbled out on to the wet, cold stones. The carriage thing screeched to a halt.

"Uh, goodbye, thank you," Maurice called distractedly. He wasn't sure what the etiquette was with a thing like that, but it never hurt to be polite.

The carriage executed a strange four-legged curtsy or bow – just the way he imagined elephants in the Far East did to let people up and down their enormous backs. Then it scuttled off in its nauseating fashion.

Snow was falling, Maurice suddenly realised. He had been so preoccupied with everything on the trip back he hadn't even noticed. Running carefully on the slick cobblestones, he made for the pub.

It seemed as if the usual crowd had been drinking there for a while that night already; the sounds of laughter and singing spilled out into the otherwise silent town.

The wind caught the door as Maurice threw it open, slamming it loudly and theatrically. It wasn't what he intended, but the resulting effect was useful: everyone stopped what they were doing and turned to stare.

"Help! Everyone, I need your help!"

"Maurice...?" the old barmaid asked, concerned.

"He took her and locked her in a dungeon!"

Damn his inability to speak clearly. Communication had never been one of the inventor's strengths... and it was definitely a liability now.

"Who?"

That was LeFou, Gaston's little friend. He wasn't a bad sort if you could get him away from the hunter. Not that bright, but fiercely loyal and game for just about anything. Exactly the sort of man you would want along on a beast-hunting expedition.

"*Belle!* We have to go! Not a minute to lose!"

He grabbed LeFou's hand and spun to leave, wildly checking the rack of guns and firearms and other weapons that were kept by the door. They would need to be heavily armed.

"Whoa, slow down, Maurice! Who's got Belle locked in a… *dungeon*?"

Suddenly, Gaston was between him and LeFou. For a big man he moved surprisingly quickly. Even in Maurice's addled state, he noticed there were odd patches of mud that had been carefully brushed off – but not entirely removed *from* – the man's inappropriately fancy trousers. Was he hunting in formal gear when he fell into a pig wallow?

A mystery for another time…

"A beast. A terrible, horrible beast!" Maurice made his arms go as wide as they could.

Gaston raised his eyebrows at the patrons at the bar, who had all turned round to listen.

"Is it a… *big* beast?" one of them asked.

"*Huge!*" Maurice said, shuddering.

"But did it have sharp, cruel fangs?" another asked.

"Yes! But it spoke like a man! And walked on two feet!"

"What about… a long, ugly snout?" a third asked.

"*Yes, yes!*" Maurice said, exasperated. Who cared what the Beast looked like in detail? It was dangerous and had his Belle. "Will you help me?"

"Of course," Gaston said politely. He gestured with his chin to the barflies. "We'll help you out."

"Oh, thank you, thank you," Maurice said with a sigh.

The inventor turned back to the door. The village was a touch-and-go place, filled with people of questionable morality, but when push came to shove, his neighbours really did…

Suddenly he found arms under his shoulders and his feet dangling off the floor.

"We'll help you *out*!" someone cried.

The door was thrown open in front of him. Maurice was pitched out into the black cold.

"No!" he shrieked, spinning round immediately.

But the door slammed in his face.

He hit it again and again as hard as he could with his fists.

"No! I *saw it*! I saw it!" he screamed. "Will no one listen to me?"

Gaston stuck his head through a window to take one last look before shutting it.

"Crazy old Maurice… hmm…"

"*I'm not crazy!*" Maurice shrieked. "Will *someone* help me?"

But the town was dead, everyone inside with their families or loved ones, doors and windows barred tight.

"I'll just have to go and rescue her myself," Belle's father said quietly, once the reality of the situation sank in.

He was a dreamer, it was true – but no inventor lasted long in his or her career by giving in to dreaming. The moment something didn't work, either due to a misunderstanding of how a metal behaved or how steam would push a certain way, you had to immediately stop and think and figure out what the cause of the problem was and start again from there. Practical, pragmatic, dogged – these were all the adjectives used to describe successful inventors.

Maurice turned round in the cold night and headed steadily for home.

He wished, however, that his wife were there to help. She was… he vaguely recalled… extremely useful and handy at times like these… even if he couldn't exactly remember how…

SHE DIDN'T SEE IT THERE BEFORE

Dawn was a paling of the black-and-blue sky to the east; the sun was at least an hour from rising. The fire was nothing but embers and Belle realised she had been shocked awake by the cold on her face. She turned over in bed and saw, to her dismay, there were no more logs in the neat stack.

Immediately she felt ashamed; only two days in a castle and already she was coming to expect service, perfect and punctual!

This is no worse than home on a winter morning, she told herself, closing her eyes and bracing herself for the quick emergence from bed that such mornings usually prompted. It was like jumping into a freezing lake.

She threw back the covers quickly, hoping against hope that the warm spot her body made would still be there after she returned with more wood. Her feet didn't slap against a floor like ice as they would have at home; there was a thick rug to protect them here. She thought with longing about what warm clothes might be in the wardrobe, but opening the thing up while it was sleeping seemed wrong. An invasion of privacy or worse.

So she crossed her arms against the frigid air and slipped her shoes over bare feet, preparing to make the long trip down to the kitchen and storerooms.

But when she threw open the door a statue was standing there.

For some reason, Belle didn't scream. She *did* jump back. It was too early in the morning, her head was too sticky and murky with sleep, and it was too cold for her to think about much else except for how cold she was.

This time the leaves were slightly more 'arranged' to copy human features… or possibly *in*human ones. Belle was reminded of the haunting Green Man images she had seen in books about ancient British churches: broad leaves flanking the face like a mane, smaller ones making a flat nose and unseeing eyes. The ivy near its 'feet' was covered with delicate white tracery of frost. *Like the other one – it had come from outside.*

"What the...? What on earth is *that*?"

Any thought Belle had that she was dreaming was immediately banished by the banal, confused words of the wardrobe.

Belle spun round and put a finger to her lips. Now was not the time to interrupt.

"Were you sent by my mother...?" she began as she turned back.

But the statue had changed in that moment: an arm was now raised, and a finger pointed to something behind Belle.

She turned to look. There was nothing really there.

"The window...?" she started to ask, turning back.

But the statue was gone.

"That," the wardrobe said, "was spooky."

Belle ignored her, too wrapped up in what was going on to care about being rude, and went over to the window.

Thin strands of pale webbing had somehow reached it, crossing lightly back and forth in front of the pane. In dismay Belle pressed her face against the glass and tried to see how much more of the castle had been covered.

A surprising amount. Thick ropes had breached the top of the perimeter walls and thin, sickly-looking runners were shooting out from them, spreading out over the open ground, as if looking for the next vertical edifice to attack.

Belle shuddered and had to fight down a surge of panic. Eventually the webs would blanket the entire castle, enshrouding it and everyone within.

Then she noticed that the view of the grounds seemed strangely foggier than the weather should have allowed. It took her a moment to realise that there was a thin film of ice caught between two of the white strands. It was rippled and crazed, and what it showed was not a blurry version of the landscape beyond, but something else entirely:

Her house, at night. A dark rider approaching it – no, *two* riders, on the same horse. Galloping at breakneck speed, pulling up at the very last minute with a silent buck and protest from the horse.

Belle drew back, terrified by this strange vision. Nothing about the situation seemed right.

The lead rider jumped down, then turned to help the second rider off. This was a tall, graceful boy who flowed off the horse like water – Belle could see this in the splash of yellow light from the now-open doorway.

"No! Don't go out!" Belle couldn't stop herself from whispering. But her mother was in the doorway now, speaking to the rider, appearing nervous. Then Maurice was coming forwards, clasping the first rider's hand...

And then the vision restarted.

"No," Belle said, frustrated. "What *is* this? What is happening? Is he a relative? Is *one* of them a relative? Is that an uncle? What is happening? Why are you showing me this? Is he the one who betrayed you? Did you move out here to get away from all of the death and violence, and he tracked you down?"

"No idea, dear," the wardrobe said with a yawn. "But if you figure it out, let me know. I'm going to get a few more winks of sleep… good luck…"

Belle stayed and watched the vision, again and again and again, for hours, all thoughts of going to get the logs forgotten. Eventually, when the inside of her mouth tasted like death and she couldn't feel her legs, she went back into bed, curled up like a mouse.

When Belle woke up the second time, the sun was high and sparkling yellow.

"Morning, Miss," the wardrobe said brightly. "You figure out what that statue was?"

"Um, no," Belle said. She struggled for words. "I feel like… I feel like this *entire* castle is full of… my mother. I don't know if she's alive or dead but it's like everything here has been… *filled* with her, somehow. Her memories. Her… *soul*, almost. She's definitely trying to tell me something."

"I wish she'd find a less creepy way of doing it. Your old dress is washed, pressed and ready to go," the wardrobe said, throwing her doors open brightly. Indeed it was. So clean and crisp it was almost new. The apron was spotless and her shirt's sleeves puffy and shining white.

Next to it was a glittering yellow ball gown and a heavy pink dress with bell sleeves so long they might have almost been tippets, with a matching fur-trimmed stole.

"Snowed last night," the wardrobe said innocently. "Thought maybe if you wanted to go skating, or…"

"*Skating?* I don't know if you've noticed or not, but we're *trapped* in the grounds of this castle now. No way out. I don't think we're getting to the river any time soon."

"Oh, there's a tiny viewing pond in the larger bailey, past the stables. I'll bet it's nice and solid by now."

Huh. That was interesting. So if she got a little too stir-crazy in the next few months, at least there were courtyards. "Thank you," Belle said, reaching for her old dress. "Maybe later."

Between her mother, the curse, the disappearance of *les charmantes* and her apology to the Beast, there was too much to do to spend time skating.

She hurried downstairs so quickly she almost didn't register the pale glowing toadstools that had begun to pop up in clusters on the steps. When a particularly bright and ghastly group of them finally caught her attention, she stopped to take a closer look.

It seemed like they were springing directly out of the grey streaks in the marble. The mottling on their stalks and umbrella tops looked like faces pressed up against cloth, screaming or trying to say something, shrouded before they were fully dead.

Belle felt her stomach turn. Some of the markings were *moving*, just a little, further making them look undead.

Part of her couldn't help thinking: *Wait, my mother worked with plants. Ivy and roses. Mushrooms aren't* technically *plants,* right*? Not like ones with leaves?*

"I need to eat something," she said aloud. That would make *everything* better, including her stomach. A chat with Mrs Potts, some bacon and a bright friendly stove would banish any lingering gloom.

But when she got there, the kitchen was as cold as her room had been the night before. The fire on the stove was so low it was almost out. Everything was still and silent. The waiting staff couldn't still be asleep, could they? Had they indulged in whatever magicked drams animated objects could after she had left last night? Were they now all passed out?

"Good morning!" Belle called cheerily.

Nothing.

Confused, she looked round the room. There, in the cabinet, was the unmistakable Mrs Potts. She was the only large white teapot with a pink-and-purple lid. Her porcelain was shiny and utterly unmoving.

Stacked next to her were all the little teacups, all but Chip, who was next to her. Like someone had placed him safely next to his mother.

"Mrs Potts?" Belle called softly. She rapped on the glass with a gentle knuckle. "Hello?"

No response.

Belle backed away into the middle of the kitchen. She spun slowly, looking all round her. It was a normal, quiet kitchen, waiting for a human to come in and breathe life into it.

Belle ran a hand through her hair, panicking. Was she still asleep?

Was she finally awake?

Was she just some poor mad girl lost in a deserted castle, imagining teapots who talked and flirty candelabra? If she ran back upstairs to 'talk' to the wardrobe, what would she be confronted with? Wood and dust?

The softest sigh came from the cabinet.

Belle almost sobbed in relief when Mrs Potts shook herself slowly, throwing off the last remnants of paralysis.

I'm not mad. That's *something.*

It was strange to think of a kitchen literally brightening but that is what it did. The oven glowed more orange, all of the chairs straightened to full attention, and sconces round the edges of the room lit themselves.

Mrs Potts spied Belle and hopped down from the cabinet anxiously.

"Oooh, my word, I've not overslept a day in all my years here!" she cried. "Get the kettle on! Lord, it's cold! My dear, I am so sorry! We'll get you something fresh and hot in a moment!" She descended to the table and spun round, directing Chip and the milk jug and a small plate of muffins and a silver dome to arrange themselves on a tray. "A beautiful day it is – I'll bet the sun melts all the snow before noon. But we'll just pour you some hot chocolate to take the morning chill off!"

"Thank you. I *love* hot chocolate. I almost never get it."

"I love chocolate, too!" Chip chimed in. "I can feel it in my cup," he added confidentially.

He was so cute and… chipper. But Belle couldn't help thinking, with a shudder, how there was a real little boy under the porcelain.

"How old were you when… all this happened?"

"*Five!*" Chip said proudly. He puffed himself out.

A little brass pot hopped itself off the stove and carefully on to the table. The cup stood very still, trying to be a serious big boy at his task while creamy, peppery hot chocolate was poured into him.

"Nicely done," Belle said, picking him up. She took a tiny sip and he giggled. Then she grabbed a couple of muffins. "I hate to eat and run but I want to get back to the library and do some more research. I don't suppose you know the name of the Enchantress who laid the curse on you… My, er, mother?"

Mrs Potts shook her spout mournfully. "What a terrible thing, not to know the name of your own mother! But I'm afraid *I* don't, either. I'll tell you, though, I'm fairly certain Mr Potts did. He said some things… dropped some hints… But by that time, it wasn't safe to have friends who were *charmantes*, certainly not if you lived at the castle. She was known to other folks here, though… you could try asking them. She came to see the king and queen three times, altogether. Magic always comes in threes."

"What?" Belle leaned forwards. "Why? Why did she come so often?"

"Well, the last time it was to curse us all," the teapot said with a dry laugh. "The time before that it was because the king and queen had summoned her, to beg her to help with the plague."

"Did she?" Belle asked breathlessly.

"No," Mrs Potts said with a sigh. "I'm not even sure if she could. Anyway, she told them no and stormed out, the way Lumière tells it."

Belle felt like she had been hit in the stomach. After accusing the *Beast's* parents of being heartless... Her own mother refused to heal the sick.

"Why did she visit the first time?"

"It was to bless the baby... the Prince, the Beast. On his birthday. Like they used to do in the old days. Ooh, I wish I'd seen that!"

"How... confusing," Belle said, trying to wrap her head around the idea of her mother blessing a prince she would eventually curse.

"Well, the king and queen didn't let her. They said it was *archaic* or some such. But it was more like *thickheaded*, if you ask me," the teapot said with a wet snort. "You can be all modern *this* and anti-magic *that* but if an enchantress offers you a free blessing on your child, you're a damn fool not to take it! That's what I think, anyway."

Didn't let her...

Belle felt something like a headache start to come on. A few days ago, she'd had no mother. Now she had a very complicated one. It was like finding out the country you live in is actually on the moon, and beholden to an entirely different set of laws and procedures.

No... Belle corrected herself. It was more than that. The mother that Belle *imagined* she had wasn't a tenth of the mother she actually turned out to be.

How could Belle, a lonely little bookworm of a country girl, ever have come from someone so great that she meted out curses and blessings like sweets and then took over an entire castle with her presence?

It didn't seem possible. It *almost* seemed like a mistake.

Well, she told herself bravely, *I may not have her* magic *power, but if I am indeed half of my mother, then I have her willpower and cunning, too. I am more up to this than any other creature in this world.*

… *Right?*

"Thank you," she said aloud to Mrs Potts before leaving.

As Belle went up the stairs to the dining room, she took a bite out of a muffin. It was still warm and moist inside, practically dissolving on her tongue. There was a delicate aftertaste of lemon and vanilla. She quickly finished the rest of it and ate the next one immediately, telling herself it was to get it all gone before entering the snack-free library.

Chip giggled as she sipped from him and tried not to wiggle too much. The hot chocolate was *very* hot.

Belle threw open the library doors dramatically so she could pretend it was the first time again. There were so many *other* books she could read on this cosy winter day. Almost too many. She narrowed her eyes and looked at it the way her father would: with a view to improvements. Rather than ladders here and there, he would have a wheeled trolley probably, with some sort of chute or pulley system to allow the lifting up and bringing down of books as gently as possible and a greater number than one person could normally carry. Or maybe a lens on wheels on a rail above the books, so you could look from the comfort of the floor quickly to see if a folio you needed was up there…

Suddenly, she noticed the Beast at the far end of the room, hunched over a book, frowning at it like he had been there for hours.

Belle tiptoed quietly down the main aisle towards him. He had a claw out and was moving it slowly across a line of text, frowning. Around him she saw some of the results of frustration: there were more than a few priceless, ancient record books shredded beyond recognition and little piles of what looked like future mouse nests.

"Beast…?" she asked in wonder.

"I'm… trying to make a time line. I went through one book already. Pretty thoroughly, I think. Noted all the references to someone who sounded like your mother." He held up a piece of paper that had so many holes in it that Belle was reminded of the constellation maps you put in front of lanterns to make the little stars glow. There were one or two giant names scrawled at the top before the pen devolved into meaningless loops and scribbles.

"I haven't written… in a while…" The look on his face was such a mix of desperation, eagerness and *forlornness* that Belle felt her heart break a little. She took the paper from him and looked at it closely.

"That's great," she said. "That's just what we need."

The Beast took a deep breath. "I… my parents…"

"I am so sorry," Belle said, putting the paper down and taking his paws in her hands. The Beast looked at them, and her, in surprise. "I didn't know. I had no idea you lost your mother and father to the fever when you were a child. I was a cad and a lout for what I said."

The Beast opened his mouth to say something.

"Thank you," eventually came out. "I'm… also sorry. I can't always control my rage," he continued haltingly, flexing his paws, trying to find the right words. "It was… *bad* last night. My mind went black. I don't remember what happened after I ran from the dining room… It's completely blank. I woke up in a corner of the basement with feathers on my muzzle."

Belle tried not to withdraw her hands immediately in horror, but to do it slowly, like she was intending to anyway. What on earth had those claws touched? What had they *done*?

"That's never happened before," the Beast said, not even noticing.

He spoke through a mouth so large he could have opened it wide and scooped her up and bitten her in half or swallowed her whole. He could snap off her head with his tusks. But he was hunched over and the hump on his back was more pronounced. His eyes, light blue and out of place among the darker colours of his body, were wide and covered with a wet film.

"I'll bet it's the curse," Belle said glumly. "You're becoming even *more* of a beast. And it's all my fault."

The Beast gave her a very wan smile. "And your mother's."

"Right." Belle slumped down next to him. "*Parents.*"

The Beast, almost unthinkingly, put his paw on her hand and squeezed. Like he was comforting *her.* She leaned into him and he adjusted, putting his arm round her shoulders.

"They're out there," he said quietly after a moment.

Belle looked round the library before she could stop herself.

"I'm sorry…?"

"*My* parents are out there," he jerked his chin gently towards the window. A strangely human gesture for such a giant chin. "I… visit them. Sometimes."

"Show me," Belle suggested gently.

Before entering the bailey, they stopped at a cloakroom. The Beast was still wearing his fancy trousers from dinner the night before but had divested himself of the shirt at some point. He swirled his old giant and ragged cape round his shoulders and fumbled at the golden clasp. But he didn't lose his temper as immediately as Belle thought he would; apparently doing this one thing properly without destroying it was important to him for some reason.

Nevertheless, she reached up and firmly did it for him. He didn't say anything, although there was a lopsided half-smile on his sad face.

She lightly swung an old cloak round her own shoulders and tied it under her neck in a movement so graceful the Beast couldn't help staring.

Then he pushed the door and went out.

Belle followed, then stumbled over the threshold. Dizzy and confused, she looked to the Beast. He grimly pointed at little piles of dirt that had somehow built up around the door and the base of the walls.

At first Belle thought of moles or other pesty rodents, but it was winter – they would have been asleep or at least unable to dig through the frozen ground.

With a skipped heartbeat, she suddenly realised what the cause of the disturbance was.

The castle was sinking.

It was being pulled down into the ground by the webs that coated the castle like white fungus and now cut them off from the rest of the world. Earth would swallow the castle whole, like it had never been there at all. The curse would make certain that the kingdom would be entirely forgotten.

Belle shivered and met the Beast's eyes, knowing that he had come to the same conclusion. Neither said a word.

She took a deep, cleansing breath, adjusted her cloak and turned away from the castle to face the outside world instead.

Belle was dazzled.

It wasn't sunny any more but still very bright, with festoons of brilliant clouds arching overhead. A light snow covered everything – the kind that was so friable and delicately balanced that it would be gone with the first warm breeze. But for now the landscape was iced in white, and white flakes were still falling from a white sky. Compared to the eternal gloom of the castle, it was positively blinding.

Even the sickly, bone-white webbing that now cloaked statues and bushes in its strangling tendrils shone with an ugly pale radiance.

The Beast began to walk and Belle followed… stepping in giant claw-shaped tracks. Her feet barely made it up to the middle of his prints.

He turned left before he led her through what might, in some ancient year, have been a courtyard filled with defensive spikes during wartime or sheep and merchants during peace, but was now a slightly overgrown strolling garden, thin and tight under the coldness of the season.

It was extremely beautiful in a shabby, overgrown sort of way. Those who followed fads – and not the actual *philosophy* of thinkers like Jean-Jacques Rousseau – would have approved wholeheartedly of the 'return to natural state' the garden was taking. Belle couldn't help smiling at the thought of either the Beast or the frustrated gardener being interested in the whims and trends of Parisian gardens.

Vines had begun to creep up everything. Birds had taken over in a way Belle was pretty sure they wouldn't when more people were in the castle. Woodpeckers loudly attacked insects in diseased trees and made their signature swooping flight paths over her head. Doves boldly congregated in twos and threes on the ground, looking for seed, unthreatened by cat or dog.

They passed under an arbour and into what at one time must have been an extremely elegant jewel box rose garden. Belle caught her breath. It wasn't huge, as she imagined the ones at Versailles and Rome were, but what it lacked in width and depth it made up for in narrow, winding paths and bushes so cleverly interplanted it looked like a maze of roses that went on forever.

Climbing roses made thick walls above prim cutting

roses, beach roses lapped at the bases of stone urns that held prize miniature roses. There were no other types of plants at all, except for a surprising number of weeds and the ivy again, creeping along the stone walkways, taking over from below.

Belle looked round nervously for gaps in the topiary… for brown, bare strips from which the more ambulatory ivy had come. But everything seemed to be… normal.

Unlike in Belle's mother's garden, it looked like winter had killed most of the flowers. They certainly hadn't been deadheaded properly and to Belle's experienced eye, it had been this way for a number of years, with canes not pruned and branches growing weak and heavy from their spent blooms and nutritionally costly rose hips.

Normally Belle would have reached over and casually broken off one of the unbelievably bright pink fruits and popped it in her mouth. Sour it might have been, but also a welcome burst of vitamins and memory of the summer sun. Hidden on a back shelf in their cottage Maurice still kept a stash of her mother's rose hip tea. He never drank it, but once in a great while she caught him holding a silken bag to his nose and inhaling its aging perfume.

The whole place made Belle sad. Not *bad* sad. Just nostalgic and a little weepy for things that were lost or that she had never had.

Like a mother.

Would her mother have taken her into the rose garden and taught her all of the names, would she have plucked a blossom and placed it in her daughter's hair? Would she have made rose hip tea for her daughter?

Would she have made raspberry leaf tea for Belle when she first began to have her monthly blood? *So that 13-year-old me wouldn't have had to research the possible balms and soothing medicines for it* by myself?

She crunched some brittle snow under her heel extra angrily with that thought.

The Beast continued to quietly crunch his way forwards through the snow. She couldn't tell if he was affected by the rose garden; he didn't seem any more or less melancholy than he normally did – when he wasn't in one of his rages. He hunched over in that way that very strongly indicated that moving upright on two feet was not only uncomfortable and unnatural for him, but at times downright painful.

Belle hurried to catch up and then immediately stopped when she saw where they were: a tiny ancient cemetery.

It was one of the most beautiful ones she had ever seen. A modern wrought iron fence, whose sharp points were leafed with gold, surrounded the small patch of land. Only the kings and queens of the castle were buried here, along with the heartbreaking bodies of some royal babies and children who had not survived for long enough to inherit the throne.

In front were the two most recent stones. They were beautifully carved marble, still fresh and icy-looking. Ornate designs of skulls and crosses and roses decorated the rounded tops of the stones and their inscriptions were carved in beautifully flowing script.

Here lie the king and queen of the castle, taken before their time.

The Beast had squatted down on his haunches to regard them more closely. He took his giant paw to brush off the little snow that had accumulated on the tops of the graves.

Belle knelt down next to him and put a hand on his shoulder.

"I was ten when they died," he said softly. "I didn't understand. They had done all these things – quarantined the kingdom, sealed us up in the castle, made us drink all of these disgusting tonics..." He chuckled slightly at the last memory. "I hated them, they made me almost throw up. No one else in the castle died, but nothing worked for my parents. From fever to death in less than three days. I wasn't allowed to touch them, I was barely allowed to see them. I never had a chance to say goodbye."

Belle was suddenly reminded of the Beast's change of heart when she was weeping, when he sent her father away. *I didn't even get a chance to say goodbye.* No wonder that had moved him.

"I was the last of the line… everyone wanted to keep me safe. Away from them and their sickness," the Beast said mournfully. "But I would have traded my life for one more embrace from my mother, a final word from my father. Without them, I didn't want to… live."

Tears coursed down Belle's cheeks. Was it better to never have had a mother – or to have one and lose one?

The Beast shook himself. "What remained of the court fled in droves after that… what good is an empty kingdom with no one to rule? What political use is a ten-year-old orphan prince in a backwards land?"

"Beast…" Belle said softly, squeezing his giant arm.

He sighed deeply.

"We mourned for a year, as was customary. And then it was time for my coronation. And the night before…"

"My mother showed up, and turned you into the Beast," Belle finished softly.

"*Turned me into?*" The Beast chuckled with despair. "You and your mother think I was well on my way to becoming one all on my own. As unfair as it was to do this to an eleven-year-old boy… why would she come the night before my coronation? She was *testing* me, to see if I would be as terrible a ruler as my parents. And I failed that test."

Belle opened her mouth to say that it still wasn't a fair

thing to do to a child. But… seen from a different angle, the larger picture, it began to make sense. The previous king and queen had turned a prosperous, happy kingdom into an empty nightmare where people were dying of plague in the streets or were beaten and 'disappeared' for being different.

Maybe her mother was just doing what she thought would protect the little that was left.

Still, it seemed a rather harsh burden for one so young.

"I *know* they were terrible rulers. Even as a child I sometimes felt like they weren't doing the right things. They turned away petitioners… their own subjects, whose houses were taken from them or were being vandalised… poor folk who were repeatedly beaten by the same thugs who always went unpunished… Sometimes they acted like the tyrants in stories my nurse read to me.

"That's why I lost my temper last night. I know you're right about them, but… They're *dead.*" His voice was beginning to degrade into a growl. "Their mistakes are *overrr.* Can't everyone just leave them alone now?"

The growl turned into a roar. He opened his mouth and howled, his tusks and teeth bare, his eyes closed. It was angry and mournful and chilling all at once – like nothing Belle had ever heard before. Like something ancient and large and lonely that haunted the woods, forever looking for something it was missing.

It had begun to snow again, she noticed, and his hot breath melted the timid flakes all around his giant head like some magical beast who breathed fire.

Belle gazed at the haunted, unkempt gardens and the mournful ancient cemetery. The air suddenly felt bitterly cold: the flakes became larger and stranger-looking. *Ashes*, Belle suddenly realised as she touched one with her finger and it remained, unmelting. Ashes from some dreadful, world-ending fire, signs of a war that consumed the land, a vision of everything ending.

Two tyrants who behaved like they had never been taught right and wrong ruling their toybox kingdom, hidden in the woods of France… and her own mother, who decided to take it upon herself to punish them and test their child. Everyone behaving like little gods.

She took a deep breath. "I am so sorry, Beast."

He gave a sad smile. "I used to have a name, a real name, before all this."

"What was it?"

"It doesn't matter now," he said, shaking his head. "Even if… even if I turned back into a person, I'll never be *that* person again."

"Oh…" Belle felt the tears welling up in her eyes and bit her lip.

"No, it's not so bad," the Beast said quietly,

putting his paw on top of her hand. To comfort *her.* "Not… not all change is bad. You are making me realise that."

Belle felt like crying for reasons she couldn't quite articulate. She realised that even if she hadn't been the one to mess up everything with the rose, even if it wasn't her own mother who laid the curse, she would still have done all she could to help him. It was a strange feeling; she never really had the opportunity to help anyone before, except for her father.

Belle put her hand on top of his paw and squeezed.

"We'll figure this all out. Together," she promised.

The Beast looked down at her in wonder for a moment. Then he put his other arm round her. She leaned into his warm side and he didn't pull away.

GASTON

The tavern, so lively not that long ago, was now gloomy and cold. It was the hour for dark things: far past midnight but not close enough to dawn for any hope of light. A fire was still burning in the enormous fireplace, banked low, more chastised and sullen than cheery.

Three lonely figures gathered around the single illuminated table, heads and shoulders bent close despite the absence of anyone around to hear.

Gaston was there, of course, his giant profile unmistakable. And next to him was his equally recognisable friend LeFou, who was sipping somewhat nervously at a tankard of *cidre*. The third man was thin, with taut, papery skin barely covering his skeleton. He seemed as ancient as a real mummy, but there was nothing frail in the way he held himself over the fancy cordial Gaston had poured. His hair was long at the back but without a ribbon confining it, the locks strangely neat and greasy. He had all of his teeth, or a very fine set of someone else's, that showed clearly whenever he talked or smiled, which was rare.

There was an odd smell about him, too – not *from* him, but a miasma around his clothes, his cloak, his hat. Something that reminded one a little too much of dangerous chemicals, vomit and decay, of urine and years. Gaston tried to move his head away without seeming impolite.

"I don't usually leave the asylum during the week – much less the middle of the night, but they said you'd make it worth my while," the old man said, completely frozen otherwise. He didn't even play with the base of the glass where his yellow fingers rested.

"Of course, Monsieur D'Arque," Gaston said as politely as he could. He wasn't used to dealing with refined gentlemen. Not that he needed to, most of the time. He pulled a small sack of coins from his coat and tossed it on the table.

At first D'Arque looked repulsed – either at the gesture or the size of the sack, it was hard to tell which. Then he reached out with a not-so-tentative hand and pulled the laces apart. His eyes glowed the same gold as whatever he found in there and a horrid smile formed on his lips.

"I'm… listening."

"It's like this," Gaston said, as if presenting a tricky and serious situation, like the capturing of an enemy castle. "I've got my heart set on marrying Belle, but she needs a little persuasion."

"A little persuasion? She turned you down flat," LeFou pointed out.

Gaston picked up the tankard of *cidre* and shoved it at his friend's mouth. LeFou burbled in protest but drank.

"Everyone knows her father's a lunatic..." the hunter continued, waving his hand nonchalantly.

"Be careful using that word," D'Arque said with a delicate menace. "Maurice is utterly harmless."

Gaston pounded his fists on the table in exasperation.

"He was in here tonight raving about some beast that is keeping Belle locked up in a castle!"

D'Arque's eyes flickered and he frowned slightly. Otherwise, he made no motion.

"Surely he was jesting."

"He seemed pretty serious to all of us," LeFou said, shaking his head. "Going on about what a *big* beast it was... with fangs and..."

"He said it could talk," Gaston interrupted, shrugging. "Like a man."

"How very unusual," D'Arque said, leaning forward. "A talking beast. Do tell me more."

"Oh, what does it matter?" the hunter roared. "The point is he is insane and Belle would do *anything* to keep him from being locked up."

"Yeah, even marry *him*," LeFou said, rolling his eyes. Gaston glowered but didn't disagree.

"I see," D'Arque said with a glittering smile. "Well, normally I would hesitate at the whole idea of throwing an innocent man into the asylum unless his beautiful daughter marries you. Even for gold. But you've piqued my curiosity… All right, I shall do it."

"Excellent! Let's drink to it!" Gaston raised his giant beer tankard for a toast and white foam spilled over the top. LeFou held up his smaller mug of *cidre*. D'Arque lifted his own delicate cordial glass, a glint of malice in his eye…

AN OLD CRIME

After a few minutes of sitting quietly but companionably in the falling snow, the Beast rose and offered his arm to her for the way back.

"While we're out here… why don't you show me the stables?" Belle ventured.

The Beast looked at her, surprised.

"Why?"

"I don't know… I just have this feeling… the disappearance of Alaric Potts… A vision that was shown to me last night involved a rider. I don't think it was a coincidence. Even if it wasn't Alaric, maybe it was something else connected to horses. And since this is the only stable we can get to, well, maybe it will spark something."

"What did the rider look like in the vision?" the Beast

asked curiously.

"It was hard to tell – it was night, and dark. He obviously knew my family. A skinny man, tall, a little bowlegged…"

"That sounds like him, I think," the Beast said, a little doubtfully. "But I was a child. Everyone was tall."

Belle laughed. "It's hard to imagine *you* being *small.*"

The Beast smiled self-consciously… and then his ears twitched. He turned, spotting what Belle would have missed: a tiny brown bird tucked deep and snug inside a ragged untrimmed topiary. While it was unclear if the Prince's beast form came from a cat or a dog or some sort of primordial aurochs, he definitely looked like he was twitching his tail, entranced by the little sparrow.

Belle slapped him delicately on the wrist.

The Beast shook himself and kept walking but he gave her a rueful sideways grin.

The stables were just outside the main collection of towers and turrets that made up the castle but still inside the grounds' outer walls. They were also the first buildings – besides Belle's apartment – being tentatively covered by the glacial spiderwebs. One main line of webbing had made its way to the corner of the ancient stone edifice and branched out into multiple strands, each slowly creeping up to the roof.

Belle tried not to panic. Without her knowing precisely what would happen, the webs still spoke of an eventual, and eerie, end to things.

In the vee of two forking strands was another pane of ice, like the one in her window. She paused to see if a vision would appear.

She was not disappointed.

It appeared to be a scene at a *tavern*, of all places – though the complete silence made the otherwise festive scene seem sad and spooky. Maurice was there, toasting two other men. One had an easy smile and a sloshing beer, the other had a thin smile and bright black eyes that seemed to burn unhealthily, like tiny coals.

"Do you see –" she started to say, but a cloud passed from the sun, the light changed, and the vision faded. They weren't strong in the daylight, apparently.

The Beast had opened the large double doors to the mews and gone in. Belle followed quickly, glad to be out of the cold. It smelled musty and old inside: no fresh tang of horse manure or newly dried hay. All of the silage and feed had crumbled to beige dust years ago, and had since been pilfered by rodents.

"So you haven't been in here in ten years," Belle said, looking in each of the stalls.

"Only to set them free," the Beast sighed. "Before that I was also here very rarely. When Alaric... disappeared, my parents eventually hired a replacement who didn't think stables were the proper place for a prince. The horses were already saddled and brought out to me for my rides. I missed being here. It was always so warm, and friendly, and the horses were so soft, and I thought it smelled nice…" But he twitched his nose unhappily.

"What was the name of your favourite horse?" Belle asked, poking at a feed trough.

"*Lightning.* He was big, and fast, and beautiful."

But he seemed distracted as he said it.

There was a small space set aside for the stablemaster and furnished with a large table for working on equipment. All sorts of tools and whips and little bags of medicines were arranged on shelves nearby. Belle poked through everything, unsure what she was looking for. For all she or anyone knew, Alaric had been knocked on the head and dragged off when he went down to the tavern for a pint. It might have had nothing to do with *les charmantes.*

Nothing looked out of order, it was all just very dusty.

"Well, I don't know," she said with a sigh. "I don't know if this is getting us anywhere…"

The Beast began to snort in big sniffs, moving his head back and forth. Alarmed, Belle backed out of the way.

"If you're hunting rats, I don't *want* to know."

"No… What's that smell?" the Beast said, wrinkling his giant nose. "It smells like… I don't know what it smells like."

Belle closed her eyes to concentrate. *The Vintner's Guide to Precisely Categorising the Wines of France* mentioned all sorts of incredibly nuanced aromas in very expensive wine: slate, bark, cherries, strange herbs, all of which she had to imagine, since *cidre* and local *vin ordinaire* were all they had in the village.

She could detect hints of hay, and cold dust, and *rat*, but that was about it.

"It just smells musty to me," she admitted.

"No, it's like… rot? Old rot?"

The Beast pushed her aside, gently, as he sort of slithered his way around the cold, stony space, moving his head like a snake or a bloodhound. Belle almost didn't want to watch; it was entirely inhuman.

"Over here," the Beast said, pointing to a corner in the largest stall. He began to scrabble at the dirt-packed floor like a pig rooting for truffles.

"Uh, I don't think…"

But then she looked at the room again, with a more discerning eye. Where he was digging, the floor was uneven, and higher than the area around it. The stones in the wall near the floor were chipped in places, like a shovel had accidentally struck in a mad attempt to mine out that part of the stables.

The dirt wasn't as hard-packed as in the other stalls,

either; it didn't take a lot of force for the Beast's claws to tear it up.

Then one of his claws snagged on something, with a terrible-sounding *rip*.

Belle jumped at the noise.

The Beast held up his paw: trailing from it was a strip of fabric. It was blue and lightweight, woven… not the sort of heavy canvas one would expect to find in a hard-working part of the castle. Not part of a saddle, or a basket, or a blanket…

It was a piece of *clothing*.

"Keep digging," Belle whispered, trying not to guess what was buried under the dirt.

The Beast threw the cloth aside and redoubled his efforts, pulling up clods of dirt like a badger. Belle found herself unconsciously leaning slightly forwards to see, despite her reluctance.

He suddenly sat back, finished.

With much gentler, slower motions he swept the now-loosened dirt away.

"There," he said sadly.

Belle leaned over his shoulder to look…

And nearly screamed.

There, at the bottom of a low trench, lay a half-rotted, dry and bony corpse.

Belle realised after a moment that she had never actually fainted.

Heroines in books and even sometimes heroes, always had violent reactions to finding skeletons or dead bodies.

But after she got over the initial fright of seeing the ivory skull bulging through the papery skin and the eye sockets and the whole thing in its rotted clothes, well, she found she was more than a little curious. She had never been this close to a body this far gone before.

The Beast's face had turned to a terrible look, somewhere between a grimace and a snarl, his teeth all bared and his lips pulled back.

He leaned over the corpse, searching the body with claws retracted. After a moment he pulled up what he had been apparently looking for: a belt buckle, bits of the leather still clinging to it. An image of a horse's head had been worked into the upper part of the clasp.

"This is… Alaric Potts," the Beast said thickly. "My parents presented this to him when he got married…"

Belle covered her mouth. For a moment she *did* feel like fainting. It was one thing to see a random corpse and quite another to realise that the person they had been talking about just minutes before was here, reduced to bone and sinew, long, long deceased. This body had been the Beast's favourite servant, father to the little teacup…

"They told me he ran away. Because of *me*!"

The Beast howled mournfully for a second time that afternoon. Belle had to cover her ears; his cry echoed inside the stables like nothing she had ever heard before.

When he finally quieted, he put the belt buckle back on the body – delicately, as if laying an amulet or sword on the body of an ancient king like Beowulf.

"But… but why was he…" Belle wanted to say *buried there*, but it was fairly obvious that it wasn't a sanctioned – or known about – burial.

The Beast, showing no reticence despite his sadness and maybe exhibiting a touch of anger, reached into the trench and carefully pulled the body out. As it twisted towards the floor, a knife could plainly be seen sticking out of his sternum.

Belle steadied herself.

"Murder," she whispered. "Plain, simple murder."

The Beast eyed the body speculatively. "Not simple," he finally said. "Stabbed from the front. Either a second person held his arms behind him, to keep him from fighting, or… he was killed by someone he knew. And didn't expect it."

Belle knelt by the body, mind whirling. She still couldn't tell if this was the rider from her vision. "What kind of knife is that?" she asked.

With less delicacy than she would have liked, the Beast pulled the metal thing out of Alaric's body.

He held it up, frowning. It was much longer and narrower than any sort of hunting, eating or other everyday knife. The entire thing – even the handle – was metal. The butt, at the end of the grip, was almost as thin as wire, and bent in a heart shape.

"Strange," the Beast said.

Belle narrowed her eyes. "It looks more like a surgeon's instrument than a knife. I've read Joseph Charrière's book on surgery – this looks like something out of that."

"Why read a book on *surgery*?" the Beast asked in distaste.

Belle shrugged. "It was the only new book at the bookshop last winter. I had nothing else to read. I wonder what it means. Was he killed by a doctor, or a doctor's assistant? Was it something he used on the horses?"

"I don't think so," the Beast said. "I don't think anything he did with the horses required anything that delicate."

Belle frowned. "Is there anything else on him that might help us out?"

The Beast's expression was unreadable. This was, she reminded herself, his favourite servant, even if he did as a child think of servants as being of a different class than kings and queens. But he must have seen the logic in her suggestion, and so he began to pat down the body, looking for anything else that might be a clue.

His eyes grew large as his claws tapped against something unexpected under the cloth of the tattered jacket. With claws extended like pincers, he pulled out what looked like a little leather-bound booklet.

Belle hastened over to his side and used her more nimble fingers to gently take it from him. She opened it slowly; its pages were beginning to fall out from dampness and rot.

"What does it say?" the Beast asked eagerly.

" 'June 4th'," she read carefully, turning to a random page. " 'Clarissa's a sweet one, but not overblessed in the department of fidelity. Sadly, not marriage material, though pleasant enough to look upon.' Ah, this is a… rather personal journal."

The Beast shrugged uncomfortably. "Keep reading."

" 'June 21st. Champion has a small abscess in his right hind leg, beneath the knee. Worried about it. All the good animal-speakers are gone… A poultice and charm from Baldrick would have fixed the poor boy right up. What to do?' "

"Horses," the Beast said with a gentle smile. "Just as important as women."

"Only for *him.* Let's see what the last entry is," Belle said, trying to sound pragmatic, not miffed. " 'August 10th.

All of the horses miserable – I know the quarantine is for the best, but I'm afraid for their sanity. I'll have to take a different one out tonight when I go to M's.'

"I wonder what 'M's' is," Belle said thoughtfully. "Whatever it is, it must be a horse-ride away."

"Is there anything about who his killer is?" the Beast asked impatiently.

"No, it doesn't say, 'Oh no, I hear my own murderer sneaking up the stairs, and he is revealing himself to be…!' "

"There aren't any stairs in the stable."

"You know what I mean. There doesn't seem to be any hint of mischief at all," she said, flipping pages. "The last pages seem to be just lists… and names of people… and places… North Country Road? South Boulder Bypass? River Run?"

"Those are the names of all the major roads in and out of the kingdom," the Beast said, reading over her shoulder. He tapped a claw at the columns of information. "I recognise some of those names… they were captains of the guards. These are lists of who was guarding which border crossing and when."

"That seems like an odd thing for a stablemaster to be interested in – unless he was smuggling," Belle said thoughtfully. She flipped further back in the book. " 'May 16th. Found a goblin-kith hiding in the hayloft.

Poor thing – a bunch of hooligans almost got her, so she tried to run away through the woods – but the border patrol turned her back. Violently. What do I do?

"'June 17th. Goblin-kith still here. People are starting to get suspicious. If word reached the king and queen... or any of them... that I was harbouring a *charmante*, who knows what would happen to me. Or her. Been sneaking her stuff from the kitchen, thanks to B's generosity and discretion.' B?" Belle asked, confused.

"Beatrice," the Beast supplied. "Mrs Beatrice Potts."

"Oh. *Beatrice*." Belle repeated the name and thought of the teapot, trying to make the human image match the porcelain one. It was hard. She went back to reading.

"'June 18th. I think I have a plan. After midnight I'll take the goblin-kith on the back of one of the bigger mounts to M's place, on the other side of the river. Either I'll try one of the old hunting paths or find out if there's a sympathetic guard on the western road. I'm sure M and his wife will help out.'..."

"He was helping the *charmantes* escape," the Beast said thoughtfully.

"But is that enough to be *murdered* for? Even by the most crazy, anti-magic person? Helping *one charmante*?"

She skipped back a few more pages, moving her finger along the text.

"'February 27th. My Wedding Day! I am going to be happy for the rest of my life with B, and hopefully she will make me a bit fatter, too!'"

"I remember that," the Beast said softly. "Everyone in the castle – I mean, all of the servants – were so happy for them. There was cake and champagne and I managed to sneak out and see a little bit of it."

"'Wish M and all had been there. They sent a rose somehow – a beautiful white one that smelled like heaven. I couldn't tell B or anyone directly that it was probably magic, of course. But I did tell her to keep it safe in her drawers.'"

Belle's eyes widened.

"Magic rose? *M's* place? It's… *Maurice.* M is for Maurice! Alaric brought the goblin to M's place on the *other side of the woods. My* place! My home! And I never *noticed* this?"

"You were a child. It was at night. Your parents kept you safe, separate from it," the Beast ventured.

Belle rubbed her forehead. Her mother, who had abandoned her and laid curses on 11-year-olds, at risk to herself and family, sheltered and provided escape for a poor creature fleeing persecution. Why was she so complicated? Why couldn't she have just been… *all* good, like a fairy godmother in a story, or *all bad*, like a witch?

She flipped back to the previous entry she had read.

"'People are starting to get suspicious. If word reached… any of them… who knows what would happen to me. Or them. I'm putting R and her family in danger…'"

The Beast looked at the corpse sceptically.

"It does seem unlikely that someone killed him because he saved one person…"

Belle shrugged. "Yes, I don't know. But my mother's disappearance… his disappearance… They knew each other, they *worked* together on this… and she warned me about *betrayal*."

The Beast raised an eyebrow. "Maybe *he* betrayed her. And *she* killed him."

"I don't think someone who curses an entire castle and animates plant statues is going to resort to sticking someone with a knife," Belle said dryly. "But if you're right about him being murdered by someone he *knew*, then it was possibly someone who also knew my mother and father. Someone who betrayed all three of them."

The Beast scruffled the back of his neck with a giant paw, his usual gesture when he was embarrassed or stumped.

"How does that help us find your mother?" he asked.

"I don't know," Belle admitted. "But it certainly changes the way things look – for me."

Maybe her mother didn't abandon them. Maybe her mother was *murdered* – or otherwise disappeared – and taken away from them. Belle felt a funny pain in her body melt, a tiny thread of resentment she hadn't realised she had had all those years. When she said, "It was fine, just Papa and me," she never realised how defensive she was being.

But her mother had never meant to leave her.

"If your mother is dead now, can we break the curse?" the Beast asked, trying to put it gently.

"I don't know. I really don't know."

She sighed and continued flipping through the journal, looking for clues.

"Listen to this: 'April 3rd. Today I am a father. Charlemagne Alistair Potts, born healthy and screaming his wee head off this morning! B is fine, healthy as one of my horses. Just think! Someday he and M's little lass could meet… I like older women, maybe my little Charles will, too!' "

She looked at the Beast expectantly. He looked, as usual, confused.

"*Chip*," she said. "Charles is *Chip*."

"Yes," the Beast said, still not understanding the depth of her reaction.

"We would have been the same age. Almost," she said impatiently. "He is five now – five forever. He was five at the time of the curse, ten years ago. He would be only really a few years younger than I am. If he aged normally. If he wasn't a… teacup."

"Oh," the Beast said, thinking about it. "Yes, he would be fifteen. Maybe my manservant. Unless he left to seek his fortune. He… never got to do that." The Beast shivered, a strange movement from him, usually so controlled until he had a rage. Sorrow filled his large eyes.

They remained silent for a moment in the half-light of the stable, staring into space, or at the dead man's journal, or at nothing at all.

After a moment Belle and the Beast turned to look at each other, at the same time, both obviously thinking the same thing.

"We have to go back. And tell Mrs Potts," Belle said gently.

"I would rather stay out here. Forever," the Beast said honestly. "I could… catch mice, maybe…"

"Perhaps it will be easier for her now, *knowing* what happened to her husband," Belle said with a sigh. Her papa had been a pallbearer and gravedigger at more than one funeral in the village. Although a social outcast, he was also considered a decent, strong-backed person who could be counted on to do what was required. Even in the modern, enlightened world of the 18th century, death and sadness and bearing bad tidings were a part of everyday life.

Belle took the Beast's arm and they walked slowly and sadly back to the castle.

TO SLEEP

The funeral was simple and sad. The Beast insisted Alaric be buried in the cemetery reserved for royalty, with a headstone remarking on what a brave and selfless man he was. All of the castle occupants stood round while an animated secretary, once a real secretary, gave the service. Many members of the staff, including Cogsworth and Lumière, got up and said a few words, praising the quality of Alaric's character and some of his more charming habits.

Despite a certain dustmaid's disgust with the stable-master's charity to one of *les charmantes*, she remained silent and pious. Belle eyed her suspiciously. Alaric had been murdered and her mother had said something about *betrayal*. While the dustmaid seemed harmless in her little prejudices, who knew what she had been like before she was all feathers…

A light snow fell, but only Belle could feel it. She looked across the strange crowd of creatures, all of whom had tried to decorate themselves with a little bit of black: a dresser wore a black doily; Cogsworth and Lumière tied black ribands round their narrower parts.

Mrs Potts wore a black cosy. She looked sad and brave with her boy, Chip, cuddled beneath her, confused and plaintive. It had been over a decade since his father had passed away; the man was merely legend or myth in the child's mind. He only knew something terrible and final had occurred to someone he was supposed to have loved.

It had taken the Beast's strength to break through frozen ground and dig down below where the earth was still soft; it was he who had to lower the hastily built coffin down into the pit. From there everyone took turns throwing in a handful of dirt as best as he or she or it could. Finally, the old gardener and his implements took over.

Mrs Potts lingered, taking a last look at the grave while everyone else filed past her to go in. Chip had already rushed on ahead with the other children, only understanding that the strange, terrible and solemn thing was over. Belle knelt in the snow in front of her.

"I am so, so sorry."

I have been saying that so often recently, she couldn't help observing sadly.

"No, child, it really is for the best that you found him," the teapot said, shaking her spout but still keeping it directed at the grave. "My mind can rest a bit now... now that I know what really happened to him. And such a hero! I always suspected, you know," she added confidentially. "He was always having me make up and steal little packets of food from the kitchen. But he never told me outright. Didn't want me or Chip getting into trouble if anything happened, I'll wager."

"It might have saved your life," Belle agreed. She and the Beast had decided not to show her the knife just yet; they would wait for a day or two while the poor woman recovered from the shock of her dead husband suddenly being found.

"It's just..." Mrs Potts trailed off helplessly. "It's just... part of me had always *hoped*, just a little, that maybe he had just... I don't know, disappeared with *les charmantes*. Kidnapped by some sort of pretty elf queen or something to the Summer Lands. That he was still alive, somewhere, and could come back some day..."

She shook herself.

Belle turned her head to wipe away a tear; it wasn't for *her*, after all, to show high emotion at this funeral. This was for Mrs Potts.

"I wonder what he would have been turned into, if he

had lived," the little teapot said thoughtfully. "A horsewhip? He never liked using them. A bridle, maybe, or a talking horseshoe – there's a funny image..."

She hopped back into the castle, shaking her head and murmuring to herself. Belle and the Beast were last to go in.

The eerie webbing had made good strides in overcoming the wall. Thick white runners criss-crossed over and under the snow across the courtyards, almost visibly eager to attack the castle itself. In places it had already begun to scale the sides, like a ghostly winter ivy.

Thinner bits of the strands ran between the main lines, supporting or strengthening them, like leaded glass. Sometimes the enclosed spaces formed by these intersections glittered exactly like glass and if the sun wasn't directly on them, they showed strange images. Each was a little slice of memory from the Enchantress, repeating over and over. Picking a rose. Casting a spell. Pouring the last of too many glasses of wine...

Belle let out a breath which she hadn't even realised she had been holding. The castle was, in a way, a living monument to the person her mother had been. Her presence infiltrated the entire place.

Belle watched, both fascinated and beginning to panic.

"It's like... my mirror..." the Beast said, his voice full of wonder – and horror. "Someone *else's* mirror."

"The webs are everywhere now. There's no stopping them," Belle whispered.

The Beast couldn't hide the look of despair that flicked across his face, adding to all the other sad and dark emotions of the day.

The two just looked at each other, wordlessly, and went in.

A light coating of snow covered both of them by then; the Beast shook himself like a dog, starting with his enormous head and then working down his neck and his chest and finally his lower half. Belle almost smiled at the light moment in an otherwise very dark day.

She hung her own cloak up on a hook. That one act seemed to take the rest of the energy out of her. She slumped against the wall, feeling like maybe it wouldn't be so bad to get pulled down into the silent, cold earth. There was nothing but misery and sadness for this terrible land – and maybe for her as well.

The Beast ran his paws through his mane in frustration. But there was nothing *beastly* about it… it was pure human. "So maybe your mother was also murdered, or something, and maybe it had something to do with Alaric. And saving the *charmantes*. But how…?"

Belle gave him a tired look. She noticed that his eyes looked raw and red.

"I think it might be time for a break. A short one," she

said, thinking. "You're at the end of your rope and frankly, so am I. We're just… going round in circles with the same thoughts."

But what to do? What *did* people do when they were trapped in an enchanted castle, terrified and dispirited, exhausted and out of ideas? Drink? Throw a party? Torture prisoners? Play cards?

She couldn't see the Beast liking, or agreeing to, any of that.

What did *she* do when she was down?

"Let's go back to the library. I think it's time for a book."

The Beast made a noise that sounded somewhere between an angry goat and a foghorn of doom.

"No, no," Belle said with a gentle smile, "*I'll* read to *you*. A story. Something to cheer us up. One of my favourites."

"It'd better be a good one," the Beast said grudgingly. "With a… a happy ending."

"You're in luck. It *is* a good one, with a happy ending. *Jack and the Beanstalk*. It's about a poor boy overcoming almost insurmountable odds, defeating a giant and living happily ever after!"

"What did the giant do to deserve getting defeated?" he demanded with a pout.

"It was a bad giant. Not like you at all. Come on!"

Someone must have heard her plan. When they got to the library, it looked like furniture was magically gliding across the floor by itself – which was entirely possible in this enchanted castle – but on closer inspection, Cogsworth and Lumière were pushing a couple of chaises and fainting couches together in front of the fire so she and the Beast could sit next to each other comfortably.

"Thank you," Belle said, more than a little suspicious of their otherwise helpful and innocent motivations. "I think we, uh, just need a little quiet time now."

"But of course, *ma chérie*," Lumière said with a bow. His flames waggled yellow. He turned to exchange a look with Cogsworth.

The little clock laughed nervously. "Of course. Just trying to make you and the master comfortable. If you need anything… we might not be available."

Belle and the Beast both blinked in surprise.

"We are arranging a little wake for the staff," Lumière explained. "If you don't mind. A fitting end for a man who enjoyed a good time."

"Of course," the Beast said gruffly. "I understand. Please open the wine cellar, with my compliments."

Lumière's flames waggled for a moment; perhaps it was his equivalent of blinking in surprise.

"Thank you, your grace," Cogsworth said swiftly, with

a bow.

Just as he dragged Lumière out through the door, Chip and a number of his little cup friends came scooting in, in a hastily arranged phalanx. They dragged the coverlet from the study with them – not noticing, in their enthusiasm, that it had unfolded and spilled out behind them.

They didn't look tired or drawn from the funeral; then again, they were teacups.

"Thank you," Belle said politely, picking up the quilt.

"Mama said you would like it, but she's busy. Are you going to marry him?" Chip asked. Loudly.

A couple of the other teacups sniggered and clicked their handles together.

"We've only just met," Belle managed, deciding it was the most politic thing to say. *Plus, you know, he's a beast.* She wondered what Père Colbert would say about such a union.

With a gentle swoosh of her hands, she bade the army of teacups go.

"Good night!" she said. "And thank you!"

"Awww," Chip moaned. "We want to hear a story, too!"

"We'll be quiet," another one piped up. Possibly a girl? It was hard to tell. She looked exactly like all the others. "We'll hop up on the table. Please?"

Belle looked at the little creatures. What a peculiar

scene – as white as eggs, all straining at her in ways porcelain just shouldn't. Dishware begging for a night-time story.

"Please," Chip said quietly. "I can't sleep. I'm sad. My papa died."

Belle felt her heart physically wrench. Even if Chip didn't know exactly what he was talking about... even if he was just using it as an excuse...

"All right. Just... try to settle down and be quiet, *d'accord*?"

"We will!" Chip promised.

Giggling and making little tinkling noises on the floor, the teacups scurried over to the marble-topped occasional table. There was a pretty woven and quilted hot pad on it, which they carefully arranged themselves on like a pile of puppies bedding down for the night.

Belle shook her head and stepped lightly over to where she thought she remembered the Myths and Legends of the World section was. Jack was an English fairy tale... the shelf for stories from that part of the world fairly sagged under their weight. She pulled out a likely looking leather-bound and portfolio-sized book with gold lettering on its spine, and lovely – if monotone – engraved illustrations on almost every page. There were many Jack stories in this one, she realised with a skipped heartbeat. Not just her favourite.

More Jack stories!

Was there no end to the wonders of this enchanted castle?

She took the book – and the one next to it, for later – and the quilt, still on the floor, over to where the sofas were set up. With a graceful turn she managed to plump herself right in the middle of the extra-wide space, and flung the coverlet over her.

It was devilishly comfortable there in front of the fire and under the warm quilt. The heat of the Beast also pressed up against her, though he chivalrously pulled his legs as far back as they would go, tucking them under his haunches like a dog, his arms resting, crossed, on the armrest – also like a dog.

"This is nice," the Beast said with a sigh. "Like… one of those paintings where a nymph or Athena is reading to the gods and goddesses."

"And here I was thinking you were an utterly uneducated beast," Belle said teasingly.

"I am a *prince*," he responded with hauteur. "I am *classically educated*.

"Plus, nymphs are pretty," he added.

Belle laughed.

"I could stare at them all day," he continued. His tone was carefully neutral, but his eyes never left hers.

And Belle found she could look back. And not blush.

And not have to look away.

Snow was still falling lightly outside. The cups were making more little tinkling noises as they shifted and waited for her to begin. It was very cosy.

She opened the book and began.

"'Once upon a time…'"

KIDNAPPING

Maurice was struggling a little in the woods. He was not as young as he once was, and he hadn't had a moment's rest for what seemed like days. Phillipe, who had shown up in his pen like nothing had ever happened, steadfastly refused to go anywhere. The horse was done with adventures, that much was obvious, even when Maurice tried to pull him along and yelled.

So the inventor marched through the cold, dark forest alone, a small lantern hanging from a stick held before him and a pack of useful things on his back – a very strange and lonely Father Christmas making his way through the dark. In it were ropes and hooks and gunpowder and what little money he had, everything he could think of to either bribe the Beast or help Belle escape secretly. He would literally scale the walls of the place to get her back, if he needed to.

Sometimes in the night, strange thoughts came to him. Like he had somehow taken this path before – besides the one time accidentally, on his way to the fair. And he kept expecting guards, or border patrols, or something… which was silly; this was deep forest and there was no one around for miles.

"*Maurice?*"

The inventor stopped in his tracks.

"There's no one around for miles," he repeated to himself.

He turned round slowly, swinging the lantern to look.

Against all probabilities, there were Gaston and LeFou holding a much larger lantern. LeFou looked miserable in the cold, Gaston like he didn't notice it at all.

"Gaston!" Belle's father cried in relief. "You came after all! How did you find me?"

The larger hunter grinned generously. "You lead us on a merry chase, Maurice. We thought you'd be home on such a cold winter's night. So then I checked the bookshop…"

At this LeFou seemed to deflate, shrinking into himself in either exhaustion, embarrassment or horror – or a strange mix of all three.

"But you weren't there, either. So I tracked you, Maurice. I tracked you like the skilled hunter I am." Gaston grinned and patted the sack and the club he carried over one shoulder.

"Well, this is great!" Maurice said. "I'm sure with you along, we can absolutely subdue the Beast. Er, where's your gun?"

"Yes, 'subdue the Beast'." Gaston laughed, too loudly. "You really are a riot, Maurice. Why don't you make it easy on all of us and just come quietly?"

"Come quietly...?"

Finally, Maurice began to read the situation as it really was: LeFou looking nervous, Gaston looking triumphant, the presence of the sack and the lack of firepower. He began to back away. "No... he's real, Gaston. I'm not making it up. Maybe it's a crazy man in a beast suit... but whatever it is, he has Belle. You *have* to help me!"

"I may not be able to, but Monsieur D'Arque hopefully will. And by helping you, he will be helping *me*," Gaston said, reaching for him, "to get *Belle*."

"*D'Arque?*"

Before he was knocked unconscious, Maurice's mind went to a funny place. It was unthinkable that D'Arque would have anything to do with this. Because...

Because...

... but he couldn't quite remember. And then it was all black.

A LEAD

Belle had strange dreams of their pet dog. Maurice was smiling happily, glad he had finally managed to provide his daughter with some sort of companion. She had found an old, brightly coloured bit of wool and carefully sewed it into a charming collar. The little mutt jumped and ran and grabbed sticks and panted and Belle, so young in the dream, clapped her chubby white hands in delight and gave it a big hug, rubbing her face in its fur.

As the night slowly let its vine-like grips off her subconscious, Belle wondered at first what happened to the family dog. She missed it.

Then she remembered that they never had a dog.

Then she realised she was lying next to a giant dog.

Then she realised it was the Beast, actually.

At some point, by the third or fourth Jack story maybe, both of them must have drifted off. She remembered the Beast's eyes being bright and open one moment, then snapping shut like a book the next. No fluttering, no fighting sleep or gently succumbing to it. Awake, then asleep, like a wild animal.

Belle was mildly shocked to have fallen asleep so quickly herself, her feet pressed comfortably up against his toasty side. The smell of fur – not bad or unclean, just *strong* – permeated the quilt.

No wonder she had dreamed about a dog.

On the table nearby, the little teacups were gently breathing and snoring, moving very little. It was ridiculously adorable – Belle didn't think she had ever seen anything so sweet and strange.

Maybe being trapped here forever, forgotten, wouldn't be so bad. Maybe they would have endless tea parties and sleepovers and story time until she was an old lady and the Beast's fur went grey. There were worse ways to spend a life…

The Beast turned and shifted, his massive size picking up a corner of the blanket and pulling the whole thing off Belle in one accidental tug. He wriggled his shoulders and then yawned… a large, horrible, nearly endless noise that stretched from his mouth until it felt like it could have consumed cities.

Belle drew back, a little nonplussed.

Eyes still closed, he gave himself a good scratch and then stretched out. But as soon as one of his great toes met her leg his eyes popped open.

The look he gave her was so surprised and chagrined she almost fell over laughing.

"*Wh–*" he began.

Belle put a finger to her lips and pointed at the teacups.

He raised a shaggy eyebrow, still a little stupid from sleep, and then nodded, suddenly understanding.

"I hadn't realised I..." he whispered, scratching the back of his neck in embarrassment. "I must have... drifted off."

"That's all right," Belle whispered back with a smile.

"It was a good story!" he protested, trying to keep his voice low. "I, I wasn't bored! It was just so comfy, and I was so sad earlier, and the fire was nice..."

"No, it's fine," Belle said, smiling. "I take it as a compliment."

They were both silent for a moment.

Suddenly it got awkward.

Belle pulled her legs closer to her in a move that was supposed to look like she was casually adjusting her dress and stretching her toes.

The Beast sat stiffly upright as if yelled at by a posture

coach, quickly putting his hind paws on the floor.

He tapped the armrest speculatively.

"We were… ah… sleeping here all night?" he ventured.

"No, just a few hours, I think."

"Huh," the Beast said cryptically.

The little cups, finally disturbed by the noise the grown-ups were making around them, began to push off each other and roll and smack whatever passed for their lips. It was like watching a cuddle of baby kittens or chicks stir awake.

"Just one more…" Chip said sleepily through a yawn.

Belle laughed. "It's time to go to bed," she said gently.

"Noooo!" he groaned.

"My mum's gonna *kill* me!" one of the other teacups swore.

As if summoned by thought, the library door creaked open as Mrs Potts herself came in. If Belle didn't know better, she would have thought the housekeeper was listening at the door. She no longer wore the black cosy but had a little mourning ribbon tied round her handle.

"All right, Chip, the sleepover is *over*," she said firmly. "Time to come over for your real bed."

"This was great, Mum!" Chip said, dancing up and down. Belle leaned forward, afraid he would throw himself off the table. "Can we do it again?"

"And can Belle read us a story again?" one of the other

cups begged. They hopped to the edge of the table and single-file, like little ducklings, hopped down, each landing with a *clink* on the floor. They were all perfectly used to this sort of thing, but Belle felt like she died a little bit each time one made the leap.

"She's very, very busy, doing important work," Mrs Potts chastised. "It was very nice of her to let you listen in but don't think you'll be making a habit out of it or anything. Off you go!"

Belle smiled. "It's all right. I'd love to read them a bedtime story now and then. They were a perfectly wonderful audience."

"Oh, I'll bet they were," Mrs Potts said, sounding like she believed precisely the opposite. "I'll send in some tea and a midnight snack… or a *petit déjeuner*, or whatever you'd like in a minute. All served on much quieter dinnerware," she promised. But as she left her movements seemed slow and awkward. Tired. Like she was running down.

"That was nice of you," the Beast said after she was gone.

"They're delightful," Belle said, sighing. "I wish I had a dozen of them at home."

"Children?" the Beast said, eyes wide and eyebrows high.

"*Talking teacups.*"

"Oh. Right. Of course. Sure." The Beast relaxed.

Then his look turned pensive. "I guess we're kind of like one of your stories, right? With the harp that talked?"

"I guess you are," Belle said thoughtfully. She had one chilling moment where she wondered if she was *still* dreaming. If the dog was real and the Beast was not. If she had fallen asleep with one of her books and hadn't quite pulled herself out of sleep yet, living out her fantasies as if they were real.

Nope, that fur smells pretty strong. She didn't think she could make that up.

"I liked that first one the best," the Beast went on to say, a little shyly. "The one that *you* liked. About the giant. You were right, he *did* deserve to be defeated."

"Yes, that's my absolute favourite," Belle said with a sigh. "Always has been, ever since I was a little girl and my father told it to me. In his version, though, the talking harp was a clockwork invention. From the time I was old enough to read I was always in Monsieur Lévi's bookshop… and he was always kind enough to let me borrow it, never made me buy it…"

The Beast's eyebrows shot up in surprise.

"What did you say?"

"He never made me buy it. I was the only one in town who loved books as much as he did, and…"

"No, no," the Beast shook his head impatiently.

"The name of the man. The bookseller."

"Monsieur Lévi...?" Belle repeated, puzzled.

"That sounds very familiar."

He dug down in between the sofa cushions, pausing to swear when threads became caught on his claws. He threw the coverlet aside on the floor, Belle would have to talk to him about that at some point, but not now, obviously, and searched more frantically. Then he looked *under* the sofa and triumphantly pulled out one of the census books.

"I saw it... in *here*, I think... Here it is!" the Beast said with triumph. He spun the book round so she could see and tapped at an entry with his claw.

Belle gasped.

Next to an entry labelled Monsieur David Lévi was *occupation: bookseller*. And there was a little symbol next to his name.

"But there's nothing magical about him..." Her voice trailed off as she saw when the entry was dated.

Over a hundred years ago. One hundred and *ten* years before this year, in fact.

"My Monsieur Lévi is some sort of immortal being who has been selling books for over a hundred years?"

"Looks like," the Beast said.

"If he's been around for that long, and he's one of *les charmantes*," Belle said, getting excited, "I'll bet he knew my mother – and can remember her!"

The Beast frowned. "What makes you think that?"

"At its height your parents' – ah, I mean *your* kingdom – wasn't *huge*," she said excitedly, holding up one of the record books. "It looks like there were only three thousand 'heads of household' recorded. You have to think that *les charmantes* would have been a small percentage of that and they probably all knew each other. Plus he somehow magically ends up living in the same village as my mother? That's too coincidental."

"Good point," the Beast said, nodding. "You know him closely, right?"

"He's only my favourite person in the whole world besides Papa."

"And he still lives in your village?"

"Yes."

"We need to go and talk to him, then."

Belle looked out of the library's window – dramatically and ironically. White webbing now crossed it. "Remember, um, *that*? We're prisoners here."

"What would Jack do, Belle?"

When did he *become the insightful one?*

She mock pouted. "I suppose he would figure out some super clever way around it."

The Beast looked at her with wry amusement.

"Since you're the clever one here and haven't come up with a cunning plan, I was going to suggest brute force. Like we're a castle under siege, fighting them off. That's what *I* know."

"That's a fair point," she ceded, smiling.

"We should… round up everything sharp and cutting," he said. "And hammers and mallets to smash the panes between them."

"Yes, sir, prince general, sir," Belle said, saluting him with a sparkle in her eye.

It made sense to try and leave through the gates that Belle had originally come through; they unlatched inwards so at least they wouldn't have to be broken through first.

But throwing them open revealed a beautiful – if disturbingly solid – obstacle: a faceted wall of crystal and ivory, ice and bone.

Some of the panes showed more scenes of her mother, and Belle was hypnotised by them at first. A particularly intriguing one was of her standing in front of a mirror and magically adjusting her hair colour and outfit colour, cocking her head to see how it looked.

"That's… so… not like me," Belle breathed.

But if she *had* a fancy glass and the power to change the way she looked on a whim, would she?

Most of the castle's staff had gathered in the courtyard to watch and help: a strange collection of objects, furniture and bric-a-brac scattered on the snowy ground. Some wore tatters of cloth like scarves, hearkening back to when they were human. Lumière and Mrs Potts stood together, out of the way; the little candelabrum had an arm held comfortingly round her rounded middle. A pile of potentially useful and inanimate ancient weaponry lay nearby.

The Beast howled and threw himself at the biggest, most fragile-looking pane in the webbing. There was a strange noise like a gong as the material bowed with his weight and then immediately straightened again.

The Beast flung himself at the window a second time, claws out to try and scratch it.

The noise that made caused Belle and everyone watching to cover their ears and shriek to drown out the terrible sound.

"War hammer," the Beast ordered.

Cogsworth directed a whole phalanx of little creatures to run forwards and hand him the ancient thing.

With a mighty cry like a titan of old, the Beast took and swung the hammer round his head three times before letting it crash into the pane.

Something happened.

Little cracks and rivulets appeared, jagged and strange, all over the crystalline sheet but not like ice or anything else natural. It started and stopped and branched out in ways that fooled the eye. In each new shard that was formed as a result of the subdividing, a new scene from Belle's mother's memory appeared. Sometimes it was the same memory, off by a fraction of a second, or from a slightly different point of view.

The Beast roared, raised the hammer, and hit it again.

A grating, splintering sound tinkled through the air. More cracks appeared.

The shards shattered into more shards.

Each, Belle suddenly noticed, was framed by a quickly growing white border of webbing.

"Wait!" she cried out, grabbing his arm and stopping him before he hit again.

He paused, confused.

"It's just reinforcing itself," she said, pointing. "Every time you smash it!"

Indeed it was true: the bone-white runners snaked along all of the broken pieces, thickening at junctions and throwing out more threads to protect what was left.

The Beast howled in rage and threw the hammer down. Everyone flinched. "Cogsworth, get the suits of armour," Belle ordered.

"Right away!" The little clock waddled off. Almost immediately the suits came marching through, in a way that would have terrified Belle if she hadn't known better. These had probably been palace guards before they were turned – even if they were unnatural golems now.

"All right. Beast – as soon as you hit it, step out of the way," Belle ordered. "As soon as he's done, one of you rush forwards and lunge, striking the glass – or whatever it is – straight on with the tip of your sword, to knock it out. Go!"

The courtyard soon sounded with a strange, regular, mechanical tone: the *whoomph bang* of the war hammer, the metallic tap of a sword point slamming into the place he had just hit. It was all as precise and perfect as a cuckoo clock from the Black Forest.

The first shard popped out and landed on the snowy ground beyond the gates.

Lumière, Cogsworth and Mrs Potts cheered.

"Keep it going!" Belle ordered. "Faster!"

The suits of armour moved more quickly now, the last one who struck quickly marching out of the way to the back of the line while the next one hit.

The Beast huffed and grunted. Something that was either drool or sweat flew off his head as he swung the hammer.

More shards popped out. More threads grew back, but they were weak and thin and frangible, like spun sugar.

They would only have a few seconds to push themselves through before the way was barred again. Belle made sure she was ready. She was wearing the fur-trimmed robe –

it had made the wardrobe so happy when she took it – and held tight to a giant hooded cloak for the Beast and a satchel of supplies, including the magic mirror.

The Beast bared his teeth and growled, slamming all of his strength into the window.

There was a strange slowing down of time; Belle saw the hammer connect to the jagged teeth and white threads that made up what was now a lacey pane – then, suddenly, the face of the hammer was through, and there was a noise like an explosion, like a bonfire gone bad, like a cannon had ripped through the courtyard. Crystals and sticky bits of cold white twigs flew everywhere and cut where they landed.

"*NOW!*" Lumière cried.

Shielding her face with her arm, Belle dived through the hole. The jagged shards sliced through her clothing and the cold immediately moved in where blood began to seep out.

She rolled out of the way on the hard ground as fast as she could. The Beast was right behind her. With a roar that echoed through the whole pine valley he crashed through like a demon madly destroying a stained-glass window in a church.

Unlike her, he landed on all four feet, and immediately shook off the bits of crystal and webbing that came with him.

Belle turned to look back: the bone-white webs were

growing faster than ever, making terrible little slithery noises in the stone and snow. Almost like they were angry about the breach. As she watched, Cogsworth, Lumière and Mrs Potts became blurry and dim when the panes re-formed themselves. Lumière gave a little wave that she could just see because of the flame at the end of his arm.

"*Good luck!*" she heard them call.

And then all was silent. Snow was falling again.

Belle stood up and adjusted her pack, trying not to be overwhelmed with how utterly sad the scene before her was. She, the one who brought down the curse, had now escaped, leaving everyone inside to their fate. She could run away now if she wanted, she could run as far as she could, to Paris even, and pretend none of this had ever happened. And because of the curse, it *would* be like it never happened. She could forget the kingdom had ever existed.

She waved, hoping the little creatures sealed inside the glass-and-bone chrysalis could see her, and tried not to cry.

The Beast saw her.

"I'll come back. Whatever happens," he promised. "I'm... king now. I need to share the fate of my people."

Somehow that only made Belle want to cry more.

"You aren't out of danger yourself," the Beast reminded her gravely. "You're in the middle of the woods with a beast as the curse grows stronger. I won't be able to control it forever."

Belle had a sudden vision of her body, and blood-stained snow, like something out of a fairy tale gone wrong. She shook her head.

"No. You would *never* hurt me."

The Beast gave a wan smile… and then leaned over and kissed her on the forehead.

"I would kill *myself* first," he whispered.

The two began to walk silently though the falling snow, their tracks back to the castle covered up like an icy wave over the sand.

REUNION

The prisoner sagged on the operating table, waiting for her next session.

Of the many, many thoughts that she had lost over the years, to time, to darkness, to pain, at least one remained: *why?*

He had actually managed to accomplish quite a bit of what he set out to do initially, using every physical 'remedy' he could think of. He injected her blood with iron. He opened her belly and placed lodestones there. He made his knives very sharp and cut open her head and tried to root around for the source of her power. He forced draughts down her throat that he insisted weren't *potions* but scientifically formulated elixirs guaranteed to grab the magic and render it inactive.

Through trial and error, through hints gleaned from elsewhere – i.e., *more* torture, of others – he had done what hadn't been achieved since the Dark Ages.

He had removed almost all of her magic.

She could feel it. Couldn't *he*, with his instruments and devices, his measuring callipers and graduated beakers, see it as well?

With a week's time and all her strength, she might, just might, be able to turn her hair colour. Or fix a single feather on the broken wing of a sparrow. Or enchant a cup of tea to stop a consumptive's cough for an hour or so.

There was almost no major transformative magic left in her, and no death magic to begin with. She wasn't an illusionist.

He had won.

So why was he still doing it?

There was a commotion somewhere in the dark; muffled screams and thuds, the pounding of boots thrusting back against some surprisingly limber and angry captive.

When she had first been kidnapped, years ago, people were brought in every week, sometimes several at a time. Some didn't even merit torture. They were brought down through the dungeon door, past all the cells and through the black door at the end of the hall, never to be seen again, never to be brought to the same prep room or same operating tables she was. But these days new victims were rare.

The noise of the fight came closer. Fleshy, softened thunks and thuds seemed to indicate this victim wasn't going along quietly.

"Villains! Ruffians!" he swore.

Her heart froze.

She *knew* that voice.

The prisoner strained to turn her head as far as the plate holding her neck would let her go, to look through the open door. She could see, despite every part of her praying for it *not* to be – and a tiny, selfish part of her wishing it was – a stout middle-aged man, straining and struggling among the three hooded thugs who sought to drag him in.

He had barely aged at all in the years since she had seen him. His hair was all grey now, to be sure, but his cheeks were as ruddy and round as they ever were.

With a gasp that scraped her lungs raw, she realised he even still had those rounded marks round his eyes from the ridiculous ugly goggles he always wore.

One of the thugs landed a solid knee in Maurice's side. He went slack, all the breath knocked out of him. As he tried to recover his head lolled to the side. And then he saw her.

His look was one of slowly dawning horror.

But not, she realised after a heartbreaking moment, one of recognition.

He didn't know his own wife. The matted, dried blood in the wreck of her hair, the scars on her brow and her gaunt cheeks made a mask of her ruined face. Her body, limp and twisted from the dreadful labours exercised upon it in this terrible prison… none of it was familiar.

Also, there was that stupid *forget* spell she had enacted to protect her family.

She felt a sob beginning in her dry, empty bosom.

"Maurice," she croaked one last time, as loudly as she could.

His eyes widened.

"*Rosalind?*" he murmured.

Then his face went red in a mask of rage and fury.

"*ROSALIND!*"

He thrust out with arms that were thick from picking up heavy pieces of metal and machinery. He kicked with legs used to pushing carts stacked with bricks and ingots when Phillipe wouldn't cooperate.

Whirling like a berserker, Maurice broke free and crawled into the operating room, to Rosalind.

He didn't waste a moment touching her cheek gently or tenderly stroking her brow; he immediately put his meaty hands round the bar that held her neck down and began to try and pry it off.

For just a moment Rosalind wondered if she wasn't

dreaming again. Like she used to when she was first thrown into the dungeon; when in the dark her fantasies became real and she could have sworn that she was actually with Maurice and Belle again and her cell was nothing but a nightmare.

The tiny details she observed while he tried to free her proved reality, however. There was a scar by his left eye that hadn't been there the last time she had seen him. Was his hair a little thinner up front? And maybe there was an extra kilo or two round his belly… maybe he was managing all right for himself, eating well as a man should at his age, enjoying himself…

And then a leather-covered baton came down cleanly on to the base of Maurice's neck.

He fell unconscious immediately, slumping to the ground like an actor in a play.

"No," Rosalind croaked, choking.

Now that he was inert, the thugs, none too gently, picked him up and carried him off like a corpse, his torso swinging lifelessly between them.

"No!" Rosalind put all her effort into trying to scream. "He has no magic!" She tried to think of the right words, words these monsters would understand. "He is… not a *charmante*! He is pure! Innocent! *LET HIM BE!*"

But the door on the far side of the room opened and clanged shut, leaving her more alone than ever.

PART III

THE PLAY'S THE THING

Coming back to the village through the snow, under the dark cloudy skies, Belle felt like she had been away for a lifetime. She had, in fact, never left the village by herself before this. There were a couple of overnight trips to fairs with her father, and once or twice during mushroom season they got swept up in the fury and spent a few nights in the forest, gathering morels and truffles and camping out. But that was all, and always with Papa.

She gazed at the snug little houses and their lights and felt around the recesses of her heart carefully, seeing if she felt any different. It *was* a lovely little place, despite the provincialism of its inhabitants. A clean and safe and pretty place to grow up. But… even as framed as it was from a distance, as perfect as any terribly twee landscape painting,

Belle felt nothing but a slight twinge of *future* nostalgia. No sadness, no missing it *yet*. The village was like an egg, she had developed there, she had been imprisoned there, she was trying to break free. But it had a pretty shell.

"So you're from here?" the Beast grunted from beneath his hood.

"Yes, but further on, over there, outside town. You can't see our house, it's hidden by the hill," she said, pointing.

Belle looked back at the dark forest out of which they had come. Because of its shape and the depth of the valley, she couldn't see even the highest points of the castle.

"It's like it's already gone," she murmured.

"Maybe it wasn't meant to be," the Beast said softly, immediately understanding what she meant. "Maybe we were always meant to disappear, one way or another."

They were silent for a moment and the snow fell.

"Come on," Belle said, shaking herself, refusing to give in to melancholy. "We should go and see Papa first. Oh, won't he be so amazed to hear about everything?"

"We go and see the bookseller first," her companion corrected gently but firmly.

"But Papa will be so worried about me!"

"*Belle.* We have little time. The castle was sinking, you saw it. Let's break the curse first and then have our happy reunions."

Belle's head drooped. He was right. If she hadn't been so impulsive and grabby to begin with, none of this would have happened. Except for her father, she had never really had to think about anyone else before or put anyone's needs above her own.

"All right. First Lévi, and then my papa."

They decided to go the more direct route across the river since they had no horse or cart. The bridge was out, the swollen, semi-frozen river swallowing it in rounded mounds of ice and rushing water. But a rope gondola was tied where the current remained swift and, while Belle worried for a moment about their combined weight, the tiny boat only dipped a little as the Beast embarked. He had obviously never seen such a thing before but as soon as she lifted the rope he got the idea and easily pulled them across, with no more effort than if he were reeling in an empty hook and line.

"Smoke," he said, frowning, when they were halfway across.

"Mmm," Belle sighed. "Everyone's in for the night, all warm and cosy."

An icy wind blew down the river, skimming the water like a dragonfly during the summer. Without a word the Beast stood closer to Belle, between her and the cold. He radiated warmth, rather like a cow or a goat but smelled much better. She almost regretted it when they stepped off the little raft and on to the gravelly path of the village proper.

Most of the shops had closed early for the cold, dark day. The streets were almost entirely empty. Still the Beast kept out of the meagre light, slinking predatorily from shadow to shadow, hiding behind lamp posts and signs. Belle wasn't sure if she should be delighted or disappointed that the few people they passed failed to recognise her. All she was doing was wearing a different, albeit new and fancy, cloak. It was like the villagers couldn't see past the red on her hood.

As she pondered this, she saw drifts of the smoke that the Beast had smelled and it wasn't normal wood smoke. It hung in the air, transparent and grey, as if from a fire that had been out for a while but still smouldered. The scent wasn't bad at all; in fact, there was something strangely familiar about it.

"It's not time for the Christmas bonfire," Belle said, puzzled. She headed off the main street to the right, where the bookshop was. The smoke grew thicker.

When they turned the corner she finally saw the source of the smoke.

Belle sank to her knees in the street with a cry.

There was almost nothing left of Monsieur Lévi's bookshop but four blackened walls, a smoking roof, and rubble and ashes.

Monsieur Lévi! And all of those books…

The fire had brushed the nearby buildings, but except for some singed roofs the little houses were fine. A few old people were sweeping and tidying up nearby; it looked like the blaze had occurred more than a day before. Strange black ashes, as thin and flat as the petals of some ugly tropical flower, fluttered easily with the slightest breath. They covered the plaza and gathered in corners, whirling around and around themselves.

On some, a few words could still be seen.

The town is covered in books, Belle thought, nearly sick with sadness. *In the only way it could be.*

One tightly bundled villager hurried by and without thinking Belle grabbed his coat. The Beast was obviously torn for a moment, but his need to hide finally outweighed his desire to comfort Belle. He slipped into the dark shadows of a nearby doorway.

"*Monsieur*," Belle cried. "What happened here?"

"Belle?" The man looked at her in surprise. It was Monsieur Sauveterre, who ran the fancier dry goods store. "Where have you been? Your father has been going quite mad about you…"

"It's a long story," Belle said impatiently, standing up. "What happened here? Where is Monsieur Lévi?"

"Yes, a shame that," the man said thoughtfully, looking at the ashen remains of the place. "Someone set it, obviously.

The fire started from within. A harmless old academic, that Lévi. I don't know who would do it."

"*Is he all right?*" Belle demanded.

The man shrugged in a particularly Gallic way. "I don't know… no one said anything about a body. I think he was away. It's probably why they set it. I have to get home, Belle. The children are waiting to eat. Go and see your father! He's worried sick about you!"

Belle let him go, collapsing back on to the street again.

The Beast was suddenly there again, looming above her, a silent shadow.

"Let's go in," she said after a moment.

Listlessly she rose and trudged over to the wrecked bookshop, stepping through what remained of the doorframe, not caring about the soot and ashes getting on her worn shoes.

"This was your… favourite place," the Beast said slowly, coming behind her.

"In the whole world. Even more than my own bed," Belle said bleakly. "Every time I came in, it was like a whole new unexplored land would be there waiting for me. Another story to step into. And Monsieur Lévi was a friend and a guide and an explorer who took me to these new places. This was *home*, as much as my own home was."

She looked at the shelves, covered in lumps and

black bricks that were once books. Very little of it looked salvageable. Even the ones that were only lightly singed had sort of compressed and crushed together with the heat of the inferno. The chairs she had loved to flop into were skeletons, their fabric and flesh burned away, only thin bony laths of wood remaining.

"Belle… I'm… sorry," the Beast said, putting a hand on her shoulder.

Belle grabbed it with both of her hands and began to cry. She couldn't stop. Tears flowed down her cheeks like rivers, quick and endless.

"I… was looking forward to seeing your favourite place," he added clumsily.

"I know," she sniffed.

"I've never been in a shop before," he continued, trying to speak lightly.

"What?" Belle asked. She wiped her face on her sleeve. "Really?"

"Really. Merchants would come to the castle and show us their wares. We never had to go and see them. And only the finest ones were let in. They had golden balls, and lead soldiers, and stuffed bears made with real bearskin and glass eyes…"

"All right, all right," Belle said, shaking her head. "I get it, Your Majesty."

"I'm just trying to… distract you."

"I know. I appreciate it." She took a deep breath and tried to shake practicality back into her arms and head. "Can you… can you smell anyone… dead? Like you did with Alaric?"

The Beast frowned and widened his nostrils. "I think maybe a couple of mice were caught up in here when it happened. But other than that, no."

Belle let a large breath out in relief.

"Well, that's something."

Belle tried to divert her grieving soul away from the sadness with the mystery of what had happened. *The moment I find out my mother was an enchantress and Lévi himself is several hundred years old… he suddenly turns up missing with his shop burned down*?

A very unlikely coincidence.

"The stairs are all right… I'm going to look upstairs," the Beast said.

Belle didn't stop him but didn't join him, either. She would feel strange going up to Lévi's private apartments herself… it would be like invading his privacy. Somehow it mattered less when someone who didn't know him did it.

"Everything seems normal up here," he called down. "Um, except for there not being a roof."

Belle put her hand to her forehead, thinking. *Where could*

Lévi be? He went several times a year to the big book fairs in cities, or on little vacations… But now? Was he somehow warned about the attack, and had he disappeared beforehand? And was it because he was a charmante*? Had the disease of the little forgotten kingdom made it here, across the river? Is nowhere safe for these people?*

Belle poked around the charred remains of his desk, where he tallied up the sums of people who actually came and bought or sold books, kept what little money he earned, and hid a small bag of pistachios he often shared with her. All of it was burned and black except for the metal hinges on his lockbox and some coins within. And something else, tarnished and grey…

A mirror. A small, yet very *familiar*-looking mirror.

It was round and pocket-sized, perfect for a gentleman's waistcoat or a lady's grooming kit. Except for some smoke damage, the object was untouched by the fire; rubbing her sleeve on the glass quickly caused it to become bright and gleaming. Tiny roses decorated the rim.

"Beast!" Belle cried out.

Silently, faster than should have been possible, the Beast was flowing down the crumbling stairs and next to her, having heard the tone in her voice.

Belle showed him the mirror, holding it in the palm of her hand.

As if brought to life by the warmth of her palm, the silver-grey surface rippled and began to show images. A girl's face appeared, filling the whole thing.

Familiar, but so young…

With a start Belle realised it was her mother. This was the first time she had seen her up close and looked directly into her green eyes.

The girl smiled in the mirror, as if satisfied. Perhaps her chin was a little pointed and cat-like for true perfection, her eyes too knowing and intelligent for an insipid romantic painting.

Belle almost dropped the mirror when the girl, her mother, nodded seriously, then pushed a stray piece of hair back over her ear.

"She looks just like you," the Beast said.

"I…" Belle wasn't sure what she was going to say. *Know?*

It looked like the girl was shaking her end of the mirror. The picture faded.

Belle had to stop herself from shaking the mirror as well, to see if it would clear. But she didn't have to; it restarted of its own accord. Unlike the Beast's mirror, it obviously didn't need to be told aloud to show something.

She saw her young mother looking bored and annoyed as her parents, Belle's grandparents, stood and talked with other adults at some sort of fancy occasion. Belle's mother wore an amazing pale pink dress with a gold sash, which she was trying very hard to keep neat and stay fancy in, even when one of her friends ran up to her and dragged her off to play.

The friend's feet had cloven hooves.

"What..." Belle began.

"Hmmm... a faun," the Beast said, only vaguely interested, like it was an unusual squirrel.

The scenes shifted faster, as if sensing Belle's impatience; while all of this was fascinating, it had nothing to do with *now* or the direness of their situation. Scenes of the kingdom, possibly through the witch's eyes: a festival, Christmas, a flood one rainy spring. A fight between two young men in which one died, struck by magical lightning. A brawl breaking out among the spectators. Palace guards rushing in to break it up, slamming the heads of the magical people against the ground, rounding them up and beating them.

More scenes of the guards looking away as *charmante* girls were nauseatingly and physically harassed by street thugs and *charmante* boys beaten up. Sometimes so badly they couldn't walk. Sometimes so badly they never got up or opened their eyes again.

"*Papa!*" Belle cried when she saw Maurice enter the scene.

She and the Beast watched the Enchantress and the inventor court; they watched them spend time with friends late into the night. Then they watched them wait for friends who never showed up. The couple turned from sunny and happy to nervous and angry as the flavour of the kingdom changed.

They saw her mother go to the palace…

"Mother. *Father*," the Beast whispered.

… and entreat the king and queen for what was obviously protection and help for *les charmantes*. They saw the king and queen turn her away.

The Beast made a noise in his throat, somewhere between a whimper and a curse and a *no*, ashamed of his own parents.

They witnessed Belle come into the world, in a little too much detail for the Beast, who had to turn away in shock.

They too experienced sadness and fear as *charmantes* left, one by one, or disappeared, and the kingdom grew bleak and frightening.

They saw fever and plague come and bodies and incense burned, and a quarantine thrown up against the outside world, too little, too late.

They saw a little family fleeing a dying kingdom.

They saw a midnight rider…

"Alaric," the Beast said mournfully.

They saw him come, again and again, to the little house in the village, often when it was dark and there was no moon – and always with a rider or two behind him. They saw Belle's parents usher the fleeing *charmantes* inside and give Alaric some food and hot wine for the trip home. They watched *les charmantes* moving on the next night, loaded up with more food and sometimes money, heading on out to the world…

"It wasn't just one *charmante*," Belle said slowly. "It was… dozens. It was like… they were helping all of them… escape… That's why there were all of those lists and tables in his notebook. He *was* smuggling. *Charmantes.* Lots of them."

Belle noticed, also, that *she* never appeared in any of the scenes with Alaric and those he rescued. Her parents did a very good job of keeping her from witnessing any of it.

Then Alaric stopped coming. They saw a pale and waxy king and queen beg Belle's mother for help, and her refusal… And Belle was torn between shame and wonder at a woman who saved some people and refused to help others…

… until the next scene, which showed the Enchantress back at home, waving her fingers and staring into the distance. The castle leapt into view again, and white sparks like rose petals gently fell over it, disappearing as they landed. A sleeping boy, the young prince, shifted in his sleep with a faint smile, receiving the sparks happily.

"She's casting a spell?" Belle asked, confused.

Then it cut to her mother handing Monsieur Lévi the little mirror and clasping her hand around his, enclosing it within.

And then the mirror faded.

THE BEAST

"It's a… diary."

The Beast spoke aloud first, guessing the truth of it. "My mirror just shows exactly what is going on in the present, right now. This shows her… memories."

"She gave this to Monsieur Lévi…" Belle turned the little mirror over in her hand, a look of wonder on her face. "Like she was asking him to keep it for her, in case something happened to her. Like she *knew*.

"She *was* thinking about me. She didn't just leave and forget me…"

"She's your mother, Belle," the Beast said gently. "She wouldn't have."

The mother she had dismissed for so many years, by magic as well as inclination, had forced her way back into her daughter's life. And she was not only a more complicated person than Belle had believed, but more *motherly*.

"What was that last spell she cast? After she left the castle?" she said, dismissing the intriguing, but immediately unhelpful, new thoughts in her head.

"None of the children or babies in the castle ever got sick with the fever. Like me. I was fine," the Beast said. "People said it was a miracle. Maybe it was your mother."

"But she let your parents die," Belle said bleakly. "I'm so sorry."

"Now what?" the Beast asked impatiently, obviously not wanting to think about it any more.

"*Now* we go to see Papa. Hopefully he can clear all this up. Maybe when we show him this it will remind him, or free his memory, or something."

"All right. To Belle's father." He held his arm out and she took it, her face growing grim as they stepped over the ashes and charcoal that had once been furniture and books.

The Beast couldn't bear seeing her so sad. "If everything goes all right... if we break the curse and I become a... *real* king... I'll rebuild the bookshop. I'll make it bigger. Maybe... maybe I'll give you your *own* bookshop."

Belle gave him a sad, pleased smile. "Thank you. I'll hold you to that."

They walked quietly for a few moments, each wrapped

deep in thought.

"There it is," Belle said after a few moments. A wide smile grew on her face and her eyes brightened as it came into view: a snug little house, as comforting and… *odd* as Belle was. None of the other houses they passed had windmills, for instance.

"Very… homey," the Beast said, trying to think of something nice to say.

"Look, a light's on!" she said excitedly. "In the kitchen! The little table lantern! He's home!"

When they got to the door, Belle reached up to push it open, then stopped and turned to the Beast.

"Ah… maybe you should let me go first," she said delicately. "The last time he saw you, you threw him in a prison cell."

The Beast immediately slumped, remembering.

"I'll say I'm sorry," he promised.

"Which is great," Belle said, squeezing his paws. "But maybe I should just bring him up to date on what's happening before you two meet again. Then I'll come out the back and get you."

"All right," he grumbled. "I'll hide in those bushes over there, behind the house."

"Thank you," she said, standing up on tiptoe to kiss him on the side of his muzzle. "I won't be a minute."

She turned and he flowed back down the path like an inky shadow, silently inserting himself among some snowy bushes to wait.

The Beast tried to listen in after Belle stepped inside, but the door was solid and there were few windows.

He growled. This was ridiculous. He was a prince, a *king* really, and here he was hiding outside in the cold. He was a beast too, huge and thunderously strong, crouched and camouflaged like a rabbit.

If he *were*… a prince… a real one, a human one… would he get to just go inside with her on his arm? What would her father say? A prince on the arm of his daughter? What would happen then? Could they… could they marry? There was no one left in the kingdom to object to him marrying below his station.

Would Belle even like him?

Did she like him *now*?

She hadn't pulled away when he had kissed her, before… and she had kissed *him* just now. That was something, right?

It was hard to think about the future or have thoughts that were complicated and abstract. He didn't want to reveal this to Belle, but it was getting harder. Any quick and thoughtless instinct, *food hunger run smell good smell bad itchy scratch it*, came first, before rational thought. It was hard to ignore.

His tail lashed, its fox-like fur whipping snow off the

leaves, a veritable cataclysm of noise to his sensitive ears.

He settled down.

Where was she? Hadn't she had enough time yet for a tearful reunion?

The Beast was never cold under his thick fur. But something about the little village and its empty streets made the Prince shiver. While he had never been in a shop before, he had certainly been elsewhere in the kingdom, on horseback or on inspection or parade or just out for a jaunt with his mother, and it had been a much busier, larger, happier town than this. Many more people and houses and buildings, and none of the people looked at strangers as suspiciously as they seemed to do here.

It seemed so chilly and quiet in this town… almost like an empty, haunted castle, turned inside out.

A carriage rumbled by, a black one. Then another, this one maybe almost black. Despite his superior vision, he had trouble differentiating colours. That was one of the reasons he liked his royal-blue-and-gold jacket; they were shades he could tell apart easily and looked nice, he thought, all bold and bright.

A couple of crows flew overhead, making the lighter *caw* that differentiated them from ravens. He liked crows. They weren't as stand-offish as their larger cousins and were much smarter than the little brown songbirds he occasionally couldn't resist snagging and gulping.

A third vehicle, an old cart, bounced and creaked its way by, driven by a sharp-eyed matron.

This was boring.

He began to whack the ground rhythmically with his left hind foot, like a buck rabbit.

"Where *is* she?" he growled. "This is taking too long."

Of all the various creatures of which his body was a hideous amalgam, *cat* wasn't one of them. He had no patience for the lie-and-wait kind of hunting.

"Gah!" he finally said, tearing himself from the bushes and loping up the path to the back door. If anyone on the road was actually looking in his direction, they would have seen little; he stuck to the shadows and hid at each available opportunity: drinking well, rock, strange giant metal contraption, wall.

He pressed his ear up to the door.

Nothing.

Surprised, he gently pushed it open with the pads of his paws.

It didn't even creak. Nothing alleviated the complete silence of the place.

The Beast entered cautiously, sniffing the air. Belle *had* been here; he caught traces of her scent. And scents of other people too: masculine, one of which could have been her papa… but he didn't think so.

Panicking, he dropped to all fours and leapt round the small house, smelling everything and poking into every corner. Nothing, nowhere.

He ran his claws through the fur on his head. Where could she have gone? What happened? How could she disappear?

His overwhelming instinct was to break out of the tiny, confining building and lope up and down the road, searching for her.

What would Belle do?

She would take stock of the situation and think of all the resources available to her and then make use of them in a logical and consistent manner.

"*I don't have anything…*" the Beast said aloud, thinking of their pack and the few provisions it had. Along with…

The magic mirror!

Eagerly he pulled it out of the bag he carried. "*Show me Belle!*" he commanded.

Immediately the screen fogged and cleared and showed Belle, tied up and struggling in a small space. A box, maybe. A large, padded one? It looked like she was bouncing around while a hooded assailant tried to hold her down.

What sort of box could she be put in that moved?

Cursing himself for a fool, the Beast ran out of the front

door and looked up and down the road. Just rounding the bend, on the road away from the village, was another black carriage. It tipped dangerously on to two wheels as it went, gaining speed.

The Beast ran after it, full pelt, on all fours.

The carriage turned off the main road and on to one that climbed up a stark, precipitous hill. This path was twisty and turny, cutting back and forth across the stony escarpment that hid the top from the land below. Thick, stunted and gnarled trees clung to the cliffs and further caused the road to take some additional twists, yet the carriage never slowed down. The Beast himself slipped once or twice in his desperation to reach Belle, and only managed to avoid falling by grabbing onto roots and scrabbling quickly.

At the top the carriage finally slowed.

The road ended at a large stone building that reminded the Beast a little of his castle. This was ugly and squat, however, with no real windows except for high up, on the top floors only. The back was built into the hill so that half of the construction was underground. The air around it smelled vile and sick, too human for such a remote and wild place. When the wind blew right, screams could be heard issuing thinly between the stones.

Rage once again overcame caution and he leapt…

… turning himself mid-air and scrambling behind a

tree when someone came out of the building to meet the carriage. Several someones, by the smell of it, with hard boots and muskets.

"Ah, I see you managed to bring our little guest. Excellent. And no worse for wear, really..."

The Prince dug his claws into his own flesh at Belle's muffled whimpers and cries. More than anything he wanted to jump up, roaring and growling and slavering, and tear everyone from gut to throat until Belle was safe.

The Beast within him roiled.

Guns who cares *guns make them pay* kill them *save Belle.*

The Prince shut his eyes, trying to force the blood in his veins to calm. It would feel so good just to give in to it, to be free and terrible...

But if he failed, what good would that do Belle, or him, or anyone still trapped in his castle?

He took a deep breath. Again, what would *Belle* do? There were too many guards, too many guns, and that building had a huge and very sturdy door. It could hide an army – an army of whatever those horrible, pitiful screaming things were.

He couldn't do anything immediately, on his own.

He needed a *plan.*

He needed reinforcements.

PAPA

Belle couldn't scream.

The gag, a clean piece of cloth, part of her mind noticed, wasn't tied tight enough to stop her breathing, but it *was* bunched up in the middle to prevent her from making any noise beyond what she could manage in the back of her throat.

She managed quite a lot.

Her father hadn't been in the house. Something had felt off from the moment she went in, she should have left immediately. She should have gone to get the Beast. But she wasn't used to having backup; of all the many resources her prodigious mind was capable of accessing, *help* wasn't one of them. She was used to doing things on her own.

Almost as silent as the Beast, her captors had descended

upon her, forcing the gag in her mouth before she could cry out, kicking her knees out from beneath her so she crumpled immediately to the floor. Someone tied a bag over her head. It was all over in less than a minute; she was picked up and rushed out of the door… the *front* door… and into what was probably a carriage from the way it moved.

She struggled against what seemed to be a pair of large, strong men and the uneven movement of the vehicle, but it was useless.

Why were they doing this? Who were they? *What had she ever done?* To anyone? Did this have anything to do with the burning of Lévi's shop? With her mother? With all of *les charmantes*? Were they actually trying to grab her father for some reason, but settled for her instead? Did her father owe someone money? Did he borrow from the wrong person to pay for his metal, his inventions?

The carriage turned off the main road and started going uphill. *Steeply* uphill.

The asylum? Belle wondered. *They're taking me to the lunatic asylum?* It was the only thing on top of the one steep hill near the village.

She began to panic, far more seriously than when they first grabbed her. Like all children in the village she had crept up the hill and sneaked a look at the place, goaded by stories and rumours. It was a frightening estate despite all of the 'modern' and 'scientific' methods Monsieur D'Arque spoke so highly of on his rare visits down to the village.

"*Eh ee OW!*" she enunciated as clearly as she could. "*I nah cwayzy! Eh ee ALK an I splain! Eease, ake a ag off!*"

The two men were silent.

Soon the carriage stopped, the door opened, and she was – surprisingly carefully – let down to the ground. A clean breeze blew; she sucked it in greedily. There wasn't much time before they moved her into the building. Belle had to think fast. She couldn't talk – she couldn't argue rationally or plead poetically with her captors, two things she excelled at.

What did one do in these situations, without a hidden knife, or a ring of invisibility, or a plan?

What would *the Beast* do?

Oh…

Something she wouldn't normally do. Something he often did. Something she *never* did.

Lose control.

"*YIYIYIYIYIYIYUAYYAGG!*"

She ululated in the back of her throat the best she could manage, having read about the technique in one of her adventure books. With the terrifying cry she spun, throwing her torso out as far as she could, her arms were tied behind her back. Like an off-centre top, she kicked and hurled herself against any solid object she came in contact with.

"What the…?"

"She really *is* a loony…"

"Ooof!"

It seemed like she actually managed to connect with some of her captors' more tender, fleshy bits.

As soon as she felt some space in the air around her, Belle turned and ran.

She could see just a tiny bit of ground by staring down her nose, a patch of light where the bag had hitched up.

All right, all I need to do now is watch for where the ground changes…

Even if she ran off the cliff, her plan was to tuck into a ball and protect her neck as best she could. There were trees and bushes to break her fall, and maybe she would luck out and land on the road, and then…

… and then someone neatly picked her up as easily as if she were a child, hands on her waist, and held her up in the air.

She kicked madly but hit nothing.

Shrieking in rage and frustration she still had to bear the indignity of being calmly and slowly carried into the building, without even a satisfying curse or jeer from her captors. The smell of chemicals hit her face: antiseptics, alcohol, and traces of the sickening, sweet solutions used to dull the senses and knock you out.

Also urine and fear.

She heard the door close solidly behind her and couldn't help letting out a sob.

Would the Beast be able to find her here? Would he even come after her?

Or would the curse just gradually take him over, leaving him to wander the wilds around the village, growing more and more beastly until someone like Gaston shot him?

"Ooo an ake a ag ff ow," she said with as much calmness as she could muster.

"Not until you're safely stowed away," one of her guards said with frightening patience. Apparently he had been doing this long enough to be able to completely understand the otherwise unintelligible words coming out of her mouth. He put a firm hand in the small of her back and gently propelled her forwards.

Belle resisted, trying to sidestep him.

"All right, missy," he said with a sigh. "We've been told not to hurt you. And we won't. But there's hurt and there's *hurt.* Beating you on the soles of your feet until you lose consciousness, for instance, won't actually leave a mark. No one will know or believe what we did, no matter what you tell or who you tell it to."

Belle swallowed a cry. Apart from in books she had

never been in the presence of someone so terrible… so *evil* before. Bullies, yes. Idiots with barbaric ideas about women and weddings, yes. But never anyone so calmly vile, who spoke of cruelties as casually as if he were talking about a game of cards.

Giving up, she slumped and let him lead her.

"There's a good girl," her captor said. "Smart, you are. Just like everyone says. You just do as you're told and everything will be fine. No one is supposed to hurt you while you're here."

While you're here. That sounded like the whole thing wasn't permanent…

Like there was a possible end to her capture. Maybe someone just *thought* she was crazy and they were going to give her some kind of test or exam, and then let her go? There were already too many jokes in town about 'crazy old Maurice' and occasional references to the asylum. Maybe someone had finally decided to act on their – incorrect – beliefs.

"Carefully now, twenty steps ahead. A bit slippery."

She had just put her toe down on the second step when someone, or something, let out a scream. Far more terrifying than her war cry; this came from the heart, as if it were being ripped out of someone while they were awake.

"Easy there, just a patient wanting his medicine,"

her guard said, pushing her forwards.

She forced herself to move. She would *not* be picked up and carried again.

Strange clangs and muffled whump*s* came from around her. She jumped at every sound, desperately trying to tilt her head and look up through the gap in her bag and failing. It was all black with only occasional flickering lamplight.

"Here we go. In you go. Number fifteen. Big and bright. Lucky girl."

She was pushed forwards harder, and down another step. This time no one told her about it and she stumbled.

Belle felt her head yanked back and her throat exposed; terror overwhelmed her as she pictured a cold knife – or disgusting lips – touching her.

But her captor was just removing the bag, and then the gag.

She spun round to confront him. But he was as large and hooded and anonymous as a giant chess piece. His companion looked exactly the same. They swung the barred door shut. Belle closed her eyes at the expected but still horrible sound of a heavy lock being drawn in place. Despite any boots they wore, her captors were silent as they walked off.

Her cell wasn't actually uncomfortable. It was large, had a stone bench for a bed with a fairly thick mattress, and a plain if functional chamber pot nearby. A little light filtered through a grate high in the wall, but most of the illumination was provided by the hanging lanterns in the hall, whose light was sickly and dim by the time it reached her room. There were more bars in the two walls perpendicular to the door, little windows to the cells next to hers.

"My whole life I've never set foot in a jail cell," Belle murmured, trying to see the humour in the situation. "In the last few weeks I've been in *two.* What a reprobate I'm becoming..."

She went to the door and tried to push her face through its window as far as it would go, looking up and down the hallway. There wasn't much to see; on the right were only a few more cells and then a wide area with equipment and supplies for the jail keepers. Leather-padded batons, trays for food, mops and the like. The hall went in the other direction at least ten or fifteen metres, with more cells, these closer together. It was hard to tell because of the darkness, but at the end seemed to be an ominous black door.

Belle sighed and went back to the other side of the room, to try the high grate that looked outside. She couldn't reach it, and it looked fairly well hammered into the wall, but maybe if she...

A spate of coughing from the cell next to her froze her in her tracks.

Familiar coughing.

She ran over to the window.

"Papa?" she called, feeling a strange sense of déjà vu.

"Belle? *No!*" His voice degenerated into another peal of coughs, but it was definitely her father. There was the sound of shuffling, and then he came out of the shadows.

"Papa," Belle said, sighing. He looked – well, not quite as terrible as he should have. There were bags under his eyes and he moved poorly, but there was also a pinkness to his cheeks and a fire in the depths of his pupils.

"You escaped from the Beast!" he said, putting his arms through the bars. She clasped his hands to her heart, touching her forehead to his skin.

"Yes. *Escaped*," she said ironically. "And then came to find you and got thrown in here. But the Beast isn't bad, Papa. It's a long story. I have to help him. What happened to *you*? Why are you here?"

"I tried to get help. To go and get you," Maurice said sadly, holding his daughter's hands. "I went to the pub... No one believed me. They threw me out. And then Gaston, that *pig*, he grabbed me. With LeFou. When I was walking through the woods, after you."

"Gaston?" Belle asked in surprise, drawing back.

"Yes! Gaston and D'Arque! They're in it together! Their plan was to kidnap me and force you to marry Gaston to get me out."

Belle ran that through her head. It didn't add up.

"But then why kidnap *me*?" she asked slowly. "I don't see another ambush wedding in here. Why would they put us together?"

"Ambush wedding…?"

"It's a *very* long story." She smiled ruefully. "Maybe you picked a bad day to go to a fair."

But… when she thought about it… if he hadn't gone and been seized by the Beast, then she wouldn't have left to look for him. She never would have found the haunted castle and met Mrs Potts and Lumière and Cogsworth… and the Prince… and had the adventure she had always longed for… Assuming they all got out of this all right, really, was it such a bad thing to have happened?

"Look, Belle, I have a lot to tell you," Maurice said, his voice shaking. "And I don't know how much time we have. I don't know what they're planning to do to us. Listen…"

He took a deep breath and looked her straight in the eye.

"Your mother was an enchantress."

Belle was suddenly overwhelmed with an urge to giggle.

"I *know*," she said, trying to limit her hysteria to a smile.

"You *know*?" Her father looked baffled, stepping away from the window as if to get a better look at her, as if he couldn't see how this was possible.

"Why didn't you ever tell me?"

"Because I… couldn't *remember*, exactly. I had difficulty remembering *her*." He shook his head. "I think it was protective, a *forget* spell in case anything ever happened to her. It would keep us safe, from knowing too much."

"How come you can remember her now?"

"Because I saw her! She's here!"

"Mother?" Belle gasped. "My mother?"

"Oh, Belle, I saw her…" He began to weep. He leaned against the wall and sobbed and choked. "Belle… she was taken from us all those years ago. She didn't leave. They took her and have been taking all the magic out of her. That's what D'Arque does, Belle. He removes magic from everything. *Everyone.* That's what those screams are! He's… torturing the magic out of them. Out of your mother. She's mangled, Belle… your beautiful, strong mother. She's a husk of bone and skin…"

Belle remembered, with nausea, the monster she had seen in the mirror that the Beast had broken. It *was* her mother. The beautiful lady with the rose and mirror who cursed the Beast was now a scrawny, scarred victim of torture that left her looking like a monster.

I thought she didn't love me. That she left me and Papa for her own reasons. But she was stolen *from us. Kidnapped and brought here.*

And even in her weakened state she still summoned the

strength to try and reach me.

"Dark," she suddenly said aloud, remembering what the vision in the mirror had said. "*Stay safe away from dark*... D'Arque! She meant stay away from *D'Arque*! She was trying to protect me!"

She put a hand to her head, feeling both overwhelmed and exhausted. "We have to get out of here," she said as calmly as she could. "Papa, we have to do something. I'll do something. I'll get all three of us out. The Beast can help..."

"The Beast who captured us?" Maurice asked, alert and sceptical.

"He's the prince Maman cursed. When he was a child. I... touched the rose she cursed him with and somehow completed the spell. I'm trying to help him break it."

Maurice looked at her, dumbfounded. Then he shook his head. "Magic always comes back on itself..."

A voice, old and female and guttural and chatty, came from up the hall. A nearly inaudible masculine grunt replied. For some reason the sound of both made Belle sick.

The newcomers approached the door and unlocked it. One was a large unmasked man wearing a plain tunic and breeches. His arms were the size of hams. The woman with him was also wearing a plain, clean outfit. They looked almost like nurses, but there was something terribly not right about the whole thing.

"Hello, girly! The doctor's all ready to examine you now!" the woman said with cheeriness that wasn't so much false as terrifying.

"No!" Maurice yelled, standing upright. "Stop. I am her father. There is nothing wrong, or magical, about her at all!"

"The doctor will get it all sorted. And don't you worry about your precious girl. I'm along here to make her feel comfortable and safe, nothing naughty or untoward happening with her."

The man unlocked the door. Belle's first urge was to get away, even if just to the back of the room.

Both 'nurses' must have guessed at what she was doing, because they sprang into the room faster than Belle could think; they were well used to people resisting. The man had Belle's hands behind her back and held tightly before she could move.

"*No!*" she shouted, throwing herself back and forth, trying to wrest herself out of his grasp.

"Now, now," the woman said, clicking her tongue. "Don't want all that acting up, do we? Might need to use the special medicine, and you *don't* want that."

"*Listen to me!*" Maurice shouted, trying to make his voice sound as authoritarian as possible. "There is nothing magical about her!"

But the two ignored him. The man pushed Belle in front of him, out of the door. She kicked and tried to throw herself sideways, blocking the way.

The man wrapped his arms round her in an obscene caricature of a hug and forced her through, upright.

"Papa!" she yelled.

"Belle! *NO!*"

THE BEAST'S NIGHTMARE

The Beast loped back to his castle on all fours. A thousand different scents tried to distract him: speedy squirrels and friendly wolves and tasty rabbits. He couldn't let them. He managed the whole trip without stopping until he got to the gates.

The walls around the castle were shining white with snow and the cobwebs. He reached out to push them aside, ready to use his full strength, but they broke easily at first touch and fell. Getting in was easy. Getting out again…

He took a moment, thinking like Belle: *he would need to get out again.* To lead everyone to a rescue, including the giant suits of armour. He needed to prepare for that.

With a growl he unsheathed his claws and tore at the webbing. They sheared easily, drifting through the air and disappearing when they finally hit the ground, like candyfloss in water. All of his frustration and anger about Belle's capture went into clearing the gate and several metres beyond on either side.

He then smashed the gates open, taking them off their hinges for good measure and hurling them as far as he could. It would be harder for the webs to cover such a huge, open gap.

He did the same for the doors into the castle itself, ripping apart as much of the webbing as he could and then smashing open the doors themselves. Icy wind and snow immediately blew into the castle, as if excited by the chance to invade and freeze the unnatural human dwelling.

"*COGSWORTH!*" he roared as soon as he was inside. "*LUMIÈRE!* Guards! To me, now!"

Nothing.

There was *nothing*.

No sound, no movement, not a hint that anything in the castle was alive.

For one insane moment he wondered if they had already left the castle, if they had decided on their own that he and Belle weren't up to the task, that they needed help. He had seen no sign of them on his trip back, hadn't smelled anything of the castle, or the smoke from

Lumière's candles.

"Hello?" he roared again. "I am your *master*, the Prince! Answer me!"

Perhaps they were in the servants' dining room, where they often gathered to avoid his wrath and console each other during the long years under the curse.

He headed that way… and then paused in the hall of the suits of armour.

They were all there, lined up, though not so perfect as they once were. The fight to get Belle and him out of the castle had left a few casualties: some had notched and damaged swords, others weren't standing quite as straight as they should have been. Almost as if they were tired.

"*Attention!*" the Prince bellowed, trying to remember his father and Cogsworth and old captains of the guard. Trying to sound empowered, not entitled.

Not one of them moved.

A slow, creeping sense of horror crawled up the Prince's spine…

… and he was not accustomed to being scared.

Unsure why it took his legs so long to move, he shuffled over to the closest suit. Reluctantly, delicately, he tapped at its helmet with a single ivory claw.

The helmet tipped and crashed to the floor, rolling and bouncing like the loudest thing in the world.

Otherwise, everything remained stationary and silent.

The suits of armour were just… suits. All life in them gone. All the people they originally were now transformed permanently into inanimate objects. *Dead.*

The Prince raced through darkened halls and silent rooms, downstairs to the kitchen.

There, sitting on the table like a slightly unusual place setting, were a cold teapot, a clock that needed to be wound, and a candelabrum whose candles had burned down to their stubs and then gone out.

The Beast howled, picking up the thing that was once Lumière and shaking it. Nothing happened. He looked round, desperate to grab another candle, to try and relight him… maybe he could rewind Cogsworth…

Then he realised he could only see at all because of his beast eyes. The kitchen was dark and cold; his little puffs of breath were making clouds that as a child he had called 'dragon smoke'.

He was all alone, in his empty, dead castle.

BELLE'S NIGHTMARE

They took Belle to a truly frightening room.

It smelled of antiseptic and alcohol and the slightly sweet overtone of nitrous oxide. And also other things, meant to cover up the stink of fear and bodily fluids. *It's a prep room*, she dimly realised. A half-dozen wheeled tables were arranged to accept bulk quantities of new patients awaiting whatever horrible surgeries D'Arque had in store for them. A counter nearby had rows of shining, spotless scalpels and knives laid out neatly on a white linen towel… along with one unscientific-looking knife, seemingly carved from black glass, curvy and sinuous like an evil snake.

"No! What is this place? Let me *go*!" Belle began to struggle in a blind panic.

"Now, now, calm yourself," the horrible female nurse

said, grabbing her ankles with surprisingly strong and cold fingers as the man lifted Belle up by her torso. He arranged the struggling girl almost gently on the nearest table, holding her down with one meaty arm while drawing up and tightening straps round her with the other.

The table was cool under her body, but not cold. A soft fleece protected her from the metal surface. This was somehow more terrifying than everything else: that steps had been taken to provide comfort for the 'patients', as if this were actually a place of succour and healing.

Once Belle was secured, the woman draped a gag loosely over her mouth. It smelled of chemicals and she tried not to breathe, recognising the foul tang of chloroform.

Then they wheeled her into the operating theatre.

Around the edges of the small and spotlessly clean room were machines that looked like Maurice's own inventions… but shrunken and horribly malformed. Like they had been sucked through an evil mirror and come out the other side utterly twisted for foul purposes. The largest one had bellows and pumps and tiny versions of pistons above a neat row of bell jars.

Belle fought against the numbing influence of the drug on the gag, kicking and trying to scream. She wanted nothing to do with those machines. *Anything* was better than whatever they hinted at. Being knocked in the head, beaten on the feet, *anything.* Traditional torture…

"Ah, there you are," a clipped and aristocratic voice called out.

Belle turned her head as far as she could to look.

It was D'Arque, the sallow-faced and skeletal head of the asylum. He was well known to the villagers despite his rare trips down into town. Frightening when he was trying to be pleasant in broad daylight, here in the depths of the asylum and its darkness, he was positively horrible.

"I'm so sorry about all this," he said, coming forwards to regard her. "I think we can be fairly certain you are pure and free of the vile, unnatural corruptions of the supernatural. But I have to be *absolutely* certain."

"What is this?" Belle demanded, trying to force the gag out of the way with her lips and chin. "Is this for Gaston? So I am *pure* enough to be his wife?"

"Gaston?" D'Arque asked, surprised. His eyebrows crawled up his scalp like two beetles trying to flee his tongue. "That foolish bull of a boy? *Please.* He is no more than a pawn. He thinks I approve of his silly wedding plans."

"Thinks...?" Belle's mind raced. The way he phrased it, it seemed like D'Arque and Gaston had some sort of long-term relationship. Aside from the old man's occasional visits to the hunter's tavern, she had no idea they really *knew* each other.

"I needed someone to feed me information about

you and your father from time to time. To make sure you weren't up to your mother's old tricks, or that your father hadn't recovered his memory and gone back to seeing old... *friends.* Unsavoury friends."

"*Les charmantes,*" Belle said slowly. "You mean *les charmantes.*"

"I do," D'Arque said, sucking in his cheeks with disappointment. "Have you learned of such abominations? That's a pity. I had hoped you would remain completely free of any... taint... of them."

"Why do you care about us?" Belle demanded. "Why not anyone else in town?"

"Let us just say that I *do* particularly care about you and Maurice, in my own way. Also, I *do* care about everyone in town," D'Arque added with concern. "But everyone else is fairly safe. Normal. Set in their ways. Boring and uneducated, but harmless."

"Except for Monsieur Lévi," Belle spat. "So you burned his shop down."

"I did nothing of the sort," D'Arque snapped. "I suspect that was the idiot, Gaston. When he went to find Maurice. I have nothing against books. I *love* books. Books are the remedy to superstition and... magic. I was so pleased with your education, your brilliance, Belle... It's a pity we have to do this, but we must be sure..."

He took off his waistcoat, folded it neatly and handed it to the nurse. Then he drew over the scariest-looking machine and began to pump at a foot pedal on it.

"No… Monsieur D'Arque… *Please…*"

"Shhh, now," D'Arque said, placing a metal cup with a tube attached over her mouth.

Belle began to scream. She thrashed and tore at the leather straps, throwing herself from side to side. Blackness began to drip over her senses.

THERE'S SOMETHING TRULY TERRIBLE INSIDE

The Beast continued to howl, always his first response when something terrible and confusing was bothering him that he couldn't literally reach out and shred with his claws. Disbelief, anger and terror had full control of his animal mind and it took all his effort not to run, shrieking, into the darkness. Away from the scene.

Giving his animal side free rein for just a moment, he turned and bounded through the castle, past the dead suits of armour, up, up and up to the West Wing. He had to see for himself. He hadn't looked at the rose at all since that night with Belle. In a strange way, he had sort of forgotten about it, what with the books and the making dinner and stories and finding out about Belle's mother. All of that to figure out how to break the curse that had turned him into a beast, yet he hadn't given a second thought to the rose...

But what was happening to his servants... his *friends*... must have something to do with the curse.

Before he even got to the table with the rose, he saw something that stopped him dead in his tracks.

The Portrait of the Beast as a Young Man, as he had taken to calling the painting in the hall; it was an image of the man he *should* have been, with dark honey hair and fingers instead of claws and a broad, handsome figure. The picture that he had tried to destroy, and Belle had tried to fix...

It now showed a beast.

Not just the Beast as he was, at that very moment, but *all* beast. Snarling, slavering, the oil paints swirled so realistically it looked like he was about to tear his way off the canvas and through the heart of whoever was viewing it. In one paw was a bloody white dove, its head missing.

The Beast fell back against the wall, feeling weak.

This is what would happen to him eventually. Soon.

His inside would match his outside. He would be nothing more than that monster in the picture, completely devoid of human reason, thought and conscience.

He covered his face with his paws, overwhelmed with the urge to weep.

Hadn't she said this might be happening? Hadn't he *felt* it, recently? If he was honest with himself?

From that blackout he had experienced after Belle angered him, to waking up with no memory of how he got the blood on his muzzle. Thankfully it was just a sparrow or another small bird, but it could be anything next time, if he even 'woke up'. He had been losing his temper more than usual, little things setting him off in a way they hadn't used to. The urge to hunt was stronger than ever. And he had barely been able to control himself on the run home, nearly overcome with the desire to run free into the woods.

Slowly, desultorily, he moved into his bedroom proper, now no longer really caring what the rose looked like. He knew in his heart the changes were becoming complete.

It wouldn't have been so bad, he thought, if the Beast he became was more like a real animal, a wolf or a horse, say. Then he could almost happily sink into oblivion, spending the rest of his days like a simple creature of nature, sleeping and hunting until old age or a bullet caught up with him.

But he wasn't a real animal. A *natural* animal. He was a monster, whose heart would become ferocious and vile, bloodthirsty and out of control. His prey wouldn't be confined to rabbits and sheep.

Despair rose up like a huge, inescapable tide. He sank down on to the floor.

He'd never, ever be able to see Belle again. He *couldn't*. For her own safety.

The thought of her made him pause.

Before he was overtaken by the curse, before he became a full-blooded monster, he had to do this one last thing. *He had to save her.*

He pulled the mirror out of his cloak.

"Magic mirror, show me Belle!" he commanded.

When the silver-grey fog cleared, he nearly crushed the mirror with fury.

Belle lay half-drugged and kicking feebly, strapped down on some sort of horrible table. An old man was shoving needles into her flesh while some sort of thug forced a bronze cone over her mouth. More men stood near the door, along with a frightful-looking hag who looked like she was enjoying the proceedings.

The Prince swore, thinking about the giant, impregnable stone building he had seen her taken to. There was no way, even in full-on berserker mode, he could break in and disable every guard.

He ran his paws through the fur on his head, frustrated. He couldn't do it alone. He needed help. And the servants were all… unavailable.

The only people around to help were the people in the village.

The people the Beast had long avoided, knowing that the insane hunters like Gaston would shoot him on sight and the closed-minded peasant folk would run screaming.

But… they liked *Belle*, right? Despite what she had said about growing up lonely, she had a few friends, like the bookshop owner. And hadn't that man in the street shown some concern about her and her father?

What it came down to was that he had no other choice.

With a determined roar, he headed back to the village.

OVERHEARD

Sounds and voices came and went like wolves drifting over dead prey and then disappearing again.

"No, the meters don't lie. It is just as I said all those years ago. She has no magic in her whatsoever..."

"*[undecipherable]*"

"...*Keep* her... she is still valuable. I believe she can lure in a far better prey: the beast Gaston was blithering about... I believe he is the one cursed long ago by her own mother... how is *that* for irony?"

Even in Belle's confused head, she wondered how he knew all about that.

She forced her eyes open.

D'Arque's face was shockingly close to her, examining her wakeful movements. She looked directly into his eyes, small and black as coals, full of intelligence and malice above his narrow crooked nose.

A dagger of familiarity drove itself into Belle's foggy brain. She had seen him in the visions in the mirror at the bookshop, in the panes between the webbing on the castle.

"In the kingdom… you were… Papa and Maman's *friend…*" she croaked. "You were friends with them! And *ALARIC POTTS*!"

She had the satisfaction of seeing D'Arque's face go pale… right before he pushed the cone over her mouth again, causing her to lose consciousness.

THIS SAME OLD TOWN

The tavern was a perfect scene of Christmas: merry yellow light glowed from the windows and poured on to the snow below and cheerful singing broke through the snug stone walls. The smells of smoky fire and bubbling cheese and spicy mulled wine overwhelmed any of the rank, oily *human* scents the tiny village had.

The Beast watched for perhaps a little too long, hiding in the shadows of a fountain. Any childlike yearning he had for that glow, to be part of humanity again, was eclipsed by his nervousness about how to begin. This was a *hunter's* tavern, for heaven's sake. The Prince could smell the cold scent of long dead, mildewing fur and the fresh, lovely stink of all sorts of game in the back dressed and hung to bleed out. If anywhere there was a less safe place for a potentially dangerous, one-of-a-kind furry monster to show up, he would have a difficult time imagining it.

This was going to be hard.

Also, the Prince had never asked for help before. Anytime. Anywhere. As beast *or* prince. He ordered people, he demanded of people, he made sure people anticipated his wishes before he even had to vocalise them.

Somehow he had to go in there and make them see the human in him before it was gone forever. He had to make sure they didn't shoot him, and then beg them to help him, a dangerous, total stranger, rescue Belle.

The Beast closed his eyes for a moment, gathering his courage.

Something he had also never had to do before.

Then he sprang up…

… and immediately forced himself to slow down. To walk on two legs up to the tavern door. To s-l-o-w-l-y push it open.

Upon his entering, the tavern fell to an immediate, and very understandable, hush.

And then a mad scramble as everyone grabbed for his musket or gun or hunting knife or anything else that could be used as a weapon. There were screams and cries and general chaos, yet all leaving a very clear area between the Beast and the rest of the room.

"*WAIT!*" the Beast roared and then cursed himself for roaring. He held out his hands, his paws, claws sheathed, harmless and empty except for the mirror. "I'm here to ask you for help. *I need your help.* Belle, Maurice's daughter, is in trouble!"

There was a strange moment of silence.

"*Belle?*"

The man who asked had his gun levelled completely motionlessly at the Beast's heart. His eyes were ice-blue and the Beast had no doubt that with the slightest flick of his finger there would be blood and fur on the wall behind him.

The scene swam in front of his eyes. *They were going to get him.* These foul-smelling omnivores with their machines and ugly teeth were going to swarm him. He had to attack first, he had to get away...

"She's in trouble," the Prince whispered, fighting the Beast within. "I need you to help me help her."

"Maurice was... right?"

This was asked by a man sitting at the bar. He hadn't grabbed a gun. In fact, he hadn't even released his hand from his tankard. He was watching everything more with interest than anything else.

"*It's the beast!*" someone else cried. "Maurice *was* right!"

"Fangs and long snout!" a third person yelled, standing

up from the bar and bracing himself for a fight. "It's him!"

The man with the deadly aimed gun looked confused. "No… There's not actually a beast…"

"*He's right there!*" an old barmaid swore.

"*YOU TOOK BELLE!*" a short man with a long ponytail swore, pointing. "*J'accuse!*"

"No!" the Beast said, backing up against the door. He wasn't one to lie, even as a spoiled child. But maybe now was not the time for setting straight confusing truths. "She's being held captive… tortured… but not by me! I came here to try and get help to rescue her!"

The fire in the giant hearth blazed high and hot. His fur was growing matte and damp and itchy. The faces in front of him were ugly and mistrustful. Hands tightened round knives and muskets. The barest hint of relieving cool came from the frosty pane of a window nearby. He looked at it longingly. The moon shone behind. He could just break out and leave, flee this pack…

"Look," he said, desperately trying to focus. He pulled out the mirror.

Everyone leapt back, perhaps thinking he had a gun or a weapon. Confusion spread from one dim face to the next as they were instead confronted with the delicate silvery object.

"Show me Belle."

There was a gasp as the mirror revealed her, and what

was happening to her.

"That *is* Belle!" the short man shouted, now pointing at the image.

Several men shuddered and turned away at what they saw. The barmaid nearly screamed in horror.

The man with the gun was slowly letting it drop to his side. "Monsieur D'Arque?" he whispered.

"What is he doing to her?" the man with his hand on the tankard demanded. "That swine!"

"I always knew he was a bad one," someone said. "He doesn't just take the insane. I *knew* it."

"Foul son of a pig!"

"Is he doing that to all of the other inmates?"

"Belle is just sort of *kooky*... not crazy... Why is he doing that?"

"I don't understand..." said the man, who the Beast finally began to understand was Gaston. Although he had only seen the hunter from a distance, he now recognised his scent. This was the killer and the wedding ambusher, who wore far too much *eau de cologne.* His handsome face was pale. "D'Arque was just supposed to capture Maurice... so Belle would marry me..."

"*What?*" the barmaid asked, the one person in the room who was actually listening to what he said.

"It made sense at the time," the short man with the

pointy finger explained.

"She wouldn't marry you so you had D'Arque, what – torture her?" the barmaid demanded.

"No, no, no!" Gaston said, aghast. He stepped forwards and went to take the mirror.

At first the Beast wanted to resist – it was *his* magic mirror. The only possession he cared about besides the golden clasp his parents gave him before they died. But it was obvious that any show of force would be met with poorly.

And besides, if it helped Belle…

He turned his head away, not wanting to breathe in Gaston's hateful scent. Before too long he wouldn't be able to resist slicing the boy's throat.

"D'Arque… he was giving me advice… he liked the idea of Belle marrying me…" Gaston was obviously feeling sick; it was apparent in the thick, throaty way he spoke. "I didn't know anything about this… He's a monster… *JUST LIKE THIS ONE RIGHT HERE!*"

Gaston suddenly pointed to the Beast, much like the short man had before. Finally, an emotion won out over Gaston's face: *rage.* His brow darkened and an angry snarl distended his otherwise pretty lips.

"What?" the Prince asked, confused.

"All I wanted was to marry Belle," Gaston growled. "I didn't know this *thing* really kidnapped her… and now suddenly she's imprisoned by D'Arque? It's obvious they're in on this together!"

The Prince felt his eyebrows knitting together and a howl of frustration coming on. "If… we were… in on it together… why would I come here and ask for help?"

"I don't trust you, beast!" the hunter growled, sighting down the barrel of his gun. He let the mirror drop – his friend caught it just before it fell to the floor. "Everyone, stand aside while I put this thing out of its misery!"

"*You* were the one in league with D'Arque!" the Prince protested.

"*You* twisted him! *You* made him do this to Belle! It wasn't anything *I* did!"

Meanwhile, the little man had been looking into the mirror with wonder. "If he *is* doing this to harmless little Belle, and Maurice," the short man said slowly, "what's he been doing to everyone else up in there? Like… my great-aunt Foufou? She was just a *little* crazy…"

"D'Arque took my cousin," someone said grimly. "Said he was a danger to us."

People began to growl and mutter, and conversations about what was happening and what was to be done began.

"But what about *him*?" Gaston demanded, jerking his chin at the Prince. "He's a… he's really a beast! We should kill him now and then figure out everything else later!

Come on!"

"He's demonic! Get him!"

"Wait. Why *did* he come to ask for help, then?"

"Put him in chains, at the very least!"

Everyone began shouting an idea or opinion. Guns were waved around as well as knives and fists.

The Beast thought desperately. What could he do? What could a beastly prince do, who couldn't order or insist these men, or charm them with wit the way Belle might have?

Suddenly, he knew.

Beg.

Yet another thing he had never done before.

He knelt down on the floor. He looked up at the crowd beseechingly. At Gaston in particular, whose eye colour, he realised, was actually not that far off from his own.

"Do whatever you like to me after we rescue Belle. I swear on my honour I will let you. Lock me up, kill me, what have you. I will turn myself in. Please, just help me get her free first."

Everyone quieted. Gaston was working his jaw, trying to decide what to do.

"Don't do it," someone said. "He's a demon bewitching you with false visions. He's a liar."

But the man didn't sound enthusiastic; he said it tiredly,

like *someone* had to say it.

Everyone else began to murmur assents.

"Gaston," the short man said, poking at his thigh. "*My aunt.*"

The hunter looked ready to kill his friend – ready to kill *anyone*, just to channel the conflicting emotions and hatred that couldn't find an outlet anywhere else. The Prince almost sympathised for a moment. *Not all beasts look like beasts.* He wondered what Gaston's own enchanted portrait would look like.

"We'll deal with *you* later," Gaston finally said, grabbing his gunpowder belt and munitions bag. "But right now, we need to save Belle!"

ESCAPE

Belle had never felt so terrible and alone in her life.

It wasn't just the pain.

It was that each of the little pains she felt now, each unusual purple bruise, each scabbing pinprick, each ache from where she had unconsciously strained against the table and the straps, was inflicted on her with *purpose.* With intent. A man had *chosen* to cause these myriad pains to her. A man had made her stomach swim and head pound and now the light from the lanterns blazed and flickered such that it sent agony through her eyes and down her spine.

And she had no idea when her tormentor would be back.

What did I, the bookworm and crazy inventor's daughter,

do to deserve any of this? she couldn't help asking the world.

She had led her quiet life reading – and then tried to rescue her father, and then tried to help the Beast after she messed up everything. She had never done anything purposefully bad to anyone beyond the mild nastinesses of childhood.

And Frédéric D'Arque had been one of her father's *friends*! Poor Papa couldn't even remember that…

The mad 'doctor' was also her mother's kidnapper and betrayer. He was responsible for stealing away one of the most important people in Belle's life.

"Maman," she wept quietly, wanting her more than ever before.

Suddenly the air felt loose around her.

Confused, she sat up.

Her restraints had fallen away.

She blinked exactly once. The old Belle would have sat and tried to figure out what had happened – she was certain that when she came to, the straps had been tight round her legs and chest and even across the top of her head.

The new Belle didn't bother, taking the opportunity to run. Who knew why D'Arque had left her and how soon he would be back.

There was no one in the prep room. Belle crept past the empty beds, trying not to breathe in the antiseptic stink.

The door out was locked, but from her side; why anyone would want to try to break *into* it was beyond her. Perhaps D'Arque was afraid of someone interrupting his experiments.

She carefully slid back the giant bolt and let the door open towards her a crack. Two corridors fed into an open area where three stools sat empty… and one was filled by a man so large she was pretty sure he had giant in his ancestry somewhere. If he were a *charmante.* He was cleaning his nails with a particularly nasty-looking knife.

She cursed and quickly let the door close quietly.

Belle looked round the prep room, panicking. There were scalpels and knives on the counter in one corner, and she took one, why not? Although, she was pretty sure it wouldn't be much good in her hands against someone so large. Otherwise, there was nothing else useful.

The only other place to go was the room from which she had come.

Belle bit her lip and forced herself to ignore the blind panic building inside her and went back into the operating room.

The machines that had been used on her loomed large and evil in one corner. Opposite them, on the other side of her blood-spattered table, was another door that she hadn't noticed before. A small one that trolley-beds could not fit through.

Belle tried the handle.

It was locked.

She closed her eyes and said a few choice words she had learned from reading novels. Then she took a deep breath. The whole building was set up more like a medieval prison than a modern hospital; the lock was not going to be that complicated. She bent down and carefully inserted the scalpel into the keyhole. Relief settled upon her when it became clear that it was indeed an old Roman-style lock without barrels – just a simple latch. A few careful twists and turns succeeded in moving it a little…

… *snikt*…

… before the knife snapped. Belle cursed; now the blade was stuck in the door and if someone came by he would immediately realise what had happened. But at least it was unlocked. She slipped in and closed the door quickly behind her.

Belle wasn't sure what she expected on the other side, but it was certainly not what she found.

Skulls.

Many skulls.

Some of the skulls were inside glass jars and still had bits of brain matter attached to them.

There was what she was pretty sure was a preserved torso in a glass coffin filled with pickling liquid. The skin over the belly and heart had been pulled back and metal tags attached to what were apparently relevant bits underneath. There were, she couldn't help noticing, six nipples on the chest, and what looked like fur beginning above the hips.

A desk covered in notes and the occasional unseemly splatter, sat strangely primly amid the horror, a beautiful long quill awaiting use in an inkpot.

Unable to help herself, Belle took a look at the notes.

Sadly, unable to find a living specimen of the were *variety. The corpse brought to me was already beginning to decay, and the brain completely unusable. Cannot confirm theory of* charmante *node. Body, however, utterly fascinating. I began with an incision…*

She turned away, unable to read more.

There was a narrow spiral staircase in the corner of the room. She made for it, hoping to escape the cloying, nauseating smell of embalming fluids.

Up and up and through the darkness it climbed, round, metal and cold. It felt like she passed several floors before coming to a place where she could step off.

She emerged, dizzy and sick, in a dark and narrow room that looked like a connecting hall at first. She took a candle out of its sconce and raised it, frowning into the gloom.

Books.

Hundreds of them. Maybe a thousand.

The cold black walls were covered in shelves, and the shelves with books.

On the Extirpation of Witches in the New World
Surprisingly Accurate Trials to Determine Associations with the Devil, as Determined by John Hathorne
Taxidermy, a Layman's Guide
The Necronomicon
The Evils of Res Supernaturae
Deconstructive Anatomy
Successful Torture Methods of the Late 11th Century

Belle picked a book at random. The page it opened to had an etching of a screaming woman with horns, being opened from gut to nose by a calm surgeon.

She dropped it, feeling tainted by its very touch.

Then reason overcame disgust and she carefully picked it up, placing it back where it belonged.

Everywhere she looked, every nook and cranny, was crammed with black leather-bound books that fairly reeked with evil – couched in a weak coating of 'science' and 'religion'.

Towards the end of the aisle were large folio-sized

journals and diaries, all of the same style as the one she had seen in D'Arque's lab. She picked the thickest, blackest one and opened it. This was entirely unillustrated, just tables of entries and notes.

Madame Annabel Salvage – female, 43 at time of entering possession. Famed 'compounder' of unlikely potions and tonics. CURED. Survived. See notes, re: charmante *node removal, blood purification.*

Anonymous – female, short, speaker to animals. CURED. Deceased.

The list went on and on. Here were all of *les charmantes* who unfortunately fell into his power, and a clear list of the experiments he performed on them to remove their magic.

"'Cured. Deceased'!" Belle spat, forgetting herself for a moment. She slammed the book back on to the shelf. She longed to destroy it, as all the good books in Monsieur Lévi's shop had been. But when they brought D'Arque before a court of law, this would be prime evidence.

Belle hurried on, holding her hand round the flame so it wouldn't go out, more determined than ever to escape, to rescue her parents, to survive and bring terrible retribution on the monster who ran this asylum.

The library door opened into a broad, well-lit area shaped like a bottleneck. She shrank against the wall as noises travelled down multiple halls to her: clinking and clanking, voices raised, the occasional shriek.

The narrow end of the room had one giant set of double doors with wide bars, allowing whoever was outside to watch what lay beyond them.

"Who's the keeper tonight?" came a voice from the other side. It was rough and male and deep. Belle thought of her masked captors.

"It's Filthy Mary," another voice said with a laugh.

"Faugh! May as well leave it alone, then."

"Don't have to tell *me* twice."

Keeping her back against it, Belle crept along the wall farthest from those voices and peeped round the corner down the first hall. There was a large locked door built into a heavy stone frame just a metre or so away. Through the grill in it she could hear the moans and cries of the now truly insane.

She passed quickly by and moved on to the next hall, praying no one was watching.

Same thing. A locked door, the cries of the deranged beyond.

Same for the next hall.

The one *after* revealed something different.

There was no locked door set into it; instead, it widened and opened into a storage area of sorts. There were piles of neatly folded, surprisingly clean laundry on shelves, unused chamber pots ready to go, shapeless robes with wide belts… and trays being laid out with bowls and bread for dinner.

Doing the laying-out was a woman whose very shape made Belle almost buckle with rage.

Without thinking, Belle ran on quiet tiptoe as fast as she could, picking up speed and slamming the older woman as hard as she could in the middle of her back.

The hateful woman fell, the one who had 'accompanied' Belle for her 'comfort' to the room of torture. Who hadn't even felt the need to wear a mask, ever.

She moaned as her face hit the table in front of her and her legs collapsed.

"What…" the woman began.

Belle grabbed the closest thing she could, a tin chamber pot, and smashed the woman across the head with it.

The woman slumped, silent and bleeding.

Belle took one moment to breathe.

She took another moment to reflect on what recent events were turning her into.

But by the third moment she was feeling all over Filthy Mary for the set of keys she knew she would have.

Voilà! Next to her kitchen knife, under her belt.

Belle took the big, black, ugly lump of keys, and the knife, and hurried to the hall.

"Everything all right out there?"

Belle froze as the guard's voice called through the bars. She thought desperately.

"Keys keep slipping through my fingers," she called back in as close to an imitation of the woman's terrible accent as she could manage. She put a nasty purr into it. "You want to come and… help me? With your *strong hands*?"

"No, go ahead," the voice said quickly.

Belle closed her eyes and allowed herself a single deep sigh of relief.

None of the rooms in this corridor was as 'nice' as the ones she and her father had been thrown into. These were a little over a metre wide, unlit and they stank. Belle went quickly through the smaller keys, trying to find a likely one. Moans increased up and down the row as the metal clinked, either from fear or expectation of gruel, it was hard to say.

When Belle finally threw the first door open, it was hard to say who was more surprised: she or the person within.

The… *person*… was small. Very small. And despite the foul conditions of the cell and the prison, Belle was pretty sure that it wasn't his *hair* that was dishevelled to the point of looking like a hedgehog's spines… The person really had a head covered with hedgehog spines.

"*GO!*" Belle said when she found her voice. She pointed to the door. "You're free!"

The poor thing blinked at her with big sticky black eyes.

It started to open its mouth.

"*Shhh!*" Belle said, finger to lips. "Go!"

At that, the creature ran. Or... *scurried.* It was hard to tell.

Belle's plan was simple: unlock all the doors as fast as she could. Let *all* the prisoners out. Find her mother and father while chaos ruled the insane asylum and the guards dealt with all the other inmates.

It wasn't great, but it was all she had.

She ran to the next cell. And the next.

Most of the prisoners were seemingly human. All had terrible cuts and scars on their heads. And some of the people were shockingly familiar.

"*Monsieur Boulanger?*" She gaped in shock. He was the present Monsieur Boulanger's father, a great old man who was said to be able to spin sugar confections so delicate and airy it was as if the angels themselves created them. But Belle hadn't heard anything about him in years.

He looked sad and faintly embarrassed. And *sick.* Pale yellow and wheezing.

Belle opened her mouth to say something. He was someone's father, just like Maurice was hers. Stolen and abandoned here...

And that's when the guards finally figured out something was going on.

"HEY! HEY! Adrien! Come here! Why isn't Mary back yet? I think we have a problem…"

Belle ran out. Hopefully the old – *charmante*? – baker would follow, but she didn't have time to find out.

She flung herself desperately from cell to cell, unlocking each as fast as her tired fingers could manage. The sounds of shouting grew louder and closer.

Finally, when she flung open the last door there was no one waiting for her… just something almost like a corpse, tied down to a hard stone bench.

It lifted its head to look at the newcomer.

With a shock, Belle recognised the monster from the image in the mirror.

"Maman!" she sobbed.

REUNION

"*Belle*," her mother croaked.

She looked 20 years older than Belle's *papa*. Scars and lines crossed her face like an ancient field, once watered with canals and streams, now dry. Her prematurely white hair was filthy and tangled and matted with old dry blood. But her eyes were bright, bright green through the crust and dirt, an angelic green that Belle remembered so clearly from her vision.

"Maman!" Belle cried again, throwing her arms round her as best she could, weeping into her. In all of her fantasies of what this moment would be like, Belle was always somehow smaller than her mother, and her mother was holding *her* in wide, comforting arms. Not the other way round.

"Belle. This day is the only thing I have lived for," her mother whispered.

Only with great effort was Belle able to master herself. She clumsily undid the buckles that kept the older woman confined. With a sigh, her mother slumped to the side, maybe being allowed to do so for the first time in years.

"We have to go," Belle said, holding her hand and squeezing. It was frail, and bony, and cold.

"Wait, just wait. Let me just *look* at you," her mother said, putting another weak and spidery hand on top of Belle's. She leaned back and blinked, as if trying to take in ten years' worth of her daughter's growth in one moment. "*You are so beautiful!* So strong! You're everything I could ever have wished for in a daughter!"

Belle tried to blink back the tears that were coming again. The shock of hearing her long-lost mother say exactly the words she had always wanted a mother to say was too much.

"*Why?*" Belle asked, unable to stop herself. "Why did you make me forget you? Why couldn't I have even the few memories of us together?"

"Not just you," the woman said with difficulty, taking wheezy breaths in between the words. "Not just me. *All charmantes.* Forgotten. Forever. To protect us. And you. No longer would any human be able to remember where we live and hunt us down. And with you and Maurice having… forgotten… *me*, and magic, you would be safe, too. Forever.

"Not that it seems to have worked."

"I'd rather *not* have been safe," Belle insisted. "I'd rather have been with you."

The woman chuckled bitterly. "Ah, I doubt that. What he's done to me for the past ten years I wouldn't wish on my worst enemy, much less my own daughter."

"But how… How was D'Arque able to do all this? How did *he* not forget about *les charmantes*?"

The woman's face fell into a distinctly frightening, smouldering frown. "He is a *charmante* as well. Or was. He hated himself and all like him… I never knew how much."

"I saw him," Belle said. "In the images… in the castle…"

"Ohh," the woman groaned. "I am such a fool. And that was my last great piece of magic. *That*. The cursing of a useless eleven-year-old human. When I felt you bring the curse down, it was like my soul was ripped in two. Magic came back on itself, and I've been punished accordingly."

She shook her head.

"With what little I have left, I tried to reach you, tried to tell you what happened. And then I freed you."

The bed. Her straps. *That's* how she had been set free. It was her mother.

The sounds of metal against metal suddenly grew loud, and the shouting; the door to the cell was opened and one of the more human-looking prisoners stuck his head in.

"*Mademoiselle*, the guards are on their way, you must flee, you and Rosalind!"

"*Rosalind*," Belle said, feeling the word on her lips. Rosalind, her mother.

"Come, you will have to help me," the older woman said, pushing herself up. "Now that I've seen your face once more I can die happy – but I'd rather not. I'd rather see *Frédéric* die first."

Belle put her arm out and carefully helped the woman whom anyone else would have thought was her *grandmother* get off the stone table and out of her cell. She almost had to carry her.

Outside it was precisely the chaos Belle had hoped for: there was a lot of running and screaming and panicking and shouting.

"We have to go and get Papa," Belle said.

"I saw him… Maurice. He would be upstairs," her mother croaked. "With the… the 'real' patients. Let's go…"

"*Belle!*"

Belle was stopped in her tracks by a strangely familiar voice calling from a cell across the way, one that was still locked.

Grasping the bars like a sad circus animal was Monsieur Lévi, the bookseller.

Belle gasped, then unlocked the door.

"That *horrid, horrid* man" Lévi swore as soon as he was free. "He promised. He *promised* me he wouldn't touch you."

Rosalind's eyes narrowed. "You made a deal with that *monster*?" she said in a surprisingly even tone for someone so otherwise weak. "We will discuss this later, Lévi. For now, perhaps you can help…"

"Absolutely." He grinned and held up his hand, producing a tiny sliver of glittering glass. "Now that I'm free, I can get everyone else out. You two go and find Maurice!"

Belle took her mother's arm and dragged her along as fast as she could. Was it her imagination, or was her mother growing stronger? Was her vitality returning, now that she was away from her cell? Or was it just the excitement of the moment?

"*STOP!*"

A guard stepped out in front of them. He had the arms of a circus strong-man and his hands could easily rip their shoulders from their sockets.

Belle raised her kitchen knife. Its thin blade looked pitiful against his sheer size and bulk.

He started to reach out…

… and then was suddenly falling over like a giant log, screaming in pain.

Belle looked down to see what knocked him over. The little hedgehog-person was curled up in a ball at his feet and grinning, spines all out. Pinpricks of blood appeared like rain all over the orderly's clean white gown.

"Thank you," Belle whispered.

The thing chattered something meaningless in response before uncurling himself and running away again.

"A *hérisser*," Rosalind murmured to herself. "Delightful people. I didn't know there were any left…"

Belle pulled her mother along. She seemed easily distracted and there was far too much going on around them to allow that to happen. Back at the main entrance to the cell blocks, inmates flooded out while guards tried to push their way in, wielding clubs and leather-covered batons. Belle closed her eyes, said a quiet prayer and dived through.

On a hunch they headed down a hall polluted by the hot and fetid air of an industrial kitchen. She was right; they were soon running through a low-ceilinged cavern of a room that smelled disastrous. Squat metal stoves warmed large, unclean black pots to boiling with soup that was no more than thin broth. Foul things occasionally bubbled to the surface with a pop of sulphurous steam.

The head cook, a giant slob of a man, leaned back on

a stool that bowed with his weight while he regarded Belle and her mother with lazy surprise.

"We were never here," Belle said, gesturing at him with her knife.

The man said nothing, giving a wide, careless shrug.

Belle pulled her mother on.

On the other side of the kitchen were the pantry and receiving hall, where loads of groceries could easily be delivered, as well as a narrow set of servants' stairs that led to the main floor.

She dashed up them, pulling her mother behind...

... and ran right into a pair of large orderlies, coming down with trays of empty bowls.

All four landed in a tangled mess, Belle's and her mother's arms and legs floating more to the top because they were smaller.

"They're escaping!" one of the orderlies said. "They're patients!"

"No one is a 'patient' here!" Belle snapped, twisting and turning to extricate herself from them. Once she rose she turned to help her mother up.

The female orderly stumbled to her feet and, putting her two hands together, backhanded Belle across the face.

Not expecting such a quick and violent attack, Belle staggered back against the wall, stunned. Blood dripped down her face.

Her mother, hunched over and ineffectual looking, only widened her green eyes in reaction to what had just happened.

The other orderly, a man, was now also up. He grabbed Belle by the shoulder, digging his fingers into the muscle between the bones there.

"*Racine*," Rosalind whispered, holding out her hand and blowing something from it.

Both orderlies' eyes popped in surprise.

They looked down at their feet. Belle was just recovering from the blow and had tears in her eyes, she couldn't see anything. But their two would-be captors didn't seem to be able to lift their legs. They began to panic, screaming in little soundless Os.

Her mother slumped and swayed, utterly exhausted.

Belle grabbed her just as she fell, ignoring her own pain.

"Dirt from the floor of my cell…" her mother murmured, stepping up the stairs with difficulty. "Filled with fungal threads…"

Belle wasn't sure if she was raving or not, but the guards couldn't follow, and that was the important point.

At the top of the stairs it was like entering another world: while not precisely light and sunny, the halls were broad and didn't stink. The stone walls were free from mould and slime, and lanterns hung at regular intervals.

"This feels familiar," Belle said thoughtfully. She ran on tiptoe down the hall, dragging her mother behind her, coming to a sudden stop as she heard a familiar voice shouting.

"No... only the monsters in the sub-basement. Everything is fine up here. Send everyone you can down!"

D'Arque.

Belle felt a hot hand of rage clamp down on her belly. The atrocities that had been committed on her family by that man... She wanted nothing more than to run at him, knife out.

Reason, still a somewhat dominant force in Belle's heart, finally prevailed.

She waited until she heard the thumping sounds of guards hurrying away, followed by the cold *click* of the old man's heeled boots on stone.

She counted an additional 50 seconds after the sound died away before stepping forwards.

As she had guessed, they were in the hub of the 'normal insane people' wing. There were halls leading off to hospital rooms, wide and almost inviting, with thin rugs. No doubt to impress visiting relatives who probably had no idea what went on below. Even the sounds were different; there were a few whimpers and moans, but those sounded plaintive. Not *tortured.*

Belle would still release everyone up here as well, after she got her father.

"*Papa?*" she called as loudly as she dared.

"*Belle?*" a voice called back, surprised.

"Maurice," Rosalind whispered.

The two women hurried over to his cell. Belle fumbled over the keys until she found the right one.

Her father practically knocked them over when he came rushing out, putting a meaty arm round each one's neck and pulling them both close.

"My girls!" he sobbed. "*My two girls.* I never… I never thought we'd be a family again."

Belle didn't want him to ever let go. Mother and father together, hugging her, one happy family like they should have been, never separated. Who knew what would happen in the next few minutes, if they didn't get out? There might not be another moment like this again…

"We have to go. Now, Papa," she finally said, regretfully disentangling herself.

"Wait, what about everyone else?" Maurice asked.

"Hey. *You,*" Belle called to a prisoner who had been watching the whole scene quietly, hands on his bars. "*Catch!*"

The man seemed only vaguely surprised when she tossed the keys to him. After he looked at them for a moment, bewildered, his eyes finally widened with understanding.

"Let's go!" Belle said, grabbing her parents by the arms.

And that's when two guards, passing by the other end of the hallway, saw them.

"*STOP!*" one of them ordered.

The prisoner with the keys hid them behind his back and tried to look innocent.

"RUN!" shouted Belle.

She dived forwards, fully expecting to pull the full weight of both her mother and father. But although he took a little to get going, Maurice soon began trotting under his own power. He let go of Belle and ran round to grab Rosalind's other arm and the two dragged her along.

They ran into the closest open room, what looked like an indoor exercise and recreation area for the non-magical patients. Leather balls and tatty decks of cards littered low, padded tables and backless chairs. Belle and her father scattered the furniture as best they could as they ran, tipping things over and hurling them behind. Belle didn't dare turn round but was gratified to hear some frustrated grunts and the crashing of furniture behind her.

Not knowing which way to go, Belle picked corridors and rooms at random. They ended up in the laundry: tubs of soapy, soupy hot water and lines of eerily stained linens blocked their way. Calmer patients worked here under the watchful eyes of house nannies, carrying piles of clothes and pushing paddles deep into steamy alkaline tubs.

"You're free!" Belle shouted at them, ducking around a scalding-hot tub.

"Run!" Maurice suggested, pushing a very skinny girl out of the way.

"*OUT OF MY LAUNDRY!*" a large woman with an imposing hat shrieked.

Rosalind did her best to keep up, holding Maurice's hand as they threaded through the maze of dirty and wet clothes.

"There should be a door ahead!" Maurice called up to Belle. "For hanging the clothes out the back!"

Belle didn't have time to wonder how he could have guessed such a thing; she changed directions around a confused-looking patient with a tall pile of white cloth in her arms. Neither managed to quite avoid each other; there was a crash and soon pillowcases and smocks were drifting to earth like angels. Belle managed to recover herself first.

"Sorry," she said, dashing away. She wasn't sure the patient even noticed.

The guards were right behind them, tearing clothing lines out of their way and swearing loudly as burning hot water splashed on to their skin.

But the door, as her father had said, was straight ahead.

"On three, Belle." Maurice bent over, aiming his shoulder at the probably locked exit. Belle did the same. "One, two, *three*!"

Father and daughter ran forwards and the doors gave under their combined weight and strength – though possibly a bit more of it was Maurice. Rosalind hurried behind as best she could.

What they ran into outside was hard to fathom.

It was dusk and difficult to make out anything clearly in the gloaming. Dozens of people were running round the asylum's formal great lawn in various stages of dress and distress. Guards were chasing after them, alternately wheedling them coyly to come back or screaming viciously and aiming at their heads with truncheons. It was a scene of hellish chaos, as painted by Bruegel or Bosch.

In the near distance, angry lights flickered, coming closer.

Is that… Gaston? Leading the villagers?

"What's going on?"

One of their pursuers had caught up to them – but just as he was about to lay a hand on Belle he became as transfixed by the odd scene as she.

Maurice took that opportunity to turn and land a blow squarely on the man's sternum; he doubled over and the inventor hit him again in the jaw. With that, he fell unconscious.

"You big bully," Maurice growled. "You're only used to picking on the weak."

"*Aunt! Aunt Foufou!*"

Belle recognised LeFou among the torch-carrying villagers. Some of the others were also looking for family members among the escaped patients. Everyone else seemed to be out for blood; there were muskets and actual pitchforks in their hands. The look in their eyes was frightening, magnified by the torchlight.

"Let's... go around this," Belle suggested. Whatever was happening it would most certainly not end well for her. Nothing involving Gaston and the villagers ever seemed to.

The little family stuck close to the asylum, running alongside it and trying to keep out of everyone's way. Unless her father had a better plan, Belle's idea was simply to get to the road or the stables and either steal a carriage or just keep going.

But when they rounded the corner, they ran almost bodily into D'Arque, who was waiting for them.

A TALE (AS OLD AS TIME)

D'Arque carried a small musket and smiled grimly.

Belle, Maurice and Rosalind turned to go back the other way but there were three big guards armed with truncheons bearing down on them with all the ominous finality of a checkmate.

"D'Arque! What is wrong with you?" Maurice demanded, turning back round.

"You mean *Frédéric*," Rosalind said wearily. "Do you remember now? Frédéric D'Arque?"

Maurice looked confused. His eyes batted in strange blinks. Something not quite natural was going on in his mind. "Frédéric…" he said slowly. "My old friend… Frédéric. D'Arque? How did I… how did I forget who you were?"

"He is, or was, a *charmante*," Rosalind said. "My own spell made you forget."

"No longer one of your kind, thank you very much," D'Arque said with a nasty smile and a nastier little bow. "I managed to cut the impurities out of myself years ago."

"But… how did you manage all this?" Maurice asked slowly. "All of these people… From here, and our home… How did you get, *kidnap*, I mean, all these people?"

"I had the full support of the king and queen," D'Arque said, drawing himself up haughtily. "They wanted to rid themselves of the *charmante* problem, but for more… strategic reasons than myself; they considered your kind a threat to their power. Once they heard of my own theories and opinion on the matter, they gave me a generous stipend, the funds to buy the old asylum, and the manpower to collect my subjects and patients."

"*You* were behind the disappearances from the beginning," Rosalind said flatly. "*You* kidnapped and killed Vashti."

"I didn't kill her," D'Arque corrected. "She took her own life, here, eventually. Sometimes they do that."

Belle watched her mother's jaw drop, her hands slowly gripping and ungripping some object she obviously no longer had.

A wand, maybe?

"Frédéric..." Maurice said slowly. "I don't understand. We were *friends*... How could you do this?"

"My apologies for borrowing your innocent self and pure daughter," he said, lowering his eyes almost convincingly. "I was after larger prey, as it were. You were just the bait."

Belle's eyes widened. "Beast. Oh, no..."

"Yes. I made the connection after Gaston told me about Maurice's 'beast in the woods'. It was the little princeling from the forgotten fairy tale kingdom, all grown up. If not into a *man*, precisely."

Rosalind narrowed her eyes. "Whatever has happened to him, it is not his fault. Leave him be."

"I cannot let a marauding monster go free in our countryside," D'Arque said, clucking his tongue. "And who are *you* telling me to leave something be, you who go marching around, cursing princes and changing *les naturel*s into something they are not? What gave you that right?"

Rosalind looked pained. "I made mistakes. I would correct them... Killing the Prince solves nothing."

Belle's curiosity made her speak up, despite all that was going on. "Monsieur Lévi said something about you promising not to touch me," she said accusingly.

"Ah, yes, well," D'Arque said, shrugging. "Lévi was one of the least harmful *charmantes*, and careful not to ever practise magic in the village. In return for his not… exposing my operations, I agreed that neither I nor any of my associates would bother you."

"But you kidnapped me *and* my father!" Belle snapped. "*And* Monsieur Lévi!"

"Well, regrettable as breaking my word is, it was for a good purpose. And only to a *charmante.* It means nothing, like promises to a bird. I needed to make sure he didn't help either Belle or the Beast, so I decided it would be best to keep him safely out of the way."

"Promises to a *bird*?" Maurice asked in disgust. "Frédéric, *we were friends.* You came to Belle's christening!"

"What?" Belle asked involuntarily. Her mind raced. If he was close enough to be at her christening… "You were *all* friends…

"*You* killed Alaric Potts."

At *that,* for the first time, D'Arque looked bothered, shaken out of his smugness.

"You knew he was helping to rescue *les charmantes* out of the kingdom… bringing them to Maman and Papa. Or maybe you didn't know what he was doing with them *until* you killed him. And when you found out, you went after Maman."

D'Arque shifted nervously, irritably, from foot to foot on his expensive, old-fashioned heels. "I never intended to hurt any man, any *human.* Least of all my old friend.

His betrayal was beyond enraging and dangerous."

"*HIS* betrayal?" Belle demanded. "You turned on your best friends! All of them!"

"*He turned on his race!*" D'Arque hissed. "Why would someone born innocent, born *pure*, help *les charmantes*? He *knew* how dangerous they were!"

"We are going to go now," Maurice said carefully. "And you are going to just let us go. I think you know just how precisely vile you are, Frédéric. You're a smart man. You always have been. You know this is the way it needs to end. Goodbye."

And Maurice put his arm round his wife's waist and his hand in his daughter's and turned round very deliberately to go.

"You are incorrect, *old friend*," D'Arque said, his voice cracking. Belle heard him cock his musket with a terrifyingly quiet *click*.

They turned back to the doctor. He had the gun carefully balanced on his forearm and was sighting down it with one eye closed. No mere gesture was this – he was aiming to kill if he had to.

Belle started to open her mouth, thinking of all sorts of reasonable and pitiable things to say, logic and begging…

And that's when the Beast came tearing out of the crowd, leaping at D'Arque's throat.

ALL TOGETHER

"*Beast!*" Belle cried.

At no point during any of her time in the castle had she seen him look like this. He was slavering, literally *slavering*, foam and spittle coming off his curved ivory teeth. His lips were pulled back, revealing black, animal-like gums. His eyes were still the unusual bright blue, but there was no trace of anything human or remotely intelligent in them. He was mad as a dog with hydrocephalus.

D'Arque got off one shot before the Beast landed on his chest, knocking him to the ground. And Belle couldn't tell where the shot had gone, if it was actually into the Beast, he didn't so much as twitch.

He crouched on the old man and lifted his claws high, prepared to rend him limb from limb with the relish of a long-starved lion.

"*Wait!*"

Belle ran forwards, pulling out of her parents' grip and running to him.

"Belle, no!" her father cried.

The Prince, while keeping the lower half of his body perfectly still, twisted in a weasel-like and inhuman way to regard Belle. He sniffed the air around her, his wet nose and tongue coming dangerously close to her cheeks.

She held very still.

"Beast, it's me," she said, slowly putting a hand out.

He eyed it suspiciously.

Belle bit her lip and gently touched his hot, furry arm.

"Remember? It's Belle. I'm Belle. I read you stories."

"*Belle*," the Beast said gruffly, in a voice that was barely intelligible.

D'Arque took that inopportune moment to move, trying to scrabble out from underneath his captor.

The Beast let out a roar and cuffed his prey on the side of the head to silence him.

"No!" Belle said, loudly and firmly. "*Stop.*"

The Beast growled.

"If you kill him, it will make you a murderer. And you aren't a murderer *or* a beast."

He looked at her with large eyes, impossible to read.

Were they uncomprehending, or thinking?

His claws twitched.

"Come back to me," Belle pleaded. "Come back to me. I know you're there. Please, come back."

The Beast blinked.

Belle made herself look into his eyes, to *hold* him there.

And he looked back. Wide-eyed but blank.

"*Please*," she whispered. "For me."

She reached out slowly and touched his mane, just above his horn. His nose twitched. Gently she stroked the little wavy lock there, smoothing it behind his ear the way she would a stray bit of her own hair.

The Beast's paw snapped up and grabbed her wrist.

Belle couldn't help wincing: his grip was as solid and strong and unyielding as stone. But he wasn't bearing down, or trying to crush her. He just… *held* her arm there.

"*Belle*," he whispered, almost a croak.

"You promised to give me my bookshop back," she said, trying not to cry. "You *promised me.* So I could read more stories about Jack. So I could read them… to *you*…"

The Beast's mouth opened strangely, his pointy teeth suddenly seeming too large and out of place inside lips that were trying to form words it couldn't remember.

Then he suddenly shook himself, like a spooked cat or dog.

He looked down at Belle, his eyes bright with intelligence.

"I *did* promise," he said, his voice growing stronger and more human. "And… a king *keeps* his promises."

Belle almost sobbed with relief.

Then the Beast leapt up and lifted the old man as well, setting him violently on his feet.

"The girl you kidnapped just saved your life," he growled. "*Thank* her."

"Oh, I do," D'Arque said, brushing himself off.

Belle was instantly suspicious of his calm and… almost theatrical demeanour. She glanced behind her. The villagers had gathered behind them and were watching everything. LeFou gave her a curious look. But Gaston was nowhere to be seen.

"I thank her very much for her human inclinations towards mercy and pity," the head of the asylum continued. "None of which you… naturally have." Then he raised his voice, directly addressing the crowd. "You see? This is what I have been protecting you all from for all of these years. The wild, crazed and *powerful* beasts that sometimes have human form."

He gave Rosalind a purposeful look.

"Despite their… familiar appearances, those born of magic and the supernatural are not human and have none of the temperance, compassion, logic or morality that we men and women do. All these years I have been trying to corral these creatures, cure them of their supernatural insanity, protect you from them. Can you imagine a world in which they are free to rampage and do as they will?"

"You, too, were one of *les charmantes*," Maurice shouted. "You could tell the future, Frédéric. You're killing your own."

"Not any more. Not one of *my* own," D'Arque said with a vile grin. He pushed his hair back, his *wig* back, to reveal a skull brutally scarred and pitted as if bone itself had been broken and removed like a jigsaw puzzle.

Belle, her father and her mother looked with horror. People in the crowd gasped in disgust.

"You see?" D'Arque replaced his wig. "I have removed the unnatural part of me that led to improper visions."

"You have removed something of yourself, too, Frédéric," Maurice said sadly. "You were never this mad before. Never *this* full of hate."

"But what about Belle?" someone from the crowd demanded. "There's nothing supernatural about her. You kidnapped her! And tortured her!"

"He tortured *all* of us!"

This was spat by the wheezing Monsieur Boulanger senior. He leaned heavily on the shoulders of his son and daughter, both of whom looked angry and ashamed.

There was a palpable shift among the crowd. The patients, clearly differentiated in their thin, pale garments, began to move forwards, a similar murder in all of their eyes.

The orderlies, nurses and thugs employed by D'Arque responded immediately, hunkering down and brandishing their truncheons.

Suddenly, one of the patients shot forwards with a scream, making right for D'Arque.

Two orderlies immediately leapt in his way, bringing their clubs down on his neck and back with a sickening thud.

A dozen muskets were raised, readied and cocked. The villagers, who had been angry without real direction before, now had a focus for their rage. They began to move menacingly forwards.

"I warn you, my guards are well-trained," D'Arque said.

"*Guards?* This is no house for the weak-minded," Monsieur LeClerc said in disgust. "My donations have been going to a… grizzly carnal house. You are an obscenity, Monsieur D'Arque."

"You aren't seeing the big picture," D'Arque spoke calmly, as if they would all understand in time. "These people are *dangerous…*"

"*HOW IS MY FATHER DANGEROUS?*" Boulanger's daughter demanded. She pulled her sleeves up her own meaty bakers' arms and advanced on him. "You said he was a danger to himself and others! We believed you!"

An orderly put himself firmly in her way.

"And my aunt!" LeFou spat. "She went in a little kooky and now she doesn't even know me!"

He had a pair of small flintlock pistols and was no unskilled shooter.

"People..." Belle began uncertainly.

"You swore," Monseiur Lévi called, coming out of the crowd to stand with Belle and her family. "You swore you would *never* go after Belle. You're a monster who breaks his word on top of everything else."

"I had to be sure Belle was pure of her mother's foul disease," D'Arque answered primly. "And honestly, she was bait to lure in the... the..."

Belle, and everyone else, waited for him to finish his statement, which was accompanied by a strange, wide-eyed look of surprise on his face.

His body jerked oddly.

"I, uhhh..."

Blood began to pool out of his stomach and onto his shirt.

He fell forwards, revealing Gaston and his dripping hunting machete.

"*I* found LeFou's aunt. Sitting in her own fouled sheets," Gaston growled into the dying man's ear as he slumped.

Then he stood up, chest out, a grim look of satisfaction

on his face.

"I have vanquished the villain who has been preying on our town and its innocent loonies," he announced loudly to the crowd. "Come, let us lock up the Beast as we agreed and put an end to this."

No one moved or said anything. Even the escaped patients among the townspeople were shocked into silence, seeing their captor so violently dispatched in front of their very eyes. A few people looked at each other uncomfortably.

"There's only one way to end this terrible story on a less sombre note," Gaston said with a sad smile. He spun to face Belle and dropped to one knee with a grin. "Let's make this the most romantic happily ever after *ever.*

"Belle, will you marry me?"

ENDINGS

Belle blinked at Gaston. So did the Prince, who, having been in full beast form a moment ago, was so surprised he didn't seem to even want to tear the hunter limb from limb. LeFou might have shaken his head and looked away out of embarrassment for his friend, but that was the only immediate reaction from anyone.

No one made any move to grab the Beast, or shoot him, or lock him up.

Belle tried to focus on *those* things. She made herself think about all the bad things that *weren't* happening at that moment, that could have been happening, instead of just the sick theatrical demonstration from a very confused man and how she was now the centre of everyone's attention.

Including... Monsieur Lévi. Who was looking at

her interestedly. Like he was fascinated to see what she would do next. Like he trusted her and knew whatever it was, it would be the right thing.

She could hear a rushing in her ears. It had been a while since she had eaten.

"Gaston, did you burn down Monsieur Lévi's bookshop?"

It was strange how her voice carried. She didn't speak loudly, only clearly. And yet her precise words rang out like she had shouted the accusation.

Gaston's eyebrows shot up in surprise.

"What? Yes! But I was looking for Maurice. D'Arque told me he might be there. And also he had said that Lévi was… not a nice person."

But even as he said these words he looked confused, realising how ridiculous they sounded.

"He *was* dangerous, really…"

Belle just kept gazing at him.

"Well, his books are dangerous!" Gaston persisted. "They turned you into what you are – a foolish girl who doesn't want to marry me! *Me*, Gaston! Every girl in the village wants to marry me! And, also, they're a fire hazard…"

Belle couldn't even begin to sort out her thoughts, or what she really wanted to say to Gaston. Her feelings ran from *kill him* to *oh, why waste the effort, he's hopeless…*

And by the way the crowd was watching him babble

on, it was obvious that the town was done with their favourite son.

A speech from her about how burning down people's stores, and books, was a terrible crime, wouldn't accomplish much at this point.

So Belle very carefully turned away from him and addressed everyone else instead.

"I will, obviously, not be marrying Gaston today, for many reasons. As he will no doubt understand when he thinks about it for a moment, less overwhelmed by recent events."

"Belle…" Gaston whispered, embarrassed.

She ignored him.

"And we will *not* be locking up the Beast," she announced loudly, walking over and putting a hand on his arm. "He is the Prince, no, *King,* of a forgotten magical land through the forest, which some of you may start to remember now. He came here to free his people, and you, from a man who has committed *many* unspeakable atrocities. D'Arque has kidnapped innocent souls both from that kingdom and this village to perform hideous experiments on them."

Belle turned so she could look as many people in the eye as she could on one sweep of her gaze.

She took a deep breath. "I recommend a thorough

search of this house and property. Besides any lingering prisoners, there may be things family members wish to see… books in the library that list all of D'Arque's victims…"

She trailed off, unsure what else to say.

Stunned and confused by the strange events of the night, the villagers chose to cling to her suggestion. It was at least a place to start to try and understand everything that had happened. The angry, sad and curious went to explore the asylum. The families of patients who still lived found them and finally took them home.

Some just stayed in groups, whispering and muttering about it all.

Gaston looked on with an obvious lack of comprehension.

"No, wait," he said to no one in particular, leaping up. "D'Arque *had* to die. I *had* to kill him. Don't you see? He was a sick man! A *murderer*! Someone had to do it…"

"*Someone*, Gaston," the butcher said. "A judge. A court of law. An *executioner*. Or maybe he would have been sentenced to rot in his own prison. Not *you*."

"He was an evil man," Monsieur Sauveterre said with disgust. "But I will not be able to close my eyes for weeks without seeing him brutally murdered before me. I just thank God my children weren't here to see it as well."

Gaston ran through the crowd, entreating other people,

but everyone turned away and refused to listen.

Belle slumped, leaning against the Beast. She felt a million years old, a million pains all over her body. It was *not*, strictly, a happy ending. Wasn't it supposed to be? Why wasn't it all neat and finished, with a 'the end'?

The Prince must have felt the same way; he stood there silently, just holding her.

Rosalind approached them cautiously, her eyes on the Beast.

"Nothing I can ever say can make up for what I did," she began after a deep breath. "I thought I was saving what was left of a kingdom. I thought I was avenging all who had been hurt by your parents' actions. And I was no better than that crazy man with the machete over there. Except that what I did had much vaster, more disastrous consequences."

The Beast looked at her for a long moment before speaking.

"Thank you," he finally said. Then his face broke into an ironic, sad smile. "I think… as my first official act… as *king*, I declare amnesty. Forgiveness for everyone."

"But not forgetting," Maurice added quickly, with a shudder. "I never want to forget anything again. That was rash, Rosalind. That forget spell."

"I thought I was protecting *les charmantes*," she

said with a sad sigh. "Instead, it seems I have hastened our extinction. But listen…" She pulled herself together, and despite the prematurely white hair, the wear and tear her poor body had undergone, Belle saw a glimpse of the woman she once was: the powerful, indomitable Enchantress. She addressed the Prince. "You managed to stop yourself from becoming a full-fledged beast. Well done! Recovering your human soul and mind on your own, I mean."

The Beast blinked.

"Permanently? I'm not going to… relapse? Go back to being a beast – I mean, in my head – again?"

"Of course not," Rosalind said impatiently. "As long as your love for Belle, and hers for you, lasts. The spell is broken, or mitigated, at least."

Belle and the Beast looked at each other, eyes wide.

The Beast suddenly began to scratch the back of his neck in embarrassment. Belle blushed.

And then she found herself almost overcome with giggles.

"It's pretty obvious," Maurice pointed out with a smile.

"Yes, another factor in my punishment," Rosalind said grimly. "Magic always comes back on itself… of course it would be my daughter who would break the spell. I am an idiot. And now here you are, her future husband. A *prince*."

"King," Maurice corrected mildly. "And really, is that such a bad thing?"

"Yes, it is. But that's beside the point. I only have the tiniest bit of magic left, children, but it's just enough to turn you human again. Like you deserve."

The Beast's eyes widened. His mouth opened and closed several times.

Belle's heart leapt, for the first time in years, it seemed. Happily ever after *was* going to happen! Just like in books! It really was!

And then the Beast asked a single question.

"What about my servants?"

Belle immediately felt like an idiot. She had entirely forgotten them in the excitement.

"It's worse now," the Beast told her. "They're all… still. All not moving, not talking. Furniture. Dead."

"Oh, no…" Belle said, horrified. "Mrs Potts…"

"Can you turn them back, too?"

Rosalind's lips thinned as she thought.

"No," she finally said. "I only have enough magic left to undo part of the curse. If I release *you* from it, there will be nothing left to help them with."

The Beast looked deep into Belle's eyes as he asked a second question.

"If you don't… turn me back, can you help them? All of them?"

"Probably," Rosalind answered promptly.

Belle felt the icy, ancient fingers of cold reality settling on her shoulders.

She nodded, almost imperceptibly. Only the Beast saw.

"Then… that's what I would rather you do." The Beast put his giant paws on Belle's shoulders and gripped her strongly. "Save my people. They were innocent when they were cursed, and still looked after the castle and me all these years. They deserve to be free."

And then he pulled Belle into his chest and hugged her as tightly as he dared. She let out one little, shuddering sob before relaxing into his embrace. Things were imperfect and terrible, but she felt safe. Somehow they would get through this.

"Oh," Rosalind said, a little surprised. "All right. If that's what you want."

Despite the Beast's desire to release the servants as soon as possible, the night was black and cold and treacherous and utterly unfit for travel, especially for Rosalind. The four made their way back to the village with everyone else and spent the night at their home, though they didn't get to sleep until almost morning. Too many curious visitors wanted to visit the strangely human beast king, and too many others with slowly returning memories came to ask about things they thought they saw as children, or in the asylum… girls with hooves for feet, boys with dancing eyes and pointed ears.

Finally Maurice bade the last guest farewell and bolted the door behind him, and the little family, plus one, slept soundly together for the first time in years. When Belle woke in the middle of the night, she could see into her parents' room by the light of the moon and stars. Maurice and Rosalind were entwined round each other.

She could hear the Beast snuffling in his sleep, curled up in front of the fire like a dog, but with a pillow under his head and an old blanket thrown over his wide shoulders. Before succumbing once again to sleep, Belle revelled, a little, in the cosiness and completeness of her home.

When the sun rose and it was warm enough, the four set off with Phillipe pulling a sleigh borrowed from someone in town.

Rosalind sat bundled in as many coats and blankets as they could find but still shivered most of the way in her weakened state. Maurice sat by her and Belle rode the poor horse, who was occasionally given a break by the very strong beast, who pulled silently and with no complaint.

The sun was high when they finally arrived, sparkling on the snow which was melting just a little bit in the warmest places. The castle was covered in drips and drops, both from icicles and the strange webs, the strands dissolving and disappearing like they had never been.

"Huh. Not bad," Rosalind said of her own handiwork.

"Maman, I was trapped there," Belle pointed out gently. "And so were all those poor people."

Her mother's face fell as she remembered the consequences of what she had done.

When they stepped inside, it was like Belle's first time: cold and black. But because she was expecting the little creatures to come forwards and greet her, it seemed even bleaker and lonelier. When they got to the kitchen, Belle took one look at the sad little tableau of candelabrum, teapot and clock and nearly burst into tears.

"They seemed so lifelike before..." Maurice said in wonder.

Rosalind was obviously quite exhausted from their journey and just beginning to warm up. She didn't hesitate or protest, however; she just kept a look of grim determination on her face and began to chant.

Belle watched her in wonder. Rosalind was complicated... not a particularly nice or compassionate person, but certainly brave and willing to do whatever needed to be done once she decided a particular route was correct. What did that make her? Not, exactly, a good person. Misguided? Uninformed? A power that should have been tempered?

This is the mother that I found. Not the mother I imagined.

A strange smell filled the air... fresh pine and spring;

not the brittle needles of solstice or Christmas, but the soft and bright green twigs of March.

Much like something waking from a frozen hibernation, the clock on the table stretched and yawned and continued stretching. It continued filling out into a fat little man with a moustache who balanced on the table. He was a little pale, but otherwise healthy and alive.

"Good... good heavens!" Cogsworth said, looking at his hand and spreading his fingers. "I'm... me again! But the curse...?"

He leapt off the table and saw the Beast and Belle, instantly divining that something wasn't quite right.

"It's a long story," Belle said. "We can tell it later."

"I await with eagerness," Cogsworth said, perhaps a *trifle* dryly. As insouciant as the little butler ever was. The Beast managed a smile.

Next was Lumière, who turned out to be a rather handsome if long-nosed fellow. He immediately swept into a bow the moment he was able, and kissed Belle on both cheeks.

"*Ma chérie...*" he said with a grin. "I do not know exactly how this happy ending came about... but I knew you would be the one to bring it!" Then he caught a view of the Beast.

He shrugged. "Eh, *bien*, nobody's perfect."

Mrs Potts was next and she was moving and twisting

about before she had even finished becoming human.

"Upon my word!" she exclaimed. "Where's my son? Chip! Do Chip next!"

Belle carefully opened the glass cabinet and brought out the little teacup and handed him to her. Within moments, Mrs Potts had a squirmy, scrambling five-year-old in her arms who was almost too big to hold.

"Chip!" the housekeeper cried, and clasped him to her bosom. Watching her in human form, Belle realised she wasn't actually that old at all; it was merely her mannerisms and speech that made her seem so. "We're ourselves again! Oh, Charles…"

The Beast and Belle exchanged smiles. If he had harboured any remaining doubts about his decision, they were long, long gone.

Rosalind's magic held out through the very last servant… the obnoxious dustmaid, who turned out to be an equally obnoxious human maid. Any interest Lumière had in her was over, ever since her declaration against *les charmantes.*

Belle was happy but shiftless, still exhausted but unable to rest. The sounds of champagne bottles being popped and laughter and music filled the castle halls as it hadn't in a century. But she didn't feel like joining in. It wasn't *her* party. She was someone who had just bumbled into a bad situation and helped, sort of, to make it right. She went up to her old room and sat on the bed, wondering what to do next.

"Hey, hon, come join us!"

The woman previously known as 'wardrobe', who was now Ann, stuck her head in. She was a very tall woman, with a good-humoured face and the cheekbones of someone who could very well have been a Joan of Arc or warrior princess in another age. Those cheeks were presently rosy with wine and she had a golden goblet in her hand.

"In a little while," Belle said politely.

"Better come soon. Won't be anything left," Ann said, toasting her before wandering off.

Belle sighed and looked out of the window at the snowy landscape below. There was one out-of-place grey smudge in the snow, in the rose garden. Just a few weeks ago she would have guessed it was a vagrant or someone else unfortunate, but now she recognised her mother. Rosalind sat hunched over, alone, looking pensive.

Belle rose and ran downstairs, stopping only to throw a cloak over her shoulders and grab one for her mother as well.

Spring was a long way off, but the bright sun had given them a hint of warmer days; everything was slick and there was a very faint sound of drips and trickles. Belle stepped carefully and noticed her shoes were cracked and worn and past ready to be mended and resoled. Or maybe the

Prince could have a new pair made for her.

That was a strange thought. It gave Belle the shivers.

Kings and beasts and enchantresses for mothers and the thing that really *seems to bother me is the idea of a boy buying me a new pair of shoes.*

She smiled to herself, but lost the expression as soon as she came close to her mother, who was sitting dolefully, regarding nothing at all.

As if they exchanged feelings, the woman brightened, however, upon seeing her daughter.

"Belle! Come sit by me," she said excitedly, moving over on the damp bench. Despite the condition of her clothes, Rosalind didn't seem to mind. Belle gingerly joined her and draped the cloak over her mother's shoulders. "We have so much catching up to do! I want to hear everything."

"What were you thinking about just now? You looked so sad," Belle asked instead.

"Oh." Rosalind shrugged, though the movement seemed to pain her. "I was thinking about what Frédéric… D'Arque… said. What if, in his own twisted way, he was right? What if *les charmantes* think differently, act differently from humans who *don't* have magic? What if we behave instinctually in ways that are basically anathema to normal society?"

Belle sighed. "What if *you*, Rosalind, my mother, act

differently from humans and everyone else? The villagers, the servants, the government? What if *you personally* hold yourself above the law as a vigilante? What if it's *just you*? You're doing the same thing D'Arque did… applying the actions of one to a whole people. That's ridiculous. Whether you're Huguenot or Catholic or Jewish or gypsy or short or have dark skin or blue skin. Everyone is different. Each person has his or her own soul and is master of his or her own destiny."

Rosalind gave her a sly look. "That's very wise, and clever. You're still an avid reader."

"Not so much in the last few days," Belle said with a smile.

"Everyone in the village still treat you as an oddball?"

"Yep." Belle stretched her legs. "Until yesterday, at least. I don't know what they think of me now."

"I'm so glad Lévi agreed to be your godfather. You two really are a perfect fit."

"I wish I had *known* he was my godfather. I wish I had known… a lot of things."

"Wishes," Rosalind sighed. "I wish I had reined in my temper more. I wish I never cursed the Prince. I wish I had pitied the king and queen instead of seeking to punish them. I was full of power and empty of wisdom. And now it's the reverse… I am empty of power and am just beginning to have the faintest traces of wisdom."

Belle didn't know what to say. She and her mother were talking like… adults. Not like a mother to a child who wants to learn how to make pastry, or is crying over a grazed knee, or needs a story read to her. Not what she ever imagined about reuniting with her maman.

There was the sound of boots crunching against the gravelly path. Belle looked up and saw as strange a sight as any she had seen in the last month: her father and the Beast, walking side by side, heads bent towards each other, engaged in conversation. Between the Beast's appearance and her father's serious look of concentration, it was hard to make the image work in her head for a moment.

"Hello, ladies," Maurice said, face breaking into a grin. "We saw you come out here… avoiding the crowds?"

"It's a little overwhelming for me," Rosalind admitted. "I am not used to them. How are your subjects, King?"

"Overindulging," the Beast said with the faintest smile. Were those lines of weariness round his eyes? Did beasts get those? "They deserve it."

"I've been thinking about your… situation," the Enchantress continued. The phrasing irked Belle a little. "The strongest charms, spells and curse reversals can be achieved by greater numbers. Like the charm at Belle's christening that failed because we were a few short. I am fairly certain the curse can be broken with an adequate gathering."

The Beast looked at Rosalind hopelessly.

"There are no *charmantes* left, except a few poor souls we freed from the asylum."

"Oh, many of them escaped before it grew too dire. All you have to do is find them," Rosalind said airily, waving her hand.

"And if we found them, where could we bring them, where they could be safe? Where they would *want* to gather in numbers?" the Beast asked pointedly. "What happened here… has happened in the New World, too. They aren't safe anywhere."

"Yes, they are," Belle said, eyes widening with an idea.

Everyone looked at her.

"Don't you see? *This* is the one place in the world they are safe!" She waved her arms around, indicating the castle and the valley. "Your curse still isn't really broken. The castle and everyone in it have been forgotten. *No one* remembers this place. You could find all *les charmantes* and bring them here. Bring them home. And get yourself… uncursed."

"Hmmm," Rosalind said, thinking. "Not bad. It's an odd idea, considering this is the place we almost came to our end… but it's intriguing. Yes, I like it. Go and find everyone and bring them home. Really, it's the least you could do after what your parents did."

Maurice might have given Rosalind a little frown at that last bit, but she shrugged.

The Beast blinked. "Go… and find them? *Me?*"

"Yes. Why not?" Belle said with a smile, reading his thoughts. "You would have to actually go out into the world you've been watching for so long in your magic mirror."

"With you," the Beast said without missing a beat. "I could do anything, with you."

Belle grinned and started to answer…

… and then saw Maurice and Rosalind, who were both watching her to see what she would do.

Belle had a family again. She had a mother, the most interesting, perplexing mother in the world, whom she had just met. There was too much to ask her, to talk about.

But this was finally her chance to go out on those adventures she had always dreamed of. Abandoned Greek islands, the hearts of never-before-seen forests, even Paris and Rome… They would travel the world looking for reclusive *charmantes* to bring home. Who knew what they might see!

It wasn't fair.

"Belle, go," her mother ordered. "If I was your age, I wouldn't have hesitated for a moment. You will always come back here, and I will always be here. And we will have those talks we need. Everyone should have a journey and everyone should also have a home too. *Go out into the world for adventure, come home for love.*"

Maurice looked a little sad. "I like having both my girls together again… but there's so much for us to do, the time will fly and you'll be back home before we know it."

"To do?" the Beast asked.

"Well, the village has a lot to cope with right now," Belle's father said with a rueful smile. "From long-lost relatives who are, or were, *charmantes*… to those who were genuinely… ah… not well. There's a lot of people who have been in what was basically prison for years and years. I think the next few months are going to be rocky, and it might need a pair of… *oddballs* to help everyone on a bit."

"And then there's your castle," Rosalind said, indicating a window out of which someone seemed to be dangling a pair of underthings like a flag. "Once all that ruckus calms down, your people have to decide what to do with themselves. I'm sure at least a few will stay on… but they may not feel like being servants any more… There's a whole world out there, and you will be gone."

The Beast regarded her thoughtfully. "I could deputise Lumière to run things in my absence, with Cogsworth…"

"Oh, that will work out well," Belle said, already imagining how it would end: with Mrs Potts making the final decisions, of course.

The Beast regarded her. "Would you come with me, Belle? Help me do this? We may not succeed… I may always be a beast."

"No," Belle said with a smile, touching him on the nose. "You will always be my prince."

"Well, you're not exactly what I wanted out of a son-in-law, because of your *parents*, not because of your form, I mean," Rosalind said quickly. "But you're certainly a fair bit better than that Gaston fellow… what is *his* story, if I may ask? Was he also a patient at the asylum?"

Belle almost choked on her laughter. "No, and that was *not* the first time he proposed to me."

"I think," Maurice said, putting his arms round the couple, "we should all have one last night together before you set out… just the four of us. There are a lot of stories to tell before we see you again."

"And most of them," Belle observed with a smile, "seem to *almost* have a happy ending."

Photo credit: Alice Licht

After the sort of introverted childhood you would expect from a writer, Liz Braswell earned a degree in Egyptology at Brown University and then promptly spent the next ten years producing video games. Finally, she caved in to fate and wrote *Snow* and *Rx* under the name Tracy Lynn, followed by the Nine Lives of Chloe King series under her real name, because by then the assassins hunting her were all dead. Liz is also the author of *Once Upon a Dream: A Twisted Tale*. She lives in Brooklyn with a husband, two children, a cat, a part-time dog, three fish and five coffee trees she insists will start producing beans any day. You can e-mail her at me@lizbraswell.com or tweet @LizBraswell.

ALSO AVAILABLE IN THE TWISTED TALES SERIES:

WHAT IF ARIEL HAD NEVER DEFEATED URSULA?

It's been five years since the infamous sea witch defeated the little mermaid... taking King Triton's life in the process. Ariel is now the voiceless queen of Atlantica, while Ursula runs Prince Eric's kingdom on land.

But when Ariel discovers that her father might still be alive, she finds herself returning to a world, and a prince, she never imagined she would see again. Will Ariel be able to overthrow the murderous villain set on destroying her home and the world she once longed to be a part of?

Follow this tale of power, love and a mermaid's quest to reclaim her voice.

ALSO AVAILABLE IN THE TWISTED TALES SERIES:

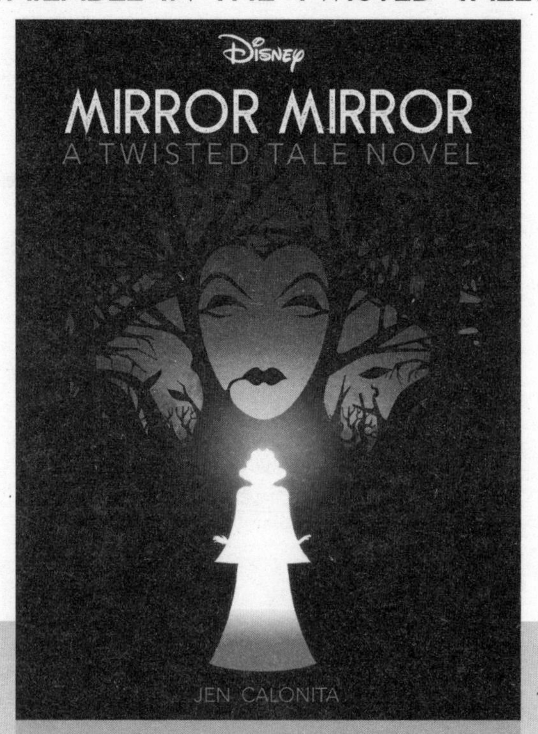

WHAT IF THE EVIL QUEEN POISONED THE PRINCE?

Following her beloved mother's death, the kingdom falls to Snow White's stepmother, known as the Evil Queen.

At first, Snow keeps her head down, hoping to make the best of things. However, when new information about her parents comes to light, and a plot to kill her goes wrong, Snow embarks on a journey to stop the Evil Queen and take back her kingdom.

Can Snow defeat an enemy who will stop at nothing to retain her power... including going after the ones Snow loves?

ALSO AVAILABLE IN THE TWISTED TALES SERIES:

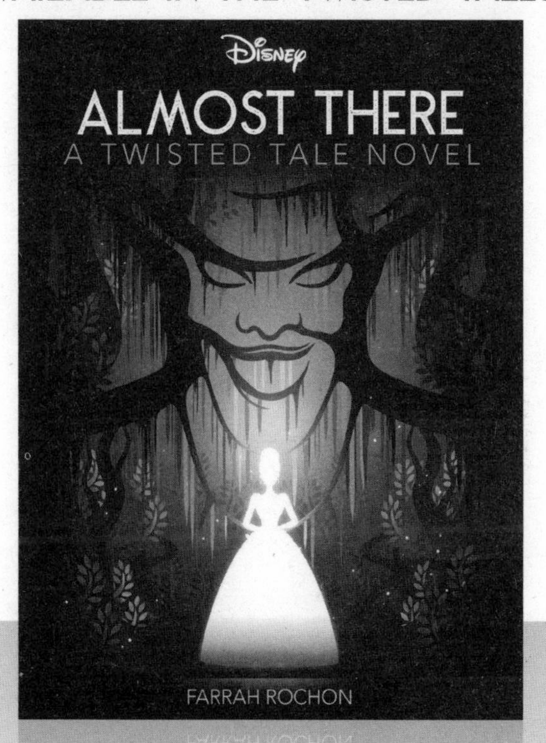

WHAT IF TIANA MADE A DEAL THAT CHANGED EVERYTHING?

When the notorious Dr. Facilier backs Tiana into a corner, she has no choice but to accept an offer that will alter the course of her life in an instant.

Soon Tiana finds herself in a new reality where all her deepest desires are realised – she finally gets her restaurant, her friends are safe and sound, and, perhaps most miraculous of all, her beloved father is still alive.

But after a while, her hometown grows increasingly eerie, and Tiana must work alongside Naveen and Charlotte to set things right – or risk losing everything she holds dear.